TEMPTING ADRIAN

"Were you jealous because you thought I was in love with him? Because you thought I wanted to make love with another man before you?"

Adrian growled deep in his throat. "Yes," he hissed. "I was mad with jealousy. I still am," he said in a warning tone.

Maisie leaned forward and kissed his lips gently. "The only man I want to make love with—have ever wanted to make love with—is you. And that is the truth, if ever I've spoken it. If you'll only take me inside, I shall prove it to you."

Adrian released her to sweep his arm beneath her legs and then turned to maneuver her through the narrow doorway . . .

Books by Heather Grothaus

THE WARRIOR

THE CHAMPION

THE HIGHLANDER

TAMING THE BEAST

NEVER KISS A STRANGER

NEVER SEDUCE A SCOUNDREL

NEVER LOVE A LORD

VALENTINE

ADRIAN

HIGHLAND BEAST
(with Hannah Howell and Victoria Dahl)

Published by Kensington Publishing Corporation

ADRIAN

The Brotherhood of Fallen Angels

Heather Grothaus

LYRICAL PRESS
Kensington Publishing Corp.
www.kensingtonbooks.com

LYRICAL PRESS BOOKS are published by

Kensington Publishing Corp.
119 West 40th Street
New York, NY 10018

All Kensington titles, imprints, and distributed lines are available at special quantity discounts for bulk purchases for sales promotion, premiums, fund-raising, educational, or institutional use.

Special book excerpts or customized printings can also be created to fit specific needs. For details, write or phone the office of the Kensington Sales Manager: Kensington Publishing Corp., 119 West 40th Street, New York, NY 10018. Attn. Sales Department. Phone: 1-800-221-2647.

Lyrical and the Lyrical logo Reg. U.S. Pat. & TM Off.

First Electronic Edition: December 2015
eISBN-13: 978-1-60183-398-3
eISBN-10: 1-60183-398-9

First Print Edition: December 2015
ISBN-13: 978-1-60183-399-0
ISBN-10: 1-60183-399-7

Printed in the United States of America

For all the good witches everywhere, in spirit and in flesh.
Believe.
~HG

Prologue

August 1179
Damascus

He fell to his knees on the packed road and swayed toward his long black shadow, his bound arms affording him no leverage. At least they had finally fallen numb. His vision blurred, the pebbles and sand and slivers of dry vegetation all seeming to melt together. He expected a blow to the back of his head at any moment. Adrian Hailsworth only hoped he would be hit hard enough to kill him.

"Get up, Adrian," Constantine Gerard ordered as he marched past. Only Constantine could still act the general with a pair of Saracen guards walking leisurely behind him.

Adrian tried to raise his head in time to catch Constantine's gaze; he wanted to say good-bye here, on the road. But he was too slow, too weak, and the Saracens already blocked his line of vision. They looked back at Adrian with knowing smirks, commenting to each other in chuckling voices.

A wide, hulking shadow eclipsed Adrian's own.

"Have no worry!" a jovial voice called out from somewhere above Adrian's head. "I will allow your friend the use of my own horse so that he might join you in the city!"

Adrian let his gaze drop back to the road, his cheek twitching, the ragged strips of his once white undershirt fluttering in the arid breeze. His chest and stomach were crusted with his own blood where Saladin's soldiers had laid beaded whips to his belly, and the hot wind tugged at the cloth where it had dried against his wounds.

The Saracen's horse clip-clopped closer so that Adrian caught a glimpse of the delicately shaped front hooves out of the corner of his right eye. Such fine horses they had here. Adrian's father and older brother would be mad to claim a pair for their stables back in England.

"Have you had enough?" the dark general asked, his voice almost kind. The tone stung Adrian's pride, as it had been none other than this very man who had ordered him whipped, bound. "Will you call out for your god to save you now?"

"I told you," Adrian rasped, his throat so dry and pinched together that the words were like blades crawling up his insides. "I am no Templar, no soldier. I am a schol—"

"I witnessed your prowess with my own eyes," the general interrupted. "It takes great skill to remove a man's head with one blow. You must have much experience."

"It takes only a sharp blade and a strong arm," Adrian choked. "My experience is limited to this day."

"Is that so?" the Saracen mused, but his words were tinged with heavy sarcasm, indicating that he did not believe Adrian's claims. "Then you should know that a soldier never forgets the face of the first man he ever kills. It pleases me to know that he will haunt your dreams. You will remember him forever."

Adrian's vision threatened to darken completely as the screams in Chastellet's bailey filled his ears once again, the sight of the wall of robed and belted Saracens advancing toward him and Constantine and the handful of Templars left standing. He felt in his numb hands the heavy hilt of the sword pressing into his flesh, slick with sweat. His friends had swung, slashed, yelled; Adrian had stood very still, his sword held before him in a two-handed grip, as the brown face rushed at him, its mouth twisted in a battle cry. The curved scimitar rising, rising . . .

One swing.

Adrian blinked, bringing himself back to the present. "Your men came into a house I built and slaughtered my friends," he rasped. Then he tilted his head and looked up at the mounted general. "I couldn't pick his head from the pile, even now."

The Saracen's boot connected with Adrian's temple, sending him into the sand at the edge of the road. He felt a faint pulling somewhere between his shoulder blades, but it was eclipsed by the blinding pain of the late sun cutting into his dry eyes.

"Though you may in time find it rather unfortunate, I remember exactly who you killed," the man said in a low, contemptuous tone, and Adrian noticed he was feeding a long coil of rope from the back of his saddle into a loop beneath his hands. "Look around you, infidel—this is *my* house. *Allah's house.* We are only ridding our pallets of vermin. With the help of one of your own," the soldier added slyly.

"That's how you knew when best to strike," Adrian commented as he struggled to come back to his knees, not in the least surprised. Adrian and Constantine had figured out as much on their own the day Chastellet had come under attack from Saladin's army—when King Baldwin and half the fighting men were away to Tiberius. "It was Felsteppe, was it not? The man who aided you?"

The Saracen clicked his tongue and shook his head, the rope in his hands now fashioned into a circlet at one end, swaying with the horse's even breaths. "So eager to turn on your brother. But no; the man who gave us the detailed plan to bring Chastellet to its knees is not called Felsteppe."

"It is," Adrian insisted. "He is one of Baldwin's generals, red-headed and—"

"Yes, yes," the soldier interrupted agreeably. "A red-haired general, his nose, long and pointy, yes?"

"Yes," Adrian said. "Glayer Felsteppe is his name."

"You are confused." The Saracen shook his head, as if disappointed for Adrian. "Our mutual friend clearly stated his name was General Constantine Gerard."

"General Gerard just passed us," Adrian rasped, his muddled brain fighting to make sense of what the soldier was saying. "He is on this very road, just ahead of us."

"Is that so?" The Saracen tossed the circlet of rope. It landed expertly around Adrian's body, catching on the ties that held his arms behind him. With a sudden flick, the rope tightened, causing Adrian to realize he hadn't lost all feeling after all. He cried out in agony.

"How convenient for Baldwin that we have his traitor in our captivity. I am certain there shall be a large ransom for him."

"Constantine did not betray Chastellet," Adrian whispered, his eyes squeezed shut. He could not fathom how his arms were still attached to his torso. If he'd had any moisture left in his body, his face would have been washed with tears.

The Saracen leaned slightly toward him in the saddle, as if eager to impart a great secret. "This I alone know. Which is why he will not live long enough to be bought." The man regained his regal posture. "Come now, soldier—if you only ask it of Allah, he will give you the strength of ten men. You can walk into Damascus with your dignity and recover in some comfort until you are ransomed."

Adrian didn't know what the Saracen's plans for him were, but from his treatment thus far, he was very sure they would involve massive pain and torture. And Constantine was going to die. What would it matter if Adrian indulged the dark man's religious delusions with a self-preserving lie? If he played along, perhaps there would be a chance to warn Constantine. A chance to plead their cases to the triumphant Saladin. The ruler was rumored to be reasonable and fair with his prisoners.

The ones who lived, any matter.

But then Adrian's mind was filled with a memory of his father, portly, graying, his beard tugged down into a point where he worried at it with his fist. Adrian knew he bore much of the responsibility for the beard's pointedness. Rather than live a life of relative ease or take the cloth as was expected of him, Herne Hailsworth's younger son had boldly decided to leave his noble home to pursue an insatiable thirst for knowledge. Everyone had thought him a fool—his father's peers, even his own brother. Quiet, odd Adrian, with his books and his stones and his measure sticks. Adrian remembered vividly the day he'd left, when his father had taken him aside.

Always be who you are, Adrian. Dare not belittle your assets in hopes of avoiding scrutiny, for it is only in bearing his own full weight that a man grows stronger.

Adrian raised his face to look squarely at the Saracen. "*I am not a soldier*. I am a scholar. A philosopher. And if any god existed to stand before me in this moment, after all he has allowed to happen *in his house*, I would spit in his face."

It was then that Adrian received the blow to his skull that he had been expecting. The hot, brown world of the Damascus Road went silent and black in an instant.

The god who did not exist was merciful in allowing unconsciousness to cling to Adrian as the Saracen soldier kept his word and used the power of his own horse to drag Adrian's limp and battered body the remainder of the way to Damascus.

* * *

The sound of ragged sobs stirred Adrian from the depths, and as he became aware of the cold stone beneath his cheek, he realized he was the source of those sobs.

His voice, cawing and raw, echoed as he writhed on the stone floor. Every inch of skin, every muscle, screamed as if they had been painstakingly scored with glowing iron. He tried to tilt his head back as he cried out again, to relieve the drawing torture on the back of his neck and spine, but he felt a wide cuff of iron dig into the base of his skull. His cry intensified.

"Adrian," a muffled voice called. "Adrian, stop. You must get hold of yourself."

Adrian thought it was perhaps Constantine who spoke, and so he tried mightily to quiet, to still, so that he could locate his friend. His cries retreated back into his throat, but he could not help the whimpers that escaped him, like dogs straining at their leads. His whole body trembled with such pain that he could not understand how he still lived.

"That's it," the voice said again, perhaps somewhere behind him. Adrian's ear canals seemed to be swollen together, muting the sounds around him but amplifying the sluggish rush of blood in his skull. "Move beyond it. Can you open your eyes? Come outside yourself."

Adrian tried to raise his eyelids, but they felt melted shut. Increasing the effort brought another round of jagged sobs, but he was rewarded with a sliver of light that made him cry out again in earnest. He felt thick wetness running down his forehead, his cheeks. He didn't know if it was blood or sweat, although he doubted the latter, as he felt as though he was in the midst of a blizzard.

Constantine? Adrian tried to say his friend's name, but all that came out was a moan of which the effort and sound pained him so that he began to weep again.

"Get hold of yourself, Adrian!" Constantine demanded, using every nuance of his military tone. "You must not surrender to it. You must fight! If you don't, you shall die."

It was his friend's last statement that brought Adrian some measure of stillness. He could not see the extent of his injuries, and he knew in some part of his fevered mind that he was only feeling a fraction of the damage that his body was suffering, but he realized that he was only hanging on to life by a fingertip. He could quiet, and then just let the pain slip away. His heart would stop beating, his pupils would contract a final time, and then Adrian Hailsworth, master architect, would simply cease to exist.

He would never again see his brother, or his father. He would never again stride through the green grass of Hereford on his visits home from his travels. He would never see the completion of the great bridge in London, the plans of which he himself had helped conceive before accepting the ill-fated charge of the great fortress Chastellet. It was to have been his final project before taking the position in Oxford, teaching generations of fresh young minds the truth about the world around them, and shining light into the darkness of superstition and myth that gripped the populace of his country.

Now that bright dream, along with his weak physical body, was flickering.

"That's right." Constantine's voice broke into his dimming thoughts once more. "Be still. Conserve your strength. You are gravely injured, it is true, but now Saladin will preserve us until we can be ransomed or traded. King Baldwin will not forsake us. We must have faith, Adrian."

While Constantine launched into a murmuring plea to an imaginary creator, Adrian let his friend's hopeful words reach his muddled consciousness. Ransom? Why did that sound false to his ears?

How convenient for Baldwin that we have his traitor in our captivity. He will not live long enough to be bought.

The king would be told that Constantine was the traitor of Chastellet. Perhaps the news had already spread. There would be no ransom.

But Constantine would never know that if Adrian let himself die.

Adrian tuned his ears to the sounds around him again, hearing Constantine's murmuring prayer for Adrian's failing body, for the preservation of Constantine's son and wife, awaiting what was to have been their father and husband's imminent return to England. He fought to crack open his eyes once more.

At first Adrian thought it was his damaged eyesight that made his surroundings so dim. But after a moment, he realized that it was the cell itself that was dark—blurry brown sandstone walls that appeared sueded with the orange and yellow torchlight washing over them. Perhaps it was night, but Adrian guessed that he and Constantine had been interred in some underground prison; the smooth, domed ceiling seemed to mimic Constantine's bowed form.

Adrian saw the thick metal collar around his friend's neck and realized then the source of the choking and pulling sensation around his own throat. But whereas Constantine was tethered to the wall behind him, preventing him from kneeling or sitting, Adrian surmised his own bond terminated on the floor nearby. He could not move anything beyond his eyeballs at the moment to test his range. Constantine's hands were free, however, and he utilized them to cross himself as he now finished his sonnet to the Great Pretend.

Adrian almost reconsidered then. What good would it do Constantine to know with certainty that he was going to die? Was it not kinder to let him believe, this last bit of time he had left, that he might be saved? That good would somehow triumph and right would win the day and he would see his little boy again? Why not let him continue in his delusion if it should bring him comfort, rather than have him die knowing that his name would be forever remembered as that of a traitor and a murderer?

Because it is a lie, Adrian told himself. *Because he deserves the truth. If ever an opportunity arose for Constantine to save himself before he was executed, he must be aware of the truth, else he might just wait patiently for his rescue unto the very moment of his death.*

Constantine saw then that Adrian's eyes were open. "Adrian?" he asked hesitantly, and Adrian realized that he must look as if he had already expired.

He gave a great effort and blinked.

Constantine Gerard's broad shoulders slumped momentarily, and Adrian thought perhaps it was with relief. "We will survive this," Constantine said firmly, his posture straightening as much as his tether would allow. Even the metal restraints weren't enough to rob the commander of the Templars from his duty to lead. "God has spared us thus far—beyond the hundreds that were killed—for a purpose. And God will see us delivered."

Adrian could only stare at his friend, leashed to the prison wall. For a moment, he wanted to believe, if only to delude himself against the inevitability of the fate that awaited them both. Adrian told himself it was the pathetic condition of his physical body that caused the wetness to leak from his eyes. Or perhaps the unspeakable pity he held for the capable and honorable Constantine. But he wept quietly all the same.

The sound of footfalls shuffled dully in the space behind Adrian's head, and then the creaking of some gate being opened. Shadows interrupted the torchlight, causing Adrian to wince. A moment later, the wicked face of the Saracen general leaned into Adrian's line of vision. His smile was bright.

"You are not dead," he said with something akin to delight. "I am impressed, infidel. I have great plans for your conversion, indeed." Then the face was gone, and a pair of metal dishes were dropped inches before his face, murky water and chunks of runny, unidentifiable stuff sloshing onto the stone and splattering Adrian's cheek.

Adrian could not register any smells from the offering through his clogged nostrils, but he saw a speck of white morsel moving, wiggling within the mottled mass of gray.

Maggots.

He focused his eyes instead upon the soft-looking leather boots of the accompanying soldiers that crossed the floor beneath voluminous robes.

"Stay where you are, infidel," the general called out to Constantine from where he still stood near Adrian's form. The soldiers quickly deposited similar metal vessels on the floor at what looked to be the very limits of Constantine's restraints. But Adrian could see a wide piece of the unleavened bread popular in this part of the world, and what was perhaps a leg of meat.

When the soldiers retreated, Constantine stepped toward the food, only barely able to drag it into his reach with the toe of one boot. The dish of water trembled wildly in his hands as he picked it up and brought it to his mouth.

The Saracen's evil countenance came into Adrian's view again, and he used one hand to push the low-rimmed bowl of rotting matter closer to Adrian's face. "Here is *your* meal, infidel. Go on—eat it."

Adrian closed his eyes against the sight of the wriggling mass.

"You must have nourishment," the voice in the darkness cajoled. "To build your strength."

"Don't eat it, Adrian," Constantine called out, his anger clear in his deep voice. "Why do you give an injured man rotting foodstuffs? Have you not done enough to him that you still seek to poison him?"

"Go on," the Saracen encouraged from beyond Adrian's eyelids. "If you do not eat, I will take away your friend's food as well."

Adrian continued to lie very still while Constantine engaged the soldier. "Take it then, for I will not eat good food while my friend is offered that which swine would refuse."

Adrian felt a painful rush of air over his skin and the Saracen's voice was directed toward the back of the cell. "Is that so? How honorable of you. Thank you for illuminating my mistake; however, this business does not concern you. It is between myself and your friend, who killed my son."

Adrian's eyes opened then, and he saw brown hands snatch the dish of water from Constantine's hands while another set whisked away the bowl of untouched food from the cell floor. His vision moved jerkily upward to see the Saracen general removing the short, beaded whip from his belt.

The man Adrian had slain at Chastellet had been the general's son?

"Will you eat, infidel?" he asked pleasantly, but now Adrian recognized the hatred burning in the man's dark eyes.

Constantine commanded, "No, Adrian. Don't."

Adrian stared at the whip, remembering its cutting song.

"Very well," the Saracen said lightly. "You leave me no choice."

In the next moment, a whistle of air preceded a clicking slap, and Adrian heard Constantine's cry escaping through clenched teeth even as he tried to contain it.

Adrian closed his eyes. Perhaps if they thought him unconscious again . . .

But only a beat of time passed before the whip's whistle and slap sounded again in the close air of the cell. Then again. And now Constantine could not withhold his shouts.

Adrian remembered the bite of the beads as they sank beneath his skin, the ripping as they retreated.

Again the whip sounded, and again Constantine screamed.

Adrian opened his eyes and saw Chastellet's general crouched against the rear wall of the cell, his forearms raised to protect his face. Adrian tried to call out for the Saracen to stop as he raised his arm again, but his throat would not work. The whip fell with a gasp, and Constantine's scream pierced Adrian's ears.

Drawing strength from an unknown source, Adrian inched his face toward the congealing mass spilled over the side of the dish before him. The scrape of the metal bowl on the sandstone floor sounded like the sharpening of a blade. He peeled his lips apart, feeling the sting of the skin as it was pulled away. For a moment he wondered that he hadn't already bitten off his tongue, for he felt nothing emerge when he willed himself to sample the rotten offering before him. But then he tasted its sour perfume, felt the liveness of the mass in his mouth, around his lips.

"Adrian, no," Constantine pleaded in a breaking voice. "It will be as poison!"

But the whip fell no more, and the Saracen's boots came into close relief as the man moved over Adrian once again and crouched down.

"Again, you surprise me, infidel," the man said, obviously pleased as he watched Adrian struggle to swallow.

Adrian gagged as the mush pushed against the sides of his throat. He fought against the urge to vomit while he held the Saracen's gaze.

"Sorry," he slurred, his voice emerging thick and garbled, unable to open his jaws wide enough to form the words properly. "Your . . . son."

The dark man blinked and his brow creased as he seemed to consider what Adrian had said. Then his eyes narrowed and he leaned forward on his haunches and spat in Adrian's face.

"Eat it," he commanded in his own raspy whisper and then shoved the dish toward Adrian's face again so that the rim bounced off his nose and upper lip. "All of it. I want to watch you."

Adrian was thankful the Saracen was between him and Constantine so that his friend was not forced to watch the grisly meal. He hoped the dark man's chuckling laughter was loud enough to mask the retching noises coming from Adrian's body.

By the time the dish was empty, Adrian knew his mind had been broken, for he was praying for a dark angel to deliver him from the hell he had finally accepted was very real indeed.

Chapter 1

February 1181
Melk, Austria

The sudden rapping on his chamber door caused Adrian to flinch. He looked immediately to the small man hunched over his lower abdomen, but Song had already raised his hands away with his typical quick grace and sat back on his heels. The faint, rhythmic pain in Adrian's body faded with the Chinese man's retreat, but irritation at being interrupted caused his temples to pound.

The rapping sounded again, and then an accented voice called through the thick wood of the door. "Ad—*Brother Adrian*?" the voice corrected, and Adrian could see in his mind the Spaniard rolling his eyes at the enforced title. "It is I, Brother Valentine."

Adrian raised himself up from the mattress on his elbows and scowled toward the door. "What do you want, Valentine?"

"There is a—" Valentine Alesander broke off, and his next words were muffled, as if he pressed his face close to the seam of door and stone wall. "Actually, I would prefer no to have this conversation in the corridor."

"I'm busy. I shall see you at supper." Adrian lay back down and motioned toward Song to resume his task. The Chinese monk leaned over Adrian's hips.

The chamber door rattled against the bolt, causing Song to once more calmly retreat and Adrian to sigh without quite the same easy acceptance.

"Victor sent me," Valentine said pointedly from the corridor. "Why do you have a lock on your door? No one else has a lock on their door."

Adrian ignored the question but gained one elbow to look toward the small, serene man whose eyes fixed upon Adrian's naked torso. "I'm sorry. Can you finish?"

Song nodded his smooth head once.

Adrian turned his face toward the door. "I'll be a moment."

"It is no trouble. I will wait."

Adrian collapsed back onto the bed and raised his forearm to lay it across his eyes. He felt the coolness of the sides of Song's palms against his skin, the faint vibrations of the monk's ministrations in the muscles of his abdomen.

He barely noticed when it was over. The mattress shifted slightly as the spare man backed down from the bed, rolling the tools of his secret and forbidden trade into a small bamboo mat. Adrian rose and swung his legs over the side of the bed, looking down at his nakedness, then raised his eyes to Song.

The Chinese bowed and then swept a downward-facing palm through the air.

"No more?" Adrian asked, looking down again. He felt hot prickles behind his eyes as he surveyed his raw and bleeding skin. But he needn't have asked because the proof was before him.

Song had fulfilled his promise.

When he looked up, the silent monk was walking toward the door. Adrian stood and attended the lacings of his chausses. "You must allow me to repay you," he said, tucking in the ties and then reaching for his undershirt.

Song paused with a half turn and shook his head. *No.*

Adrian swept his shirt over his head. "I insist," he said as he emerged through the neck hole. "Perhaps some herb, or . . . coin? What do you have need of?"

Adrian expected only continued silence from the Chinese man, and so he was surprised when Song seemed to consider the offer Adrian had put forth. He raised his face to regard Adrian directly, and the tilt of his dark, sparkling eyes gave him an elfin look.

"You must live to fulfill your purpose," he said, his voice as low as a whisper but with no hint of breathiness. "It is only my duty to give you the protection of the old ones. The honor of it is payment enough." He bowed again before reaching for the door.

Adrian might have been touched by the quiet man's concern had it not shamed him to admit that he needed Song's ignorant charms to protect him against scars that were terrifyingly real—both physically and mentally.

He held the door open while Song gave Valentine his own small bow and then moved past him down the corridor on silent, sandaled feet. Adrian ignored the Spaniard's raised eyebrows as he turned back into the barren cell to retrieve his long brown habit from a peg in the wall. It was the only bit of decoration in the stone chamber.

"Why shouldn't I have a lock on my door?" Adrian asked instead. "You have a lock on *your* door."

"I do," Valentine acquiesced. "But I also have a secret wife in an abbey full of monks." His ever-present smirk deepened as he tossed a glance out the door and into the corridor where Song had disappeared. "Perhaps I am no the only one to have a secret, yes? Song *is* very petite. Although I always imagined you with someone less"—he rolled one hand in the air as if searching for the right word—"bald."

Adrian pulled his head through the habit and then turned to reach for his cincture. He drew up the yards of brown wool around his hips, securing it carefully below his tender skin. "You have a message?" he prompted, not willing in that moment to engage the Spaniard in repartee.

"Victor has called a meeting," Valentine said, his eyes catching on the squares of blood-smeared linen left on Adrian's thin mattress. "There has been some word. Adrian, are you injured?"

"No. Perhaps your wife's inquiries have seen early success."

"Hmm," Valentine murmured, his gaze still studying the bloody scraps of cloth. "Then what is—"

"When and where?" Adrian asked.

Valentine at last dragged his face toward Adrian's. "Now, of course. I do no need to tell you where."

Thankfully, the Spaniard's inquisition ceased once he and Adrian were in the corridor. It was not the first time Adrian had been grateful for Melk's enforced silence, and he utilized the time it took to maneuver through the abbey's corridors on the way to the library to form a hypothesis about the news Victor would impart.

Valentine's wife, Mary Beckham, had sent a score of identical letters chronicling the facts of her husband's and his friends' entrapment to the most powerful contacts in the English and Christian Holy Land rule. The missives were to gain their destinations by a circuitous route, first traveling to Vienna to be handed off to Father Victor's trusted compatriots and then scattering across the map as letters contained within letters, visiting tens of burgs and switching bearers countless times before reaching the hands each were intended for. Adrian wondered, though, that they could be receiving good news in such a short span of time. The messages had only left Melk two months earlier.

He fidgeted with his cincture, which had ridden up and was now rubbing against his skin. Valentine's keen eyes caught the movement, and Adrian could tell that his curiosity was straining at its lead once more. Fortunately, they were just passing the wide stone archway that housed the set of shallow steps leading to the abbey's lower levels, and some beast from below chose that moment to send a bloodcurdling scream ricocheting up the stone passage.

The men exchanged glances but of course said nothing, and Valentine's interest in Adrian's discomfort was effectively interrupted.

They neared the entry hall of the abbey, and after glancing around to be certain there were no witnesses, Valentine took the lead and stepped up onto a stone pedestal where a ten-foot-tall statue of St. Michael seemed to be keeping watch over the guardhouse beyond the gate. The Spaniard slipped into the dark arch of what appeared to be no more than a shallow inset behind the statue, but the depression was only an illusion; the stones were actually set back nearly two feet from the surrounding arch, and in truth it was this hidden opening that the archangel protected.

Although Adrian estimated the statue to weigh several tons; one man laying his weight to a certain wind-tossed fold at the rear of Michael's heavenly garment would cause the angel to tilt backward, his wide wings effectively sealing off the secret entrance to the even more secret chamber above.

Adrian quickly followed Valentine into the tight-winding stone staircase, which widened after the first turn just enough to accommodate the width of a man. But the stones still brushed both Adrian's shoulders with every step, and the feeling of imprisonment made his already inflamed skin crawl. There was no light source, so that by the time Adrian had taken ten steps, he and Valentine were ascending in pitch blackness. It was only for a pair of moments though, and then Adrian heard Valentine's huff of breath as he pushed at the door at the pinnacle of the stairs.

The stone slab moved soundlessly, and as Adrian passed into the secret library and slowly swung the massive entry shut, he marveled as always at the ingenious hinge on which it hung. Removing one small iron pin would cause the entire slab to settle fully into the deep groove in the floor, wedging into the invisibly tapered stone jamb, where it could never again be opened.

Trapping humanity's knowledge—and its noble but unfortunate savior—inside for an unknown eternity.

A quick glance around the room affirmed that all were gathered at the table that dominated the secret library. Valentine took his usual seat nearest the door, next to the huge blond Norseman. Roman, once Adrian's stone master at Chastellet, sat turning a smooth obelisk of granite in his fingers. Roman shared his side of the table with Melk's abbot, Victor, who studied his folded hands. Constantine sat opposite Valentine, with his back toward the one window of the library. His wide shoulders were hunched as his forearms braced him on the table, his head hanging.

It had become his common stance since just before the first snowfall, when he'd learned that his wife and son had been murdered. As if he could barely muster the strength to remain upright under his burden of grief, the once formidable general of Chastellet appeared beaten.

None of the men looked up at Adrian and Valentine's arrival, although Roman did give Valentine a sideways glance that, had Adrian been in a more generous mood, he might have taken the time to interpret. But as it was, with being interrupted and still experiencing a good deal of discomfort from Song's labors, the only things Adrian was interested in were his separate chair next to the window beyond Constantine and the decanter atop the nearby side table. He seized the second and lowered himself carefully into the first, picking up the cup he'd left on the stone sill that morning and filling it with rich red wine.

He had drunk half the wine and still the library was stuffed with its muffled silence. It was unusual for the old abbot to summon the men during the light of day—they typically only came together after the evening prayers had faded away with the incense and the other monks were abed. Obviously something of import had occurred, but Adrian was not in a hurry to hear whatever it was. The library was his haven, and unused as he was to sharing it, he was content enough to let the quiet stand.

He moved his cup to his left hand and picked up the manuscript of philosophy he'd laid on the sill earlier, his place between the vellum pages marked by one of Lou's cast-off tail feathers. It then crossed Adrian's mind that he'd not seen the hunting falcon upon entering the library, and he deduced that Roman had been summoned in such a hurried fashion that he'd been forced to leave Lou behind in the mews.

This realization caused Adrian to raise his eyebrows for a moment, but then he rested the book on his thighs and grasped the hard rib of the feather, using it as a lever to find where he'd left off. He'd read halfway down the page of minuscule text, painstakingly translating the Greek characters, when Victor at last spoke.

"I had a visitor today," the abbot began in his usual quiet voice, although his tone was even more subdued and measured than usual. "In the red confessional."

Adrian's eyes came to pause over the word μυστικό.

Mystikó.

Secret.

A visitor to the red confessional could mean only one thing: Someone had come to Melk bearing one of Chastellet's gold coins, which Father Victor had distributed to confessors the world over. If anyone's sins or problems could be traced back to the massacre at Jacob's Ford, and the framing of the four men now in hiding at Melk, they would be directed to the abbey on the Danube.

The red confessional was the place where Mary Beckham had come seeking help, and she had led Valentine directly to the betrayer of Chastellet—and the accuser of the four—Glayer Felsteppe.

Although the news roused Adrian's interest, he wondered of what import the visitor could truly be. After all, Valentine had pierced Glayer Felsteppe through the heart. He could cause no further damage than what he'd already accomplished before his death.

From where Adrian sat, trapped inside a broken body ruled by a withering mind, it was more than enough.

As if all the men's thoughts mirrored Adrian's own, no one prompted the abbot for details or made guesses as to the visitor's identity, letting Victor take his time.

"The lady-in-waiting to the queen of a small pagan island kingdom off the northern Scots coast," Victor said in the same measured tone.

"Another woman?" Adrian blurted out and looked up from his page, unable to contain his irritation. Blasted women. Always muddling things with emotion and need and want. Confounding issues with sentiments and frivolous desires. "I do hope this one isn't looking for an errant husband as well, else I'll be tempted to believe you've sent forth love potions rather than gold, Victor."

Adrian could feel Valentine's scowl on the back of his head, and it made him smirk. He raised his cup again.

"It's actually the island's king who is missing."

Adrian snorted. "I knew it. So the queen is the one with the errant husband. Can they not keep track of their men?"

"No, no—the queen's deposed brother," Victor corrected. "The royal family experienced a coup of sorts some months ago." He sounded deeply disturbed. "I am not being clear. Forgive me. I was not expecting such a thing, and it has confused my thoughts." The abbot took a breath. "Queen Maighread was encouraged to steal the throne by a foreigner, promising her military protection for her home, which has withstood several conquering attempts in history for its rich resources and position as a stronghold. Similar offers had been made to the king for years from various municipalities, but he always refused, choosing to keep his people autonomous from a larger rule."

"The foreigner, he is English," Valentine surmised.

"Indeed," Victor said. "After the queen gained control, her supposed benefactor then changed colors, demanding the sum of the kingdom's fortune by the time he returns by ship after the seas thaw, else the army that accompanies him will seize control of the island rather than protect it."

Adrian shut his book in disgust. "I regret that I have little sympathy for this queen thus far. She is reaping what she's sown. I say tell the maid to return to her queen with the advice that she hand her fortune of peat and goats over to this challenger so that she—and we—may be left out of it."

"That is the crux of what spurred her maid to flee the island; even if Queen Maighread wished to pay the fortune, no one has been able to locate it thus far."

"Good for the king," Adrian muttered. "I only hope he's gotten himself off to a pleasant, civilized city."

"The king didn't take it, Adrian. The fortune is said to be hidden somewhere within the royal castle," Victor supplied.

"Oh, come now, Victor," Adrian demanded, at last swiveling in his chair despite his discomfort to address the room. "Said *fortune* is likely only threepence stuck to the wall with some daub behind a tapestry. This has nothing to do with us."

Like the sound of an ancient tree creaking from the strain of a mighty wind, Constantine's voice at last emerged from his hunched posture. "What is this kingdom called, Victor?"

The abbot's mouth thinned, as if his body wanted to prevent its speaking. "Wyldonna."

Adrian threw back his head and began to laugh. In truth, it was the perfect answer. "Oh, Father—I'm afraid you've been had."

But Constantine obviously failed to see the humor, as his voice remained raspy and devoid of any mirth. "Victor, Wyldonna is a myth."

Victor nodded, his thin cheeks growing ruddy. "I have heard the tales myself."

"Wyldonna?" Valentine repeated.

Roman turned to his friend. "My people called it Valdunna. It is a magical island that no one can find, although if one manages to locate it, they never want to leave. It's populated by fairies, mystical creatures. Merpeople make their homes there when the seas freeze in winter. Shipwrecked sailors wash up on shore and are never heard from again. My mother often told me I would be stolen off to Valdunna if I strayed too far from home of an evening." Roman sent the abbot an apologetic glance.

"I see," Valentine said, sitting back in his chair. Adrian thought the Spaniard also looked sorry for the old abbot.

Instead of sympathy, Adrian felt irritation and disillusionment. Up to this point, he'd thought Victor a man of marked intelligence and cunning, even if he did subscribe to such a thing as religion. Now he couldn't be sure. "I hope you didn't tell this woman—who is obviously troubled—that we would assist her in this . . . this . . ." Adrian found himself at a loss for words.

"Goose hunt," Constantine supplied in an emotionless voice.

Adrian held his cup toward Constantine's back in salute. "Thank you, yes. Goose hunt." He drained his cup. A complete waste of the afternoon, although he wouldn't admit to himself that he'd nothing else to do any matter.

Victor was nodding his head. "I thought the same as you all when I first heard her tale. My only concern was who she had received the

Chastellet coin from, because whoever had given it to her had used very poor judgment." Then the abbot pinned Constantine's bowed head with his gaze. "Until she told me the name of her blackmailer."

"No, wait, wait," Adrian rushed, holding up his right palm. "Allow me to guess: Jack o' Kent."

"Adrian," Constantine chastised in a low tone.

"I wish it was," Victor whispered to the tabletop. He looked to Valentine for a moment, causing the Spaniard to crease his brow in concern. And then the abbot stretched out his hand and grasped Constantine's forearm.

"The man threatening Wyldonna is Glayer Felsteppe."

Chapter 2

The library was tomb silent for several moments as the name of Chastellet's betrayer and the scourge of the four laymen gathered there sank into the thousands of pages lining the walls and was absorbed, as if the mere mention of it could not withstand the air.

"Glayer Felsteppe is dead," Valentine said in a quiet voice. "My aim was true. *He fell*."

"He survived," Victor said softly, his kind gaze still regarding Constantine's bowed head. "It seems as though the troubles you and Lady Mary gave him at Beckham Hall were enough to incur Henry's irritation. He has taken on the task of securing Wyldonna for the English king in order to repay the wealth loaned to him from your wife's estate."

Valentine shook his head. "No. He is *dead*. He must be."

"It would not be the first time you had erroneously judged a man to be at the end of his life," Adrian said sharply, but then felt an uncomfortable welling of regret as the Spaniard dropped his gaze to his hands. It hadn't been ignorance that prompted Valentine to proclaim Adrian's impending and inevitable death; by all that was rational and true, Adrian should never have survived the escape from Saladin's dungeon.

Even though it had fallen to Valentine to carry back the news of the deaths of Constantine's wife and son years since that hellish time, at least Valentine had been able to assure his friend that he had personally brought an end to the fiend who had committed the atrocity.

Now, Constantine Gerard's family was still dead, but Glayer Felsteppe lived.

"What does this woman want us to do?" Roman asked hesitantly.

"If Felsteppe is not to return to her land until spring, that is a long time to wait."

"She wishes assistance in locating the Wyldonian fortune," Victor said, releasing Constantine's forearm with a sigh. Whatever reaction the abbot had been looking for from the general was not forthcoming. "The queen has no choice but to pay the price Felsteppe demands, else her people will be massacred."

"Unless we take care of Glayer Felsteppe once and for all when he returns to collect his spoils," Roman guessed.

Victor nodded. "That was my thought."

Adrian had felt the blackness growing in him since hearing Felsteppe's name spoken aloud. It was taking all his concentration to keep the rage under control.

"What would you have us do, Victor?" he bit out. "Go about some scraggly Scot rock, overturning stones in search of a tiny coin chest?"

"The legend of Wyldonna speaks of a great fortune hidden somewhere within the castle itself, perhaps protected by an enchantment."

Adrian sighed in disgust and replaced his cup on the sill as he gained his feet. He'd had quite enough. If he listened to much more, his temper would get the better of him.

Victor continued as Adrian shelved the manuscript. "I thought Roman might go, because he is most familiar with the northern hemisphere. Lady Maisie says that the castle itself is something of an enchantment—with rooms that seem to disappear at will, corridors that continue endlessly, hidden trapdoors that lead to inaccessible dungeons."

"Ridiculous," Adrian muttered and walked toward the stone doorway.

"Of course I will go," Roman said from the room behind Adrian. "If I must, I will tear the stones from the walls."

Adrian came to a halt and spun on the room. "There won't be any need for that, Roman. It's simple building design—you of anyone else here should realize that. An interior wall always has *something* behind it. An *inaccessible dungeon* must have a *ceiling*. Corridors lead *somewhere*, even if it's to a solid wall. Which, referencing my first point, has *something* behind it!" He was nearly shouting his arguments now.

"But . . . it's enchanted," Victor said.

"I'll go," Roman repeated firmly, turning his face toward the abbot. "I know the legends. Perhaps I can—"

Adrian snorted. "Perhaps you can be stung by this paltry queen's illusions? What will you do when she insists the *enchantment* requires a blood sacrifice?" He waggled his fingers in the air.

"I'm no fool, Adrian," Roman said with his formidable brows lowering.

Constantine's declaration cut into a ready rejoinder that Adrian would later be glad was never spoken.

"I will go."

All eyes turned to the general, who still regarded the smooth oiled wood of the table.

"If Glayer Felsteppe lives, he owes me a great, great debt. One that is not payable with his pathetic life, but I would take it all the same."

"If it is even Glayer Felsteppe who threatens this . . . this woman!" Adrian insisted. "Her mythical kingdom could be a hovel outside Edinburgh. Her fantastic fortune a plated spoon one of Felsteppe's deserters stole from her. It's a goose hunt. Or a trap." Adrian paused. "And, forgive me for saying so, but you are in no condition to be placed in a position requiring clear judgment."

Stan's head rose, and his deep, pained eyes warned Adrian. "Explain to me why I have not the right to exact my revenge on the man who murdered my son. My little boy, who was not quite six years."

"I didn't say you hadn't the *right*," Adrian defended. "Of course you have the *right*. Nay, above anyone else in this room, you have the responsibility to see that scum wiped from the earth. But Stan, you must see the logic in my argument: your mourning is so deep, so impenetrable—you are not yourself. Just because you want to believe that you will meet Glayer Felsteppe face-to-face and see him dead"— he turned to acknowledge each man in the room—"because *you* want to believe it, to finish what you started in Beckhamshire; because *you* want to believe, to save Constantine this suffering; because *you* want to believe, if only to show that there is something magical about this dreadful, miserable earthly existence."

Adrian turned back to Constantine. "Does not mean it is so. I do believe that if any can lead us to redemption—regain at least part of what we lost that terrible day at Chastellet—it is you, Stan. But you would put yourself, and us, in danger if you take on this fool's errand. You have been weakened by your loss. Your mental state is not sound."

Roman's gruff voice cut through the tension. "I think you've said quite enough, Adrian."

But Constantine acted as though the Norseman hadn't spoken. "Weak now, am I, Aid? Not mentally sound, you say?"

Adrian squared his jaw. "From all I have learned of the mind, that is my opinion. Yes."

"Physician, heal thyself," Constantine said in a low voice.

Adrian frowned. "This is not about me."

Valentine leaned forward in his chair, one elbow on the table. "It seems to me that all you have learned of the mind has been through personal experience, yes? Do you no hide yourself away in this very room, day after day, choosing to lose yourself in your precious learning? Do you no limp about, feeling sorry for yourself? At least Stan's behavior is justified. You are a coward."

"Yes," Roman added, warming to the idea the Spaniard was undoubtedly alluding to. "When it is you who has the most knowledge of building, by your own arrogant admission."

"And," even Victor seemed eager for the sacrifice, "if we are all such fools for believing in anything that cannot be grasped in the hand, you are the best candidate to take on the task. Surely your superior intellect could not be led astray."

Every pair of eyes was fixed to him now, and Adrian wondered at their sudden hostility. He'd only been trying to save Constantine's life by pointing out the obvious. Now they were attacking him.

Adrian looked at them all in turn and realized he was nodding his head. He held out his palms. "You want me to go?"

Constantine's scowl relented a bit. "You don't have to go, Adrian."

"No," Valentine said with a whiff of disgust in his tone. "If Glayer Felsteppe survived my blade, he is unlikely to be bragged to death."

"Oh, he is capable of tactics more deadly than that, aren't you, Adrian?" Roman said quietly, and when Adrian met the Norseman's ice blue eyes he once more saw the splash of blood, heard the clang of swords beneath the hellish cries of attack, smelled the sweat contained within the bowl of Chastellet's sunbaked walls.

Adrian again felt Roman's shoulders beneath him as he was carried—more dead than alive—from Saladin's prison.

"Fine," Adrian said, holding Roman's gaze for a heartbeat longer. Then he looked to Victor. "When am I to depart for this imaginary island?"

Victor seemed more than a little surprised. "Within the hour."

Inside, Adrian paused. He had not expected to leave so soon. Actually, he'd not expected to leave at all. Ever.

"Very well," he said. He gave the men seated around the table a nod. "I shall gather my things."

Victor called out to Adrian as he reached the stone slab. "We shall meet you in the courtyard, while the brethren are at their suppers. Lady Maisie's ship is moored downriver. You should reach it by nightfall."

"Ship, you say? What a shame. I'd hoped we'd be traveling by unicorn." Adrian paused with his hand on the latch and spoke over his shoulder. "Don't bother with seeing me off. I've little use for sentimental farewells when I'm being exiled."

Then he swung the door open and escaped into the black vortex of the stairwell.

Maisie Lindsey paced back and forth between two tall, winged angels in the courtyard of the abbey, her boots crunching on the gravel, made louder by the snow packed between the stones. The hood of her black cape was drawn up, doing much to shield her ears and the sides of her face from the biting wind swirling up off the Danube, and yet each time she spun on her heel to change directions, she caught sight of the stone eyes of the statues, staring at her reproachfully.

"Stop it," she muttered up at the one currently before her as she turned her back.

Crunch, crunch, crunch. The layers of her rose- and cream-colored skirts flaring out in front of her with each step.

What was taking him so long? She prepared to turn again, and saw the disappointed moue of yet another angel.

"Stop," she gritted out through her teeth. "I doona have any choice, do I?"

The hollowed stone pupils twitched forward with a little sandy whisper to regard the winter-stilled courtyard once more.

Maisie heaved a great sigh and turned to continue her pacing.

Then she saw the lone figure emerging from between the columned archways, his telltale monk's robes kicking up above the gravel path. He walked with a limp.

"Oh, good," she mumbled. "He's crippled." She noticed the man regarded her openly as he approached. Stared at her, actually, and his impertinence caused her to bristle.

She glanced up at the statue next to her and then glared at it until even the great angel had to avert his gaze.

The monk reached her at last, his hooded brown eyes appraising her suspiciously. He could have at least shaved. Maisie mustered a thin smile and tried to enunciate her words clearly. "Good day. Do you speak any English?"

One of the monk's eyebrows rose. "I do. Would you care for me to teach it to you?"

Maisie frowned; his accent was clearly of the far southern island. "I thought you were Norse."

"Do I look Norse?"

Now it was Maisie's turn to raise an eyebrow. "Nay. Actually you look a bit of a weasel, so I couldna be certain. You're quite rude for having just met a lady."

"Forgive me; I assumed the qualifier of your title 'in-waiting' absolved me of the burden of chivalry until a later time. And you *did* just refer to me as a weasel."

"I didna. I only said you had the look of a weasel. Whether you actually are one or nae remains to be seen."

"What exactly is that supposed to mean?"

She cocked her head and the wind chose that moment to reach inside her hood and pull forth a ringlet of her red curls. "Are you certain you speak English?"

He gave her a ghost of a smile, then. "Adrian Hailsworth."

"Lady Maisie Lindsey."

"Quite a musical name. Where are the horses, Maisie Lindsey?"

"*Lady* Maisie," she corrected. "They are in their stables, I assume."

Adrian Hailsworth began limping toward the wide gates of the abbey, and so she had no choice but to follow.

"The stable closer to the river, or in the east of the village?"

"The stables wherever one who keeps horses should live, I suppose," she clarified as they passed through the wrought-iron posterns.

The monk halted, turned to look at her. "You walked here?"

"I would have flown, but my arms were weary from such a long swim," she quipped.

Adrian's eyes narrowed. "How far? In case you haven't noticed, I am in possession of an old injury that is aggravated by overexercise."

Maisie started walking again, turning away from the town and heading south down the sloped motte. "Only a pair of hours. If we hurry, we can be at the ship well before midnight."

"I can't walk for two hours."

She stopped and turned around, looking down at his legs. Then she looked up at the monk. "Why nae? Your leg is fine."

"It's not *fine*," he growled.

She growled back. "Can I request another monk? This one seems to be broken."

They stared at each other for several moments before Adrian Hailsworth at last broke the standoff. "No, you can't request another monk. This isn't a market. It's an abbey."

Maisie looked over Adrian's tall form toward the statues in the courtyard. The ones she could still see from beyond the wall—perhaps six—were all cheeky enough to have turned their very heads to watch her depart. "Fallen Angels Abbey," she murmured grimly.

Adrian turned his head to see where she looked, and at his movement, the statues faced forward once more, as if completely well-mannered. "Hmm," he mused, and then regarded Maisie with a faint look of surprise. "That's actually more fitting than you know."

"I likely know more than you would think is fitting," she said quickly, and then turned away and began walking down the frozen hillside again, mentally kicking herself.

"Come on," she called over her shoulder. "If I've nae returned by midnight, the ship will leave without us."

"Is that part of the fairy tale?" he challenged.

"Oh, aye," she said, tossing her head and rolling her eyes at the stark winter landscape. Then she muttered under her breath, "Just wait until you meet me dragon."

Chapter 3

Barely a quarter of an hour had passed before Adrian was kicking himself for his hasty decision to leave Melk. The dark winter sky rushed toward full dark at an astonishing pace, the wind picking up and blasting mean little flurries from the low roiling clouds as the last of the meager daylight seemed to leach from the bone-chilling air.

Ahead of him, Maisie Lindsey navigated the rocky path along the river as if she possessed hooves at the terminus of her legs rather than feet. It took all of Adrian's concentration to merely keep her in his sight, her black cape blending into the jagged shadows as she rolled ahead of him like fog. After a full hour, his leg screamed and pulled with each step, and his buttock began to cramp.

As far as Adrian knew, Maisie Lindsey had not bothered to glance back at him once to be sure he still followed. If she had, Adrian would have tried to engage her in conversation; perhaps then she would slow her pace somewhat. But he would be damned if he would call out to her to beg for reprieve. The way she had looked at him and called him broken outside the courtyard at Melk had stung more than Adrian cared to admit. Although as the wind rushed in his ears and his heart pounded in his chest, as night fell and the cold settled into his bones with an ache that was nearly audible, Adrian was seriously considering bending and picking up a handful of rocks to throw at her. Anything to get her to slow down.

Sweat ran in rivulets down his temples, dripped from his nose; the cold air seared his lungs. A rock turned beneath his boot as he stepped on it and Adrian slid sideways, falling onto the path with a breathy grunt.

He didn't think she had noticed that he'd fallen until he heard the fast little crunches of her footfalls drawing nearer to him in the dark.

"What?" she demanded. "What is it? What's this about?"

Adrian struggled to gain his feet in as dignified a manner as he could manage. It was a trial, as it seemed his right leg no longer wanted to bend at all now.

"I thought I spied a jewel in the road," he said through his teeth, giving a little hop onto his left leg.

He could see the darker shadow of her outline as she placed her hands on her hips. "What?"

"I slipped." Adrian sighed. "My leg is—"

His explanation was cut off as Maisie Lindsey gave a great sigh and abruptly left the path to approach the sparse woods to their left. She returned in a moment with what appeared in the darkness to be a long branch. She snapped off the reedy tip and spindly twigs jutting out from its sides and then stomped the thick end onto the road twice—Adrian could feel the reverberations through the soles of his own boots. Then she thrust it at him.

"Here you are," she said and then spun on her heel. "Now, hurry. We're almost there."

Adrian reluctantly braced himself against the makeshift walking stick and stepped forward with his right foot. He was amazed to discover that the discomfort was lessened by half, and in moments, he had nearly caught up with Maisie Lindsey.

He was disappointed in himself that he hadn't thought of the thing earlier—after all, it was simply a matter of physics. If the crutch was taking half of the burden of his stride, it would only make sense that his discomfort would be lessened by at least as much, not even considering the completely mental reassurance the stick provided as a way to test out his footfalls on the black road before he stepped. Such a simple, brilliant solution.

Regardless of the thousands of manuscripts at his disposal, life at the abbey was obviously causing Adrian's brain to rot.

To his further astonishment, the longer he walked, the less he felt any discomfort at all. It seemed only moments had passed when Maisie Lindsey veered suddenly to the right ahead of him. Adrian could smell the dormant cold of the river before he crested the edge of the path and looked down to find Maisie's goatlike shadow skittering over the rocks, but what he saw was, again, not what he expected.

This surely could not be Maisie Lindsey's ship—the one that was to navigate the North Sea to the Scots coast in winter. The long black shape on the inky water below seemed little more than a strange, cylindrical raft without even a mast at its center.

Maisie Lindsey stopped at the edge of the river and turned to look back at him. "What are you waiting for? Come on!" Then she gave a great leap onto the vessel itself, not bothering to wait to see if Adrian would follow.

Which he did, and as he drew nearer to the narrow ship, he saw the long oars jutting from the side nearest the riverbank, the slightly domed shape of the deck with its square depression in the center of the vessel, hinting at cabin areas to either side. Not even a railing could be seen, nor a wheel for steering. Its general shape reminded Adrian of the long Norse ships he had seen on occasion, but up close, it was apparent that this vessel was wider, although its keel appeared so shallow as to be nearly flat.

"Come on!" Maisie Lindsey repeated, waving to him from the center of the odd ship. A single lantern hung on a hook to the side of a short black doorway behind her, and as Adrian gathered himself for the short leap from the rocks to the ship, the oars protruding from the side of the ship lifted and turned in unison, showing Adrian the sharp, blond wooden edges.

The sudden synchronic movement unsettled him, and he hesitated.

"Adrian!" Maisie called out. "If you doona get on, you'll be left behind!"

Adrian's eyes flicked back to the twenty oars on the side of the ship facing him, and as if they were obeying a command from Maisie Lindsey, the paddles turned flat edge, moved forward as one entity, and cut into the water.

"Adrian!" Maisie called again.

Adrian dropped his staff and leapt onto the ship just as it began to turn into the river. He fell heavily onto his right side but gained his feet quickly, only noticing as he did so that he had not cried out in agony.

His leg felt fine.

He took a moment to look across the width of the ship—perhaps a span of only fifteen feet—and saw an identical set of oars on the far side of the vessel, moving in perfect, silent unison with its counterparts on portside.

Adrian turned to inquire of Maisie Lindsey as to the miraculous nature of this unique ship, but she was gone, the low black square of the doorway the only clue as to where she had disappeared.

Adrian turned back toward the river once more, looking around at the land that was blurring into a black wash as the vessel picked up unlikely speed. The frigid air blasted Adrian's skin, but his stance on the decking was sure; it was as if the ship glided through the river as a bird in the air.

This is starting off to be quite a strange adventure indeed, he said to himself, not realizing the small smile that had sneaked across his mouth.

Then he ducked into the black doorway to find Maisie Lindsey.

Maisie threw off her cape onto the low chair as she came into the cabin and lit the lanterns without thinking. She held her breath and spun around, but Adrian Hailsworth had yet to follow her down the short ladder. She would have to mind herself a bit until he got used to her. It would not do to have him attempt to throw himself overboard into the sea halfway to Wyldonna. Maisie would have to turn around and go back to Melk to fetch a replacement, and there just simply wasn't time for that nonsense.

She raked her fingers up into the tangle of curls caught at her crown and blew out a stiff breath as she looked across the tall cauldron to the table laid for two on the other side of the cabin. Her shoulders slumped as she stared at the white fish with lingonberry relish on the metal trenchers, the chalices she knew contained fermented, spiced goats' milk.

She'd been expecting a Norseman.

Maisie glanced over her shoulder to make certain she was still alone as she strode past the cauldron, absently patting its rim twice as she passed. She heard the whoosh and crackle of the flames behind her as she lifted the heavy lid of her provisions trunk at the table's edge. She turned quickly and squatted down to peer out the doorway and saw the outline of Adrian Hailsworth's body coming toward the entrance to the cabin. Then she rose and pulled the meal from the tabletop into the trunk with both arms, resulting in a terrible crash, and then dropped the lid of the provisions trunk closed, just as the Englishman gave a shout of alarm.

"Watch yourself," Maisie called out. "'Tis a ladder rather than steps."

"Yes, I see that now," he said wryly, backing down the short set of rungs.

"Close the hatch, if you would," Maisie said. She watched him carefully as he slid the thick, square wooden panel into place and latched the bolt.

Englishman, Englishman. Long away from home, probably missing Cook's hearty meals. A meat pie, then. And . . . and what?

Adrian turned to face the cabin, and his look of amazement at the tidy space was impossible to miss. "Where was this ship built? I've never seen any of its kind—it's neither a longship nor a cog. But the oars . . . ?" He moved deeper into the cabin toward her, his eyes taking in every corner of the wood-paneled room.

"It's called a crawler," Maisie supplied, continuing to watch him closely. It was important to get this right. "I'd wager you willna see another of its kind, as they're only made on Wyldonna." Ah ha! She reached for the lid of the provisions trunk and swung it open, reaching inside until she felt the handle of a jug. Maisie lifted it out and gestured toward the Englishman. "Mead?"

He paused and looked at her with raised eyebrows. "Truly?"

Maisie couldn't help her smug smile as she reached into the trunk again and withdrew two chalices with her free hand. "Made with the finest honey." She set the cups on the tabletop and poured as he came around the cauldron toward the table. "Wyldonian weather is unpredictable. Crawlers must be ready to navigate water, ice, snow; the smaller ones can be pulled by animals if need be."

Adrian Hailsworth picked up one of the chalices but, to Maisie's surprise, he waited for her to bring her own cup to her mouth. The manners of a nobleman, she noted.

"But the friction on the wood," he said. "It would seem that the ships would spend more time in repair than in use if used as sleds on ice or turf." He took a drink and then swallowed, looking in surprise at his cup. "I'll be damned, but this is good."

Maisie couldn't help her small smile. At least she'd gotten one thing right today. "That would be true if the bottoms werena clad."

"Clad?"

"Copper."

Adrian stared at her for a moment, and then his eyes went back to his cup. "Amazing," he muttered, bringing the chalice to his lips and turning away from her to survey the cabin once more. "Where are the oarsmen?"

Maisie set her cup on the table and reached into the trunk. What would one keep a mince pie in? "Oarsmen?"

"Yes, I can't guess where there would be enough room on either side to house so many, and yet the ship itself doesn't appear deep enough for them to be below us. One would think we would be right on top of them."

"One would, would they nae?" Maisie huffed a laugh as she laid a hand on a package wrapped in rough-woven cloth. It seemed as likely as anything. She brought out the dish and set it on the table.

Adrian turned back toward the table, although by now he was on the far side of the cauldron. "I should like a full tour of the bilge in the daylight."

"Oh, I doona know if that's possible," Maisie hedged as she unwrapped the cloth from the metal dish. "Nae much room for visitors. Mince?" She tilted the crusty top toward the Englishman and gave him what she hoped was her most beguiling smile.

Adrian Hailsworth's eyes narrowed and his mouth turned down in a slight frown. "That's a mince pie?"

"Well, er . . ." Maisie felt her smile falter as she glanced down at the pastry-topped dish. "I believe it's mince. Do you nae care for mince? Would you prefer fish?"

"Not at all," Adrian said hesitantly, his frown still firmly in place. "I've not had mince pie in ages—it's my favorite, actually. Cook at home made the most delicious mince I've ever tasted."

"Oh, good!" Maisie sighed. "I'm quite certain it is mince, then. Yes. Absolutely sure." Maisie clasped her hands at her waist and tried to force another cheerful smile at him when he made no further move toward the table. "Are you . . . are you nae hungry?" Her teeth felt like they would crack.

Adrian frowned at the pie, at the cup in his hand, turned his scowl about the cabin, and then his brown eyes landed fully on Maisie.

"I am," he said. "It's only . . ." He cocked his head and looked suspiciously at her.

Maisie wanted to scream. But she swallowed down her impatience. "It's only what?"

"I must say, I was regretting my acceptance of this mission from the moment I found you pacing in the abbey's bailey. I was quite certain this would be a fool's errand and that I would find myself at the mercy of a savage people. But, so far, I have been treated to a marvel of seafaring engineering, the pleasure of my favorite food and drink, and the promise of—"

Maisie allowed her smile to widen. "A comfortable journey with a beautiful woman?"

Adrian hesitated. "I was going to say the promise of a riddle to solve." Maisie tried to keep her lips from pursing as she felt the tips of her ears heat.

"Let's just eat, shall we?" she suggested, pulling out her chair and sitting. "After we've dined, I will show you the drawings of Wyldonna Castle, and you can get right to your riddle, Brother Adrian."

He pulled out his chair and sat. "I should probably tell you, in case you haven't already guessed—I'm not actually a monk. It's best you have no illusions about who I am or what I can do for you."

Maisie paused, the knife in her hand poised over the pie. Then she smiled, and cut Adrian Hailsworth a very generous piece.

Adrian looked carefully at the sketches spread over the tabletop now that their—admittedly delicious—supper had been cleared. The drawings were amateurish, yes, but strong and remarkably detailed, with a separate page for each level of the castle. He glanced up at Maisie Lindsey, startled for a moment at how near to him she stood. He'd not noticed her moving toward him and now she leaned over the table with one slender arm holding her aright, her head cocked as she surveyed the print, her riotous hair slinking over her shoulder in springy, bold curls. She smelled like fields of heather.

He quickly drew his gaze back to the stack of parchment, flipping up a corner of the topmost one to glance at one beneath for comparison. "Are these renderings quite complete?"

"Aye," Maisie said. "Laid down by the queen's own hand."

He couldn't help but glance up at the woman again, and she answered his unasked question straightaway.

"Nae one else knows the castle better than she. Perhaps the king, but . . ." She shrugged.

Adrian ran his finger along a maze of parallel lines. "Corridors?"

"Aye."

He flipped the top two sheets back and forth several times. "What of this chamber here?" He pointed to a square that seemed to jut out from the castle wall—too deep to be a garderobe—then flipped to the page beneath. "There is nothing that corresponds to the level below. What's beneath it?"

"Nothing."

Adrian looked up at her, feeling his eyebrow raise. "Nothing?"

She gave him something of an indulgent look while waggling her fingers back and forth. "There is air. And fifty feet below"—she abruptly swept her palm down to the tabletop—"rocks."

He shook his head with a sigh and then tapped circular shapes sketched at six wide angles of the perimeter. "And these?"

"Towers," Maisie supplied as she leaned closer to him, bringing a rush of her scent with her. She pointed to four in quick succession. "These have stairs."

He looked sideways at her. "How do you gain the top of the other two?"

"You doona."

Adrian glanced at the drawing again. The two towers were at opposite ends of the print. Decorative, then? Structural? It would seem likely if the towers were at right angle corners of a square construction, but this castle seemed to be hexagonal—why build two useless towers?

He dismissed the idea for the time being. It was likely this queen's lady was only mistaken as to the castle's components. "Have you been in service to the queen long?"

"Nae," Maisie said, obviously losing interest in the drawing and walking across the cabin to sit in an odd chair, low to the ground with long arms. The back and seat were tilted at an angle, so that its occupant seemed to recline. She stared up at the close, planked ceiling. "Only after Glayer Felsteppe left Wyldonna."

Adrian nodded as his suspicions were confirmed. "It seems rather a dangerous mission to put upon someone just entered into service."

"Well, I suppose she's known me all my life," Maisie said contemplatively. "There was nae one—absolutely nae one—else to trust. I'm doing what I must to save my home—our home," she emphasized.

"The fate of all of magical Wyldonna rests on the efforts of a brave but humble lady-in-waiting," Adrian said, unable to help his smirk. "It does sound like something of a tale, you must agree."

Maisie Lindsey let her head roll against the wood back of the chair to regard him. Her forearm lay across the rest, her palm up, and even from across the cabin Adrian could make out the bright blue veins just beneath her ivory skin.

"Aye. Or a legend." She regarded him for a moment. "I know you doona believe any of it."

Adrian looked back to the drawings. When he answered her, his voice was intentionally gruff. "You're right—I don't."

She sighed from her chair, and her voice sounded weary. "You will."

Chapter 4

Maisie did not slip easily into slumber that night, even though she was fatigued beyond measure when she crawled into her berth behind the thick woven curtain in one corner of the cabin. Adrian Hailsworth seemed to find a bit of difficulty falling asleep himself, if the tossing and turning she heard from the opposite corner of the cabin was any indication. She tensed at every little sound he made at first, but then, when the cabin was quite still, signaling that he at last slept, Maisie found that she actually missed the evidence that there was another human being on the crawler with her. She had been alone for weeks before fetching Adrian Hailsworth from Melk. But the simple knowledge of his presence must have given her some measure of comfort, for when she finally succumbed to exhaustion, she slept deeply.

So deeply, in fact, that she had not heard the Englishman rise before her, and she only came awake—quite at once—when she heard him struggling with the hatch.

"Oh, nay. Nay, nay, nay," she mumbled as she fought to disentangle herself from her covers, pedaling her feet against their strangling hold and then throwing back the curtain before she had come to stand properly.

Her vision was still clouded with sleep, the dimness of the cabin lit by only the cauldron hampering her ability to see beyond it. She staggered forward, one hand rubbing at her eyes, the other held before her.

"What is it?" she called groggily. "What's wrong?"

There was a pause in the cursing and scraping. "This blasted hatch is stuck." She heard two thuds as his feet assumedly came from the ladder back to the floor, and then she saw his outline move toward her. His brown monk's robes were gone, leaving him clothed in a white undershirt and brown chausses and his boots. The stubble on his jaw had increased from yesterday, and Maisie found his appearance quite large and startlingly masculine. "Likely the humidity," he added.

"The what?" Maisie turned away from him to approach her provisions trunk beyond the table. She squatted down and lifted the lid, in search of a jug of cider.

"The moisture in the air," he said, his footsteps coming up behind her. She closed the trunk quickly and then used a hand on the edge of the table to help her to stand. "From being on the water. Ofttimes wood—"

She waved a hand to cut him off. "Yes, yes," she said gruffly, and poured a measure of the crisp drink into a cup.

He seemed to be waiting for her to say something further, and when she only attended to her drink, he continued. "I'll need a hammer, or a lever of some sort."

Maisie looked up at him, her irritation barely in check. Couldn't he see she'd just come from bed? "A lever? Whatever for?"

He stared at her, blinked once. "To pry loose the latch."

"Why would you want to pry loose the latch?" she insisted, squinting at him and then dragging a chair from the table to sit down.

"Why would I—?" he broke off and adjusted his stance to place his hands on his hips. Maisie tried not to look at him. "So that I might open the door, is why."

"There's naught up there," she half-groaned, rubbing her eyes once more. "And we're going at such a speed that 'tis unsafe to be above deck."

"I've sailed on many a swift ship, Lady Maisie," Adrian insisted. "And this one cannot even claim sails. I assure you, I am more than capable of keeping my legs beneath me while we navigate a river."

"You've nae been on a ship with me before," she muttered into her hands.

"What?"

"I said, it will be a bit before we can open the door." She lowered her hands and looked at him at last. "It will loosen eventually."

"I need it to loosen now," he said and turned to walk about the cabin, his head craning and swiveling, peering onto the shelves and in the corners. "Have you a thick blade or a metal wedge?"

"Nay."

"A sturdy spoon would do."

"Why are you in such a hurry to get above?" she insisted as he strode toward her curtained area. "Get away from there!"

Adrian grabbed a fistful of the curtain and yanked it open fully, peering inside the private enclosure where she'd slept.

He turned on his heel and faced her, and Maisie at last saw the wild look in his eyes.

"I can't be contained in small areas," he said, and she noted the rapid rise and fall of his chest.

"You were fine all the night while you were sleeping," she pointed out, bewildered.

"That's because I thought I could easily depart if I chose to," he said as his eyes fell onto her provisions trunk.

She realized his intent in the same moment that he had made his decision, and Maisie stood from her chair with a scrape and turned to block his access to the trunk.

"There's naught in there," she said, barely stopping herself from flinging her arms wide. "I'll nae have you rifling through my things, messing up the order of them."

"There must be a utensil of some sort," he said as he kept advancing. Maisie saw then that his panic was authentic and he would not be denied, and so she did hold forth one palm.

"I'll look," she said, and was grateful when he at last came to a halt only inches from her fingertips. "Just . . . just wait a moment." She drew a deep breath. Great Gods, what an encounter to contend with first thing in the morn. "All right?"

"Are you going to look or not?" he demanded.

"Aye!" she shouted. "Would you sit down before you cause me to leap from my skin? Have a drink!"

"I'll wait here, thank you," he said between his teeth.

Maisie sighed while sending him a glare, and then turned to once more squat down before the trunk. She lifted the lid only enough to slip her right arm inside and stir her hand around.

Biscuits; oats; wine. Another meat pie? He was unlikely to be treated to another of those anytime soon, the weasel. More wine. That felt as grass—what was that doing in there? Fur?

"Ouch!" She withdrew her hand and stuck her finger in her mouth. "Little bastard bit me," she whispered.

"What was that?" Adrian asked from behind her.

She withdrew her finger and glanced down at the bloody crescent at its tip. "Nothing," she tossed over her shoulder and reached back inside the trunk. She reminded herself to be careful of her thoughts. Now she had two weasels to attend to. "Pricked myself with a knife, is all." *I'll wring your bloody neck should you try that again, you squelchy puss.*

"A knife will do nicely," he said pointedly.

"Fine," she muttered, thinking to herself that, in other circumstances, she might be tempted to use a knife on Adrian Hailsworth. A rather large one. In the next instant her fingers curled around a smooth wooden handle. "A knife it is." She pulled out the requested item and was as surprised as Adrian Hailsworth seemed to be at the foot-long blade she held forth.

"Here you are," she said as calmly as she could manage as her cheeks flamed.

The Englishman's eyebrows rose as he took possession of the weapon. "I thought you said you didn't have anything of the sort." He turned away at once.

"I didna know for certain," she reasoned. "What use would I have for a knife of such a length?"

"Indeed," he muttered, climbing the short ladder. "I thought as much myself."

Maisie heard a scrabbling from inside the trunk, and so turned and delivered a swift kick to the side of the wood. She hoped Adrian Hailsworth could not hear the replying squeak. She glanced toward the hatch to make certain he was not looking at her before she patted the top of the trunk twice.

The scrabbling noises ceased, and Maisie wondered briefly if weasels could swim before she turned to give her full attention to the Englishman currently hacking at the latch of her door. "I wouldna do that if I were you . . . er, I'm nae exactly certain what to call you."

"My name is Adrian." He glanced back at her. "If I damage the ship, I shall repair it. I'm quite good with mechanics."

"Obviously, since you are clearly adept at operating a sliding door."

"Strange sense of humor you have for a lady-in-waiting."

"Do what you will. But doona say I didna warn you." She had little choice but to help him, unless she wanted the hatch reduced to splinters. It would never yield to him, any matter.

Maisie took her place at the table once more, and calmly picked up her cup. She held it toward Adrian Hailsworth's back in silent salute. "*Fosgail*," she whispered and then took a drink.

Adrian wasn't sure he'd be able to get the ridiculously long blade between the pin and the hasp to provide a suitable fulcrum without breaking off the knife tip and further incurring Maisie Lindsey's wrath, but no sooner had he managed to wedge a sliver of the metal against the wood than it slid open as if oiled. The knife slipped free, surprising him into giving a huff of breath.

"There we are," he said, hearing the smug satisfaction in his own voice as his panic began to lift like a fog. In another moment he would be free.

He backed down one rung of the ladder, the knife still held in his left hand, and released the latch with his right. Then he gripped the hasp and slid the hatch open.

He was nearly knocked from the ladder by the gale of icy rain and seawater that blasted through the opening, the wind screaming into the cabin like a banshee, sucking the warmth from the air and drenching him at once. Adrian threw up his right forearm to shield his eyes while he coughed and gasped, mindful of the miniature sword he still held in his other hand. He squinted through the punishing onslaught at the ice-crusted deck of the crawler ship as it seemed to rise up before him on the crest of a massive wave. He clutched at the ladder as he was thrown backward, and heard Maisie Lindsey cursing in quite an unladylike manner behind him as the sounds of furnishings sliding about the cabin reached his ears.

But Adrian braved the storm in disbelief, regaining his forfeited step and squinting through the tempest, attempting to make sense of what he was seeing: the ice and sleet of a full-on winter storm, sheeting the twenty-foot gray waves of the open sea. Try as he might, he could discern nothing beyond the ship's oars, waving in the air like insect legs, as they came upon another mountainous crest. No land at all.

They were on an ocean, when they should have still been floating leisurely down the Danube River.

"Will you shut the bloody door before we're drowned?" Maisie Lindsey shouted behind him, shaking Adrian from his shock and prompting him to slide the hatch door back to the left. A challenge, as the slender groove that housed it was already filled with freezing slush.

He shoved the pin home and backed down the ladder, noticing at once how the ship seemed to right itself on the waves, as if the storm beyond the hatch had suddenly ceased with the closing of the hatch. But his very bones shivered inside his soaked skin and his legs trembled atop his boots, which splashed to the floor in what appeared to be at least three inches of water, chunks of slush bobbing like ghostly anemones around his ankles.

Maisie Lindsey still sat at the small square table, but now her feet were drawn up onto the seat, away from the water swirling around her chair legs, her knees up by her chin and her skirts draping like a tent. She was shaking her head at him ruefully, her cup still clasped in her hand as she rested her elbows across the apex of her knees.

"Happy now, are you?" she asked. "Look at the mess I shall have to clean up, and I've nae even had my oatcake yet."

"What," he began in a voice that was slightly more civil than a growl, "was in that mead you gave me?"

Her brow crinkled as if he had spoken a foreign language.

"How long was I asleep?" he demanded as he splashed through the water toward the table.

"How should I know?" she replied in an irritated tone. "You woke before me."

He reached the table and slammed both palms down on the top, the knife blade clattering ominously. "You poisoned me."

"I'm thinking now that would have been a grand idea, but nay, I didna *poison* you," she said with a roll of her eyes, seeming completely unaffected by his anger.

"There is no other explanation," Adrian continued. "We departed Melk only last night—perhaps as few as seven hours ago. And yet when I look out yonder hatch, my eyes find no land."

Maisie blinked at him and then gave a shrug with one shoulder. "So?"

"*So?*" he repeated. "*So?*! We should be in the middle of a river, not the sea!"

"I told you the crawler was fleet." She brought the cup to her mouth again and sipped calmly.

"*No* ship is that fast," he insisted, banging his hands on the tabletop again for emphasis.

"Stop doing that. It pains my head."

He leaned toward her. "And why aren't we being tossed about the cabin like stones in a crate? The storm beyond is unlike anything I've ever witnessed at sea. We should be broken up at any moment by the waves and ice!"

"I *told you*," she said, her words muffled as she rubbed a hand across her face, either to help push the last vestiges of sleep from her countenance or in irritation, Adrian couldn't tell at the moment. "Ice, water, land—it makes nae difference. The crawler *goes*."

"And *I'm* telling *you*," he said, "that where we are right now is an impossibility!" He slammed his hands on the table a third time.

He heard the screech and slosh of wood through water too late to brace himself as the chair caught him behind the knees, forcing his legs to bend and his arse to fall into the seat as his stomach was pushed into the table. The knife clattered away from his flailing hands.

"An impossibility, is it?" she asked calmly, one burnished eyebrow raised. "Why is that? Because you demand that it's impossible?"

Adrian's stomach felt as though it was little more than the opening to a gaping pit. How had the ship moved so that the chair slid beneath him with such force but he hadn't felt the sudden listing himself? And why had Maisie Lindsey failed to even wobble atop her perch?

"It's simply a matter of physics," he said, noticing that his voice was much calmer now, despite the anxiety he felt in his middle. "Melk is six hundred miles to the North Sea, depending on the route you take and the weather. Even in a nimble vessel such as this, that trip could take no less that a fortnight."

"And yet here we are," Maisie mused, eyeing him.

"Facts are facts," Adrian insisted. "You must have poisoned me so that I slept through the first portion of the journey. Although why you would do such a thing, I cannot fathom."

"I didna poison you," she said calmly. "I have nae knowledge of the distance we are travelling, and that suits my purpose. I must return with you to Wyldonna in two days' time."

"Two days?" Adrian repeated. "But it will take at least—"

"Nay!" Maisie shouted, holding her palm toward him. "Nay, doona say anything. I doona wish to know how long you *think* it should take us. We shall arrive in two days, unless you insist upon opening the hatch again and sinking us. I can only do so much."

Adrian felt the blood leave his face. "You mean I'm trapped in here for at least two days?"

Maisie shrugged. "I suppose you could swim back, if you choose."

"Swim the North Sea in an ice storm," he clarified.

The corners of her mouth turned down slightly as she considered. "I wouldna be so confident that the North Sea is our exact location." She looked at him keenly for a moment. "I will tell you, though, that once we've arrived at Wyldonna, you willna be free to go until you've fulfilled your reason for being there."

Adrian felt his own eyebrows raise. "Really? And who is charged with holding me captive? You? I can promise you I've been liberated from more formidable captors than a female member of the lesser nobility."

Maisie Lindsey shook her head and her red curls bounced, although her eyes flashed with anger. "The island herself willna let you go."

"That's an old wives' tale," Adrian scoffed. "If the island even exists."

She continued to hold his gaze, as if debating whether to tell him something he might or might not want to know. In the end, though, she only shrugged again.

"Facts are facts, are they nae?"

Chapter 5

"**Y**ou'd best change out of those wet things before you catch your death," Maisie said to him after she had finished the cider in her cup. She needed to clean up the cabin a bit after Adrian's stubborn insistence in opening the hatch, and the way things had gone thus far that morning, it would be better if he hid himself away behind his curtain whilst she did. "I assume you brought another suit of clothes with you."

"Just my robes from the abbey," he said tightly, and she couldn't help but notice the way his hands were clenching rhythmically on the tabletop. He refused to meet her gaze.

Maisie set her cup down and gathered her skirts into her fists before lowering her feet into the icy water still flowing about the cabin.

"That's better than naught, I suppose," she said as she waded through ankle-high seawater to her provisions trunk. "I am a bit surprised that a man of your station only claims one simple shirt and chausses, though, even if he is pretending at being a monk."

"What do you mean?" he asked in a guarded tone as she pulled out the jug of mead from the night before. Luckily, nothing bit her this time.

"You're from a noble family," she said, rising and coming back to the table to set the jug before him. "Or am I mistaken?"

"No," he said slowly, eyeing the mead suspiciously. Apparently he'd decided the drink wasn't poisoned after all—or perhaps he was hoping that it was—for he reached for the neck of the jug and poured a healthy measure into the cup he'd abandoned hours ago. "I can claim a courtesy title, although I don't use it. My older brother is lord."

Maisie paused to look at him closely. The skin around his lips was white, as if he was exerting tremendous self-control by only sitting there. "You wish it was you?"

He glanced up at her over the rim of his cup. "Wish I were lord?" She nodded, and he gave a frown. "God, no. Why on earth would I wish to be saddled with the running of a keep and preserving the livelihood of all who live under my rule?" He took a drink, hiding his gaze for a moment.

Maisie felt a bit small after his sensible explanation, but thankfully he was not interested in her motives enough to question her. He set his cup down but picked up the jug as he moved around the table toward his curtained partition, gesturing toward her with the mead. "You don't mind, do you?"

"Nay. Toss your clothes out and I will hang them up near the cauldron to dry," she offered. "Your boots might take a while longer."

His reply was the hush of brass rings as he jerked the curtain shut after him.

Maisie raised an eyebrow at the curtain but then quickly turned toward the cabin to begin her tasks. She didn't know how long she would have.

First things first: the water situation.

She had no choice but to drop the hem of her skirts as she brought both palms together in front of her waist and then moved them away from each other in a sweeping motion as she splashed toward the cauldron. Her toes were already numb. She patted the rim twice as the sound of gurgling water echoed in the wooden cabin, and soon flames leapt above the metal bowl, replacing the flickering glow that had warmed the cabin through the night. Little rivulets of water tickled the arches of her feet inside her slippers as the floor seemed to suck up the moisture, and so she balanced precariously on one foot, then the other, as she slipped them off. The boards beneath her feet were scratchy and damp.

What a bothersome man he was turning out to be.

As if turning her thoughts toward him again had roused him, Adrian called from behind the curtain. "What of you? Have you any family?"

"I've a brother. We're twins, actually," Maisie supplied, although she was rather surprised at how readily she answered him. She waved her slippers over the flames in the cauldron in turn.

"Twins? You must be close."

"Nae of late," she replied, pausing to bend down and slip the toasty warm shoes onto her frozen feet. "He . . . doesna approve of my new role."

"Not an admirer of the queen, is he?"

"Of her actions, rather."

Adrian grunted from behind the curtain. "I must say that I share his opinion from the little I've been told." The brass rings tinkled as a bundle of dripping clothes was thrust through the narrow opening between the curtain and the wall.

Maisie crossed the cabin with a frown. "What have you been told?" She reached out to take the clothes and caught a glimpse of Adrian Hailsworth's wrist and forearm—the latter crosshatched with dark black markings.

Her stomach did a neat flip in her abdomen.

But before she could study the shapes, he pulled his arm back in.

"That she instigated a coup against the king and has now found herself in a quandary of her own making. One that she needs my help to extricate herself from. Isn't that the gist of it?" His boots thunked to the floor, one after the other.

Maisie shook herself from the shock the sight of his arm had given her. She had likely only imagined what she saw any matter.

"There's more to it than that. You shouldna judge her so harshly before you know the whole of it." She reluctantly picked up the worn leather boots, feeling the rumblings of new anger grow as she saw herself in the role of laundress for this particularly arrogant Englishman. "She is a good woman."

He harrumphed.

"She is," Maisie insisted, turning away from the curtain before she did or said something she would very soon after regret. She tried not to think of the purpose for Adrian Hailsworth's journey to Wyldonna. "You'll see. She meant nae harm to the king or her people. Quite the opposite."

"Any who aligns himself with the likes of Glayer Felsteppe cannot have selfless motivations. He is a liar and a murderer and a traitor."

Maisie dropped the boots to the floor and felt her cheeks heat, and not only from the flames in the cauldron as she reached up high to hang Adrian's clothes from the hooks in the ceiling.

"I'm certain she didna ken his full character when first they met."

"I'm certain she was only interested in whatever he promised her when they did," he shot back from behind the curtain.

Maisie spun to face the embroidered cloth. "It's easy to see why it was your brother who was made lord and nae you."

"Yes, it's called primogeniture," he said with a sigh, and Maisie could picture him stretching out on the narrow bunk. "Had I the misfortune to have been born first, I assure you that I would have gladly forfeited the title."

"Rather disrespectful to your father's legacy." She sniffed, lifting her nose into the air and admittedly feeling quite superior.

"It would have been more disrespectful to have taken on a role for which I am ill-equipped," Adrian Hailsworth said blithely. "I've never had any desire to rule or to manage. I want only to read and think and learn and build. To be left alone, really."

Maisie blinked at the curtain. For a moment she wondered what it would be like to be so very certain of your own person, your dreams and talents and desires. To be certain of them, and to have the means to act upon them without fear of the consequences.

But then she remembered where she had found Adrian Hailsworth.

"Then why did you agree to come to Wyldonna's aid?" she asked, fearing it was unwise to learn too much about this man's motives and character, but at the same time unable to withstand her curiosity about him.

Silence filled the cabin of the crawler for several heartbeats.

"I don't really know," he said at last.

And Maisie did not believe him in the least.

"I'll send your clothes through once they've dried," she offered.

He didn't answer her, and so she turned from the curtain to face Adrian's wet and dripping garments hanging from the ceiling. She could have seen them bone dry in an instant, but she needed some distance from this man, whose firm ideals seemed to take up so much room both on the crawler and in Maisie's head. Glancing over her shoulder to make certain he wasn't spying on her, she reached up and took hold of the hem of each garment in her hands and concentrated.

After a moment, she dropped her hands with a frustrated sigh. They weren't even his clothes, unless he transformed into an aged tailor in the night. Likely they'd been fashioned for him shortly before he'd left Melk.

Then Maisie's gaze fell on the old, worn boots she'd dropped on the floor near the cauldron. One had fallen over onto its side, and although the leather that fashioned the whole of the thing was so worn that it was almost black with age and oil, the boots sported obvious new soles. On the upright shoe, darker splotches punctuated the toe area, as though the stains had not been tended to right away, and had permeated the leather. Maisie crouched down and touched a finger to one of the free-form discolorations. She drew her hand back to her chest in a fist.

Blood. Adrian's blood.

Maisie looked over her shoulder once more, and this time the frown that creased her brow was more quizzical than angry.

I want only to read and think and learn and build.

How had it come to pass that a man who proclaimed to be a scholar had seen so much of his own blood spilled upon his boots? And although fine footwear was dear to come by regardless of your station, why would he choose to retain boots in which such a tragedy had occurred? Even going so far as to have them resoled?

Maisie could have touched the stains again, learned more about the misfortune that had at one time likely caused Adrian Hailsworth a great deal of pain. But her cheeks heated again and she stood, returning her attention to the straightening of the rest of the cabin. She had no need to know anything further of him. It was none of her affair.

But as she went about her chores a tiny, traitorous voice murmured to her that she didn't want to know only because, if Maisie had her way, Adrian Hailsworth would soon find himself on the receiving end of considerably more misfortune.

Adrian stared at the low, planked ceiling above his berth, concentrating on his breathing. In, one, two; out, three, four. After several moments, he had stretched his inhalations and exhalations to a count of eight and didn't feel quite so much like clawing his way out of his own skin.

That is, as long as he kept himself from thinking about the fact that he was trapped inside a tiny, windowless boat, in the middle of an ice storm at sea, with no means of escape whatsoever.

Back to the beginning, then. He raised his head and took a swig from the jug, then lay back down. *In, one, two; out, three, four . . .*

Better to turn his mind to the riddle of how he had arrived at his present predicament rather than the what of it. The most likely answer was that he had indeed slept through the first portion of their journey. After all, that was precisely how Valentine Alesander had dealt with his seasick woman on their journey to England. Mary Beckham had slept for days, none the worse for wear. But why would Maisie Lindsey deny it?

Who wants to admit they're a poisoner?

True, but it's not as if I wasn't ever going to notice. Did she think I was dim-witted, perhaps?

Any fool not giving pause at the idea of a journey from Austria to Scotland taking only three days is likely too mentally inconvenienced to draw breath continuously, let alone to put both legs in chausses. I do doubt she requested the aid of an idiot.

In, one, two, three, four; out, one, two, three, four . . .

It's likely she did poison me; she only hasn't got up the courage to admit it yet. After all, if I took it badly—which I did—I could have brought her to some harm.

Perhaps, yes. But I'm not very hungry, am I? As one might expect after having been asleep for the better part of a fortnight.

Adrian reached up with his left hand and rubbed at his jaw. He hadn't shaved in a pair of days before leaving the abbey—much to Victor's dismay, likely—and yet he wasn't sporting a full beard. Like Herne Hailsworth, Adrian could manifest an admirable face of hair in only a handful of days.

She could have shaved me, I suppose.

It doesn't seem to be in her nature to care for others in such a personal manner. Rather . . . unfeminine. No, that wasn't an accurate description. Reserved, perhaps, was better.

She wouldn't have been caring for me, necessarily; she would have been covering her tracks. Although she did provide a fine meal last night. Or whenever it really was.

In, one, two, three, four, five, six, seven, eight . . .

I, too, would be especially nice to someone I was persuading to ingest poison.

Touché.

Adrian turned over the various points both for and against the idea that he'd been poisoned by Maisie Lindsey in his head for the better part of an hour. Each time he'd thought he'd come up with a definitive answer to the question of how long he'd slept since last crawling into the berth, some other bit of reason would rise and defeat it. He was soon forced to accept the only logical conclusion: He had only slept the length of one typical night.

But how, then, had they come to already be at sea?

Snippets of his last conversation with his friends in Melk's secret library flew unbidden through his mind.

It is a magical island . . .

Enchanted . . .

Populated by fairies, mystical creatures . . .

Adrian closed his eyes with a self-deprecating grin. He probably really should have a bit to eat before imbibing any more mead. Perhaps there would be another mince pie waiting for him once his clothes were dry.

The ghost of a smile remained on his lips as he drifted off into a relaxed slumber.

The scrape and clang of a gate caused his eyes to snap back open almost instantly, but the planked ceiling and hollow silence of the crawler had been replaced by sandstone sueded with torchlight and the faint screams of prisoners hidden away by twisting corridors. There was Constantine, tethered by his neck to the wall, his mane of hair now matted and dark, his face lined with sweat and grime and worry, his clothes hanging on his once sturdy frame like so many old rags tossed over a winter-nuded bush. The smell of Adrian's own rotting body washed over him like a familiar perfume, and the agony of his injuries bloomed once more with vivid intensity.

With one painful blink, Maisie Lindsey and her poison were forgotten as if they'd never existed, and Adrian was once more crumpled on the floor of the Damascene dungeon, where a large robed bundle now rolled awkwardly with some force into the wall opposite the cell door.

The door slammed shut, and the bundle of robes unfurled itself to reveal what appeared to be one of Saladin's own soldiers.

The man got to his feet with a groan, brushed himself off, and then placed his hands on his hips, looking from Constantine to Adrian and then back to Constantine.

"Gerard and Hailsworth, I presume?" he said in perfect English, accented with the spicy flavor of the Spanish shore.

Constantine's eyes narrowed. *"I don't know what you think to learn from us, but we have nothing to tell you."*

"I am no spy, my friend, although very soon Saladin will likely think me one. And I have your *friend to thank for it."*

Adrian's ears itched at the mention of a friend. He and Constantine had no friends in the Holy Land any longer. They were all dead. Unless the Spaniard was referring to Glayer Felsteppe...

As if Constantine had read Adrian's mind, he demanded, *"What friend?"*

"The giant." The Spaniard slid down the sandstone wall to sit on the floor near Adrian's blood-blackened boots. He kept his irritated expression, one knee bent up, his other leg stretched out before him, allowing his robes to reveal a pair of finely tooled leather boots of his own. He threw out an arm in disgust. *"The white monster. He attacked me in Chastellet's bailey! Demanded I show him the way to Damascus so that he might rescue his friends."* Then he waved a hand, as if dismissing the whole episode. *"Bah. I knew it would no work."*

Constantine's eyes met Adrian's for an instant before turning back to the Spaniard. *"The giant—was he called Roman Berg?"*

"Yes! Roman Berg!" The dark-skinned man spat the name like an expletive. *"He gave me a sack of coin to attempt to bribe the guards for your release. Now I have no coin, no horse, and will quite likely suffer a traitor's death along with the two of you."* The Spaniard swung his head toward Adrian and looked him up and down uninterestedly. *"Well, perhaps no you. I doubt you will survive the three days you have left before they are to kill you, my friend."*

Adrian's heart beat faster in his chest, causing the thrums of constant pain to turn into a stabbing vibration. If his throat was not now swollen nearly shut, he would have unleashed a barrage of questions at this man.

Fortunately, Chastellet's general was not so hampered. *"We die in three days?"*

The Spaniard shrugged.

"Where is Roman? Was he also captured?" Constantine demanded in a low voice, his eyes flicking toward the cell door.

"No, no," the Spaniard said. *"I am no so stupid as to try to infiltrate a Muslim dungeon with a man who resembles the transfigured Christ. I left him in some caves outside the city. So he is safe, but I! I*

have the misfortune to encounter the one guard in all of Damascus who accuses me of horse thievery!" He gave a growl of complete frustration.

"Why would a guard say you stole a horse?"

The Spaniard rolled his eyes. "Perhaps it was because I stole his horse, yes? And because I had asked after the notorious betrayers of Chastellet, it has been assumed that I am in league with you. I wish I'd never heard of that hellish place! I should have known better once I saw the scavengers! Mierda!"

If it was possible, Adrian's heart beat even faster, causing black spots to dance before his eyes as the Spaniard continued to rail at his misfortune, although Adrian could not interpret exactly what he was saying; the man's passion had caused his speech to resort to his native Spanish. But Adrian knew if he didn't calm his own self, his body would shut down in order to preserve his pathetic mortality and he would become unconscious. He began breathing in and out slowly, counting each inhalation to two, then each exhalation. The spots began to fade when he reached a count of four.

Roman was just outside of Damascus. He had survived that last horrible day, when Adrian had thought for certain that the huge Norseman's arms had been ripped from his body before he was tossed beneath the churning hooves of the Arab horses.

Roman had found his way to Damascus, with coin.

"What think you, Adrian?" Constantine asked in a low voice, as if the Spaniard's animated, foreign discourse on the shortened span of his future had rendered the two friends quite alone. "Will Roman Berg come for us?"

Adrian forced his chin up, then down deliberately, the best nod he could muster. As the side of his skull ground against the gritty floor, he felt the lump that was his ear holding firm. He doubted he would keep it, if he lived.

The mad barrage of Spanish suddenly ceased. "Surely he will no attempt entry into Damascus," he said in disbelief, and Adrian was unsettled at the way this man had managed to rage loudly in a foreign language and at the same time listen keenly to Constantine's quiet English question.

Who was this Spaniard?

The dark man continued, "No matter his size, he can no hope to penetrate such formidable armed defenses. And even if he possesses the madness to try—which, I must admit, is likely—he may no arrive before—" The Spaniard drew the flat of his palm across his throat while making a ripping sound through his teeth.

"He is our only hope at this point," Constantine said gravely, his eyes never leaving Adrian.

"Yes," the Spaniard mused agreeably. "Yes, I can see how that is true. Well then, I will hope, too." He dragged his seated posture closer to Adrian, coming to rest between his legs and the wall, and made a great show of craning his neck to inspect the state of the man lying before him. "It is too bad, what has been done to you, my friend. I will help you."

From the very periphery of his vision, Adrian saw the Spaniard reach into his boot and withdraw a slender dagger. He had only a moment's thought for how this man had managed to smuggle a blade into a Damascene dungeon before he made an instinctive, strangled sound in his throat as the Spaniard moved even closer to him.

Constantine, too, called out in alarm, "What are you doing?"

"Do no fear," the Spaniard said mildly as the blade disappeared behind Adrian's hip. In a moment, Adrian's torso rocked back and forth, and he felt a heavy weight descend against his ribs. "I would no further harm this man. I was only freeing him from such cruel bonds. He is unable to use any force at all against our captors, even without them."

Adrian saw the Spaniard wipe the sticky black mass from his blade with the hem of his keffiyeh before replacing the dagger in his boot. Then Adrian realized the weight he'd felt against his ribs was his own arm. He tried to urge his shoulder forward but could not.

The dark man leaned over Adrian slightly and flipped up one of the ragged pieces of cloth—once the fine shirt of a nobleman—from Adrian's torso. The man winced. "Do you see?" he said over his shoulder toward Constantine. "I am sorry, my friend."

Adrian told himself that he would not look down. He would keep his gaze on Constantine only. There was no benefit to knowing what atrocity had developed of his own body. Once Roman had come, it would be addressed. But then Constantine blanched a horrible white and his throat convulsed.

And Adrian looked down.

The sliver of stomach the Spaniard had revealed showed black, putrid crevasses where he had been scourged and the meat of him where *the road had stripped away the top layer of his skin. But the rotting wounds were not empty.*

They were alive with wriggling white worms.

He lost consciousness in the dungeon as his eyes came open in the quiet wooden berth, his breath trapped in his chest so that he wheezed and creaked like a cart wheel. His lungs strained, his throat constricted, and he felt the tight bands once more around his arms.

He looked down wildly, as if expecting to see the thin strips of leather once more gouging his flesh, but what he saw were pale, slender fingers encircling the shallow deformations of his arm over the bold, black patterns laid down by Brother Song.

Adrian's eyes traveled up the ivory sleeve to behold not Valentine Alesander's swarthy visage but Maisie Lindsey's pale, terrified face.

Chapter 6

Although she would have given all she could claim in the world to be free of the feel of him, Maisie could not seem to release Adrian Hailsworth's arm; it was as if their flesh had melted together. She knew her mouth was hanging open, her eyes wide and glistening, for she could see them as clearly and objectively as she could see Adrian's chest still lurching, seeking the breath he could not find.

And yet his terror had somehow crawled inside her and was now trapped, like a mouse inside the long slender body of a snake, where it bulged and twisted grotesquely as she continued to stare at him. Her own breath was lost somewhere in a land where only sand and heat and violent revenge lived, and so unfamiliar with this foreign place was she that Maisie could not think of where to look for it.

Adrian's dried clothes hung limp in her right fist, the clothes that were not truly his but fashioned recently by some other man who had never known such horrors. Maisie mustered all her will in order to raise her right hand from her side as Adrian's own fists clutched at the bedclothes, and his torso strained from the thin pallet as another strangled wheeze came from him. His garments entered her line of sight and Maisie wrenched her eyes from Adrian's gaze and then released his arm with a gasp, her breath flooding her brain with swirling colors.

She had to act quickly now. She knew that her touch had likely made things much worse for him—more vivid than any memories or nightmares he had likely been plagued with for so long. She dropped the clothes onto his heaving body and clapped her palms to either side of his face, staring once more into his wild eyes but no longer seeing death.

"Adrian! Adrian!" she said, her nose nearly touching his. "Listen to me: breathe easy. There is nae preventing your breath—your throat is clear and open. Look, look!" Maisie drew a deep, loud inhalation through her nose, her nostrils flaring, and then blew it out her mouth into his reddened face, sweat breaking on his forehead like sea foam. "Like that. Shh, shh!" She repeated the inhalation, blew against his skin. "Doona struggle—let it come. It's right there." She inhaled again deeply.

Maisie heard the reedy whistle of air as he tried to draw breath. His lips barely parted on his exhalation, the weak breath making a popping sound through his dried lips.

"There it is. Easy, now," she coaxed, surprised at how calm she sounded when her knees felt as though they would fail and spill her to the floor at any moment. "Breathe in—you ken how. One, two . . ." She nodded quickly as his next breath hissed into his body. "Out, three, four." His exhalation caused his lips to tremble.

Two more times he managed to inhale, and Maisie slowly peeled her hands from his damp face, fighting the wave of nausea that crashed over her as she swayed aright. The ruddiness of his complexion was fading, and behind it she saw a flash of some emotion she could not name. Perhaps it was shame at being caught in such a vulnerable moment by a woman who was nothing more than an irritating stranger to him—one who he was trapped with for the time being at that.

She told herself that she would leave him to recover in private quickly, so as to preserve what dignity he had left, but she knew in her heart that it was she who could not bear to face him in that moment.

"Here are your clothes," she tried to say matter-of-factly, her gaze flitting away to the bundle of cloth atop his stomach. "There is a meal laid when you wish it." She turned to leave.

"I apologize," he called out after her, making her pause.

Against every shred of self-preservation within her screaming at her to keep walking, she glanced over her shoulder at him.

His brown eyes were clear now, no longer flickering with ghostly torchlight. "For frightening you. I'm neither ill nor mad, if that's at all reassuring." He spoke bitterly, as if he had not only moments ago relived what must be the most horrifying moment of his life, with her to witness it. As if it meant nothing, the pain he had felt, the terror of seeing his own imminent death with his very eyes.

As if what had happened to him—what was still happening to him—was nothing more than a petty annoyance.

Her breath caught in her throat, the beginnings of a sob churning in her chest. She daren't speak, and so she ducked out of his berth without a word.

Maisie crossed the floor to the cauldron, the very ends of her red curls trembling with the overwhelming emotions she felt. She paused long enough to stomp her right foot firmly on the boards under her feet and then pat the cauldron twice. The flames leapt up by half their size again, instantly warming her face and causing the air in the cabin to expand as she crossed to her chair and retrieved her cloak where she'd left it the night before.

It seemed like years ago, now.

She began fastening the frog at her throat as she crossed to the ladder, whispering, "*Fosgail*," as she went. The frog was not cooperating, and so she was forced to tuck her chin and look down, releasing a fat, fast tear as she did so. She swiped it away as she reached for the sides of the ladder and made her way through the open hatch to the deck of the crawler. She purposefully left the door open behind her; Adrian Hailsworth did not deserve to be trapped anywhere ever again.

Still, she hoped they hadn't stopped in the midst of another storm. Or pirates. She hated pirates.

But neither storm nor pirates greeted her upon the abbreviated deck of the crawler—only a thick, gray fog and the quiet lapping of the water upon the hull of the ship. Maisie drew a deep, hitching breath of the cold, humid air. She turned in each direction, but she could see no farther than a quarter length of the vessel. She had no idea where they were, what lay beyond the fog in whatever direction she must go.

It had all seemed so clear to her a month ago. Looking back now, she couldn't help but be frightened by the suspicion that she had made the very worst possible decisions at every opportunity. If she had actually sought to make things as bad as they could be, it could not have placed her in a worse predicament than she now found herself in.

Why, oh, why had the skinny old abbot sent *this* man?

Maisie could not return to Wyldonna with Adrian Hailsworth.

Neither could she return to Wyldonna without him.

She saw once more in her mind the strange, black markings under her fingers where she'd gripped his forearm, like those of the ancient Picts. Maisie again found it difficult to catch her breath as the lines of verse danced in her mind like the swirling gray fog.

> *Out of the mist she returned unseen,*
> *And none could ken where she had been.*
> *Beware the Painted Man, my child,*
> *Who trades the death of the Queen . . .*

Why couldn't she have just tossed the clothes atop his dreaming form when she'd peeked behind the curtain and seen that he slept? Instead she'd been drawn by his hitching breaths, the odd way he'd held his arms, the fear etched upon his strained face. Perhaps it was because she'd been so foolish as to have touched his boots, but once more the urge to know had overcome her, especially when she'd spied the dark lines and swirls peeking out from the wide bell of his sleeve.

Maisie could not afford to care one whit for this strange, brusque, damaged man. She had a duty to fulfill. But if her conscience had been twisted uncomfortably by the events of the past months, now it was being torturously crushed. Adrian Hailsworth had escaped death once, although how Maisie could not fathom. But the marks she'd glimpsed on his arm had confirmed her worst fear: he was the Painted Man. If she returned with him to Wyldonna, as she had promised to do, Adrian Hailsworth would die.

And if he did not, the Queen of Wyldonna must.

She heard Adrian's footsteps coming up the ladder behind her and so she faced into the misty wind in an attempt to give a mundane reason for her splotchy face.

He came to stand beside her, and she could see from the corner of her eye that he had once more donned the plain shirt and chausses he'd worn earlier, hiding his arms from her. It was a long moment before he spoke.

"Why have we stopped?"

"I needed to rest," Maisie said.

If he thought her answer strange, he made no mention of it.

For the good of all living things, both in spirit and in flesh . . .

"Do you wish to return to the abbey?" Maisie asked quickly, before she could lose her nerve. She didn't dare look at him, though.

"What's this now?" he asked with mild surprise. "Wasn't it only this morn you were going on and on about your terrible hurry to return to this island of your queen? How, once I'd arrived, I'd not be allowed to leave?"

"That's why I'm asking you now," she said shortly. "Before we draw any closer."

"How close are we?"

"Close enough."

He was quiet again for several moments and Maisie could almost hear the swift working of his mind. It made her nervous, as if he would somehow logically decipher the truth on his own, which was impossible. Anything he might learn, Maisie must tell him, for logic had no hand in any of it.

So it was with great surprise that she received his words when he did at last speak.

"You don't think I'm competent to help you," he said. "After . . . what you witnessed." Maisie turned her head to look at him, her eyebrows raised. His mouth was pressed into a thin line. "What man who behaves in such a manner is possessed of the skills necessary to aid a queen with any effectiveness, is that not it?"

"Nay," she said slowly, her eyebrows drawing together. "I'm giving you opportunity to extricate yourself from a thoroughly dangerous, perhaps life-threatening situation."

"Because you have come to the conclusion that I lack the fortitude and skills to be of any use in a situation such as that."

Maisie gave a quick sigh of irritation. "Hear me now: I doona often avail myself of the characteristics of charity or compassion. But I am telling you that you have nae obligation to the problems that plague the people and rulers of Wyldonna. In fact, there is more than a better chance that you may have been . . . misled into accompanying me in the first place."

"I see. Now I am deserving of your charity and compassion," he spat, completely missing the point that Maisie had been trying to make. "Kindly hear *me*, Lady Maisie: Glayer Felsteppe killed my best friend's wife and son. He has caused me to be estranged from my own family, whom I've not seen in better than five years, and has quite possibly ruined them by now any matter. He is responsible for the deaths of hundreds of loyal men, and very nearly cost me my own.

"If aiding your queen brings Glayer Felsteppe within my reach, then rest assured that I will see that he is brought to justice in one way or another. Regardless of what you might now think of me, I am not weak. I am not an invalid. And I will not be told that I am incompetent at any task I set myself to, especially by a recently appointed, glorified lady's maid who never bothered to learn to press out the creases in a shirt properly when laundering it."

Maisie's hands were clenched into fists by the time he was finished. And she found she no longer felt as much compassion as she had a moment before. Which was all for the good, she supposed.

"This is your last chance," she said. "Do we continue on from here, there shall be nae turning back." *For either of us*, she said to herself.

"Is there or is there not a vast fortune hidden in Wyldonna Castle?" he demanded.

"That is the legend," Maisie replied.

"What shall I be paid for my services, besides the opportunity to capture Glayer Felsteppe should he return?"

"The queen is prepared to grant you anything you wish."

"Ah-ah," he cautioned, holding a finger toward her. "Careful. You should know, my expertise is renowned. Your queen should not promise a reward she may be unable to fulfill."

"Anything you wish," Maisie repeated. "*If* you can find it."

"If it's there, I shall find it."

"Perhaps. But let it be understood that, from this moment onward, it is your decision to continue. I gave you a choice."

"You really don't think I'm capable, do you?" he asked, his eyes like molten pools. The wind picked up his hair and pulled it behind his head. Maisie saw the thick scar that twisted along his earlobe. The top edge of it was missing altogether.

She knew he'd caught her looking at his disfigurement, and so she brought her gaze back to his eyes. "I doona know what I think at the moment."

His jaw tensed. "Where have you put the plans? I'll need to study them again so that I might form a strategy of the most likely places to search once we land."

"They're in a locked crate in my berth."

He nodded at her once and then turned back toward the hatch, calling to her over his shoulder, "Fetch them. And give the oarsmen orders to resume. I'd not delay any longer than necessary." He turned on the top rung to retreat down the ladder and Maisie watched him with a raised eyebrow.

Once his dark head had disappeared from sight, Maisie walked to the side of the crawler and peered over at the waves caressing the smooth, pale wood.

"You heard the man," she said sardonically, and twenty oars shot to attention from the hull. She tapped the toe of her slipper twice on the deck, and her ears were immediately filled with the shush and slosh of the long arms straining against the water. She wobbled a bit on her feet when the wind began to increase and put out her hands for balance as she turned toward the hatch and backed down the ladder.

Halfway down, Maisie paused to slide the door into place securely, shutting out the view of the sky fading quickly to night, and what looked like a million shooting stars streaking over the deck above.

Adrian pored over the amateurish plans for hours by the light of the lantern over the table, which, for what reason he couldn't fathom, didn't so much as wobble or cast a cross shadow. Maisie Lindsey scooted a bowl containing a hunk of bread and some sort of rich stew close to his elbow at one point, although Adrian could not recall any evidence of her cooking over the strange, cauldronlike heating apparatus in the cabin. He told himself he was only preoccupied with the maddening drawings before him.

Regardless, the stew was delicious.

The drawings couldn't be accurate, which frustrated him. How was he to appropriately plan for the search when it was clear the renderings of Wyldonna Castle were incomplete or incorrect? No structure of this mad design could possibly stand. Whatever chambers were missing or unexplored and thereby unaccounted for on the sketches could very well be the best locations to pursue, but he could not count on them until he was in the place itself. For now, he would be forced to plan with what he had.

Adrian traced a finger between two lines representing a corridor—obviously the wing of the castle that held the royal apartments. Clearly noted was the queen's chamber, and down a bit and across the way, a large square room labeled "Malcolm."

Adrian lifted his head and glanced about the cabin, his vision blurry from his intense concentration. "Who is Malcolm?"

The redhead was sitting in her queer chair, her arms laid carefully along the wooden rests, staring at him unabashedly. "The king."

"The king, yes, of course," Adrian mumbled, half to himself. Then he directed his voice to Maisie again. "Where is he exactly?"

She shrugged.

"No one knows?"

"Likely he does."

He frowned at her. "Not helpful, Lady Maisie."

"If we knew where he was, we'd have little use for you now, would we?"

Adrian decided to ignore the baiting remark. "When did he leave the island?"

"He didna leave the island."

Adrian sat back in his chair with a loud sigh, rubbing his hands over his eyes and then dropping his palms to his thighs. His back ached from hunching over the tabletop. "Has no one searched? I have seen maps of the Scot coast; there is no island of such magnitude that a healthy-sized search party could not cover in a pair of days."

"The queen looked for him."

"Only the queen?"

"There wasna anyone else."

He stared at her and she stared back, and Adrian noticed suddenly how remarkably attractive Maisie Lindsey was just then, half-reclining in her low chair, her riotous red hair falling over both shoulders to below her small, high breasts, her dainty feet crossed at the ankles. Adrian found himself intrigued at the way she seemed utterly at ease, studying him openly as if he were a painting or sculpture.

"What do you mean, there wasn't anyone else?"

"Nearly everyone abandoned the castle after they learned of the queen's pact with Glayer Felsteppe."

Adrian snorted. "Loyal lot."

"They hate her. They have reason to, I suppose." Maisie shrugged again and continued to stare at him. She appeared different this night than the way she'd behaved since they'd met. Sadder. Resigned. Adrian found himself with the odd urge to comfort her.

"Then she must doubly appreciate your devotion."

"I hate her, too."

That gave him cause to smile and he cocked his head. "At least you stayed."

"Did I?"

His smile broadened into a grin. It was true. Maisie Lindsey had likely traveled farther from Wyldonna than any of the others who had merely abandoned their posts at the castle.

She didn't return his smile but cocked her head, mirroring his pose. "What are the markings on your arm?"

Adrian felt his grin fade and he dropped his eyes back to the drawings on the tabletop, sitting up in the hard wooden chair once more. "I don't know what you're talking about."

"I saw them, Adrian," she chided. "When you were having your—" her palms came away from the armrests and turned toward each other, as if she could somehow manifest the correct word—"nightmare." The palms fell back down.

Adrian sniffed, shuffled through the leaves of parchment before him, cleared his throat. "I have . . . scars."

"From what?"

He kept his eyes trained on the drawings, although he wasn't actually looking at them. "I was taken prisoner in the Holy Land more than two years ago and obliged to remain a guest of Saladin for some time. The hospitality of his generals was quite lacking."

"Scars are nae black."

Adrian sighed and at last raised his eyes to meet Maisie's once more. "No. They aren't."

Her gaze was like flashing emeralds in the lanternlight. "Both arms?"

"Yes."

"May I see them?"

"No."

They continued to stare at each other until Maisie suddenly folded and rose from the chair. She approached him slowly, carefully, but deliberately, as if he was a wild animal she didn't wish to spook.

Perhaps he was.

She came to a stop at the edge of the table, so near Adrian's chair that the skirts of her gown spilled over his boots. Adrian continued to stare at the drawings before him, but his vision was of no use as his other senses could only detect the woman's presence so near to him, like a promise of heather-scented danger, but one that would thrill rather than frighten.

She trailed a pale hand along the splintered end of the table, her little oval fingertips barely grazing the wood until they met Adrian's right elbow. She grasped a fold of his sleeve and rubbed it between her thumb and finger.

"How did you get them?"

"A Chinese," Adrian said brusquely, feeling the heat of her skin through the linen. "He had the misfortune to happen upon me the day I saw the extent of the effect my injuries had left on my body. He offered to help . . . assuage some of my distress at my appearance. It is a talent of his culture, though forbidden in the West. Especially in a cloister of monks."

"More than your arms."

It wasn't a question, but Adrian answered her anyway. "Yes."

Her fingertips trailed up his right arm then, her touch so light and yet so full of energy that the hair on the back of his neck raised.

"May I see them?" she asked again.

"No."

"Why?" The question was not asked in a demanding manner. Her fingertips skimmed across his shoulders and she moved around his chair in order to complete the path her hand wanted to follow down his left arm. "Does it shame you?"

Adrian felt heat come from his neck. "It's not a fit sight for a woman."

"I'm nae easily frightened."

He looked up at her then, and saw that her gaze was already on his face. "But you're frightened of Wyldonna. Of your own home. Of the queen?"

Her trailing fingers slowed to a halt over the folds of linen at his elbow. "Aye."

Adrian frowned. "Would she harm you?"

"If she has to." Her fingers picked up their journey once more, dragging her smooth nails down his sleeve to the edge, her eyes never leaving Adrian's. "Perhaps I need some of your black paint myself. To protect me." She slid one finger under the seam of linen at his wrist, testing him.

Adrian reached across with his right hand and grasped her wrist, and it was as if desire for her broke over him like a rogue wave. The hum generated by their skin pressed together was nearly audible to Adrian, the sensation penetrating his very bones.

"No," he said quietly, struggling to keep his voice level to disguise the way the feel of her was affecting him.

She didn't pull away from him, and Adrian did not release her. Could she, too, feel the strange energy between them? Regardless, she must be taught that she could not press him. His mind and his decisions were his own, and they were resolute.

And yet she managed to turn her wrist in his grasp so that her fingers were open, her palm lying up, the veins in her delicate wrist exposed to him like an offering.

"You canna run from your fears forever," she said quietly.

"Neither can you," he said, his confusion with the feelings her touch roused in him causing his voice to roughen with anger.

"I'm nae," she replied and at last pulled her arm away. Adrian let her cool skin slip through his fingers and the hum faded from his bones. "I'm running at mine."

She moved away from the table, and Adrian could hear her footsteps behind him, then the ringing of the metal clasps as she pulled open the curtain to her berth.

"Good night." The rings sang again.

Adrian stared down at the end of his sleeve where Maisie had touched him and then at his own hand, which had pressed her skin. His flesh was still pricked with tingles.

And he wondered if ink would be enough to protect either of them from whatever awaited their arrival at Wyldonna.

Chapter 7

The Englishman was once more already awake and about the cabin when Maisie exited her berth the next morning, although he barely acknowledged her presence, and she extended him the same courtesy. His only comment was that, in seeking to break his fast, he had been unable to access her provisions trunk, and Maisie was glad she'd had the forethought to seal it the day before. Citing the stickiness of wood at sea, she made a show of struggling with the lid before she opened it and produced suitable rations for both of them.

He spent the day studying the drawings again, and although Maisie doubted anyone could be so academically single-minded, the task seemed to keep him sufficiently distracted from the fact that he was still confined within the crawler. He paced a bit at times, true, but it appeared to her as if he was working through imagined scenarios in his mind rather than trying to escape invisible demons. His brow furrowed beneath the fall of his dark hair and he seemed oblivious to her presence, even when she gave up trying to occupy herself and surrendered to the urge to observe him openly from her chair while she waited for the unpleasantness she knew was to come.

Maisie heard the song before Adrian. She had felt Wyldonna in her bones hours before the watery moans penetrated the hull of the ship, and so she expected them, but a shiver raced up her spine all the same. She couldn't help but think of her fate should the thickness of the crawler's wood not stand between her and what sang in the icy water beyond.

Adrian heard the mourning wails then, his face raising from the parchment on the tabletop. He turned toward her, and his ever-present frown deepened, increasing his look of solemn handsomeness.

"Do you hear that?"

Maisie nodded.

He seemed to concentrate on the sound, turning his head slightly away from her for a moment before muttering, "Change in water temperature, perhaps. Or depth." His eyes flicked to her again, demanding an answer before his mouth could form the question. "Are we near the coast?"

"We are," she said, content for the moment to continue watching him in peace. Likely the last peace she would know for some time.

He nodded and returned his attention to the drawings.

The howls grew incrementally louder as the minutes passed, and although to Maisie's ears they were piercing, vicious screams, she knew they would sound much differently to Adrian.

As if on prompt, he looked up again, his expression now more puzzled than annoyed.

"What *is* that?" he insisted quietly and stood, the motion shoving the chair back and away from him. Maisie watched the way his body became attuned to the sound filtering through the cabin, the way his head cocked. He turned to her suddenly. "I want to go above." And before she could answer him yes or no, he was striding across the floor and had gained the ladder.

"You canna," she called out mildly, unconcerned for his safety. He would never be able to open the hatch until she bade it open.

He tried anyway, jerking at the latch with frustrated grunts. "It's stuck again," he growled, backing down the ladder swiftly. "Where is the knife?"

"The knife didna open it last time and it willna open it now," Maisie said, watching him as he strode toward the provisions trunk and dropped to one knee. He struggled similarly with that piece for several moments while the squeals grew louder in the close space, before shoving the heavy trunk away with a vicious curse. His growing distress was clear.

"Sit down, Adrian. We'll land soon, and any discomfort you feel will be over."

But rather than heed her advice, his now wild eyes landed on the wooden chair he had so recently vacated. He seized the back of it and carried it toward the ladder, springing into a jog halfway across the floor. He drew the chair sideways over his head and flung it at the hatch with a shout.

Maisie didn't flinch as the chair broke into scores of pieces, but

Adrian cried out in fury when he saw that the door was unscathed. As the screeches grew even louder, he clapped his palms over his ears and swung toward her, his face twisted in agonized ecstasy.

"*What is it?*" he demanded again. "I must know!"

"Sirens," Maisie replied, careful to meet his eyes directly.

He winced, as if the answer confused him and the confusion brought him pain. "No."

She didn't argue with him; it would do no good. The only way he would believe was to see the heartless creatures with his own eyes, and should that occur, his satisfaction would be short-lived before he met a grisly death.

Then, suddenly, the song was gone, as if the cries were threads snipped off by a sharp blade. Adrian lowered his hands and blinked, his eyes dazed as they seemed to search the air above his head.

"What happened?" he asked. "Where did it go?"

Maisie closed her eyes. *Please* . . .

A loud, hollow thump shook the crawler, the sound echoing as if a mighty drum had been struck. And then Maisie did flinch.

They knew she was aboard.

Another thump, then a pair, and then it was as if all the sounds of hell were unleashed on Maisie Lindsey's vessel—the wails of the sirens returned with a blast as a thousand hammers seemed to pound the wood with the intention of destroying it.

Maisie could imagine the cloudy-white hands beyond with their toothlike claws, beating on the hull of the crawler, seeking her.

Adrian shouted something, but Maisie could not decipher his words through the thunder and piercing squeals. When two strong hands gripped her upper arms and shook her, she opened her eyes to see his panicked face.

"We've run upon rocks!" he yelled. "We must go above before the ship breaks apart!"

She only shook her head at him, pressing her mouth into a line.

"Maisie!" he demanded, shaking her again. "If we stay here, we'll die!"

"Nay!" she shouted back into his face. "Here, we are safe! But if I open that door, we are both dead in an instant!"

His expression was pained, although she could not tell if it was from the irresistible lure of the song he heard or the thought that the crawler would burst apart at any moment, flooding the interior with seawater and drowning them both.

He shook her again, as if it would convince her.

Maisie wrenched her arms up to mirror his hold on her. "Nay!"

They stayed frozen in their postures for what seemed to Maisie to be an hour, with the deafening roar of fish belly skin beating against the wood and the hellish, hungry screams buffeting them in their desperate embrace. Maisie didn't know if Adrian clung to her out of fear or fury, but she didn't care as long as he clung to her.

He was *real*. And he was holding on to her.

Then, like a ripple of water receding from the shore, the crashing blows against the hull began to fall away from the crawler, from the end of the cabin where the sleeping berths lay, all along the sides as if they were moving through a barrier. The cries began to fade away as well until only the sounds of Adrian's labored breaths filled Maisie's ears.

Save for one final scream, risked by the bravest or most vengeful of the creatures, which seemed to explode inside the cabin.

"Traitor!"

Maisie swallowed as the scream's echo faded into unnatural silence, and she saw the look of recognition come across Adrian's face. He'd heard.

Then the cabin gave a violent lurch, tossing most of the contents on its sides, and Maisie and Adrian tumbled to the floor still gripping each other.

The crawler had landed.

Adrian's eardrums felt achy and swollen inside his head as he helped Maisie to stand, and then released her to kick his way through the pieces of broken chair and shove the overturned table aside. Only the cauldron, sitting within an iron frame that allowed it to sway, was left aright, and its flames continued to crackle.

The drawings had slid to the floor—which Adrian guessed to now be at a thirty-degree angle—and come to rest near the trunk where Maisie kept the food stores. He was disoriented, and so he squatted with his hip braced against the trunk to help maintain his balance as he quickly shuffled the pages together and then rolled them.

He dared a glance at Maisie. She had thrown back the curtain to her bunk and was looping the long strap of a satchel over her red curls to rest on one shoulder. Her arms reached out and her pale, delicate fingers began plucking items from around the narrow bunk like birds pecking at the ground, tucking this and that quickly inside the bag.

Adrian's head throbbed. *Sirens . . .*

He stood just as Maisie turned from her berth. She looked at him expectantly.

"Well?" she said. "Are you coming or nae?"

He hesitated. "Won't there be someone to meet us?"

Her delicate features hardened. "I hope nae. Although if you doona hurry, we may indeed have to contend with some rather unpleasant individuals. It willna be long before word of my return spreads."

Adrian's mind fairly tripped over itself with the questions he wanted to ask, but he had doubts that he would believe any answer Maisie Lindsey gave him, so he only nodded his understanding and stepped to his own compartment to retrieve his few belongings.

They crossed to the ladder, and Adrian let the lady precede him. She laid a hand to the latch and the door slid open, as if the track it sat in had been greased. She looked over her shoulder and blew a quick breath through her lips before completing the climb.

Adrian looked over his own shoulder and saw that the flames in the cauldron were gone. No smoke curled from the vessel, no smell of spent fuel wafted on the air. The fire had simply vanished as if it had never been lit.

Sirens . . .

Adrian shook the mad ideas from his head and followed the woman through the doorway.

He wasn't certain what he had expected upon his arrival at Wyldonna, but it was not what he saw as he stepped onto the deck of the listing crawler. For one, it was nighttime. But the sky was not the inky black pricked with stars he was accustomed to. Instead, it was a dull charcoal color, almost misty, and there was no starlight to cheer it.

The gloom was not so thick, though, that he could not make out the coast upon which they'd landed—steep and rocky, with the jagged black outlines of coniferous trees crowding down to the shore and blocking out his view of the horizon to either side. The crawler had come to rest on a sliver of rocky beach, and Adrian was surprised that the oars he expected to see protruding from the port side of the vessel were already gone. Likely pulled inside by weary crew, eager to disembark, he told himself. There was a long dock perhaps only ten feet from where they'd made land, but it was empty, standing in the gloom like a ruin.

Adrian turned to look over the roof of the cabin behind him at the sea beyond. Indeed, it was blanketed by a heavy fog, and he decided that the strange light of the place could be attributed to nothing more magical than low clouds. The water was flat, oddly still. No sound came from it save the common lapping at the shore.

Sirens . . .

"Adrian."

His head turned back quickly at the sound of his name, spoken in a low but urgent tone. Maisie Lindsey wore an intense expression on her face, and in that moment, Adrian considered that the queen had made a wise choice in champions. All the lady would require to complete the picture of a mythical Gaelic woman warrior was a weapon.

"Listen to me verra carefully," she said and took his hand. He looked down at it briefly; she was gripping him hard. "Once we step down from the crawler, you mustna release my hand. Until we are safely inside the castle, it is imperative that you keep hold of me."

"It's not that dark, Lady Maisie," he said. "I've found my way along roads in deeper night than this."

"It isna night," she snipped. "It's just before supper."

Adrian looked up at the sky again. "That's impossible."

"Winter in Wyldonna means almost constant darkness," Maisie said. "And it's nae your losing your way I fear; the folk who live in the wood will sense that an outsider has come onto the island."

Adrian felt his brows raise. "They would challenge my presence?"

"Nay," she said levelly, meeting his eyes in the gloom. "Some would just eat you."

"Eat me?"

"Shh." She nodded. "As long as you remain joined with me until we are in the castle, you'll be safe. But we must hurry nonetheless. I'm only slightly safer than you right now, especially since some already know I've returned." She turned toward the low side of the crawler, pulling him along.

"The sirens," Adrian said in a flat tone, following her to the edge. "And I thought it was me they sought. My ego is crushed."

She shot him a look. "You step down first—you're taller than me. But doona let go," she hastened to add.

Adrian gave her a mocking bow. "As you wish, Your Highness."

Maisie Lindsey frowned at him but came easily into his arms after his boots had crunched down on the rocky beach. She turned away from him immediately and began pulling him up the steep incline, toward a slender path Adrian could see amidst a tangle of winter-naked briars at the foot of the hill.

"The sirens have an endless craving for men's blood, true, but they forgot about you quickly—it's me they wanted."

"Why, you're nearly as popular as the queen," he said, trying to make his voice light, although it was taking an enormous amount of concentration to navigate the path behind Maisie, who skipped up the shadowy and sliding track as if it were nothing more treacherous than a set of well-made stairs. Adrian's leg began to ache as he tried to avoid weighing on her arm.

"Aye," she muttered.

"Where are the sirens now?" he pressed, measuring his breaths so that the words didn't come out as gasps.

"In the sea, of course," she said with what sounded like forced patience. "They canna come ashore unless they are with a creature of warm blood, or upon a vessel to the dock, thank the gods. Ships that wander too close to Wyldonna are a danger and a nuisance to us. Heavy storms blow pirates and mercenary ships off course, and soon after our hall will stink of sirens, airing their petty complaints."

He came to a stop, his chest heaving, but he kept a firm grip on Maisie's hand, yanking her to a halt.

"What are you doing?" she demanded, tugging at him. "Come on!"

"You expect me to believe that sirens actually exist?"

"You asked. Now come on." She tugged at him again, and because he'd had a moment to catch his breath and no further reason really to delay the trek, Adrian followed.

"What about the folk in the wood who would . . . eat me, was it?" Even he heard the snideness in his tone.

"Aye, eat you, they would," she replied. "Pech; a pair of Tallmadegeons that we know of, but there could be more than that now. The worst of the lot—and the most dangerous to you—are the afternhangers. The most ancient of the Cat Sìth."

"Oh, certainly. Felines are terribly frightening. But no minotaur?" he needled.

"Doona be ridiculous," she said. "Nae one calls them that anymore."

"My apologies."

Adrian didn't know why this beautiful young woman, who otherwise seemed to have a very sensible mind about her, insisted on feeding him such fables. Was it not enough that he'd come to this desolate Scots isle? Not enough that he was here to help her desperate queen, regardless of the insignificance of Wyldonna's troubles to the rest of the world? Adrian had committed his aid regardless; his ultimate goal was to trap Glayer Felsteppe. Why must she try to make the island and its people something fantastic and dreadful and so obviously untrue?

Ahead of him, Maisie gave a little cry that sounded like dismay and then swayed to a halt. Adrian looked up to see the cause of the delay, and at first he thought he was witnessing the phenomenon of colored lights in the sky that were rumored to frequent the northernmost parts of the map.

Lazy, pulsing blue sheets seemed to billow above the dark spires of the treetops, flapping away the misty gray like a rug being aired and allowing piercing dots of starlight to briefly flash. But the blue glow was concentrated at a point, and as Adrian looked more closely, his chest heaving from the climb, he could make out what appeared to be a lone spire reaching higher than the tallest arrow tops of the pines. His guide began walking once more, but now her steps were measured, almost hesitant, and one by one the trees crowding the path moved aside until the blue glow cast their shadows long and black on the path behind them. Adrian's mouth fell open despite himself.

It could only be Wyldonna Castle. And it was glowing.

He guessed the structure must be seven full stories to the uppermost turret, and the construction appeared to be chiseled stone, but there was no gray or brown or even red to the rock that comprised this place, only a soft, shimmering blue, like the horizon just after sunset. Adrian could see the apexes of the towers that had been in the drawing—six in all—with numerous flapping pennants. Tall dark shadows—the insets of windows—crawled over the castle like insects, and some of the openings were filled with brighter, welcoming light, beckoning to him to discover the secrets that lay inside.

The castle itself seemed to cling to the cliff, as if it had once been a living thing that had scaled the side of the rocky isle and then perched there on the edge. Adrian could not fathom how such a massive and ornately built palace had been built in such a treacherous location.

There was no drawbridge, no moat, and no need for one. Only a tall, arched wooden door at the end of the path, and no guards at that. He strained his ears; faint music wafted on the breeze. The blue glow caressed and retreated along the track like the waves on the beach below, almost keeping measure with the ghostly tune, and Adrian could hardly wait to see if the light had a feel. His skin crawled in anticipation of the blue glow.

But then Maisie suddenly pulled him from the path and into the woods, breaking into a run.

Chapter 8

Maisie nearly dragged Adrian through the stiff underbrush of the wood as she rushed around the perimeter of the castle, hidden by the bare, solemn trees. At least she hoped they were hidden. If they were detected and stopped, it would be too late. It might be too late now.

The castle was already glowing.

She willed her legs to move faster, using all her senses to keep her feet beneath her as her heavy skirts sought to tangle between her knees and catch on the branches she forced her way through.

"Hurry, hurry, Adrian!" she gasped, feeling the perspiration between their joined fingers, icy cold as she gripped him.

"Where are we going?" he panted, yanking on her arm every score or so strides when he stumbled.

"To the castle." She hauled him aright without stopping, feeling that her arm would be pulled from her shoulder. "Nae far now."

Maisie saw the sliver of shadow nestled against the base of the castle, and once they had come opposite it in the wood, she darted to the right, breaking cover from the trees and sprinting across the perimeter of yard. Her head swiveled left and right as she ran, but she saw no one. She glanced up; no figures stood at the lowermost windows.

Everyone was most likely too busy enjoying a lively feast.

They were going at such a speed that she had to throw out her free hand against the old door to keep from crashing fully into its spongy, damp wood. Adrian rammed against her, but she couldn't care as her fingers sought the primitive lever. Her fingernails scrabbled against the almost furry-feeling wood, and her eyes watered as a thick, wet sliver found its way beneath a fingernail.

"They're not blue," Adrian said behind her, and then she felt her arm being pulled away from the side of her body as he stepped to the castle wall, examining the stones with his fingertips, his head circling as he looked up and around him. "Where is the light coming from?"

The lever at last moved and Maisie threw her shoulder into the door, nearly dragging Adrian from his feet as she pulled him sideways through the opening.

The vestibule was pitch black, but Maisie didn't care. She shook herself free of Adrian Hailsworth's grip and squatted to the floor, placing both her palms on the worn, damp stones, which seemed to vibrate almost imperceptibly beneath her skin.

"I'm here," she whispered through her gulping pants, her eyes closed, hot tears swelling behind the lids. "I'm here."

"Lady Maisie?" Adrian ventured. "Are you . . . unwell?"

"I'm fine," she said, feeling a sense of calm come over her. She removed her hands from the stones and then swiped a forearm across her eyes as she rose. "Let's go."

She turned a sharp left into the deeper darkness of a corner, leaving Adrian Hailsworth to follow her by the sounds of her footfalls and voice.

"Mind your step," she warned as she mounted the narrow, twisting stairs. His hiss of breath and muffled curse told her that she'd spoken too late.

"I don't recall seeing this on the plans," he said pointedly.

"Perhaps you didna look well enough."

Her feet skimmed up the risers, and even though she could not see in this unlighted and nearly forgotten part of Wyldonna Castle, Maisie knew exactly where she was in her ascent. She heard Adrian's gasping breaths behind her as she reached the tiny landing and felt for the latch.

"Hurry," she urged into the darkness, her whisper echoing over his head.

"Right . . . behind you," he panted, and then she could feel his presence at her side.

She opened the door onto further blackness, but then reached out a hand and pushed the heavy tapestry aside, leaning out into the dim light of the corridor.

"Pull the door," she said as she stepped from the stairwell and held the thick weaving so that Adrian could duck though. Then she let the tapestry fall back with a flap and turned to lead the Englishman quickly down the corridor.

The sight of her door standing open ahead caused her footsteps only the tiniest hesitation. Her chamber had been breached. Perhaps thieves were even now inside, looting, stealing whatever they fancied. A fury burned in her heart.

She hoped they were still there.

Maisie fairly flew through her doorway, her satchel swinging wide and then banging into her hip as she came to a stop inside her chamber, her right arm already extended. But then it fell limp at her side as Adrian came to a halt near her, and both of them took in the sight of the man seated on the side of her high bed.

His wide hands were braced on his thighs, his head cocked and his bearded face regarding the woven rug on the floor. His face looked calm, pensive even, and that caused Maisie's recent aspirations of indignation to shrivel up and retreat behind her knotted stomach. The man had not looked up at her arrival.

"Malcolm," Maisie breathed. And then she sank into a deep curtsy.

"Malcolm?" Adrian echoed above her. "*King* Malcolm? Malcolm the *Missing*?"

"There's nae need for all that now, lass," Malcolm said, ignoring Adrian's comments. "I'm nae the king any longer, am I?"

Maisie rose and forced herself to straighten her posture, lift her chin. "Where have you been? I wasted such time—"

"Where've *I* been?" he interrupted. "Well, I suppose I might ask the same of you, lass. Since you obviously havena deserted the isle as was again rumored."

"Of course I didna desert the island," she hissed, feeling a touch of her ire return even as her face heated with humiliation. "Or you. I'm still loyal to you, regardless of what you might think. Of what those . . . those monsters have told you. You knew enough to come back to the castle this night. *You* deserted *me!*"

"I did think you gone," he admitted with a nod. His green eyes were bloodshot, evidence of the spirits he'd been drinking. "You had only perhaps a handful of moments left, did you know? The celebration had already begun." His eyes glanced toward the doorway. "They're still making merry. They havena realized."

Maisie swallowed. She'd known she'd been almost out of time, but she hadn't known it had been down to a matter of moments. "I know they hate me. But what I did was for the good of us all. *Spirit and flesh*," she emphasized.

"Where've ye been, Maisie?" Malcolm repeated quietly, ignoring the quote from the old vows. And then his gaze at last went to Adrian, who had been observing the exchange keenly without comment. "And who's this you've brung with you?"

She swallowed again and cleared her throat, turning slightly to indicate the Englishman at her side. "Adrian Hailsworth, Malcolm of Wyldonna."

Adrian gave a brief but courteous nod.

But Malcolm did not acknowledge Adrian, instead turning flashing, incredulous eyes upon Maisie once more. "Och, lass, what have you done? Bringing a *man* to Wyldonna?"

"He's come to find the treasure, Malcolm," Maisie rushed. "I wanted to tell you, but none could find you. Or they wouldna tell me where you—"

"Have you gone *mad*?" he demanded, rising from the side of the bed. "It's bad enough we have that bloodthirsty demon Felsteppe to fend off, but now his brother as well? Would that you had deserted us, rather than deliver our very destruction into the castle!"

"Nay!" Maisie insisted and then, in desperation, she reached back and seized one of Adrian Hailsworth's hands. Before he could protest, she shoved up his sleeve past his elbow, revealing the swirling black designs on his skin. "Look, Malcolm! Look!"

His green eyes flicked to Adrian's arm and then back again, where his gaze lingered, his eyes widening. Then he looked up and met Maisie's eyes as Adrian shook himself free of her grip.

"The Painted Man," Malcolm whispered, and his jaw tensed, as if he ground his teeth together.

"I would never desert you when I am the only one who can help," Maisie insisted. "Do you see?"

He was shaking his head at her before she could finish speaking. "You fool," he said low and then began walking toward her. "You bloody little fool!" He seized her arms and shook her. "Why would you do such a thing? Why?" he demanded.

Adrian Hailsworth was suddenly in between Maisie and Malcolm, shoving the bearded man away. Malcolm was likely quite surprised at the brazenness of the Englishman, so that he released Maisie without protest.

"Now, see here," Adrian said. "I can understand you're upset; I am certain it's quite a blow to be usurped by your own sister. But this woman has done nothing save what she was bade to do by her queen, and she has shown great courage in bringing me here to help your people. She does not deserve such rough treatment, even if she is only the queen's lady. I assure you, I will air my own complaints with the woman as quickly as I can join her."

Malcolm looked at Adrian; then his eyes found Maisie. "What is he going on about?"

"He knows he was brought here to help locate the Wyldonna treasure," Maisie supplied. "At the queen's request."

Malcolm's eyebrows rose and he looked back to the Englishman. "Is that so?"

"Quite," Adrian replied. "So if one of you would be ever so kind as to go to the trouble to present me to Queen Maighread, I would be grateful."

Maisie's cheeks heated and her stomach did a neat flip as Malcolm huffed a breath of a laugh. "Nae trouble at all, lad," he said. He held out one of his wide palms toward Maisie. "You're in Her Majesty's verra presence."

Maisie dared a look at Adrian, whose face was turned fully toward her now, his slender brows drawn down in their usual frown of concentration, but there was now something more sinister behind those brown eyes.

"Adrian . . . Hailsworth, is it?" Malcolm continued deferentially. "The Queen of Wyldonna, Maighread Lindsey. Me own dear sister."

Maighread Lindsey's blush was not the delicate wash of pink of a noblewoman; it was raw and red and splotchy, made even more virulent a shade by the proximity of her copper hair. She dropped her face toward the floor for only a moment, and then, as if realizing the meek and guilty pose for what it was, pulled her chin up with a jerk. She squared her shoulders and looked Adrian in the eyes.

Anger borne of humiliation strained at Adrian's chest. "You lied to me."

"Nay," she said quickly. "I didna. I lied to your abbot."

Adrian ticked through his memories of their conversations since meeting at Melk and granted that, no, perhaps she hadn't outright lied to him. Everything she'd said referencing the queen of Wyldonna had likely been referencing Maisie herself. But she had withheld information from him all the same.

"I couldna verra well reveal that the Queen of Wyldonna was about on her own, now could I?" she pressed. "One slip from your priest could have brought an army of my enemies in pursuit."

"Enemies?" Adrian repeated. "You mean Glayer Felsteppe?"

Maighread huffed a laugh. "If it was only him, I wouldna have been so worried."

Maisie's twin brother had apparently composed himself enough to rejoin the conversation. "Have you heard tales of Wyldonna, Hailsworth?"

"If you mean the myths of its magical populace, yes," Adrian said.

"Some of the stories are nae more than myth now, aye," the bearded man acquiesced. "But long ago, all living creatures were Wyldonians. Each season, some chose nae to remain under our rule or protection, and many of the fools then grew bitter in their life in the Outland. When they were denied return, they convinced themselves it was through fault of the Lindseys that they were hunted and persecuted. They came to believe they were exiled from paradise when it was their choice to leave."

Adrian felt his eyebrows raise. From what little he'd seen of this dark, rocky isle, he couldn't imagine anyone referring to it as a paradise. Madness must obviously be a familial trait. He looked back at Maighread, who was watching her brother with a look of . . . perhaps sorrow. Adrian couldn't tell. Nor did he care at the moment.

"I gave my word that I would aid the queen of Wyldonna in locating the island's treasure. Obviously, the king no longer needs locating."

Maighread's eyes widened. "You're nae thinking to try to leave, are you? I already told you—"

"Enough with the tales," Adrian said, slashing a palm through the air. "As I told *you*, my cooperation was based on the completely self-ish objective of cornering and apprehending Glayer Felsteppe. He is still coming, is he not?"

Maighread nodded, her eyes still wide.

"Then I will stay," Adrian said, feeling very magnanimous indeed at his generosity of spirit.

"And you will still search for the treasure," Maighread added.

"It will be something to occupy my mind until spring, when Felsteppe returns, even if it is a goose hunt."

"Nae so arbitrary a time as spring," Maighread said with a wince.

"I beg your pardon?"

"She said nae spring," Malcolm repeated loudly. "Felsteppe is to return to Wyldonna less than one month from today—at Ostara."

Adrian looked to Maighread again.

"With an army," Malcolm added.

Adrian nodded his acknowledgment, but his eyes were still on the redhead. She stared back at him without flinching. Unapologetic. Bold.

Malcolm sighed. "Which means I must return to my plans." He turned toward his sister, who pulled her gaze away from Adrian's.

"Can you nae wait, Malcolm? Perhaps he can find—"

"I will defend Wyldonna to my last breath," Malcolm told her with a glare. "*For the good of all living things, both in spirit and in flesh.* You've all but sealed your fate, you ken?" He glanced at Adrian. "I do hope he finds the gold. 'Twould pain my heart for all eternity should . . ." The bearded man broke off and then abruptly quit the room, pulling the door behind him in a slam that caused Maisie to flinch.

Adrian crossed his arms over his chest. "What else haven't you told me?"

Maisie only looked at him for a moment and then sighed, shaking her head. She swerved around him toward the bed, where she pulled the strap of her satchel over her head and swung it onto the coverlet.

"Nae now, Adrian," she said, and he could hear the fatigue in her voice. "Let us both retire for the evening. It's been a long and per-ilous journey."

"It's only been three days," Adrian pointed out. "I'm quite fine. Rather feeling like conversation."

"It's been a bit longer than three days for me," she snipped. "And longer still than the mere distance I've come with you. Your insatiable thirst for knowledge will have to wait."

"You owe me an explanation," he demanded.

Maighread whipped around on him. "I doona owe you anything," she growled, and there was no trace of the Maisie Lindsey Adrian had thought he was becoming accustomed to on the crawler ship. "You agreed to come through your own free will when twice given the opportunity to decline. I will share the details of my dilemma after I have rested and have my wits about me once more. Regardless of the scorn you hold for the fantasy you believe Wyldonna to be, I am queen here, and at least in my own chamber, my wishes are to be obeyed. I am tired. I am going to bed. And so are you."

She walked to the hearth and crouched down before the flames, hugging her knees, the fight gone out of her quickly. The dull gray stone that comprised the hearth on the floor before the fire was carved into the shape of a fantastically long lizard, its back sporting a row of perfectly aligned and proportioned spikes amidst a field of flawless, monochromatic scales. Adrian thought perhaps the spikes were utilized to prop an iron or stake upon, and the body of the lizard ensured that no stray embers or logs would roll onto the wooden floor. Quite a decorative and fanciful fitting for such an otherwise foreboding chamber.

She turned her head to look at him, and her eyes reflected the dancing firelight. She didn't look like a queen to him then, more like a frightened young woman who was dreadfully burdened and alone. Adrian's hunger to know nearly threatened to consume him, and he briefly entertained the idea of going to her there on the hearth, pressing her until she yielded to him the explanations he sought. If he touched her as she'd touched him on the crawler . . .

"Go!" she demanded.

"Go where?" he said in vexation, his fantasy dissolving with her brusque command. "Am I to sleep on the floor at your feet?"

"Go with Reid," she said as she turned back to the fire.

"Go with Reid? Is that some strange Wyldonian equivalent to 'Go with God'?" Adrian held his palms out from his sides, waiting for a response, but none came.

A muffled pounding fairly shook the wooden door of the chamber then, as if someone was attempting to gain entrance to the queen's residence with a quilted battering ram. Assuming the visitor could only be for him—which made him feel a bit better about being forced to answer the door as if he were a servant—Adrian dropped his hands and turned on his heel to cross the floor. He pulled the door open and found himself staring into his own dull reflection in a huge brass buckle.

Adrian's eyes traveled up, up, up a wide expanse of rough brown cloth until he was forced to tilt his head back. And still he had to lean into the corridor to look past the lintel of the door frame.

A sallow-skinned face, as large as a bushel basket, with thick, glossy black hair looked down at him.

"Good evening, Man," the thing said in an accent that was distinctly Rhine. "I'm Reid."

Adrian tried to swallow, but the awkward angle of his head forced him to tilt his chin down first in order to accomplish that necessary task. He reluctantly looked back up and was dismayed to see little dots dancing in his vision. He threw a hand up to brace himself on the door frame. Then Adrian suddenly shut the door.

He leaned his forehead against the frame for a moment, his hand still on the latch, his eyes closed.

In, one, two; out, three, four.

He opened the door again, and once more the brass buckle reflected his slack face. Adrian looked up again.

"Man?" the giant inquired.

Adrian attempted to respond, but nothing came out except a wheeze. This . . . *creature* would make Roman Berg seem a child. Adrian cleared his throat. "Yes?" His voice was still little more than a squeak.

"This way, if you please." He turned to Adrian's right and began walking slowly down the corridor. The wooden boards of the passage bowed like unfastened planks under the giant's feet.

Adrian looked back over his shoulder at Maighread, still crouched by the fire. She had laid a hand on the carved hearth stone, and her chin was tucked down against her forearm. She seemed to be whispering something into the flames as her fingers danced along the spikes. She paid him no heed, and although Adrian suddenly preferred to stay here in the chamber with her—sleeping on the floor if need be—rather than follow the colossal Reid through the dim corridor, he told himself that he was being ridiculous.

The man was obviously a biological anomaly. Adrian scolded

himself; he should feel pity for the poor creature, relegated by his misfortune to serving in the dark corridors of the castle so as not to frighten the rest of the populace.

Adrian reached for the door handle and pulled it after him, but in the instant before the wood met the jamb, his mind played a further mean trick on him, making it seem as though the carved gray eyelids of the hearth stone opened and looked directly at him with glittering gold irises.

Chapter 9

Adrian followed the freakishly large Reid down the corridor, keeping his gaze on the floorboards, partly to avoid tripping on the upturned ends the giant created with each step, but mostly to avoid staring at the poor man. The scholarly part of Adrian wanted to observe the way the man moved, the mechanics of his limbs in correlation to his extreme height. But he was certain that Reid received enough ogling in his everyday life and so Adrian nobly withheld his curiosity.

They passed a dark doorway on the opposite side of the corridor from Maighread Lindsey's chamber, and Adrian did glance up then to peer inside. The door was open, but no fire glowed inside the chamber, and he wondered what the room was until he recalled the specifics of this part of the castle from the drawings he'd studied. It had to be Malcolm's chamber, although it was obvious the king was no longer keeping residence within the royal wing.

Adrian never broke stride as he dug into his satchel and withdrew the rolled-up sheets of parchment. Glancing up only occasionally—secure enough in the massive presence ahead of him to alert him to a turn or a stop—he impatiently riffled through the curled corners until he had located the sheet that detailed this floor. Adrian turned the map to orient it in the direction in which he was headed.

Yes, that had been Malcolm Lindsey's chamber. They'd just made a left-hand turn, and so—yes, here they were. Reid had come to a stop to one side of another open doorway and now gestured graciously for Adrian to enter.

What a dear being, Adrian thought. He gave the man a nod as he passed into the room, well lit with a blazing fire in the hearth and a brace of candles on a table where a covered platter and pitcher and cup awaited him. Despite his general skepticism, Adrian was grateful for the luxuries and the swift consideration shown him by Wyldonna's servants. He turned, expecting Reid to enter behind him, a word of thanks at the ready.

But the giant remained in the corridor, facing the opening now and so tall that Adrian could not see his face. He stepped back to the doorway and leaned out to look up at Reid.

"My thanks. Very kind of you."

The giant stared down at Adrian, as if examining him. He said nothing, but Adrian sensed an air of forced reserve. His sallow skin was like the peel of an overripe pear, hairless and smooth, but flecked with nearly imperceptible brown dots. His eyebrows were thick and black and glossy, like his hair, his fleshy lips like strips of cooked liver.

A thoroughly unattractive individual.

"Well, then," Adrian said, discomfort creeping up his spine. Perhaps the man was mentally damaged as well, although his welcome moments ago had seemed quite lucid. "Good night." Adrian waited a breath longer, and when it seemed apparent that the man was unwilling or unable to respond, he felt behind him for the door handle.

But the crisp edges of the man's accent sliced through the air before Adrian could close the door.

"If I was permitted to speak to you, I would return your courtesy by wishing you a most pleasant evening as well," Reid rushed.

Adrian paused and looked around the lintel again at the man, who now appeared a bit more relaxed. Reid clasped his hands in front of his enormous buckle and stared at the stones of the wall above Adrian's door as he gave a quiet but impressive sigh.

"I see," Adrian said, although he did not. "I assure you that your acknowledgment would have been deeply appreciated. Were you permitted to speak to me, of course."

Reid nodded, a faint quirk to his mouth.

Adrian opened his mouth but then thought better of it and instead pulled himself back inside the room and slowly closed the door on the giant, who made no move to depart. He waited a moment, his hand on the latch, before easing the door open a crack. The doorway was still blocked by the man's girth, although he now faced away from the door, and Adrian's view was comprised entirely of the man's considerable backside.

He closed the door again and turned to lean back against it. Adrian shook his head firmly and blew out a strong breath before pulling himself aright. He took off his satchel as he crossed the floor toward the table, where he laid the plans of Wyldonna Castle near the platter. He looped his strap over the back of the chair with one hand while he tilted up the domed cover on the platter with his other. The smell of cooked fish wafted up in a cloud of steam and Adrian sniffed appreciatively before replacing the cover and removing his cloak, eager to be done with his ablutions and attend his meal.

There was a small stand with a washing bowl and linens against the longest, empty wall, and it was while he splashed his face with water that he realized the chamber contained no windows. According to the drawings, its location along the corridor should have placed the chamber on an outside wall, unless there was another small chamber or walkway behind it that Adrian had missed.

By the time he had made use of the chamber pot and crossed back to the table, the domed platter had been forgotten save for the moment it took for him to push it aside so that Adrian could once more unfurl Wyldonna's plans. He used the pewter chalice and the rounded eating knife to hold the curling pages flat while he poured himself a full cup of wine from the carafe that he'd only just discovered tucked behind the water pitcher. Then he traded the chalice for the carafe on the parchment edge and drank deeply, studying the lines and scribbles from the corner of one eye.

He sighed with relief at the refreshing life the sweet wine brought him and set the chalice away, bracing his hands on the tabletop and leaning closer to the parchment. His face tilted this way and that, confirming his location before he placed one finger atop the rectangle that signified his chamber and then drew the pointer finger of his other hand down the long line of the exterior wall. He looked up and ahead: hearth. He looked over his shoulder: solid stone. To his left: doorway. To his right where he'd washed up: solid stone.

Adrian picked up his chalice and walked to the wall that should separate him from the grounds—and a direct view of the sea. He took a long drink and looked up at the stones, his eyes searching for any anomaly. But the wall was perfect. No window.

Which meant no escape, save that of the door.

Adrian's heart began to pound, but he walked in a deliberately calm manner to the door again and pulled at the latch. It opened freely, and Reid's wide presence still filled the opening. The giant turned to look down past his shoulder at Adrian, his brows like horses' tails raised in question.

Adrian raised the cup. "The wine is delicious. My compliments," he said, and then shut the door, his heartbeat slowing to normal once more.

He wasn't trapped in the room, then. Just being guarded. He walked back toward the table, draining his cup on the way.

Guarded from escaping, or guarded from harm?

Why must it be either? I came here of my own free will, and because my presence is at the queen's request to help the very people who live here be freed from Glayer Felsteppe's threats, who would wish to harm me?

He filled the cup again and lifted it halfway to his mouth.

What about the creatures in the wood?

What creatures? I saw nothing at all either on the trail or in the wood that would lead me to believe there was anything more threatening than rats populating the forest.

He drank the wine, noting again the interesting salty-sweet flavor, like berries wet with the sea. In a moment, the cup was again empty. He refilled it.

Malcolm, then. He seemed none too pleased with my presence.

Doubtful he would be pleased with any stranger with whom his sister—who had overthrown his rule—had returned. Hadn't he said he thought her a deserter? The people were feasting at her absence. Maisie herself—should he refer to her now as Maighread?—had said she was widely hated.

The sirens . . . ?

Traitor!

Nonsense.

Adrian drank again. Filling his mouth with the wine and swishing it around while he looked down into the chalice. It really was very good wine. Perhaps the best he'd ever had.

Besides, Maisie said the sirens couldn't come onto Wyldonna without the aid of a vessel or a mortal.

I'm a mortal, and we came directly ashore on a vessel, did we not? Bollocks! You're half-pissed already. Have a bite, idiot.

Adrian chuckled to himself and reached for the twisted handle of the domed cover, but the thing seemed to duck from beneath his fingers, causing his hand to slide off the side of the dish and send the eating knife clattering to the floor. He bent and picked it up with a muttered curse and then nearly fell to the floor himself as the room seemed to tilt and rotate a quarter turn.

Suddenly he was facing the bed, the coverlet flickering invitingly with the shadows cast by the hearth.

That is a grand idea.

Adrian staggered toward the plush haven, pausing to lean his backside against the mattress while he struggled with the laces of his old boots.

He really should have burned them long ago. But it seemed disloyal to . . . himself, he supposed.

He wrenched off the last boot with a huff and then pulled his shirt over his head, tossing it into an untidy heap on the floor before seizing the edge of the coverlet and pulling it aside. Crawling between the thick bedding felt like sliding beneath a warm wave—odd, as the chamber had been chilly only a moment before. But he laid his head on smooth, silky linen and didn't care as he drifted deeper into the blankets, buoyed along by the rising and falling of his own chest, the tide of his blood rushing in his ears.

A low moaning caused his eyes to snap open. It took him a moment, staring at the faint shadows on the ceiling, to remember where he was. No sandstone—only wood.

No nightmare, only Wyldonna.

The room was darker than it had been, and Adrian realized he had fallen into bed without making certain the candles were out. They had obviously burned down, and he was glad he hadn't set fire to the castle on his first night in residence.

Then he heard the moan again, low and guttural, and his eyes narrowed against the darkness, listening intently.

It was a woman, but she didn't sound as if she were whimpering in pain. The moan was replaced by breathy panting, then a sigh. His manhood stirred.

Those were the unmistakable sounds of a woman being well bedded. But they were so clear; it sounded as if she was in his very chamber.

Adrian sat upright in bed and looked around with a frown. And then he gave a start as his eyes fell on the long wall of his chamber. It was a dream, after all. It must be.

There was a window.

And beyond that window, a woman pressed up against the cloudy glass, her bright yellow hair glowing as if the moonlight shone upon her alone. It fell in waves to either side of her peachy complexion, rosy, slender cheekbones leading down to a delicately pointed chin. He could not tell the color of her eyes from his bed, but her lashes were the same striking shade as her hair. Then he realized the wavy golden strands flowed over naked shoulders, and her bared breasts were flattened against the window as she began to undulate there, her arms spread between the stone inset. Long, rubbery-looking nipples the color of the inside of a shell rolled against the glass.

The passionate moans filled the room again as the woman's mouth opened and she swirled her tongue against the translucent barrier, raising up enough for Adrian to see her navel, which appeared to be studded with a pearl. He swallowed and then kicked the coverings away as he stumbled out of bed and to the window, barechested and barefooted.

"Ohhh," the woman moaned with a wicked smile, her eyes greedily taking in Adrian's torso. He realized then that Brother Song's designs were completely visible, and yet he didn't remember removing his shirt. He also didn't care, as the laces of his chausses strained with desire. His own nipples hardened as he placed his hands over the glass, where the woman continued to writhe, now hunching her back and moving her hips back and forth so that Adrian could just see the juncture of her thighs. She was completely nude.

And she seemed to be hovering in the air.

As if she could sense his thoughts, the woman stepped one foot and then the other onto the stone ledge, squatting low and baring her most intimate parts to Adrian boldly. She licked the window again as she brought her hand to herself.

Adrian looked wildly around the perimeter of the glass, but there was no way to open it. It was set into the frame with molding, and there was neither latch nor hinge. He slapped his hands against the glass and gave a bark of frustration.

The woman laughed. Then she withdrew her hand from her raunchy ministrations and rapped lightly on the glass with her knuckles, raising her eyebrows in innocent question.

"I can't get out!" Adrian groaned and slapped the window again, causing it to shudder.

The woman smiled brightly and then turned her fist sideways and pantomimed striking the glass harder.

Break the window . . .

Her hips pumped faster now, her panting so loud that Adrian could almost feel the heat of it in his ear. She began to grunt like an animal, in rhythm to her movements. His eyes were locked on her body, and all he cared about, all he could think of, was possessing that body.

This terrible dream. This intoxicating dream. He had to have relief. He pulled back both fists, ready to shatter the glass and pull her over the ledge atop him.

A cold blast of air rushed over his naked back as a voice cried out, "Adrian! Nay!"

He looked over his shoulder with a menacing growl and saw Maisie Lindsey standing just inside the room, his door swinging shut behind her. Her red hair was undone, curling over the shoulders of her gauzy ivory dressing gown, and her right arm was extended toward him.

"Doona break the glass. She is not what she appears, and if she reaches you, she will devour you."

"Get out of my dream, Maisie Lindsey," he growled at her and then turned back to the window, where the yellow-haired vixen was now hissing in the direction over Adrian's shoulder, baring tiny pointed teeth at the Queen of Wyldonna.

Adrian couldn't have agreed more. He raised his fists and swung them, but the skin of his fists only grazed the glass as something seized him around his chest and yanked him backward.

It was Maisie Lindsey's arms, although only in a dream could she have crossed the floor so quickly and soundlessly. He threw her off, but she slid under his arm to wrap herself around him, craning her neck to bring her face before his.

"Adrian, look at me! Look!" He glanced down at her face, and for an instant, the draw of the woman at the window was interrupted. "She would be your death. I'll show you."

Maisie looked over her shoulder toward the window, her arms still wrapped around Adrian's torso like thin iron bands, his erection pressing into her soft stomach. "Reveal yourself!" she commanded.

The yellow-haired woman screamed in fury and seemed to flicker like a candle flame in a draft.

"Reveal yourself!" Maisie shouted.

And then it was Adrian who screamed, as a demon appeared in the woman's place at the window ledge. Its skin was like whale blubber, with long, stretched-out breasts that were secured halfway down their deflated length against her belly by what looked like a belt of seaweed. Its hair was no longer yellow but a sickly gray green, and when her lipless mouth gaped in rage again, Adrian could only see one long, pointed tooth in the middle of its upper jaw. Its black eyes were glossy, like hematite, and the darkness took up the whole of its shallow sockets, reflecting Adrian and the white wraith that was Maisie Lindsey wrapped protectively around him.

Adrian brought his own arms around Maisie's shoulders and pulled her even closer to him. The nightmare had gone too deep for him now, and so he eagerly retreated back into his slumber, the warmth of the queen's embrace staying until he was aware of nothing else.

Maisie climbed back into bed with a weary sigh, pulling the covers high over her shoulder as she turned onto her side to watch the coals glowing. She knew Dragon was observing her in return, waiting perhaps for word of what had gone on in Adrian Hailsworth's chamber, but Maisie ignored her, and soon the gray creature rested her head on her claws again and closed her eyes.

Her illusion had not been strong enough. Maisie had considered placing Adrian in the dungeon for his own safety, but after seeing the nightmare of his past and how he'd suffered through captivity—and how being contained still greatly disturbed him—she thought perhaps the glamour on the wall and the giant at the door would be enough to ward off any danger.

Poor Reid. He thought he'd failed.

Poor Adrian. Maisie hoped the Englishman would not remember the events that had transpired in his chamber on his first night. How stupid of her.

How stupid not to consider that the crawler had been occupied upon landing on the beach, especially after the brazen shout of the siren. The creature had been clever enough to quickly hide before Maisie had emerged from the cabin, likely leaping from the deck to the trees so as to avoid touching the rocky shore. Had Maisie seen it, she would have destroyed it at once for its blatant defiance of the law. How it had managed to place the sea wine into Adrian's chamber was yet unknown. It didn't matter really now. As reward for her stupidity, she could now add at least one more to the roster of her enemies inhabiting the island.

If there was one positive mark on such an otherwise dreadful homecoming, it was that she'd seen the black symbols on Adrian's skin. Not well, for she had been concentrating on preventing him from offering himself to the siren. But she'd seen enough before her arms had gone around his hot, bare skin to know that the designs had been laid down with wisdom.

Could Adrian Hailsworth save her—save Wyldonna? Maisie didn't know. But she did know that if he failed, he would likely lose his life, black markings or nay. Glayer Felsteppe was a demon, true, but he had no magic in him to defend against.

If Adrian succeeded, Wyldonna, at least, would be saved.

Beware the Painted Man, my child,
Who trades the death of the Queen.

Her own brother was against her, feeling betrayed and bitter. The folk who lived in the wood and sea and supported him were therefore also against her, thinking she had betrayed her kin and king.

Perhaps eventually the Englishman, too, would agree with Malcolm that Maisie had made an enormous mistake. If that happened, she would truly be on her own.

But at least until the morrow, Adrian Hailsworth was on her side and, foolish as it might be, she felt he was enough.

Maisie rolled over away from the light and closed her eyes, the memory of the Englishman's strong, painted arms around her pulling her down into sleep at last.

Chapter 10

Adrian's eyes snapped open and he blinked at the shadowed, unfamiliar ceiling above his head.

Not sandstone—only wood.

Not the crawler—Wyldonna.

He frowned to himself and his head ached dully as if he were trying to remember something he ought. He couldn't recall even crawling into bed the night before, although he must have done just that shortly upon entering; his boots and shoes were missing from his person.

He did remember his dream of Maighread Lindsey, though. She was in his arms and she wanted him.

Adrian sat up and was startled to see the ugly Reid sitting in what appeared to be a chair made of logs near the window, through which it appeared night still maintained a firm grip on the island. He didn't think he'd noticed the glazed square when he'd arrived, but because there would be little to see beyond the panes in a land cloaked in a habitual dusk, Adrian didn't think much of it.

There was no window last night.

Don't be ridiculous.

No wonder the large man was so malformed; body and mind needed sunlight to properly thrive. Although that did not explain Maighread Lindsey's fierce beauty.

The giant stood and gave a stiff nod of his enormous head. "Good morrow, Man. The queen has requested your presence in the hall once you have dressed and eaten. I hope you find the meal more satisfactory than last eve's fare."

Adrian frowned. He hadn't eaten at all last night, had he? No, he was certain he had drunk wine, but . . . he couldn't remember anything at all after that.

There was no window.

"I assure you I meant no slight by my lack of attention to last night's offering," he said, throwing back the covers and swinging his legs over the side of the bed. "I apologize. Please tell the queen that I will answer her summons very soon." He looked up at the man, expecting him to make his exit and leave Adrian to ready himself in peace.

"I will accompany you," Reid said, with another stiff nod of his head. Adrian noticed the way the man's eyes flicked over the marks on his flank before he turned away toward the window, as if suddenly interested in the shadows that cloaked the land beyond.

A demon in the window . . .

Adrian shook his head to clear it as he fought the urge to argue with the man. He was unused to having an audience while he dressed in his private chamber, and he obviously needed some time to order his chaotic and unlikely thoughts. There were no personal servants for the humble brethren at Melk, and Adrian had become accustomed to being alone. He preferred it, actually. But since it was likely Reid was only following orders, he would not press the proper man into disobedience.

His eyes fell on the chair, where the shirt he had apparently discarded the night before lay neatly folded, the hem just grazing the tops of his boots resting neatly in pair. He stood from the bed and moved to his clothes, pulling on his shirt and then pouring a cup of cider from the pitcher on the table and taking a drink.

He would not press the man to leave him, but he did have questions.

"Am I a prisoner, then?" he asked as he turned to take a seat on the chair and attend to the donning of his boots. He looked over his shoulder and saw Reid glance back in the same manner, but the man gave no answer. "I only ask because you seem to have been given clear instructions to keep me under guard."

"You are an esteemed guest," he answered haltingly. "My presence is for . . . your comfort."

"And yet you are not permitted to speak to me," Adrian countered. Reid gave no answer, and so Adrian made a wager with himself and muttered, "Incredibly rude manner with which to treat an esteemed guest."

A glance over his shoulder rewarded him with the sight of the man's torso swelling up, as if it was taking all of Reid's self-control not to burst.

"I have been advised," Reid said very slowly, very carefully, "that any questions you have should first be addressed to the queen."

"I see," Adrian said, working now on his other boot. "Can we not then act as learned men, discussing such mundane things that apply to our lives? I do find conversation with a person of intelligence to be quite stimulating."

"As do I," Reid answered right away.

"For instance," Adrian said, spinning around on his seat to address his platter of oatcakes and honey, "I must say that I found myself quite taken aback at your stature."

"As was my mother," Reid replied. Adrian chuckled, but, to his surprise, the man continued. "It was only to my benefit as a child, however, for she tended to dote on me and protect me from my brothers due to my stunted size."

Adrian paused, an oatcake halfway to his mouth while the man continued in a musing tone.

"As I grew older, it became quite clear that I was not likely to marry in our tribe due to my slight physique. But the Lindseys showed my kin great kindness in employing me within the castle. I am the only one of my kind able to enter the palace, you see, and so it is also my honor to represent our tribe at court."

Adrian blinked. "Your tribe."

Reid turned and gave Adrian a haughty look. "Yes. I might be a small giant, but I am a giant nonetheless."

Adrian considered the oatcake still in his hand before laying it carefully on the platter, untasted. He picked up the cider.

"And you?" Reid inquired. "You are a man, and yet you . . . you . . ."

Adrian swallowed and looked at the . . . *giant.* "Yes?"

"Your skin is painted. Are you a piece blood?"

"I beg your pardon?"

"I mean you no offense," Reid said, turning and giving Adrian a bow. "I only assumed that since you were marked, your tribe is one of exile. I apologize."

"No offense," Adrian assured him vaguely. "These marks were given to me by a man who was once a prince in his land. They are meant to cover the scars I bear."

"Protection." Reid nodded solemnly. "Of course. Were you banished by your people?"

"No," Adrian said with a shake of his head, although he was more than a bit surprised that the man had used the very term also employed by Song to describe his marks. And hadn't Adrian felt his friends were exiling him from the library on the day he left Melk? "I wasn't banished. I—"

"Your family was in exile then, and you shunned them. I see."

"*No*," Adrian insisted, his mind tangling in the intricacies of meaning that could make Reid's statement true. "My father is a respected English noble. I haven't seen him in many years because I have been unjustly accused of a crime."

Reid nodded, a bit of smugness creeping around his mouth. "So you *were* banished."

"*No!*" Adrian stood from the table. "Any matter. I should not keep the queen waiting."

"Very good." Reid bowed. "This way, Man."

"There's no need to call me Man," Adrian said crossly at the giant's wide back as he followed him from the chamber. "You may address me as Adrian."

Reid ducked through the doorway and into the corridor. "It would be highly improper for me to address a Man guest by his given name," Reid advised. He strode down the passage ahead of Adrian, causing the floorboards to undulate so that Adrian was forced to lift his feet with each step. "But it is completely forbidden for me to do so with a piece blood."

Adrian sighed and shook his head. "I'm not a piece blood, whatever that is."

"I would not readily admit to it either," Reid confided.

Adrian determined that drawing the obviously unstable Reid into conversation had been a mistake. For a brief moment in his chamber he had almost considered that the huge man had been part of a race of gigantic creatures. Pretty manners could cover much insanity, he reasoned to himself as he followed the servant through a senseless maze. Up stairs, down sloping corridors—Adrian was fairly certain they journeyed underground at one point—until they finally emerged into a long narrow hall.

Unlike the manor homes he was familiar with in England, Wyldonna's hall boasted no elevated dais with a lord's table. Instead, a longer trestle sat directly on the floor parallel to the chamber's side walls and was flanked perpendicularly to either side by shorter tables. Fantastic tapestries and plaid cloths in patterns and colors Adrian had never seen combined were hung from the high ceiling like banners— at least fifty of them, by Adrian's quick guess. There were no rushes on the floor; the stones gleamed as if they had been polished and were set so carefully and finely together that they gave the illusion of being one massive slab of smooth rock.

Two circular pits in the floor at either end of the long room were home to tall open fires that warmed the space and added to the glow of the candles set along the center of the trestle table. Queen Maighread sat in a plain chair in the center of one side of the table, her back to him, but Adrian could see that her manner of dress and appointment was vastly different than that of the woman with whom he'd traveled to Wyldonna. Gone was the simple gown and tumbling curls, re- placed with a deep red velvet and hair twisted atop her head beneath a thin crown of hammered silver. When she turned her head at the sound of their entrance, Adrian nearly faltered in his step at her regal bearing.

This was the woman he'd likened to a laundress.

Across from Maighread—to Adrian's surprise—sat her brother, the recently deposed Malcolm. He did not appear pleased to be in the hall with his sister, and Adrian noted that his entrance had seemed to interrupt a rather heated conversation between the siblings.

Adrian stopped several feet from the table and gave a bow. "Queen Maighread." He rose and nodded to the woman's brother. "Lindsey. Good day."

"Hailsworth." Malcolm's eye flicked over Adrian's person, per- haps resentful, perhaps only just a remainder of the argument Adrian had interrupted.

"Good day, Lord Hailsworth," Maighread said. "I hope your ac- commodations were adequate. I fear the servants were nae aware we would be hosting a guest at the castle."

Lord Hailsworth now, was he?

Malcolm snorted. "Maisie doesna feel it necessary to inform any- one of anything, 'twould seem. You've likely begun to notice a pat- tern."

Her head whipped around to regard her brother. "It is a foolish waste of time to inform those who willna listen."

"You called for me," Adrian interrupted, not caring at all to become an observer of their row.

"Yes," Maisie said, once more facing Adrian, and he saw the effort it took her to compose herself. "I thought you should hear what transpired at Glayer Felsteppe's arrival at Wyldonna, because your presence here has a personal aim as well as a philanthropic one." She gestured toward a chair at her side with one slender, pale hand. "Please join us."

"I assure you my motives are not philanthropic in the least," Adrian countered, ignoring the place she had indicated and instead dragging the chair closest to him to sit at the end of the trestle, where he could observe both Maisie and Malcolm simultaneously. Although her presence seemed to affect him more deeply each time they were together, he did not want to give the woman the impression that he could be so easily ordered about, nor would he join Wyldonna's erstwhile king.

He was no one's lackey, and he would make that clear.

"The reason I agreed to come here—the only reason—is that your troubles are connected to a man who is the greatest enemy of myself and my friends." Adrian looked at the siblings in turn. "If any can help you, I am confident it is I, but my priority remains ensuring Glayer Felsteppe is held accountable for his actions."

"I admire that," Malcolm said gruffly and then glanced at his sister. "He doesna hide his motivations behind a guise of helping others." It was a blatant dig, although Adrian did not understand entirely the implication.

Maisie ignored Malcolm. "Fair enough. Shall we begin, or do you have any pressing questions that you would like answered first?"

Windows.

Sirens.

Did you, too, dream of me last night?

Adrian shifted in his chair. "Let us begin."

Maisie turned to Malcolm. "Well? Yours was the first encounter with him that day."

The bearded man placed his elbows on the trestle and folded his hands together. "I didna know he and his men were ashore until late

in the day. There are always so many strangers about, so many peti-
tions to be answered, no one paid him any heed. Likely he knew that
would be the circumstance, and he used it to his advantage."

"What circumstance?" Adrian asked. "As I understood it, Wyldonna is impossible to find and even more difficult to land."

"It was Yule," Maisie explained. "There are only four times of the
year that Wyldonna can be deliberately located—either at the solstices or the equinoxes: Ostara, Midsummer, Autumn, and Yule. That
is how, over the centuries, the stories and legends of our land were
spread."

Malcolm nodded agreement, and Adrian was relieved that he
would not have to contend with the brother and sister pecking at each
other the entirety of the meeting. "It's when those who wish to do so
may leave Wyldonna and those who have already left—voluntarily or
otherwise—can return to visit their families and petition for return.
Most are turned away, either because of the seriousness of their law-
breaking or because they return with wives or husbands and children.
Piece bloods canna survive here."

At this, Adrian's interest was piqued, and so he interrupted. "Piece
bloods?"

Maisie's fine brow furrowed. "Many Wyldonians marry out of
their tribe once away from the island. They soon find that life away
from Wyldonna is difficult and foreign and they wish to return to the
safety of their home. But once they have intermarried with man—"
she paused—"or . . . *others*, and borne children, they canna return."

Adrian returned her frown. "Are you so enamored with your-
selves that you cannot abide outsiders in your realm?"

"It isna that at all, lad," Malcolm said earnestly, and Adrian found
it amusing that the king referred to him as a lad when Adrian guessed
himself at least five years the man's senior. "It's for their own good."

"Piece blood means their blood isna whole," Maisie went on.
"They might have man's blood with a piece of Wyldonna, or Wyldonian blood containing a piece of man's."

Adrian's eyebrows rose. "So?"

"So," Malcolm drawled, "they doona have enough magic to defend themselves. It's worse with the ones who are mostly Wyldonian—the piece of man rises up in the worst ways."

"Magic," Adrian repeated flatly.

"Men are ambitious, power hungry," Malcom said, ignoring

Adrian's skepticism. "They are never satisfied with their station. On the few occasions when piece bloods have been allowed to remain and were fortunate enough to nae cross ways with the woodland folk, they have been unable to resist the temptation of seizing Wyldonna's power and wealth for their own purposes."

"As Glayer Felsteppe wishes to do," Maisie pointed out.

Adrian shook his head. "Glayer Felsteppe is not of this place. He's the youngest son of an impoverished family from the south of England. How do you explain his discovery of your proclaimed magical island? And why wasn't he devoured soon after stepping foot ashore?"

Malcolm leaned back in his chair and boldly watched his sister, as if highly interested in her answer.

Maisie's eyes shifted to Malcolm only for an instant before coming back to Adrian. "We believe he was led here by one of our own, who had left Wyldonna at Midsummer. Likely he was offered a great sum to do so."

"That doesn't at all explain how Felsteppe learned of Wyldonna," Adrian retorted, refusing to budge. Something weighty hung in the air between Maisie and her brother, and Adrian wished to know what it was.

But to his surprise, Malcolm rescued the woman. "He is a man who has surrounded himself with desperate men. Has he nae been to war in the East? In your holy Jerusalem?"

"He was there, yes," Adrian conceded, "although he managed to escape the worst of the fighting through lie and illusion, and by ingratiating himself to the Christian king there. A warrior he is not."

Malcolm nodded. "The armies, though; they are well-known for utilizing mercenaries."

Adrian conceded the point with his own nod.

Maisie then picked up the conversation. "Many piece bloods and exiles who are turned away from Wyldonna find securing livelihoods difficult. Because of their unique . . . gifts, a large majority of the males become paid soldiers. Some become criminals. And they are quite successful."

Malcolm leaned forward again. "We can be certain Felsteppe came across one of these exiles. After learning about Wyldonna, he concocted his scheme to gain the fortune for his own use."

"He needs the treasure," Maisie emphasized. "To find you and your friends."

Adrian was still. "You know he is searching for me."

Maisie nodded hesitantly.

"You knew it when you came to the abbey."

"I didna know who exactly I would find there," Maisie hedged. "But I knew Melk would give the assistance I sought."

Constantine would not be happy with this turn of events. Adrian gave himself a moment to compose himself before continuing.

"What I don't understand," he began slowly, "is why Felsteppe would demand the fortune and then leave? Why not take over Wyldonna in the moment Malcolm refused him rather than threaten you with his return?"

"Two reasons," Malcolm supplied, the fire returning to his green eyes. "First, he came to the island with only a handful of men—nae enough to properly challenge us. Perhaps he was nae completely convinced that Wyldonna truly existed. And second . . . well . . ." He looked to Maisie.

She would not meet Adrian's eyes. "I promised Felsteppe the reward my brother denied him in exchange for leaving Wyldonna and its people in peace. He only needed to give me the time to secure it."

"She took my throne, said the vows, and made a deal with a devil," Malcolm clarified.

Maisie slapped her hand on the table and turned to face her brother. "Your bloody pride would have brought war to Wyldonna and destroyed us all! If Wyldonna is nae more, it would be disastrous to the whole world, Malcolm!"

Malcolm rose from his chair and thundered, "Doona *dare* speak to me of what is best for this island, lass! I was *king*! *I* decide what is best for Wyldonna! The trouble is nae with my pride but that you have naught of the stuff. Your only thought now is to save your own arse, Maighread Lindsey, but *I'll* nae be intimidated by some *Englishman*."

"You promised him Wyldonna's treasure," Adrian prompted Maisie, trying not to be offended.

"Aye," Malcolm instead sneered the answer and turned toward Adrian. "And if it canna be found, she's promised to deliver to him the only other thing he desires more than riches." Malcolm leaned forward and pointed a finger at Adrian's chest.

"*You.*"

Chapter 11

The silence of the hall fell around the trestle table as Malcolm's stomping footfalls receded from the chamber. After a moment, the echoing slam of a door seemed to shake the dust from the tapestries before allowing the quiet to creep around Maisie again. It was just as well that her brother left her here with Adrian; his part of the tale was told, and there could be no benefit to anyone should he have stayed. They likely would have ended up at each other's throats again.

Maisie kept her eyes on her folded hands atop the trestle, but she could feel the weight of Adrian's gaze on her as surely as if it were a tangible, hot thing, pressing against the side of her face. Her ear began to tingle. And yet she waited.

"What did Malcolm mean exactly, Maighread?" Adrian asked at last, his voice pensive, curious. Her heart skipped when he addressed her by her given name. "That you promised Felsteppe someone capable of aiding him in his search for the men he was looking for, much as I am aiding you?"

She shook her head and then drew a deep, silent breath, keeping her eyes on her tightly folded hands. She noticed her nail beds had turned white. "I told him that *I* would help him. If he would leave Wyldonna in peace and not return to the island with the army he threatened, I would either find the men he sought or provide him with the means to do so himself, by way of Wyldonna's fortune."

"But," Adrian began, "how did you know where to—?"

"I didna," she said tightly. "After Felsteppe left Wyldonna, I sought Malcolm to tell him that I thought I had bought us some time against war. I needed his help. His advice." She huffed a laugh. "But seizing the throne is nae a friendly action, and he took it as a gesture of betrayal. Rightly so, I suppose, although I'd hoped to explain myself. But Malcolm has a . . . talent for disappearing. And the folk most loyal to him did their best to foil my efforts to find him. When they began attacking me personally, I knew I was nae longer safe here."

She looked up. "I left Wyldonna on the crawler for the mainland. For Scotland. I had nae idea where I was going, but I trusted that it was the right place. I landed on the shores of a monastery and begged shelter. The abbot there saw my distress, and when he offered me counsel, I told him that Glayer Felsteppe had threatened my family. I didna know what else to do." Adrian was looking at her so intensely, she had to swallow before she continued. "Almost as soon as I spoke his name, the abbot gave me the coin and directed me to Victor, and to Melk. I could feel as soon as I met Victor that he was hiding the four of you." She shrugged.

"And I only confirmed it for you while we were on the crawler," Adrian said bitterly. "You wouldn't have known I was one of the men Felsteppe was seeking otherwise."

"Aye, I would have," Maisie whispered. She brought her eyes back to her hands. "There was nae need for you to confirm anything once I had seen your nightmare."

He was quiet for a moment. "I don't know what you mean."

"The prison. Your . . . injuries." She looked up at him again and felt tears coming into her eyes. "I saw everything through your eyes. The Spaniard—Valentine. Constantine."

Adrian's eyes went hard. "That's impossible," he said. "If you were so certain I was one of the four Felsteppe sought, why then would you stop the crawler—offer to return me back Melk? Did you experience a sudden attack of conscience?"

"I suppose," she said quietly. "For what it's worth, I'm sorry."

"You're not sorry," he said. "It was your intention all along to offer me up as a sacrifice to Glayer Felsteppe."

"That's true," she conceded. "I had convinced myself that the life of one man was a small price to pay in order to save my people. But I didna know . . . I didna know then what he'd done, Adrian. What had happened to you."

"You don't now know what happened to me, and I don't want your pity."

"It's nae pity," she said, shaking her head. "I only wish Victor had chosen one of the others. Perhaps then . . ."

"Perhaps then you could have killed the man who is to soon become a father instead? Or the man who has lost his wife and son at Felsteppe's very hands? What about the man who rescued the three of us from torture and death that was only hours away?" Adrian stood from his chair. "Victor *didn't* choose me to come here. It was *my* choice."

"Was it, though?" She looked at him, and for a moment she wondered what kind of magic he possessed that he wasn't even aware of. Maisie could feel the force of him from half the length of the trestle. "The way I see it, you were the only one who could have come. You were meant for this time from the moment you were born."

"Because I'm the Painted Man?" he said with a breath of mirthless laughter. "I assure you the markings I bear are far too recent to have anything to do with this wretched place and its troubles."

"Perhaps. But you *are* the Painted Man," she said and nearly choked on the words. "And you are here now. You will save Wyldonna, through one means or another. I believe that."

"By either finding the treasure or surrendering to Glayer Felsteppe?"

"Surrender was nae part of the bargain," she offered with a slight smile. It was enough to disarm him the tiniest bit, and so she took the opportunity to make peace. "I've already done what I promised— I've brought you to Wyldonna. What Felsteppe can or canna do with you will be his trouble."

"Oh, he will have trouble," Adrian said. "And now I see no reason to carry on with the search. Once Felsteppe arrives, I will deal with him."

"You against him and the army he brings?" Maisie queried. "Nay. Would that I give him the fortune he craves and send him on his way with you in secret pursuit rather than force his hand against either of us. It's the least I can do—payment, if you will—for misleading you so."

Adrian grasped the back of the chair and leaned against it, considering the stones for several moments. Then he nodded curtly and met her eyes once again. "Then there is nothing for it but that I find the treasure."

Maisie nodded. "Aye."

"But I still have one more question," he said. "If the people of Wyldonna—the island itself—is so very enchanted, why did you not simply turn Felsteppe into a toad or what have you?"

Maisie gave him a brief smile. "It's one of the drawbacks of being Wyldonian royalty, I suppose. The rulers of the island canna use magic. Not even to defend ourselves. It wouldna be very fair to have a king or queen who can exert their will on their people through force, would it?"

Adrian looked askance. "Oh, I see. So you won't be able to conjure up a spell for me to prove your mystical claims."

"Not while I'm on the island," she said, knowing he didn't believe one whit of her explanation by the depth of his smirk. His mouth was remarkably alluring.

"What will you do once Felsteppe is no longer a threat? Concede the throne back to your brother?"

Maisie stood, busying herself with straightening her voluminous skirts and reinserting the chair beneath the trestle. "Ah, nay. I fear I'm saddled with the chore now."

"Will you marry, then? Produce offspring for the realm?"

She turned to him with a smile. "Are you offering for the queen's hand, Adrian Hailsworth?"

To her surprise and delight, Adrian grew stiff and flustered. "I'm only curious."

"Nay, I shallna marry," she said, taking pity on him but liking the sight of him at odds.

"Why not?"

"There's none for me to marry," she said simply. "Malcolm either. We are the last of our kind. Once we are both gone, rule will go to the tribe that is agreed upon by all at the funeral council."

He looked at her for a long moment. "You can't marry outside of your . . . tribe. That would create—"

"Piece bloods," she finished for him. "Who canna survive on Wyldonna, let alone be allowed to rule. So you see, this is much more to me than staving off an aggression from a foreign invader. Saving Wyldonna is the legacy I will leave for Malcolm and for our people."

"That's rather . . . dismal," Adrian finished. "Especially because you seem certain your brother will outlive you."

She gave him another tight smile and started to turn away. She was surprised when she felt his hand circling the upper part of her arm, staying her and pulling her back to face him.

Maisie looked down at his fingers curled around the fabric of her gown and then up into Adrian's face with what she hoped was a haughty stare, conveying her displeasure at the idea that he should be brazen enough to lay a hand on her in her own hall.

But what Maisie truly felt was the urge to wrap herself around Adrian Hailsworth's strong body as she had done last night. She wanted to beg his forgiveness for what she'd done.

He ignored her glare. "Do you believe that? That your brother will survive you to regain the throne?"

"It's naught but another story to you, Adrian," she said at last. "You wouldna yet believe it."

"Yet?" he pressed, and Maisie thought he drew her to him such an infinitesimal amount, he likely didn't realize he'd done so.

"Stay awhile," she said, letting her lips curve wryly, a genuine expression at last. "You might learn a thing or two."

He looked into her eyes a moment longer, and his fingers gentled around her arm. He released her suddenly and straightened his posture.

"I had planned to start with the turrets today. Would you care to accompany me?"

Maisie realized there was nothing else she'd rather do.

They began at the uppermost level of Wyldonna Castle: the eastern turret. Accessing it involved climbing a dizzying amount of spiraling steps, and it seemed to Adrian that they ascended for an hour, him following along behind Maisie's wide, heavy skirts. Her pace was slow, steady—for his benefit, he guessed—but even though he was winded when they at last reached the arched wooden door at the top of the steps, he was surprised that his fatigue was only perhaps half of what he'd thought it would be.

She struggled with the heavy door for a moment, huffing and throwing her shoulder into it. Adrian winced when he thought of the punishment she was inflicting on her slight flesh.

"Here," he said brusquely, grasping her elbow and returning the candle she'd bade him carry. "Allow me."

She looked down at him with a touch of surprise before shuffling aside and then down one step to allow him access to the door.

The latch was a wooden knob carved into the shape of a blossoming flower, and Adrian had to push down hard and heave against the door twice before it inched open with a pair of tight shrieks. Maisie followed him into the room, the candle lifted high, and the chamber was instantly filled with slinking shadows that seemed to cringe away from the light behind listing piles of broken furniture and busted baskets of discarded unknowns.

Adrian pulled the plans from his satchel and stepped into the center of the room, holding the parchments open before him while Maisie held the candle over his shoulder. He turned in a semicircle and then back, forcing the smaller redhead to scurry along at his side.

"I told you," she said, and the scent of her wafted up like a clutch of blooms. "Nothing up here for ages." She lowered the candle when Adrian let the parchments roll into his palms.

He walked to the single narrow window and looked out, first in one direction and then the other. Nothing but gloom, and perhaps the distant, flat flash of the gray sea. The bare branches of trees mingled with the arrow points of the pines, comprising the whole of the desolate landscape. Adrian couldn't see so much as a forgotten leaf stirring, let alone signs that there were any other living beings on Wyldonna save for Maisie and himself.

"Where is everyone?" he challenged suddenly. He didn't know why, but it had somehow become important to Adrian that Maisie tell him the truth about the island. He had no reason not to believe any part of her tale save for her insistence that Wyldonna was some magical place. If she would lie to him about the very nature of her home, he felt he could not trust her with anything, especially if Glayer Felsteppe was returning to Wyldonna shortly.

"Everyone who?" she asked.

He turned to her, and her eyes were wide, reflecting the candlelight as if they contained all the sparkling stars missing from the bleak sky beyond the window. He gestured toward the same. "The people." He waved a hand toward the open and shadowed doorway. "The servants. The only persons I've seen since coming ashore have been your brother and a single manservant."

She frowned at him a bit, and Adrian was fascinated by the little crease that formed between her auburn brows. "The servants are about their duties, I'm certain. There arnna many to see anymore, I fear. Everyone else?" She stepped to the window and looked out, drew a deep breath. "They're down there. In their homes. Helping Malcolm, some of them. Likely as nae in the mountain itself." She shrugged and looked up at him.

Adrian looked out the window and a feeling of frustration came over him. Why did she insist on playing this childish game with him?

"Then why do I not see a single plume of smoke from a chimney? Why do I not hear a dog's bark? A sheep's bleat?" He held his hand toward the scene before him. "Wyldonna appears deserted. And I cannot help . . ." He closed his mouth abruptly.

"What?" she pressed.

He looked down at her, but he didn't see any wariness in her expression, any hint of deception. "I cannot help but wonder if this kingdom is . . . something you and your brother might have constructed. In your minds," he added haltingly.

To his surprise, her eyebrows shot up and she grinned. "You think we're mad?"

"Perhaps it's the air here." He looked away from her abruptly and heard himself trying to explain. "Or the isolation. It oft does strange things to people."

He looked back at her when she laughed merrily, and saw that she had brought one hand up to cover her lips. Adrian wished she wouldn't—he liked to look at her mouth when she smiled.

"I forgot!" she exclaimed on a chuckle.

"You forgot?" he prompted.

Maisie nodded and stepped closer to Adrian. The sudden closeness of her startled him, but he did not move away.

"I canna do magic, but I can certainly reveal what is right before your eyes. Wyldonna is enchanted, Adrian. So that if any might accidentally find themselves ashore by way of misadventure, they would think themselves to have come upon a barren and desolate place of little comfort. It really is for their protection, as well as ours." She raised the arm not holding the candle and placed her hand over his eyes.

Adrian didn't duck away. The skin of her palm felt like silk across the bridge of his nose. "What are you about?"

"Tell me what you saw when you looked out the window."

"Ah . . ." The smell of her skin, the feel of it upon his face tangled his thoughts. "Nothing, really."

"Nothing at all?"

He cleared his throat. "There isn't much to see in the blasted darkness. The outline of trees. Perhaps the sea at a distance. Rocks. The slope of the cliff. Fog."

"All right," she said, and he could hear the smile in her voice. "Now I shall tell you what is actually there: cottages in the wood, doors to burrows nestled against the hill. Halfway down the cliff is a set of sea caves; you should see the torches of those going about their business on the paths. Beyond that, there are at least twenty crawlers moored in the bay. Are you ready to see them?"

"Oh, certainly," Adrian said, his answer not sounding at all confident.

Maisie removed her hand, and the first thing Adrian saw was her smile. Then he turned his face toward the window once more. What he saw gave him such a start that he braced both palms against the stone sill and blinked several times.

It was just as she'd described, only ... so much more than what mere words could convey. The fog still hung in the air, but now it was not the dense, dirty cloud that reflected the bleak landscape but seemed to be more of a mist made of sparkling frost. It hung in the treetops, which were no longer skeletal fingers and stark points of black but boughs laden with crystalline drops of moisture, reflecting the glitter of the mist like tiny jeweled buds.

And below the protective, twinkling canopy, rounded roofs shimmered mossy green over the squat, sturdy rock walls of the cottages, happy columns of smoke drifting lazily up to mingle with the mist. He was too far above for his vision to make out any individuals who might be about, but he did see little sparks of light—the torches Maisie had suggested—bobbing through the gloom that was not so much bleak now as peaceful. The sea glistened silver beyond the cliff; the dark slashes in the water must be the crawlers.

Adrian blinked again several times. What he was seeing was impossible. He had only a moment ago looked out this very window, with his same eyes, and seen nothing. Now a new world had been revealed to him. It could not be sorcery; that was only manipulating facts in order to force someone to believe that which was otherwise untrue. He was being manipulated. Driven mad and manipulated.

He turned to her. "How did you first start?"

Maisie's smile didn't falter, although her eyes crinkled a bit. "Start what?"

"Priming me to believe that Wyldonna was deserted so that my mind would not recognize anything else?"

Now the smile did fall away and was replaced with a frown. "I did nae such thing. I've just now explained to you why you saw things as you did: It was the enchantment. Now you are open to seeing what is truly here."

"Rubbish," he bit out. "It's a mind trick. A mental rub-your-tum-and-pat-your-head child's game. *Tell me how you did it.*"

"I didna do anything," she insisted, and her brows drew farther down. The candle in her hand wobbled. "You're seeing what is there because you know what is there. I told you."

"Ships, houses don't simply appear out of nothing," Adrian argued, feeling his blood pound in his veins. Why must she lie? It affected him more than he dared admit.

"They didna appear—they were there the whole of the time. Your mind couldna acknowledge them. Just because you canna see something doesna mean it doesna exist."

He gave a scornful laugh. "Yes, it does, I'm afraid."

"Oh, really?" she challenged, setting her hand on her hip. "So if I step out of this chamber and close the door between us, I shall cease to exist because you canna see me? That's rather infantile logic for such a learned man."

"It's not the same thing in the least," he argued, drawing himself up stiffly at her gentle insult. "Because you would move to a different location and set a barrier between us. Yonder village did not move."

"All right then," Maisie acquiesced. "What about love? Can you see love?"

"A physical manifestation of it, yes," he replied. "An embrace, a kiss."

"Ah-ah, but you can have an embrace or a kiss without love, would you nae agree? Either of those in itself is nae actually love. What of loyalty? Can you touch loyalty? Tote it in your satchel?"

"Of course not," he scoffed.

"So, according to you, neither love nor loyalty actually exist."

"Those are both . . . emotions. Feelings," he argued but was a bit alarmed to feel his feet beginning to slide on the terrain of his stance. "You manifest them through a myriad of actions that, while not in themselves solid objects to be manipulated physically, are attributed to and originate from a definite thing."

"What about pain?" Maisie threw at him. "People doona manifest pain if they've any sanity about them. But you are perhaps one of the best witnesses I've ever known that pain is real. Show me pain then, Adrian. I want to touch it."

He felt his face heat. She was goading him. "You want me to hurt you? Strike you?"

"Of course nae. I'm only trying to explain: What you saw through the window—both instances—were manifestations of what Wyldonna is. You can call it whatever you like, but I doona think you have been of the habit to deny what you can see with your own eyes."

His breathing was fast and shallow. This woman was challenging the very meaning of his life: his years of scholarship and learning, honing his mind to a knifepoint, his discernment irreproachable.

"I can see that this is difficult for you to comprehend," she said more calmly now. "But comprehend it you must. There are things here—beings, enchantments—that you willna be able to explain away with all your extensive knowledge. They just *are*. So you must also understand that what looks like an idyllic woodland beyond these walls is actually very deadly for you." She paused. "For us both, at the moment. And it's why you must promise that you willna venture outside the castle without me or Reid."

"That's a clever attempt to prevent me from leaving you and your pathetic people once I've tired of your lies," he sneered.

"I find myself growing quite tired of your impertinence," she tossed back, leaning toward him. "I am queen here and I willna have someone accuse me of falsehoods—especially a pompous, ignorant Englishman who doesna yet know a duvenet from an afternhanger."

Adrian leaned in as well, until their noses where only inches apart.

"Do it again then," he challenged.

"Do what?" she said through her teeth.

"Show me something I can't presently see with my own eyes."

Maisie drew herself aright again and stared at him for a moment. Then she set the candle holder on the windowsill. "Fine." She turned to him and held out her left palm, face up.

Adrian looked down at it and then at her face. "What?"

"What do you see?" she asked in exasperation.

"*Nothing*," he enunciated.

She pressed her lips together into a line and nodded. "Watch."

To Adrian's astonishment, a faint glow began to grow in the center of her cupped palm. Soft yellowish light through which he could see her skin. He glanced over his shoulder to be certain the candle was completely behind him and that his body blocked any direct light. Then he looked back to her quickly, unwilling to give her even a moment to commit some sleight of hand.

The glow had grown taller, like the sun rising out of the sea, the yellow now shimmering just around the edges of a circular green ball the size of a walnut—lighter in color than moss, but not the verdant green of fresh pasture. He glanced up at Maisie's face, but her eyes were fixed on him.

"I don't understand," he began, but Maisie began to speak.

"Malcolm Lindsey," she said, and no sooner had the words left her lips than the ball in her hand grew slightly. It was now the size of Adrian's fist.

"Wyldonna," she said next, and the ball seemed to swell again. "Glayer Felsteppe." Now the sphere was the size of a small squash, and it had a black, inky center.

"What would happen if you said my name?" he asked distractedly, studying closely the way the light moved, the exponentiality of its growth.

She took a deep breath and then whispered, "Adrian Hailsworth." The green glow exploded between them, filling up the space separating them, Maisie's face only visible now through the wavering black at the center of the swirling green phantasm.

"What is it?" Adrian asked quietly, his eyes taking in the entirety of the phenomenon brought on by the speaking of names. It seemed some sort of energy. Like . . . cholers or temperament, perhaps?

"This," Maisie said quietly, "is my fear. It is with me all the time. Only you canna see it." Her last words were barely audible.

Adrian stared at her. His was the last name she'd mentioned, and had been the name that caused the green glow to grow unchecked.

She was afraid of him. Very afraid.

Without pausing to think of a good reason why he would do such a thing, Adrian slapped Maisie's palm away, causing the glowing green sphere to disintegrate in a shower of sparkling dust before it vanished completely.

They held each other's gazes for a pair of heartbeats, and then Adrian began to have that familiar sensation of his chest constricting, his breathing becoming labored. He felt trapped in the turret room with this woman. This beautiful, enigmatic queen who was afraid of him and at the same time manipulating his mind and emotions so that he could not tell reality from fantasy.

"I want to search alone," he said, fighting to control his words and hide the wheeze from her.

"You have my leave to go where you would anywhere within the castle," was all she said, although her eyes were sad now.

And again Adrian was surprised at her.

He only nodded sharply and then turned on his heel to exit the turret room without bothering to take the candle. It didn't matter. Once he was afoot on the long spiral stairs, he fairly flew down them, his breath clawing at his chest for freedom, the dank air between the stones pressing coldly at his nostrils, seeking an entrance that was not to be had.

He stumbled onto level flooring and kept going, turning left and right, heedless to the maps of the place that were tucked into his satchel, until he found himself in the long narrow hall once more. He strode through an aisle between the tables, his hand shooting out to steady himself once before plunging into the darkness of the doorway through which Malcolm had escaped earlier.

He found himself in a tiny vestibule lit by twin torches to either side of a tall wooden door, and Adrian knew at once it was the door he'd seen at his approach through the woods. He wrenched at the handle and swung the door wide.

Adrian stepped into the darkness outside the castle.

Chapter 12

Adrian stumbled through the archway, and after the heavy wooden door bounced off the interior stone wall, it began to swing closed slowly behind him while he stooped in the dooryard, his hands braced on his knees. His breath tore into and out of him, his chest like a bellows. His satchel hung down from around his neck, swinging like a lazy pendulum with every gasp. The air was thick and cold and sweet, rich with the smell of the sea and damp rocks nestled in soil. After several moments the fragrance had revived him so that he could stand aright and survey his surroundings.

At the level of the castle foundation, he could only see the cusp of the cliff and the fall of the wood rushing over, the gloom belying the hours until sunset. Still the mist prevailed, softening the edges of the tree line even further and deepening the sparkling shadows. But when he turned to face Wyldonna Castle, the light of the fog seemed to be reflected in the stones—no longer glowing blue—and his vision improved so that he could make out the shape and detail of the structure quite well. Adrian went to one knee and retrieved the plans of the castle from his satchel.

He began to walk deosil around the palace, moving off toward the wood from which he'd first emerged with Maisie Lindsey and to the left of the main door that was now closed to him. Adrian didn't care. At the moment the last thing he wanted to think of was the woman who was somewhere within those walls. She confused him, smothered him with her myths, her illusions. The castle was only stones and mortar—things he knew well, things he could touch and study and understand.

The more he studied Maisie Lindsey, the less he knew.

He looked from the plans up along the walls, noting that there were several holes on the western wall of the castle—the opposite side on which his own chamber was located—that did not correspond to the drawing in his hand. A chill raced up his spine, and the sudden fright of it caused him to stop in his tracks.

Unaccounted windows . . .

Adrian shook his head to clear it of the ridiculous sensation that he was forgetting something important. He hadn't been here long enough to forget anything. He looked back to the plans.

Yes—here. He ran his finger along the parallel lines of a long corridor that appeared to extend between the southwest and western tower. Then he looked up at the wall again. Four openings, so small they might be nothing more than symmetrical pockmarks in the mortar, save that they were evenly spaced. Large weep holes? He flipped through the sheaves again, locating the floors above and below the corridor, and then looked back up at the windows. A gallery, perhaps?

No, the marks were too high on the wall to belong to the corridor. The openings should be somewhere within the royal wing of the castle.

Adrian dropped again to one knee and riffled through his bag, seeking the tightly wrapped parcel of his inkpot and quill. It took him several moments to undo the numerous layers of soft waterproof skins around the corked bottle, but then he set the open pot atop one corner of the parchment unrolled on the stiff grass and edged his knee onto the other side while he brought out a blade to refine his quill. He dipped the tip into the dark liquid and began to sketch on the drawing.

On the corridor of the plan, he made markings to indicate the windows, and then above and below the space; his lines superimposed on the drawing, he quickly added the features of the exterior wall between the towers. He gave his additions several moments to dry, checking and rechecking his sketches, before carefully rerolling the parchment and returning it and his tools to his bag.

It was as good a start as any. Now he would be able to compare the exterior and interior of that space, as soon as he found his way to the corridor between the towers. He stood and looked up at the wall again. It was the side of the castle where the queen's chambers lay, and he thought briefly of the set of steps that had brought them to the corridor leading to her room the night before. It had to have been the western tower, although Adrian was sure that was one Maisie had claimed led nowhere. It certainly had led to the corridor of the royal wing, but he couldn't recall that the steps had continued on past the entrance hidden behind the tapestry.

He looked all the way up to the top of the tower. A turret similar to the one he'd just escaped loomed in the mist. Adrian then searched the shadows for the side entrance through which he and Maisie had entered the castle. But the wall where it should be was conspicuously blank.

He frowned, one more of crossness than confusion. He'd have to walk around to the front of the castle now, and he wasn't at all sure how to get back around to the western wing. The vestibule had led only to the east and to the hall.

Adrian turned to his right to begin the trek when a rustling in the underbrush behind him caused him to halt. He looked through the dark stripes of the trees but could see nothing except the continuous fog.

Probably a bird.

He began walking again only to stop almost instantly when the rustling sounded once more, this time more insistent and closer, louder.

That is no bird.

He turned fully toward the wood and for a moment wished he'd thought to grab one of the torches in the vestibule. He peered into the darkness, his eyes straining.

"Who's there?" he called out. He took a step closer to the fringe of wood.

The rustling was now a crunching, interspersed with the snapping of twigs—like the sound of hunting dogs rolling on a scent.

Or a much larger animal boldly shuffling through the underbrush toward him.

Adrian heard a breathy snort, and then the rumblings of a low growl. It grew louder but deeper, like bubbles escaping a victim trapped far below the surface of the water. He began backing slowly away from the wood, his eyes never leaving the dark shadows, but the growls seemed to advance toward him even as the rustling stopped.

And then darkness launched itself from darkness with a scream, and a large, long mass streaked into the castle dooryard toward Adrian. He stumbled and fell to his backside as the shadow landed and stilled—a shadow with two shining yellow eyes—and then he scrambled backward and gathered his feet beneath him once more. He hesitated against turning and running, exposing his back for the kill, but he did take a cautious step away.

The shadow took up its hair-raising growl once more and closed the short distance Adrian had created with one slow, graceful step. Adrian paused.

The shadow halted. It was long and low, like a big cat, but its color was unfathomable in the gloom. Its head was wide and squat and the pointed shadows near the sides of its head gave the indication of ears folded back. A long waving tail swept the grass behind the thing's haunches like a thick rope. Another yawning scream showed gleaming fangs in the mist and the sight of them brought a sick hollow to Adrian's stomach.

They would eat you . . .

Adrian didn't know what manner of beast he faced, but he decided in that moment that it wasn't absolutely necessary for him to know the details to understand that the creature meant to pounce—and soon. He didn't dare glance behind him to gauge the proximity of the castle door. He wished he had some sort of weapon in hand. Even his quill could have been rammed into an eye.

An identical shriek called from the black wood, answering the scream of the beast in the dooryard. Perhaps in the next moment there would be two of them. Adrian instantly conjured the dark image of himself being ripped to shreds between the pair, his body like an old rag amongst hounds.

He thought he was nearly at the southwest corner. If he turned and sprinted as hard as he could, he might make it as far as the door. He knew he didn't have much chance, but it was better than standing there, waiting to be devoured.

The beast must have sensed him tensing to move for it crouched lower, the burbling growl erupting from it like hot lava.

Adrian slid his left foot backward.

The beast slunk toward him with its right paw.

Right foot . . .

Left paw . . .

Placing his weight on the foot behind him, Adrian turned and erupted into a run. The castle door appeared tiny, so far away it might as well have been the gates of London. He had gone perhaps five strides when he heard the soft thuds of pads on the grass, like the earth whispering, and then he was struck on his shoulder blades with what seemed like two hot anvils and pitched forward onto his satchel, the breath going out of him.

The paws slid off to either side of his body and Adrian twisted on the ground, dragging his bag up to guard his face even as the beast swiped at him, its long claws ripping through the soft leather and shredding the contents within. He felt the thing's hot breath as it lunged forward and its jaws clamped down on the satchel. He noted faintly the sound of crunching glass and crinkling paper.

Apparently the beast did not have a taste for the satchel, for it reared up slightly on its haunches, a scream of frustration ripping through Adrian's eardrums. Another swipe of paw completely severed the strap around Adrian's neck, and the tips of sharp claws caught the gusset of his shirt, ripping it open cleanly and exposing the whole of his chest and abdomen to the mist and the castle stones and the beast towering over him that would soon end his life.

But then the creature suddenly twisted and squealed as if stuck with a hot poker, falling backward over its own haunches and fighting awkwardly to get its legs beneath its muscled bulk. It scrabbled away at least two lengths from Adrian's prone body and crouched there hissing, its ropelike tail snaking between its rear legs and curving up to its chest.

Adrian raised up on his elbows and then scrambled to his own feet, the remnants of his satchel falling away and his shirt hanging from him by only its sleeves and one shoulder. The animal crouched lower and hissed again before taking a sidling step away from him.

He looked over his shoulder. There was nothing, no one, behind him. No giant Reid to come to his rescue; the castle door remained closed. His eyes flew back to the animal hugging the ground ten paces from him.

Adrian's mind clicked and whirred. He took a single step toward the beast. It cringed and whined at his movement.

He steeled himself against the logic that was screaming at him to dash to the castle and bolt himself inside. Then he held his arms out from his sides and marched toward the animal with a roar of his own.

The beast gave a sharp yelp and sprang from its crouch, but away from Adrian. It ate up the ground in the dooryard with its long, graceful lopes and dove into the black wood, directly over a pair of identical yellow eyes. In a flash, those eyes vanished too, to the fading sounds of a swift retreat through the underbrush.

Adrian stopped in the sudden stillness of the yard, feeling a blast of power come over him as his heart hammered his hot blood through his veins. The hush of the waves beyond the cliff were echoed in his own breaths, and he felt as if he were expanding, growing. Perhaps it was the elation of escaping death, perhaps it was part of his ego that would have him believe there was something powerful about his person that had frightened the beasts away. Whatever it was, he closed his eyes, felt it fully, reveled in it while the salty cool air of Wyldonna rushed into him.

"You're a bleedin' idiot."

Adrian's eyes snapped open at the sound of the man's voice, and his searching eyes caught a small red glow grow and then dim along the side of a shadowed tree.

"Malcolm?" he asked, squinting toward the gloom.

"Aye, lad." Then the shadow pushed itself away from the tree that it had been leaning against—one leg propped, smoking a long, thin pipe no less—and revealed itself to indeed be the displaced king of Wyldonna. One hand was tucked up in his armpit, the pipe held masterfully intertwined in the fingers of his other hand. "'Tis I."

Adrian's brows lowered. "Were you watching me the whole time?"

"I was," the bearded man continued around puffs from the stem. His next words were accompanied past his lips with white smoke. "I'd marked you for dead, certain as the sea meets the shore. Would have inconvenienced Maisie more than a mite when her champion was eaten in her own dooryard, nae even a full day after coming to her rescue."

"You were just going to stand there while I was mauled by those . . . those . . ." Adrian's words failed him.

"You were warned," Malcolm cut in, but his tone was neither condescending nor smug. In fact, he seemed rather surprised. "There was naught I could have done to save you, be certain. I've nae more power here now than you."

Adrian's eyes narrowed. "The queen says there are more loyal to you than she. That they hid you, are even now helping you plan a war."

"Does she now? The queens says . . ." Malcolm shrugged, and Adrian noticed that the man's eyes were studying Song's marks, now laid bare by the beast's swiping claws. He puffed at his pipe again and then suddenly gestured over his shoulder with the stem as he turned toward the wood. "Come on, then."

Adrian looked over his shoulder at the castle. It could have been deserted for all the movement he saw. "You want me to go with you?"

"You're eager to ken what I'm about, are you nae?" Malcolm paused inside the fringe of trees.

"I am," he answered. "But what about . . . those beasts? Are there more of their kind where we're going?"

"Oh, aye." Malcolm chuckled. "And some even stranger still, to your virgin eyes. But if afternhangers flee you, you have little to fear from the rest of our folk."

Adrian's eyebrows rose. Those beasts had been the afternhangers—the Cat Sith—Maisie had warned him about?

Malcolm looked at Adrian's torso again and waved his pipe stem toward him. "Although there's nae much to it any longer, I'd remove the rest of your blouse, were I you." Then he turned into the wood again and disappeared into the darkness.

Adrian glanced over his shoulder at the castle once more as he slid the remnants of his shirt from his arms and let it fall to the grass near his destroyed satchel. He wouldn't be gone long.

Well, he hoped he wouldn't be gone long, following a man who, only moments before, had been content to witness Adrian's bloody death, and who possibly carried a hunger for revenge against the woman in the castle whom Adrian had come here to help. He was only going into a strange, perpetually dark forest. Full of afternhangers and God knew what else.

He couldn't help but chuckle at this last thought. Wouldn't God be surprised at the strangeness afoot on Wyldonna, if he existed?

Adrian had to trot a bit to catch up to Malcolm's trail.

He wanted to *know* for himself . . .

Maisie ate the midday meal alone, begging off even kind Reid's offer of company. She felt like a fool, an idiot, for trying to reach Adrian Hailsworth. Why not just let him search, let him be, leave him to his own stubborn closed-mindedness?

Because of the way his skin felt beneath your hands, a voice whispered in her mind. *The way he looks at you, talks to you, like you have a mind inside your head and are not simply the king's sister. The way he argues with you, pushes you for answers, like you are not the queen.*

Because he is the Painted Man . . .

She shook her head and looked down at her wooden bowl, where she had done little but push the bits of fish around with her knife tip. He had had enough time to himself now, and Maisie wanted to see what he had found.

She was certainly not seeking him because she longed for the sound of his voice in her ears once more.

She wiped the blade on the small cloth beneath her place and returned it to its sheath before standing from the table and leaving her deserted hall for the west wing. Adrian had likely started there, as far from the eastern tower—and her—as he could think to get.

She roamed the corridors and stairwells for over an hour, only passing one pair of servant girls along the northern walkway. They were a full head shorter than Maisie, although grown women by Wyldonna's measure, and she couldn't help but glance enviously at their delicate, pointed ears and the feminine slant to their eyes as they bobbed their heads to the queen. They belonged. Their tribe was healthy and vibrant and would inhabit Wyldonna for generations to come.

Maisie told herself she was only imagining the whispered twitters that trailed behind them in the corridor, but her face heated all the same.

She began walking faster, her brows drawing closer together with each empty chamber, each deserted corridor. Perhaps they were merely missing each other. She entered the stairs of the southwest tower and began to climb, pushing the door of the turret open and glancing inside.

Empty.

Maisie sighed and was about to close the door and head back down the stairs when she felt the sudden urge to see if anyone was about the grounds. She crossed the small diameter of wooden floor to the window and leaned her elbows upon the sill to raise up on her toes and peer out of the glassless opening.

There they all were, far below her—the people who were once her friends. Going about their business without so much as a thought for Maisie, unless it was a wish of misfortune. The baser creatures, especially. Naught would please them more than to see her destroyed, because she had betrayed the mighty, saintly Malcolm.

Maisie snorted. Aye, the man who would have them all fight to the death to preserve a wooden farthing he'd nowhere to spend.

Her eyes roamed away from the cluster of the woodland village to the treetops, and then she leaned farther up on her toes to survey the grounds around the castle proper. Her eyes caught on something light-colored and she frowned, squinting at it. As she looked, she thought she could make out darker objects strewn alongside the white thing.

Her heart skipped half a beat, but then she shook her head in denial. No, it couldn't have been Adrian. She had expressly forbidden him from leaving the castle without her or Reid, and Reid would have asked permission before going off with the Painted Man. Maisie had explained to Adrian about some of the folk of the isle, and how dangerous they were to him.

And he hadn't believed a word she'd said.

Maisie swept from the tower room and down the twisting stairs, running past the elfin girls again so quickly that they were forced to press themselves against the walls to prevent being run over. At last she came to the vestibule and wrenched open the door, running out into the yard and toward the crumpled pile on the grass.

Her skirts swung around her legs as she came to a stop. Maisie dropped to her knees and picked up the rent pieces of cloth, holding them before her. It was Adrian's shirt.

She looked around her and saw his satchel and its contents in pieces on the ground, including scraps of parchment on which slivers of drawings made in her own hand could be seen.

"Great gods," she breathed, running her fingertips along the shredded cloth. In that instant she could smell the beasts, feel Adrian's fear, hear their gurgling growls. "Afternhangers."

She bent and scooped up what remained of Adrian Hailsworth's presence in the yard and then stood with her arms laden. She turned in a circle, searching for him, feeling for him, and then faced the wood once more, her knees beginning to tremble.

She took a hesitant step forward, feeling the trees watching her. She swallowed the catch in her throat.

"Adrian!" she called out to the wood, which grew darker with each passing moment.

Hysteria tried to climb her spine, wrap its skeletal arms around her neck. She shook it off, juggled the items in her arms to swipe at her eyes. Then she stepped closer to the edge of the wood.

"Adrian!"

His name echoed on and on. The only answer to her calls was the sighing of the sea far below. Her eyes scanned the darkened ground around her and Maisie could discern the wide, rumpled path of crushed grass. Something—or things—had passed back and forth over the yard between the wood and the pile of Adrian's ruined things.

Had something also been dragged? A man's thrashing body, perhaps?

She had two choices: She could return to the castle and wait, see if he somehow returned. If he didn't? He was dead. Maisie told herself that was the most likely result any matter. But then what would she do?

She tried to see into the dark shadows as she contemplated her other option. She could search for him—for his body at least. If he wasn't already dead, perhaps there was still something she could do to save him. But what if she was caught up by the same creatures who had taken Adrian? Trapped in the dark wood, there would be none to hear her screams. And even if her cries for help were heard, Maisie wondered whether they would be answered by the folk dwelling beyond the trees. She could die at the teeth and claws of those she was already risking her life to protect.

But if Adrian Hailsworth was dead, her life was forfeit any matter.

She thought briefly of returning to the castle to locate Reid. He would be a measure of protection for her, but at what cost with the time if might take to find him? She knew the stunted giant would answer her plea without hesitation, but by then it could be too late, and the consequences for Reid might be dire.

She had brought Adrian Hailsworth to Wyldonna, and so she alone was responsible for his safety.

Maisie let the bundle of linen and leather and parchment fall away as she walked into the wood.

Chapter 13

The smoke from Malcolm Lindsey's pipe was like a white, spicy beacon in the shimmery darkness of the steep woodland path, and Adrian followed its wafting trail as it curled into his nostrils and seemed to pull him along. His bare skin prickled in the damp, but the effect was already fading, and Adrian gave a moment's notice to the fact that he really didn't feel cold at all, despite half of his body being exposed to the chill air of a northern island in late winter.

In fact, he realized, he hadn't been cold since his arrival on the island; he'd left his cloak in his borrowed chamber and it had never occurred to him that he would need it. His vision jarred and bumped as he tromped down the path behind Malcolm, and Adrian opened his mouth to send forth a short *ha* of breath.

Steam billowed before his face.

So, yes, it *was* cold here. Only *he* wasn't cold. Actually, he felt quite comfortable. Perhaps it was the side of the island he was currently traversing—a blocking of the wind? A sheltering of the deep valley?

He had no more time to consider the possible reasons why he was suddenly immune to such a winter clime, for it was then that Adrian followed Malcolm from the wood, emerging on the narrow dirt track between the idyllic cottages Adrian had seen from the turret window earlier in the day.

Up close, they were even more charming than he'd guessed—tidy little stone homes with deep, rounded overhangs to protect the foundations from the dripping damp mist that seemed to permeate everything here. Solid wooden doors, rich with oil, matched sturdy shutters flanking the little windows, and the dooryards of the cottages were stamped flat, swept clean between the mossy round stones seemingly placed there more for aesthetics than to actually mark boundaries between the plots.

Some of the doors stood open, and as he passed, Adrian could see the cozy glow of peat fires reflecting off the daubed walls in the tidy interiors, shadowed inhabitants going about their domestic tasks just the same as anyone would expect. In one yard, a small boy was perched on a stool with a blanket draped about his shoulders, a woman in long skirts going round him with a blade, plucking at his curling blond hair with one hand and trimming with the knife in her other. It seemed a typical scene to Adrian, and the sight of these people afforded him a measure of comfort until he drew nearer to them.

The woman glanced up at their approach and nodded with a preoccupied smile but then glanced back at Adrian, her eyes wide. The boy's mouth fell open into an *O* as he stared at Adrian's bare skin, and it was then that Adrian noticed the boy's pointed ear beneath the fringe of recently trimmed hair, the almond shape of his and his mother's eyes. The woman turned, staring blatantly at him as he passed, while the boy began to chatter excitedly in a language Adrian did not understand.

Adrian nodded to the woman.

After he and Malcolm had passed, Adrian glanced back over his shoulder in time to see the woman hurrying to the cottage next door, her son close at her heels in his flapping makeshift cape.

Soon the sound of doors scraping open filled the narrow track between the cottages, and Adrian heard the tromp of footfalls behind him. He turned again to witness the humble street filling with people who emerged from the homes and animal sheds, from around corners and between structures, some still carrying the tools of the day's chores—long pitchforks, axes, mallets.

They were following them, and talking quietly to one another in the strange tongue. Adrian had a moment of worry; was Malcolm leading him into an ambush?

Adrian looked ahead again to see Malcolm's profile turned toward him, the crinkles at the corners of his eyes over his beard betraying his smile. The man gestured with his pipe.

"You've nae need to fear," he said, as if reading Adrian's mind. "They're as curious of you as you are of them, I'd wager. The tale of the Painted Man is an old one, and all have heard its telling since they were bairns. They've waited a long time for you, lad."

Adrian frowned, readying to ask Malcolm to clarify his comment. Surely he didn't mean to equate the marks on Adrian's skin with some fairy-tale story told to children. He was only a man desperate to escape a hellish past by covering his scars with a pagan art form. If anything, it was pathetic. He would not allow Malcolm to portray him as something he was not in order to perpetuate a bit of island lore.

But the thought was whisked from his mind as his eyes caught sight of a man coming to stand at the edge of the track, leaning one elbow atop the handle of his long pitchfork, hooking his other fingers over the sharp curve of a jutting hip. Adrian looked down the man's heavy breeches to where their frayed hems ended at his hairy, slender midcalf—

Above a pair of hooves.

Before the idea of what he was seeing could fully penetrate his brain, the road ahead was widening between two rounded hills into a common area overlooking the sea, and the dusky dirt track was being painted with low, slinking shadows of huge catlike creatures. A bale fire in the center of the common lit up the lithe range of their sliding shoulders as the creatures crisscrossed the path ahead, their low growls burbling over the sounds of the sea beyond. They watched Adrian boldly.

Afternhangers. At least a score of them.

"Malcolm?" Adrian asked.

"All's well," Malcolm said cheerily and forged ahead toward the feline beasts, each bigger than a man.

The afternhangers scattered as Adrian and Malcolm drew near, many of them giving graceful leaps onto the hillsides sheltering the common, some padding and bounding away to the farside of the bale fire, around which large flat stones and halved logs were arranged in concentric circles. The fire flickered up the wide chimney created by the hills, and Adrian could at last see clearly the nature of the beast who had attacked him.

Their fur was silky-looking, gleaming like polished chestnuts in the firelight. Every feature on the big cats' faces was the same rich auburn color—their flat, soft-looking noses, even the long whiskers that jutted from rounded muzzles—save for the yellow eyes and the insides of their pointed ears, which were a satiny, disturbing black.

One of the beasts had the audacity to give a quiet shriek at him, and Adrian saw that the inside of the afternhanger's mouth—tongue, gums—was also the deep color of ebony around gleaming yellow teeth.

The fleeting image of hell contained inside a satiny skin occurred to Adrian, and although he wanted to look away from the afternhanger, he met its glittering eyes. The animal shrieked again and averted its gaze, getting up to circle its perch as if suddenly uncomfortable.

Ahead of Adrian, Malcolm chuckled.

He followed the erstwhile king of Wyldonna to the far side of the common, where Malcolm stopped beside a low carved seat that appeared to have been fashioned from a stump. The bearded man's back was to the sea far below, and Adrian took a moment to look out over the water, which was only a lighter shade of dusk beyond the fire's glow. His brow furrowed as he thought he saw bobbing yellow lights beneath the waves, glowing and shimmering between the still shadows of the crawlers.

What were they?

Sirens . . .

Adrian shook his head and turned back around to see the common now crowded with the folk who had followed him, their numbers growing as shadows emerged from hidden tracks stretching along the hillsides, pushing handcarts or dragging skids, which they left at the edge of the meeting space. Adrian saw long white beards, the outlines of pointed caps. He heard the ruffling and flapping of wings as what appeared to be massive white birds with long spindly legs and draping translucent feathers dropped from the gloom to light on the boulders above the pacing afternhangers.

There was a quiet murmuring in the air, hovering over the balefire, and all the wildly differing pairs of eyes—yellow and slanted and round and black—were trained on Adrian's torso.

He felt another wash of gooseflesh erupt on his skin, but it was not due to the chill in the air.

The folk eased down onto the benches and stones in pairs and clusters until all the seats were filled and the area fringing the common was staggered with the shadows of those left to stand. The murmuring died away to leave the perfect whispers of the waves on the beach and the wind in the trees. The air was crackly, charged, expectant.

"*Les geants?*" Malcolm asked into the crowd.

"Still within the mountain, sire," the man with the beastly cloven feet answered with extreme deference and a nod of his head, which Adrian now noticed was rather long at the upper jaw.

Malcolm grunted. "They shall hear well enough, then." He stepped away from Adrian toward the balefire and put his back to it, joining the crowd of strange folk to regard Adrian openly. To say that Adrian felt on display would be too mild.

"Wyldonna," Malcolm said solemnly but firmly, his eyes meeting Adrian's. "Your queen has delivered to us the Painted Man."

A gasp swept through the crowd, and a moment later, those gathered there lowered into a bow behind Malcolm.

Adrian frowned as the people—he didn't know what else to refer to them as—rose from their subjective postures. He didn't know what to make of what he was seeing, but he would not allow Malcolm Lindsey to perpetuate a myth to further his own agenda against his sister. There could be no other reason for this gathering, no other reason for the man to bring him before the people of Wyldonna.

It was a blatant attempt to wrench power back to himself.

"No," Adrian called out, scanning the crowd, his eyes glancing over and largely ignoring Malcolm. "I am not part of your legend, whatever it may be. I am an Englishman; my name is Adrian Hailsworth. I did indeed come to your island at Queen Maighread's request, but it is only to assist you in your fight against the one who threatens your peace. My presence cannot be attributed to any tale you've been told."

Malcolm chuckled, and Adrian had no choice but to regard the bearded man again. "That *is* the tale, lad. And it is one older than you, older than me, older than—" he held out his arms and half-turned in either direction—"everything here. That you doona believe it doesna mean it isna true. You have come at the point of Wyldonna's history when everything here is in danger of being destroyed. You are marked with the magic signs. You are the Painted Man."

"What do you mean?" Adrian demanded. "I was not born with these marks."

Malcolm Lindsey only nodded, as the crowd behind him whispered excitedly among themselves. "No one is born with marks like that, lad. You were chosen because you proved yourself worthy. You earned your magic."

"Proved myself worthy to whom?" Adrian demanded with a snort.

The bearded man spread his arms wide and looked up and around him—at the woods, the horizon, the sky shrouded with mist—before he let his hands drop and met Adrian's gaze again. "By all that is."

"That's what you call God, I suppose." He shook his head in frustration when Malcolm's easy smile only deepened. Then Adrian held up a palm. "I've not *earned* any magic. I'm *not* magic."

The little boy who had been having his trim—and who now sported a coif that was decidedly lopsided—grinned at Adrian good-naturedly, the glow of the fire flickering over his gap-toothed gesture of goodwill. It was almost as if Adrian had told him a marvelous joke, and although the lad didn't truly believe it, he appreciated the humor all the same.

"Everyone's magic, Man."

"No. They're not," Adrian said, causing the boy's grin to falter. A quiet gasp swept through the crowd. Adrian looked around to find Malcolm again. "Was there something you wished to show me, or was this all only a ploy to parade me before the people so that whatever actions you plan to take against your sister would seem justified by some ancient nonsense?"

"I've something to show you," Malcolm said easily. "Our folk have been working hard to construct a machine of war to defend us against our enemy when he returns." He gestured to Adrian's right, along the craggy cliff where Adrian could just make out the dark oval entrances of the sea caves. "In the mountain."

Adrian was intrigued despite himself. "A machine of war? How would you come by knowledge of such a thing? I would think you would attend to any trespassers by casting a spell on him or setting your wild beasts on his men." Adrian couldn't help but glance at the afternhangers, who had draped themselves over the rocks.

"Although we are removed from the world," Malcolm said, "we are nae ignorant of it. Many of our folk have journeyed abroad; some have gone as far as to enjoin with man in pursuit of livelihood." He paused. "And as to why we canna simply dispatch Felsteppe upon his arrival—why we must resort to such crude and mundane methods—surely Maisie told you that he will come on the equinox."

"She did," Adrian allowed.

"It is only one of four days of the year when we can neither prevent Wyldonna from being landed nor can we keep anyone who wishes to go."

"You can't use magic against him," Adrian reiterated.

"Not until he has proven himself a threat."

Adrian's eyebrows rose. "I'd say returning to the island with ships full of armed men constitutes a threat."

"Nae if his ships and men do naught but sit in the harbor," Malcolm argued.

"But then how many of those men will know how and when exactly to return to Wyldonna on their own?"

Malcolm smiled. "Which is why I was keen to show you what we've built."

"Adrian!"

The echo of his name seemed to vibrate the ground beneath his feet as it swirled out of the wood and whooshed down the dirt track between the cottages to wash over Adrian, and he felt a surge of energy in his bones. He lifted his chin, his eyes scanning the black beyond the village as if he could somehow see her in the darkness.

Maighread Lindsey was calling for him. And he could . . . *feel* her.

Malcolm's head cocked and he winked at Adrian. "Perhaps another time, though."

"I'm here," Adrian argued, dragging his attention back to the king and trying to ignore the vibration in his core that brought vivid red curls and the scent of heather to the forefront of his senses. "Show me now."

He held up his palms. "The queen calls. It was she who summoned you to Wyldonna, so it is she you must obey."

"She's not my queen," Adrian bristled. "I shall wait for her to join us so we might both know your plans in full. Surely if you wish to reveal to a stranger the secrets of your offense, you have considered putting to rest this feud with your sister—one who shares the goal of saving your people from this threat."

Malcolm shook his head. "Maisie doesna think me capable of saving Wyldonna. She isna interested in my plans, else she never would have betrayed us to Felsteppe and taken the throne for herself."

"I'm not certain that's true," Adrian hedged. He had no interest really in helping two stubborn siblings remedy their quarrel; he only wanted to bring the truth to light. It was all Adrian ever wanted to do.

"I am," Malcolm said solemnly.

Before Adrian could comment further, the crowd gathered around the fire rose from their seats and turned en masse back toward the cottages.

"Come on, then," Malcolm said with something akin to resignation, repeating the phrase he'd used to draw Adrian into the wood an hour earlier. And once again Adrian felt he had little choice but to follow the bearded man around the balefire.

She was striding down the narrow track when he at last saw the physical manifestation of the summons he still felt thrumming through him, her red curls bouncing behind her, her pale skin gleaming in the mist. Maisie's arms swung freely at her sides, her cape billowing in her wake, and her green eyes seemed to pierce the gloom as her gaze landed on Adrian.

She stopped perhaps forty feet from the common; as close as she was prepared to come, apparently. The folk to either side of Malcolm Lindsey and Adrian bowed or curtsied deeply, and then, in the next moment, the spaces between the villagers were filled with the tools of their workday, pointed at their queen. Axes and forks and blades all mingled with the mist as a sort of grim expectation descended upon the crowd.

"Come nae farther, Maighread Lindsey," her brother warned.

"What the bloody hell are you doing?" Adrian demanded, looking around him at the folk who now wore shared expressions of angry distrust. "This is your queen."

Maisie ignored them all. "I've come for what is mine."

"You thought him dead, did you nae?" Malcolm said, in a tone that was not quite taunting, not quite curious. "You doona truly believe in your own miracle."

Adrian bristled at the way he was being spoken about, as if he were nothing more than an object to be quarreled over, although Maisie Lindsey's words caused a resurgence in the zinging vibrations in his bones. Did he belong to her now? By some insane logic, the idea did not sound so impossible.

And if it was true, that he belonged to her, did she not then belong to him?

What was this madness that had seized him?

"You ken as well as I the dangers Wyldonna poses to Outlanders," Maisie accused. "That you would bring him into the midst of the folk shows your disregard for his safety." She looked at the crowd. "The safety of you all." Her eyes landed on Adrian. "He set the afternhangers on you."

"The afternhangers do what they will," Malcolm argued. "And I couldna have set anyone upon anyone had the Painted Man nae made himself vulnerable. As it was, he brought them to heel in his own manner. You've nae reason to fear for him here. He is free to go where he would."

As if the beasts were resentful at being reminded of their defeat in the castle yard, they gained their feet and were now crowded together at the cusps of the hills they occupied, staring down hungrily at the red-haired woman on the road below them.

"You doona command him, Malcolm," Maisie said, but her eyes flicked to the beasts above her.

Adrian had had enough. "And neither do you," he said, stepping into the space between the queen and the crowd. The feline creatures shrank back from the edges of the hills with angry hisses. "Your brother has offered to show me his plans for turning Felsteppe and his men away. I think you should listen to him."

Maisie looked at Adrian as if he too had sprouted cloven feet. And then her brows lowered in Malcolm's direction. "I'm certain he was keen to win you to his side. We will talk about it later. Come with me now, Adrian. Please."

"I appreciate your concern for my safety," he began, but then stopped when he realized Maisie was no longer looking at him.

The afternhangers had apparently dismissed Adrian, and they were now crouching over the road again, their long tails swishing through the air. Maisie's face was going from one group to the other, speaking to them in a language that sounded strongly Gaelic.

To his surprise, the creature closest to the queen peeled its lips back from its black gums and shrieked before replying in the same tongue, its voice sounding dark and scratchy but remarkably human. Adrian felt his legs go rubbery.

Malcolm leaned toward him so that their shoulders touched. "I believe 'tis *you* who should be concerned for *her* safety, lad."

Then Maisie took a sudden step back on the road, her eyes going from cliff to cliff, her already pale face seemingly devoid of all blood now. One by one, the afternhangers leapt from the rocks to land silently on the dirt road, separating Adrian from Maisie. The bold one in the lead—had it been the very creature that attacked Adrian?—spoke again, and the pack of beasts began to growl as if in anticipation.

He had frightened away the monster earlier. But could he deny a score of the hellish things? Why weren't Maisie's own brother or the other folk doing anything to prevent the impending attack on Wyldonna's queen?

Whatever the reason, Adrian had no doubt that the vicious beasts would strike the defenseless woman and possibly kill her before him and the crowd. Someone had to do something.

Wasn't that the reason she had brought him to Wyldonna in the first place? To do something?

"Stop!" he called out, raising a hand and striding toward the rear of the pack. Behind him, he heard the crowd gasp again. "Leave her."

The afternhangers paid him no heed though, and so as he reached the slinking monsters nearest to him, he swung his raised hand and landed a slap to a sleek rump. The blow met the animal's flesh with a crack, and to Adrian's astonishment, the afternhanger tumbled over into its neighbor like a stone rolled down a hill, sending three of the beasts kicking and sprawling in a heap. Adrian's palm felt as though it had just seized a hot coal.

The rest of the pack swung on him with furious shrieks, and all the hair on Adrian's body tried to stand up. But they were slinking back from him to either side of the road, even as the bold one spoke to Adrian.

"You presume to touch us?" Its black tongue flicked the English words easily, and its whiskered cheek pads flinched away from its fangs as it added contemptuously, *"Man?"*

"I have no quarrel with you as of yet, save for the loss of my belongings," Adrian said, coming to stand between Maisie and the apparent leader of the Cat Sith. "But if you harm her, you will answer to me."

The beast hissed, like a breath of laughter. "The only thing Man is good for is killing. Stand against us again, Man, and you will learn."

"I stand before you now," Adrian taunted, his blood heating where once alarm had chilled him. He stepped toward the beast, even as he felt Maisie Lindsey's fingers trail down the skin of his back, as if trying to stay him. "She brought me here and I will not allow you to harm her."

The afternhanger continued to slink away as its brethren leapt back onto the rocks of the hillside.

"You'll not be protected forever, Man," the beast warned with a snarl.

Adrian let the threat hang in the air unchallenged as the creature turned and crept into the shadow of the rocks. And then he looked to the crowd who were watching him with something akin to bewildered horror. All except Malcolm Lindsey, who kept his enigmatic smile.

"You will not share your plan with me now?" Adrian asked.

The bearded man shook his head. "We yet have time," he said. "I'd wager you'll seek me out when you see that you must. I'll be here when you're ready."

The answer sounded enough like the afternhangers' threat to anger Adrian, and so he turned without answer and began striding back up the road between the cottages, seizing Maisie Lindsey's hand as he passed and pulling her along with him.

He paid no heed to the cumulative gasp of the crowd behind him.

Chapter 14

Maisie let Adrian Hailsworth lead her up the dirt track until they reached the fringe of wood beyond the last cottage, her heart in her throat. Several trail heads led into the forest here and Adrian slowed.

Maisie pulled her hand from his grasp as she passed him, feeling as though the chill in the air had increased twofold at the loss of his touch. Another moment of his skin on hers and Maisie feared she would have turned fully into his arms, begging him to hold her and kiss her and tell her she would be safe.

"It's this way," she said instead, hitching up the front of her skirts with both hands and mounting the steep trail without needing to mind her step.

How many thousands of times had her feet traversed this path since she'd learned to walk, scampering to and from the village to play with her friends and visit the folk, participating in woodland games or digging in the coarse sand of the beach below? Those journeys had been filled with smiles and happy shrieks and breathless laughter.

Now she climbed toward the castle with tears of humiliation and hurt in her eyes. She had no friends on Wyldonna anymore, save the unfathomable, shirtless Englishman who traversed the path with her.

By the time she emerged from the wood onto the castle yard, Adrian Hailsworth close at her heels, Maisie's eyes were dry. She was thankful for that as she saw the hulking black outline of Reid against the torch glow from the open door behind him. He appeared to be holding Adrian's ruined belongings in his huge hands, and they hung between his fingers like scraps.

Seeing the shredded shirt and leather bag reminded her that Adrian

Hailsworth could have died that evening. By all rights, he should be dead at that very moment. But not only was he marching behind her, shirtless, his black marks camouflaging him in the night, he had shown himself superior to the most deadly inhabitants of Wyldonna—the afternhangers. He had more likely than not saved her from their claws. Her own brother had not even raised a finger to defend her.

Adrian had made a grave enemy tonight in having the audacity to strike one of the creatures. Maisie's stomach tumbled at the idea that he had made such a risk for her alone.

"My queen," Reid greeted her as she neared, his deep solemn voice betraying his concern. "Is aught amiss? When I found you not within—"

"I'm sorry to have worried you," she said as she swept past him. "My brother thought it a good time to introduce Lord Hailsworth to the folk." She headed for the castle door without slowing, wishing to lock herself away from the night, the wood, the ones below who now shunned her.

The only place she was safe, and could keep Adrian Hailsworth to herself.

"My thanks, Reid," Adrian said behind her, and she heard both pairs of feet follow her into the vestibule before the door shut firmly.

Maisie breathed a silent sigh of relief as she came into the hall, even though that long chamber was populated by the puny crowd of servants reluctantly charged to care for her. They were clustered together and looking at her with wide eyes as she entered, Reid and Adrian following in her wake. She ignored them all, heading for the doorway that led to the central corridor.

Malcolm had tried to win Adrian to his side. To turn him against her? Well, fair was fair. And she'd never been very good at keeping cautious any matter.

"Maighread," Adrian called out behind her.

Maisie stopped and spun around in the center of the aisle, her cape swirling around her feet.

For a moment, he only looked at her, as if he had forgotten what he was going to say. Maisie took that heartbeat of time to appraise him as well, his muscled, slender waist covered with the bold black marks of his magic. He seemed larger now, his body half-bared to her, than when she'd first seen him in the courtyard of Melk in his monk's robes. His jaw was nearly covered with stubble that was rapidly becoming a beard, his hair curled at his collarbone. He looked as if he could have been born on the island.

Maisie felt her stomach clench with desire. The same desire she recognized in Adrian Hailsworth's dark eyes.

His saving her had not been a simple act of chivalry—he felt the want of her, too.

"I have questions," Adrian began again, and she could see him attempting to gain control of himself. "About what just transpired below."

"And I mean to give you answers," she replied, not caring if he saw her recklessness. "If you will follow me."

One of the elfin girls stepped hesitantly from the knot of her friends. She gave a slight curtsy in Adrian's direction.

"Perhaps Man first desires a drink?" she asked sweetly.

One of the other girls joined her. "Or a bit to eat?"

By the way they fluttered their long eyelashes, one would think them to be afflicted. But Maisie was oddly glad to see that she was not the only one affected by Adrian Hailsworth's presence, even if it meant her own maids were trying to steal the Painted Man away from her.

Adrian was changing. Wyldonna was changing him.

Reid sent the servant girls a glare that had them scattering back into the clutch of maids. "I will serve Man should he have need. Be gone from here and back to your duties before the queen dismisses the lot of you."

Adrian had barely glanced at the girls; his attention was for Maisie alone, and it thrilled her. "Where are we going?"

"The library," she said.

"Library?" He blinked, then cocked his head. "You have a library? That wasn't on the plans."

Maisie couldn't help the ghost of a smile that pulled at her mouth as she turned. She could feel his heightened excitement rolling off him like a wave. "This way," she said, then swept from the hall, slightly giddy at the sound of Adrian's footfalls gaining on her.

Adrian could hardly contain his anticipation as he followed Maisie's slender form down the dim corridor. Her curls streamed behind her in the wake of her swift passing, and Adrian's nostrils were filled with the scent of her, so strong and vivid it was almost as if he could taste her fragrance. He could not explain the feeling that had come over him since his encounter with the afternhangers and the villagers in the common, but he felt . . . amazing. Whole and powerful and full of life.

And it had taken the greater portion of his will not to seize the queen of Wyldonna and kiss her in her own hall when her eyes had fallen upon his bare skin like a touch. He'd not felt such strong desire for a woman since before arriving at Jacob's Ford more than three years ago, and now he wanted Maisie Lindsey.

Which was completely foolish and unreasonable. So he busied himself with the idea that his eagerness was not for the woman who led him down the corridor but for the location alone to which she was leading him.

She stopped at an ornately carved door, and Adrian's heart skipped as her cape slid behind her, revealing the fit of her bodice over high breasts and flat stomach. But he told himself he was only anxious for what lay behind the door. Volumes and volumes, he told himself. Everything he needed to know. And then he could push the lustful thoughts of her from his mind.

She glanced at him. "Are you certain you want this?"

I've come for what is mine.

Adrian's blood boiled. "It's the only thing I can think about."

Her breasts lifted and fell with her sigh. Then she pushed the door open, and he followed her in, actually daring to lay his fingertips along the side of her waist as if to hurry her along. But his hand wanted to slip around her midriff, pull her to him in the privacy of the black chamber . . .

He stepped away into the space properly and felt his eyebrows raise as he scanned the dark corners.

He heard her moving about behind him, and a moment later a yellow glow spilled around his boots as she lit a candle, but it did little to improve his view. Then she was at his side once more.

"I thought you said we were going to the library."

"Aye," she replied, raising the candle and gesturing about her. "This is the library."

Adrian's eyes took in the windowless stone walls, devoid of shelves, the small square table and single wooden chair—both covered in what appeared to be a hundred years' worth of dust. In the center of the tabletop rested an odd raised platform, similar to the ones used by the brethren at Melk when copying manuscripts. He had to admit to himself, he'd fantasized at the possibility of taking Maisie Lindsey in the castle library. But—

"Where are the books?"

"Books?" she repeated with a frown. "There are nae books on Wyldonna. There is *book*."

"Book," he said flatly.

"Yes, book. One." She walked to the table and set down her candle before swiping her palm across the raised square, sending a fall of dust onto the floor. It was then that Adrian could make out the leather cover, it's embossing filled with packed gray years. "This one."

He gained her side then and set the remains of his belongings in the seat of the chair before leaning over the only object in the room besides the candle and wooden furnishings. He slid the flame closer so that he could make out the marks on the cover, but there were no words—only swirls of age-softened black.

"What's in it?" he asked, his fingertips skimming the designs, his eyes seeking to form a logical pattern from the marks.

"Everything," Maisie said simply and quietly.

He turned his head to look at her. Her eyes were raking over his skin, and he could feel the twist of his guts with the intimacy wrapped around them. In that instant, the library—if one were so generous as to refer to the chamber as such—ceased to matter.

"Everything?" he prompted, more sharply than he'd intended, but he needed to distract himself from his desire for her.

"Wyldonna's history. Stories. The lineage of the crown." Then, to his amazement, she actually stepped closer to him, placing her hand on the curve of his shoulder to urge him to stand upright.

He did so, turning toward her, and she reached out her hands, her fingers skimming the marks on his chest and stomach, his forearms, much in the same manner as he had been stroking the now forgotten tome on the table. It was as if she was coming to him in a dream once more, touching him as he'd wished she would.

"Maisie," he said in a low voice, wanting to warn her.

"I canna help it," she said, and indeed her voice sounded mystified. "I've wanted to look at you, to touch you, since first seeing your marks on the crawler. Doona deny me, Adrian. I'm the queen, after all. I must see. You must let me. It's the magic."

He reached up and grasped both her wrists in his hands and then jerked her to him. If he wasn't very careful now, he would lose control. "It's not magic. And you mustn't be so bold. I have been without a woman for a long time. Where is your fear of me now, in this room with no one to protect you?"

"I still fear you," she confessed, and then her tongue wet her lips as she looked up at him. "But nae for the reasons you hope. You are the only one who will protect me."

"Shall I kiss you, then?" he challenged. "Will that give you reason to fear me?"

She shook her head and turned her face up, daring him. "In truth, it's the only thing that shall make me feel safe."

Adrian felt his brows draw together even as his left hand released her wrist to pull her against him fully. "That isn't logical, Maisie. For should I dare, I shan't stop with only a kiss."

"I know," she breathed and let her hand slide over his ribs to his spine. "It's meant to be, though, Adrian. Let it."

He tasted her bottom lip and sensation exploded behind his eyes. "We are meant to make love?" he pressed, feeling his control slipping away like silk through a keyhole. "You can't believe that."

Maisie nodded. "Your marks," she said, and then pressed her lips to each side of his mouth before whispering against his lips, "Match the book."

A hint of alarm went through his body then, even as Maisie kissed him fully and his will to deny her disappeared. He grasped her tiny waist and returned her attention even as his mind rioted.

It was impossible.

He wanted her so badly.

The island was rotting his brain.

She wanted him just as badly.

Maisie pulled away from him only far enough to speak again. "Come with me to my room."

He shook his head. "I suspect you've a dragon in your room. And mine is closer." Then he kissed her again.

When he pulled away from her next, it was to bend and sweep her legs over his arm. He strode to the door and turned so that she could reach behind her and open it, and then he was carrying her through the corridor as she ran her hands through this hair, pressing her mouth to his jaw.

Adrian's vison had blurred at the edges, and only a small circle of the way before him was clear. He didn't know how he navigated the castle, but he made the turns instinctively, bounding up stairs with Maisie in his arms as if she weighed no more than a feather. He felt stronger then than he ever had the whole of his life, as if he could carry her to the ends of the earth if that was where their bed lay.

But in only moments they were in his borrowed chamber. He kicked the door closed behind him and then crossed to his bed, where he lay her down on the mattress and followed. She was already reaching for him as he bent his face to her décolleté, his lips running over her perfect skin, breathing deeply of her scent, his nostrils flaring like a wild beast.

No sooner had the likeness occurred to him than he was tearing at her beautiful gown, snapping the closure of her cape with both hands rather than attend to the delicate frog. And Maisie did not protest.

For a brief moment, he wondered whether he had gone mad. Or if some strange magic had indeed taken hold of him, rendering him incapable of coherent thought. The woman beneath him was not some cheap fancy to use for his ease; he would not leave her in the morn with a coin and a friendly farewell. She was a queen, and they would be in each other's proximity until the business Adrian had been summoned to attend to was finished. But that thought only increased his desire as it occurred to him that he could have her again on the morrow, and the day after, and the next. . . .

She pulled his head down so that their mouths met, and Adrian continued to pull at her clothes while they kissed, his hands pressing the flesh he found, smooth and warm and soft. He'd not felt such base urgency in years—perhaps he'd never felt it to such an extreme. All he knew was that he must possess this woman soon—now.

He didn't bother to remove the little clothing he was still wearing, or his boots. Rather, he removed his hand from her while their mouths were still joined and loosened the laces of his chausses as she made little anxious sounds in the back of her throat, urging him on. In an instant he had freed himself and then jerked her leg higher, climbing over her. He entered her with little caution, pulling away from her mouth and giving a shout at her readiness, even as he pushed at the resistance he felt.

He was her first.

And so he stroked her face, kissed her temple tenderly, but still she did not protest or refuse him. Instead, she urged him in his race, her fingernails raking the skin over his buttocks, but he doubted he could have stopped had the room been afire. Her scent, the scent of their joining, enveloped him, set off shuddering white light behind his eyes, which only grew brighter and brighter until it was also a roar of noise in his ears like an ever-falling wave. He was drowning in her body, in the feel of her around him, and in that moment, he would have forsaken anything he had ever held dear for what he was experiencing.

He could feel his time rushing over him, his pace increasing, and still Maisie encouraged him, her delicate fingers running up his stomach and over his chest, locking together around his neck and pulling herself up against him. He looked down at her and saw that her eyes were open, watching him brazenly, her lips parted as her head rocked on the coverlet.

"Adrian," she whispered.

It pushed him over the edge and he hung there suspended, joined with Maisie Lindsey in a space that was neither of the earth or the heavens but somehow existed apart from even time. The roar in his brain faded like rain moving away over the land, to be replaced with his loud, pounding heartbeat and another similar thrum but smaller, like a bird's wings.

He realized it was her heart, and he could hear it—feel it—in his own veins.

It startled him so that he slid from her and backed off the bed, swaying on his feet and panting as he looked at her, so bedraggled and nude before him. It was only his own heartbeat that jarred his vision now, but he was not soothed. She was watching him solemnly, and in that moment, Adrian Hailsworth was unable to access his logic, his reason. He could not explain what had just happened between him and Maisie; he could not explain what he felt even now, looking at the queen whose virginity he'd taken so swiftly and callously.

But he knew he wanted her again already. And if he continued to stand at her bedside, it would perhaps only be a moment before he was atop her once more.

Adrian began retying his chausses.

She didn't say anything, and neither did Adrian as he turned and left the chamber, closing the door behind him.

Chapter 15

The candle had not even spent itself a quarter of the way when Adrian returned to Wyldonna's pathetic library. He shut himself inside and moved to the chair to slide his arms into the sleeves of his destroyed shirt. It couldn't cover his chest, but it gave him some measure of warmth against the chill that had overcome him since leaving Maisie Lindsey's warm body.

He wondered suddenly—absurdly—if, in the moment he donned his shirt, she had pulled his coverlet over her body, feeling the chill as he had.

He sought to push the image of her lying on his bed, ready for him to take her again, from his mind. He couldn't process what had happened between them now; his thoughts were a jumble. The only thing he knew to do when in that state was to order his ideas with fact.

Adrian piled the scraps of his satchel and belongings on a far corner of the table before pulling the thick, dusty tome toward him and sitting on the chair. He adjusted the candle's position and ran his left palm over the leather cover of the book, studying the designs for a moment, reading them with his fingertips. And then he looked down at his abdomen.

Maisie was right—the patterns were remarkably similar. He held out his arms, sliding what was left of the sleeves to his elbows; there, too, the lines and swirls matched. He knew a moment of unease but shook it off. Nothing was proven yet. The designs could be of ancient origin, well known and widely used at one time but forgotten now.

He took hold of the edge of the book's cover—it appeared to be wood wrapped in leather—and pulled it open. The first page was creamy tinged vellum, covered in a rendering of a large castle, boasting six turrets that appeared to be perched at the top of a mountain.

But even for the similarity of construction, this could not be Wyldonna Castle; the palace in the drawing stretched to either side of the main structure in two massive wings ringed with smaller towers, and a gatehouse complete with portcullis in the foreground.

Adrian's eyes went to a small bit of Latin text beneath the drawing. *For the good of all living things, both in spirit and in flesh.*

He turned the page and was presented with a small colorful drawing of what appeared to be a red cat inside a little square in the upper left corner of the page. He translated the text next to the image: *of the Cat Sìth, from the Eastern tribes, creature of revenge. Red of skin, black innards. Feeds on warm flesh. Protector of the crown. Prideful. Loyal unto death.*

Adrian's eyes studied the little drawing once more. It could only be an afternhanger.

He scanned the next page, where another small rendering decorated the corner—this one of a brown hairy-looking creature, accompanied by another description of origin, traits.

Adrian flipped through several thick pages: centaur, elf, dragon, giant, griffin, kelpie—Adrian saw countless creatures he was familiar with only through myth, and even more descriptions and likenesses of those he'd never even heard of before.

It was like a bestiary of sorts. But that was only the first part of the book. Midway through, it seemed the tome was taken over by poetry, mythology, parables. He skimmed and turned pages mindlessly, taking in a word or two along with the intricate illustrations, until his eyes caught a glimpse of what appeared to be a drawing of a man.

A nude man with a shock of dark hair, his skin covered in swirling patterns of black. Adrian swallowed the lump in his throat as he read the words beneath the sketch.

> *A stranger came to fall the Towers*
> *And scatter all the Kin.*
> *The King met battle with the foes*
> *But naught could he win.*
> *For his crown was flung across the seas,*
> *Stolen in the Blue.*
> *The imprisoned Man so took her hand*
> *And commanded that she rule.*
> *Out of the mist she returned unseen,*

> *And none could ken where she had been.*
> *Beware the Painted Man, my child,*
> *Who trades the death of the Queen . . .*

This was the legend the people of Wyldonna held him to. Adrian had to admit he could see the correlation—even down to the idea that he had been a man imprisoned. Now the gasp he'd heard upon taking Maisie's hand and quitting the village made sense. But how long ago had this rhyme been set down? A hundred years or more? Surely Malcolm and the rest of the folk didn't actually think he had come to Wyldonna to kill Maisie so that rule could be returned to her brother?

Adrian frowned and turned the page so that he would not have to look at the crude drawing of the man whose skin was decorated so similarly to his own.

What he discovered next in the book appeared to be a lineage of sorts rendered in art, with another drawing of a six-turreted castle and a web of names leading from windows and doors, from stone to stone. He looked closely at the names, noting that the dates shared similar patterns. Coronations, perhaps? They all seemed to occur exclusively during four months of the year.

The months of the solstices and equinoxes.

Adrian turned the page and saw yet another castle, but this one was missing the gatehouse, although the names continued.

The next page—the east wing was smaller by half.

The next page—the turrets grew taller, as it seemed two entire floors had been removed from the uppermost levels of the castle.

Adrian kept going—page after page after page—until he came to the last drawing and realized it was an accurate depiction of what Wyldonna looked like at that very moment. He thought the lineage contained only one name—Malcolm—until he saw the parenthesis after the king's title.

Maighread, d.

Adrian looked up from the page again with a shiver. If anyone could attest that Maisie Lindsey's blood ran hot in her veins that day, it was Adrian. He looked back at her name closely and realized the date.

It was the spring equinox, yet more proof that the legend was false. It was almost exactly a year since the last spring festival, and Maighread Lindsey was still very much alive. The next would mark Glayer Felsteppe's return to Wyldonna.

He thought for a moment. Maisie had taken the throne from Malcolm on one of the only days Felsteppe could have found the island, the winter solstice.

Perhaps the lineage was not a history but a foretelling?

Adrian shut the book with a dusty slam.

That was impossible. There were no such things as prophecies, magic predictions—fate.

But what of the things he had seen on the island that he would have heretofore pronounced impossible? The creatures and beings here; they couldn't really exist in the manner that everyone claimed, could they? They were nothing more than an anomaly of breeding. Of isolation.

Weren't they?

Adrian stood from the chair and looked down at the dusty book as if it might at once come alive and attack him. What of the changes he had felt coming over himself since arriving at Wyldonna? His increase in strength and health, his immunity to the elements. His boldness in confronting the wild beasts of the island. Nothing more than him regaining his manhood after such mental torture and physical injury of course.

But what if they weren't? What if everything Maisie Lindsey had ever told him, shown him, was true?

What if Adrian's presence insured that the queen of Wyldonna would die?

Saving Wyldonna is the legacy I will leave for Malcolm and for our people.

His mind could not accept it. He had spent the bulk of his life gathering the knowledge to dispel such superstitions. There were undeniable laws that governed the actions and characteristics of every living thing on earth—and of the elements, of nature itself. It was the old ways that sought to explain away what was yet unknown by attributing it to magic or fate or some ancient curse, not the learned way. Not Adrian's way.

Why had it been he who had come to Wyldonna and not Roman Berg, as was originally intended?

How could the marks Song had applied so painstakingly on

Adrian's skin over the course of months match so precisely to an ancient tome found on a forgotten Scots isle?

What of the mythical creatures contained in Wyldonna's bestiary—some of which Adrian had read about during his courses of study in mythology? He had always thought them parables or weak attempts to explain that which the ancients had not yet discovered, but were those scholars of old then fools? The great minds of history who had laid the groundwork for modern academics—were they naught but superstitious alchemists? Magicians?

Of course not, Adrian thought to himself. They were geniuses. Forerunners in the art of science.

Why, then, was Adrian so very certain that Wyldonna's ways were impossible, while at the same time he could not come up with a logical explanation for them? Why was the light of the sun warm? He didn't know. Some thought it was magic, but that was impossible because it couldn't be proven.

But Adrian realized he could not disprove it either.

If he was truly the scholar he claimed to be, the only logical thing to do was to consider the evidence as it was presented. By ignoring what his own eyes could see before him, what he could touch and study, he was behaving exactly as the superstitious fools whom he held in contempt. He had been unable to explain Wyldonna's mysterious characteristics, and so he had dismissed them as impossible even when their existence was undeniable by his own standards.

Could he forgive himself if he continued to pretend that the events that were unfolding around him were impossible and Maisie Lindsey died because of it?

Adrian gathered the remnants of his satchel and its contents beneath one arm and then took Wyldonna's history from the table. He had reached the door and opened it before realizing he'd forgotten to blow out the candle, and so he turned back.

But the flame was already extinguished, the wick sending up a curl of black smoke.

A draft caused by swiftly opening the door had blown it out.

No.

For the first time since arriving on Wyldonna, Adrian applied the logic of the island: He was finished in the library, he was taking the only book it contained, so there was no need for the flame. It had ceased to exist because it was unnecessary.

What else might cease to exist once its usefulness had been met? The drawings of the ever-diminishing castles contained in the book beneath his arm came to mind.

Maighread, d.

Not if the Painted Man could help it.

Maisie swept her hand beneath the murky surface of the warm water of her bath, watching the ripples as they broke against her knees and chest. The fragrant steam soothed her as much as anything could. The fire in her hearth crackled, and Dragon rested in her usual place, as still as the stones that she so resembled. Maisie's chamber should have been peaceful to her.

But beneath the curls piled atop her head, Maisie's mind was a whirlwind.

Adrian Hailsworth was still somewhere in the castle, of that she was certain. But what he intended to do since they had made love hours ago she did not know, and it was that uncertainty that caused her unease.

Her chamber door opened then, without even the small courtesy of a warning knock, and he appeared as if she had summoned him by mere thought. Which wasn't true, because she had thought of nothing but him since he'd left her on his bed, and she'd not managed to catch sight of him the rest of the day. It was late now; everyone else had retired. He closed the door behind him and stood there looking at her in the bath, her nakedness concealed by the water, Wyldonna's book cradled in one elbow, a roll of parchment in his other hand.

"Good evening," he said at last.

"Good evening," she returned. Her eyes went to the unknown documents he held. "I see Reid was able to supply you with what you needed. He told me before supper that you had requested his assistance."

"The afternhangers destroyed your plans," he said, motioning with the parchment. "I had need to redraw them as best I could."

She waved her hand through the water again, continuing to watch him.

"Thank you for the shirt."

"You're welcome to it." Maisie let a little smile come over her mouth. "Although I prefer you without it, I fear I would soon be without female servants of any sort were I to allow you about the castle unclothed."

He returned her smile, and Maisie's heart skipped a beat.

"The marks disconcert them."

She chuckled. "I doona think it's the marks that disconcert them but the chest that bears them. I canna blame them when I am so affected by it myself."

Adrian's jaw clenched. "Would that you refrain from such talk until I have told you what I came here for. The sight of you so bare has me already at my limits."

"You didna come here just for me?" Maisie smiled at him. "State your intentions then, so that we might converse quickly and have it over with."

He walked to her bed and put down the items he carried, and Maisie heard the scrape of Dragon as she rose from her post. Maisie couldn't see the long, low creature beneath the high sides of her tub, but she could guess at her location by the way Adrian's eyes tracked along the floor. She was going under the bed.

He seemed to struggle with something for a moment, as if debating what he would next say and how he would say it. "How old is it?" Adrian asked at last.

"She," Maisie clarified. "Verra old."

"Older than you?"

Maisie laughed. "Older than anything living today, I'd wager. Dragon is the last of her tribe as well."

"I've seen creatures somewhat like it—*her*," he corrected. "During my travels through Egypt. They live in the rivers there."

"Piece bloods," Maisie said, fishing her rag from the bottom of the tub and feeling for the slippery cake of soap she'd forgotten. "Perhaps of her line, long ago. It's why they have taken up residence near such wealth."

"Dragon," Adrian mused. "*From below and above the earth. Guardian of treasure, particularly of gold.*"

Maisie was not surprised. She had guessed what had kept him hidden from her sight the remainder of the day. "You've been reading." She swiped the soap across her collarbone and followed it with the rag.

"Yes. Have you thought that it—*she*—is perhaps the guardian of Wyldonna's lost fortune?"

"Of course." Maisie moved to wash her arms, turning her wrists to watch the firelight gleam over her wet skin. "Each generation makes an attempt to turn this chamber over, seeking that which is nae here. Nothing has ever been found of course. Besides, unlike her ancestors, Dragon is small. If Wyldonna's treasure is as vast as the tales tell, she couldna hide it verra well, could she? Just because dragons have guarded fortunes in the past doesna mean that they must."

Adrian hummed, neither in agreement nor argument.

"Why did you seize the throne from Malcolm?"

Maisie stilled in her ministrations, her eyes falling on the folds of the sudsy rag in her hand. "I had to. He would bring Man's war to Wyldonna." She looked up at him. "One day it will all be gone, but it has been left to me to preserve it for as long as possible."

"Even if that means sacrificing yourself?"

He *had* been reading. "Without Wyldonna, I would cease to exist any matter."

"I don't think that's true," Adrian said, perching on the edge of her mattress. "You could have stayed in Melk. Or even Scotland. Your brother thought you would."

"Malcolm hoped I would, aye," Maisie said, lifting her right foot and washing from her knee over her shin. "But I wouldna have survived long. A lone woman who appears one day from nowhere, with no mundane skills of any good use, no pedigree to recommend her." She had learned that lesson the hard way.

"What about your . . . magic? Surely you could use it to support yourself, gain yourself what you needed."

She glanced at him as her stomach lurched. "And be burned alive when my abilities were discovered by the wrong person? Or attacked by a vengeful piece blood or exile who would know me?" She attended her left leg now, trying very hard to avoid his gaze even as she longed to look at him again. "Any matter, magic doesna exist, according to Adrian Hailsworth."

Adrian hummed again. Then he asked, "How are you to die? Am I to kill you?"

Maisie shrugged. "You, Glayer Felsteppe, the afternhangers. Perhaps the island itself shall swallow me up, or the sirens shall seize me and drag me down."

"I would never harm you, Maisie. Surely you understand that after . . . after this afternoon."

"I understand that Glayer Felsteppe was your priority in coming here. You made that verra clear. He is a dangerous man who threatens nae only you and your friends but also Wyldonna, which is the source of all magic for the entire world." She dropped her foot back into the water with a little splash and looked at him again. "I would hope that destroying him means more to you now than ever before."

"I don't see why you have to die in order to stop him," Adrian said.

Maisie wanted to hope, with every fiber of her being, that he was right. But he still didn't fully understand, and so she said nothing.

"If Wyldonna's fortune cannot be found, we must fight him."

"How?" Maisie demanded. "We canna use the island against him on the equinox."

"No, but the folk of this place—the giants, the afternhangers, especially—they possess great skills by the nature of their very existence. Size and strength and teeth and claw."

"You speak as Malcolm," she scoffed.

"He has a plan," Adrian pressed. "He and the folk are building machines of war, perhaps the likes of which I have seen used and could help engineer."

She shook her head and rose to her feet in the tub, water sluicing down her body as she began to wash her torso, uncaring that Adrian watched her boldly. He had already seen her in the most intimate setting possible. Let him watch her wash the last traces of him from her skin before he replaced them.

"Nay. I willna have Wyldonna's people killed in a futile attempt to save my own life and then the island be destroyed all the same. Adrian, I took a vow, and nae a light one: *For the good of all living things—*"

"*Both in spirit and in flesh*," he finished. "I know. But you brought me here, and so you have to trust me."

She let the rag drop into the water. "I brought you here to trade your life for Wyldonna's survival."

He rose from the bed, his brows lowered. "It matters not to me what promise you made. The only way I would accompany Glayer Felsteppe anywhere without protest is if I was nothing more than a dead body."

Her fists clenched. "I'm certain that is a possibility!"

He shrugged, his gaze running over her body like the droplets of water that raced down her skin. "I'll begin searching the castle again on the morrow. And I shall seek this fortune your book tells of for a fortnight. If I should not find it by then, I must go to the village. To see Malcolm," he clarified. "Perhaps you will be more receptive to his plans if my search is unsuccessful."

"I doona care to hear of his foolish scheme," she said. "Nae now. Nae ever."

He picked up the toweling from the end of her bed and began walking toward the tub. "I could convince you to listen, I'm certain."

She raised her arms to his neck as he swirled the towel around her body and pulled her to him.

"Do what you will," she said against his mouth. "I doona wish to talk anymore tonight."

He kissed her and then pulled away. "Oh, we've finished talking." He lifted her from the tub and she wrapped her dripping legs around his waist. His hands went to the still tender flesh beneath the edge of the towel.

"Good," she said, nipping at his neck. "Then take off that damned shirt."

Chapter 16

A fortnight passes very quickly when mind and body are well-occupied, Adrian soon realized.

Each day of his interment at Melk had seemed a month. Endless, never-changing routines of waking and reading and drinking enough to be numbed to his misery so that he might sleep without nightmares.

But the fortnight at Wyldonna—it passed with the swiftness of a smile and a wink. Adrian would rise from his bed, break his fast, and spend the days combing the corridors and dank chambers of the castle, often with the giant Reid at his side. They would partake of the noon meal in the company of the island's beautiful queen, during which the trio would discuss what had—or had not—been discovered during the morning efforts. And then Adrian and the queen would retire to her chamber for an hour or two's deeper, wordless investigation. The search would then happily commence until supper, when Maisie would subsequently accompany Adrian to his room until the black sky beyond his window was the darkest it could become.

During those fleeting days, he had discovered walled cells of old bones, trapdoors leading beneath the castle where secret springs flowed. One chamber contained nothing but a battered-looking golden chalice resting on a stone pedestal in the center of the room. Adrian had stared at it for a very long time with a queer ache in his heart before finally closing the door gently and carefully repositioning the tapestry that hid it.

Forgotten halls; a corridor filled to the ceiling with what appeared to be twisted stubs of horn, which threatened to avalanche on Adrian when Reid had wrenched the old door open. Try as he may, Adrian could never locate the far end of that particular corridor.

One of the towers Maisie had explained to him as inaccessible turned out to be nothing but a tall, echoing cylinder, empty to the very top of its conical roof; the other had been filled solid with mortared stone.

Adrian found a pelt fashioned with sleeves at the bottom of an ancient crate. He found an enameled pin Maisie had misplaced when she was a girl. He found a pair of Reid's enormous braies airing on the windowsill of an unused chamber, and also found that giants could run remarkably fast when pursuing a man who waved them like a flag through the main hall. He had discovered ancient tapestries; primitive carvings; long lengths of exotic silk.

But he had found no treasure.

Lying in his bed with Maisie on the last evening of the fortnight, he reminded her of his promise to seek out Malcolm. She did not deny him, but neither did she encourage him, instead choosing to pull his naked body atop hers once again.

Adrian did not resist. Choosing to ignore, for at least a while longer, that the equinox would arrive in two days.

He had no trouble finding the correct path that led into the village the next morning, and felt a tinge of pride that he had refused Reid's courteous offer of escort. In fact, Adrian didn't hesitate at all when he came to the edge of the wood, walking between the trees and into the deeper dark of the forest as if he had gone that way a hundred times before. And although he was immediately surrounded by sounds that were both foreign and familiar—the calls of birds, but no birds he'd heard before—rather than becoming anxious at what might be watching him from the safety of the trees and underbrush, he was alert and curious, training his eyes to scan the murky shadows for a glimpse at whatever strange creatures resided there. He wasn't afraid.

He'd left his shirt at the castle. He wasn't certain he needed to put his marks on display after nearly all the folk had seen him, but the attack of the afternhanger had only been stopped at the sight of the black designs, and although Adrian felt a heady increase in confidence as his long falling strides ate up the steep downward path through the wood and the mist kissed his bare skin, he wasn't foolish.

Any matter, he found he was growing quite fond of glancing down and seeing the evidence of his survival tattooed on his skin; the lines seemed crisper somehow, darker, a primal part of him now. Adrian didn't know if that was due to the fact that the wounds from

Song's art were at last completely healed or if the air of Wyldonna emboldened them.

Were they magic?

Was he?

After the past fortnight he'd spent with Maisie Lindsey, he was inclined to at least entertain the idea, if only humorously. They'd made love a score of times, and Adrian had to admit his stamina had not lagged in the least. In fact, it seemed that each time he took her, his desire for her grew tenfold. Even as they lay in each other's arms at the verge of each dawn, Maisie dosing easily with her head on his chest, Adrian already anticipated the coming night.

And likely the afternoon as well.

He hadn't thought about what the future would hold once he left Wyldonna. There had been no declarations of tender feelings between himself and Maisie, no promises of devotion. They were certainly no longer at odds with each other. Indeed, their uneasy relationship had seemed to grow into something akin to friendship, stewarded by the hours they spent in each other's beds. Adrian told himself that was tenderness enough for him, and by the way Maisie had flown from his chamber before Reid could discover them that morning, the arrangement suited her as well.

The only instances that had perplexed him from their encounters were the glimpses of Dragon he'd caught when in Maisie's chamber. The creature always seemed fast to hide herself away at his arrival, and then, at his departure, she'd once more take up her post as seemingly part of the hearth.

Did the beast not trust him? Was it because he was a stranger, Man? Or was it the marks on his body perhaps? Dragon had never growled at him, if that was something she was actually wont to do; the bestiary wasn't explicit on that account. But she had certainly kept herself hidden away from him.

Likely as not, being such an old creature, she simply didn't have the patience for his foolishness with her young queen.

Or perhaps she was simply a modest dragon.

Adrian grinned to himself as he came out of the wood and onto the wider dirt path between the cottages. As if he'd been waiting for Adrian, the little boy he'd first encountered the day he'd followed Malcolm to the village was sitting in the middle of the road, arranging a circle of stones and sticks. He looked up with a gap-toothed grin as Adrian emerged, and Adrian noticed his golden hair had been put to rights at some point.

"Good day, Man!" the boy said, scrambling to his feet with nearly a hop of exuberance.

"Good day," Adrian returned, unable to help his grin. The child's happy appearance was infectious.

"Have you come to battle the afternhanger?" He scrabbled at the air with his fingers hooked like claws and gave a mewling roar before dropping his arms back down with an exaggerated flap. "I know where they be this time of day."

"Not today," Adrian said, walking past the boy. "Thank you for the offer, though."

The boy turned and fell in step with Adrian, craning his head to look up into Adrian's face. "My name's Edel." He gave a little leap that turned him to face Adrian, and now he walked backward. "Well, my true name is Edel, but me mam oft calls me Eddy."

"Because it's shorter?" Adrian teased.

The boy gave Adrian an indulgent grin much like when he'd informed him that everyone was magic. "It isn't shorter, Man."

"I jest," Adrian allowed. "My name is Adrian, not Man."

"Are you nae a man?"

"Yes."

"You're the Painted Man."

"Some say that."

"You're a man and you're painted. You must be the Painted Man."

"Perhaps I'm *a* painted man. Not necessarily *the* painted man."

"Hmm." Edel considered this. "Where are you going then, if not to battle the afternhanger?"

"I've come to see the king. Do you know where he is?"

"Same place as the afternhangers—in the mountain. He's always in the mountain." Another little hop brought the lad to walk alongside Adrian once more, but this time on his right side. "I can take you, if you like. *Les geants* will hardly let you pass on your own."

"I would be grateful," Adrian accepted. He glanced down at the lad, unable to help but notice again Edel's subtly pointed ears. He seemed small for one who possessed such a mastery of language. Adrian was not well familiar with young children, but surely this boy could be no older than five or six years. "How old are you, Edel?"

"Nine winters," he said proudly. And then, as if he thought it only polite to return the query, he asked Adrian, "How old be you?"

"Oh, I am very old," Adrian said in a grave tone as they neared the common, its balefire still blazing. They skirted the edge of the pit farther from the sea cliff before Edel led the way onto a hilly track that cut across the steep slope beneath the castle. The path was edged with low, thick shrubs, their branches too dense to penetrate even without their foliage. "*Thirty-three* winters."

Edel looked back over his shoulder. "Huh! I would have guessed you at least two score."

Adrian huffed a laugh. "And I would have guessed you no more than six."

But the boy didn't seem offended, swiping at the brush as if he brandished an invisible sword as he led the way. "I reckon you haven't seen many elves, is why." He glanced back again briefly, his eyes going to Adrian's right ear. "Although one might mistake you for a piece-blood elf, should they see that."

"I was injured," Adrian supplied easily, finding himself unbothered at the mention of his mangled auricle.

The boy hopped around once more to walk the path backward, and Adrian was impressed at how sure-footed the lad was. "In a battle, I'd wager. Were you shot with an arrow?" He brought up his arms, aiming an imaginary bow, then let his pretend projectile fly toward Adrian's head with a whistle of air.

"It was after a battle," he allowed, "but no weapon did this damage. I was dragged by a horse."

Edel's tilted eyes rounded. "A horse? Have you ever ridden one?"

It amused Adrian that the boy was more intrigued at the mention of the animal than the punishing torture Adrian had endured.

"Of course. My father and brother raised horses at our home in England, and I had several of my own by the time I was your age." Ahead, Adrian could see the face of the cliff growing, it's rocky side draped with mosses and vines. "Are there no horses on Wyldonna?"

"Nay." Edel hopped around to face forward once more, speaking to Adrian over his narrow shoulder. "There used to be. Lots. Mam says before I was born and the island was large, there were herds. They've all gone now."

Perhaps the castle wasn't the only thing that was growing smaller.

Edel turned to the left, up a short incline littered with loose shards

of rock. "I'll have a horse one day, though. When I go to the Outland."

Adrian was intrigued. "You'll leave Wyldonna?"

"Perhaps when I'm twelve," Edel supplied musingly, and then
quickly looked over his shoulder. "Doona tell me mam, though. Me
brothers have all gone, and she thinks me to be the one she'll keep."

"Why do you want to go?" Adrian pressed. "You seem happy
enough here, and the Outland can be a dangerous place." He reached
up to touch his ear unconsciously, but he caught himself and let his
hand fall.

"There's nae future here for me," Edel said, his tone becoming
one of a much more mature age. "Naught left to hunt besides mice
and birds. Naught to explore. Only sea, all around. I dream of forests
that never end, and deep lakes with fat fishes you can reach in and
grab with your very hand." The boy mimicked the motion before
looking back at Adrian, as if for reassurance. "The Outland has many
forests."

"Parts of it," Adrian answered faintly, as he had just caught sight
of the man—the giant—standing with his back against the side of the
cliff.

Reid had been truthful; his size was nothing compared to the massive individual the elfin boy was cheerfully leading Adrian toward.
Adrian guessed him to be no less than twenty feet tall and perhaps
five feet across at the chest, over which arms like tree trunks rested.
Like Reid, the man's skin was mottled yellow, and he had the same
thick black hair.

"Then it's the Outland for me for certain," Edel said with finality,
as if he and Adrian had just decided a very serious matter. The boy
raised a hand to the giant and continued walking toward him even
though Adrian had stopped while still a good distance away in order
to avoid straining his neck. "Good day, Cairn! Man's come to see the
king." The boy proceeded to clamber atop the giant's instep, perching
on the rounded toe of his boot. He swung his bare feet over the edge,
his spindly arms braced to either side of his thighs.

The giant tucked his chin and looked down at the lad, who appeared no larger than an insect on that massive boot. "Edel," he said
gravely, his voice like an argument of boulders. "You are not to be
about the caves alone."

Edel tilted his face sideways as he flung out his arm to indicate Adrian. "I'm nae alone; I'm with Man."

Adrian thought the grimace on Cairn's face might have been an indulgent smile. But then the grimace fell away as the giant's arms dropped to his sides and he regarded Adrian with a grim expression.

"Good day, Man," the giant said, and then he bowed stiffly, an act that seemed to take a full minute. "Forgive my insolence. It is rare that Wyldonna is host to such an esteemed guest. I am Cairn."

If the short time Adrian had known Reid taught him anything, it was that giants valued courtesy, and so Adrian returned the man's bow with one of his own. "Adrian Hailsworth, at your service. I beg your pardon for any inconvenience caused by my unannounced arrival."

Cairn's massive hairy eyebrows rose, and Adrian thought he saw a spark of delight in the giant's eyes. "It will be my supreme honor to lead you to His Majesty. There is no inconvenience—King Malcolm thought perhaps you might call. This way, if you please." The giant turned smoothly and ducked into an opening perhaps only a foot or two shorter than the crown of his head.

Such a large opening would require a large guard, Adrian thought to himself.

Edel went to his stomach with a joyful whoop, spreading his arms and legs wide and clinging to the top of the giant's boot as he enjoyed the ride.

Adrian followed the largest and smallest males he'd ever met into the side of the mountain, his vision temporarily disabled by the intense blackness of the cave after the bland fog of the exterior. But after a moment, the torches lashed to the rocky walls inside normalized his sight, and he saw that they were entering a huge terraced cavern whose ceiling was perhaps fifty feet above Adrian's head. As he followed Cairn to the edge of the corridor, where the floor appeared to fall abruptly away to nothing, the muffled sounds he'd heard outside the cave bloomed into the echoing noise of industry and construction.

Adrian came to the giant's side and looked down over the precipice. The cavern began some fifty feet below his boots, the terraces revealing themselves to be wide, spiraling paths carved from the rock itself, winding to the floor of the mountain. The paths were currently populated with the traffic of scores of individuals pushing carts, dragging skids, hefting large woven baskets filled with unknown contents. Hammering and sawing, chopping and crashing sounds wafted up like fragrances, flavored with the familiar shouts and curses of men well into the task of construction.

And, as Edel had foretold, several afternhangers lounged about the rim, watching the industry below with apathy. Adrian would have been loath to admit his relief that they seemed to pay him little attention.

From his own perch atop the perimeter, Adrian saw great wooden skeletons spread out across the floor below, some with rigging and ties for ribs, and wide wooden platforms for skulls. Wyldonna's folk swarmed over the structures like ants, the hundreds of tiny torchlights heating the bowl and sending up the warm glow of steam and sweat. The far end of the basin was devoid of construction, but the stone was crumbled, large chunks of the wall itself fallen away and lying in a heap on the graveled floor.

In an instant, Adrian knew what the king had been building.

Edel's excited voice drew Adrian's attention. "Can I help today, Cairn?"

"That permission is not mine to give," Cairn said reproachfully, and then he looked down at Adrian. "If you please, Man." He turned to his right and started down one of the gentle curving terraces.

Adrian followed.

It took him several moments to habituate himself to the spiral of the path without almost falling to his death; in that time, he nearly walked off the unguarded walkway twice, and bounced off the mountain's wall once, the view of the building going on beneath him so intriguing that he could barely take his eyes from it. But there was a rhythm to the curve, how it sloped and turned, and by the time the trio reached the bottom of the cavern, Adrian thought he could have walked it blindfolded, it was so well-engineered.

Once upon the floor proper, the skeletons grew to massive proportions, rivaling the great Cairn for breadth and height. Adrian followed the giant and elf through a corridor of sorts between two projects, and he found himself turning on his feet, walking backward, craning his head, trying to see all the things at once.

"Ah, Hailsworth." The sound of Malcolm's voice dragged Adrian's attention back to the floor, and he saw the bearded man back down a short height of scaffolding, his pipe clenched in his teeth. Malcolm tossed the hammer in his hand onto the lowest platform of the scaffold and then brushed his palms together while Adrian approached.

Adrian took the king's forearm in his own. "Malcolm. I must admit I'm quite astounded at the enterprise you have hidden away."

Malcolm chuckled and released Adrian's arm to take his pipe stem from his mouth. "We are nae making children's slings from driftwood, if that was your thought. Or what Maisie would have you believe. Surely it is she who has delayed your visit to my mountain."

Adrian did not wish to discuss the king's sister at the moment, fearing that Malcolm might somehow deduce what had been going on in his castle between the Painted Man and the woman who had stolen his throne. And so he walked closer to the structure from which Malcolm had just come down, running his hand along the base of the machine.

"I've been searching for the treasure of course." He looked over his shoulder as Malcolm joined him. "Who designed the trebuchet?"

"I did." Malcolm drew on his pipe as he gazed with pride along the long throwing arm of the siege engine Edel was currently scaling. "A pair of Wyldonian brothers—duvenets—left the island to try their fortune in the Outland. They didna care for the place. But their time in captivity gained them this knowledge, and together we replicated the machine in plans."

Adrian remembered seeing the entry in the bestiary; duvenets were creatures that could supposedly change their shapes into that of a number of beasts—bear, wolf, fox.

"In captivity, you say?"

Malcolm nodded. "Aye. They were mistaken for primitives and taken as slaves for an army."

"Their distaste, then, is understandable." Adrian caught a glimpse through the bones of the dormant trebuchet of a dark-skinned man walking along the cavern floor with a bundle of long hewn boards upon his shoulder. The duvenet met Adrian's gaze and gave an acknowledging nod, which Adrian returned in kind. "I have seen many trebuchets, and this one appears at least equal to if not superior in construction to the best of them."

"Your kindness is well-met, lad. In truth, I never wished for a need of such wisdom, though grateful I am of it now." He glanced at Adrian from the corner of his eye and gave a sly wink. "And I canna say the building of them hasna brought me some pleasure."

Adrian chuckled, feeling oddly at home here in the depths of the mountain with this man who should be king, surrounded by a population of beings whose mere existence was largely unbelievable. Adrian thoroughly understood the excitement and satisfaction that could be derived from constructing a thing of your own ingenuity. He realized that he and Malcolm were little more than a pair of overgrown boys, playing about with wooden bricks.

Malcolm turned to him fully just then, an eager glint in his green eyes. "Are you keen to see it at work?"

Adrian's grin widened, as it seemed the king had just affirmed his thought. "Do elves have pointed ears?"

The king roared with laughter. "That they do, lad! That they do!" Malcolm clapped his shoulder and then turned away and gestured with his pipe toward the ruined side of the cavern.

Cairn stepped to the edge of the trebuchet from where he had politely removed himself from earshot and allowed Edel to scamper on to his hand so that the elf boy could be lifted to the giant's shoulder, out of harm's way. Then they followed Adrian, who now walked alongside the king.

The workers busied on the engine Adrian and the group approached noticed the king's imminent arrival and sprang into action at the wave of his hand, rolling the massive frame to the far end of the floor of the cavern. Tall wheeled carts filled with rock were pushed near the rear of the dormant trebuchet, and several workers appeared to assist without direction, obviously fulfilling roles in which they were well-versed. A short, squat being with a long beard and a round cap ran in a humorous, waddling manner up the pathway from the floor, and Adrian would have chuckled at the sight of him until he turned to look down upon the cavern, revealing his scowling, warty face.

Troll, Adrian realized.

The troll cupped his hands around his mouth and bellowed into the space, "Ready!" The word robustly chased itself in echo, eliminating the need for the man to repeat himself.

Back on the cavern floor, two more giants had joined the endeavor, one drawing back the launch arm and locking it into place while the other braced the counterweight. A group of trolls began loading the trebuchet with the rocks from the carts.

Malcolm nodded to the troll still on the path above, and the little man shouted once more.

"Firing!"

One of the giants took hold of the rope attached to the brace beneath the counterweight and pulled.

The counterweight dropped, causing the launch arm to fly forward with an earsplitting crack. The mountain itself seemed to tremble less than a heartbeat later, as hundreds of pounds of rock smashed into the already ruined cavern wall and exploded in a cloud of pulverized stone.

A cheer went up from the floor, an echoing roar of triumph, and Adrian was not hesitant to add his own voice to the celebration. The engine had worked perfectly, and it buoyed Adrian's hope for the success of Wyldonna in defending itself against Glayer Felsteppe.

"Well done!" Adrian said enthusiastically to the king as the giants rolled the spent machine away. The king was smiling broadly and waving his pipe stem appreciatively at the workers who returned to their duties. "How many do you have?"

"Three," Malcolm said, with more than a touch of pride in his voice.

Adrian nodded and shadowed the king as he began walking around the perimeter of the cavern floor. "What else?"

Malcolm drew on his pipe and looked at Adrian with a frown. "What else? What else do we need, lad? You saw for yourself the destruction of which only one of them is capable. We have *three*. Felsteppe's army willna set boot on Wyldonna come the equinox."

"They are fine machines," Adrian allowed. "But I'm certain you will not be surprised when I tell you that I have come to you this day because I have yet to find the island's fortune."

"Nay, I'm nae surprised," Malcolm admitted.

"What if Felsteppe does return with the army he promised? On four ships? Six? Trebuchet are undoubtedly deadly in range, but they aren't terribly accurate at a distance. They are often used by ships when attacking a sea hold, but rarely the other way 'round for the simple reason that there is a considerable more amount of water to hit than ship."

"He could arrive bearing machines of his own, is your meaning," Malcolm said.

Adrian inclined his head while he winced. "I doubt it. The type of ship that could carry a machine of such size is almost never taken in the open water for any length. What I mean to say is that you must have other means of defense if Felsteppe brings soldiers to attack Wyldonna."

"Nae man can match an elf with a bow, neither for accuracy nor speed. They shall be posted along the cliff with full quivers."

Adrian nodded but pressed further. "What else?"

Malcolm thought a moment. "I supposed *les geants* could simply overturn the boats."

"Good," Adrian said. "Have they armor?"

"Armor?" Malcolm repeated. "They're giants, lad."

"Aye. And a single bee's sting is naught but a nuisance to most. However, if the hive should swarm upon a man who has intentions for the nest . . ." He let his meaning fill in the remainder of his sentence.

"We've nae means to make mail for such beings on Wyldonna," Malcolm allowed. "I doona know if any forge would exist."

"Wood, then," Adrian suggested. "Shields, helms?"

Malcolm nodded, his brow furrowed in thought. "There may be time for that yet."

"What of the afternhangers?" Adrian said, glancing up at the cavern's rim. "Surely their viciousness is of use in protecting the island."

Malcolm shrugged with an expression of dismissal. "Afternhangers are selfish beasts. Aye, they are bloodthirsty, but they canna be directed. I will speak with their leader, but I wouldna count on their help. Besides—" Malcolm paused to relight his pipe, puffing on it several times before the smoke again swirled around his head. "Unless Felsteppe makes an outright move to attack us, we canna harm him."

"You can do nothing against him? Even when he has threatened you so?"

"He's asked for our gold," Malcolm clarified. "And if it should be found and given to him, and he leaves us in peace, that would be the end of it."

"But you believe there is no gold to be found," Adrian said.

"Precisely. And neither do I believe he'd leave us in peace, nae matter the reward he was given."

Adrian found himself walking up the path toward the upper part of the cavern alongside this man who was revealing himself to be surprisingly intuitive. His mind worked laboriously on the riddle of this strange place, this strange people.

"Which is why you went straightaway for your plans of war. You already knew that if Felsteppe returned and was not given what he asked for, he would attempt to occupy Wyldonna by force, giving you recourse for retaliation."

Malcolm nodded. "Aye. If Maisie would have trusted me, you wouldna be involved at all. But she did a foolish thing in leaving and seeks to justify it."

Adrian frowned. "But I thought the tale of the Painted Man was a foretelling. You mean she wasn't meant to seek me out and bring me back?"

"It's less a foretelling than a warning," Malcolm explained. "Maisie is gambling with her life and yours. There's naught that can be done about it now. It's already been set in motion."

"Beware the Painted Man, who trades the death of the queen?"

Malcolm nodded again as the two men walked toward the opening in the mountain, and the weak light of day beyond. The sky was so much lighter than when he'd arrived on the island.

"I still don't understand," Adrian said, stopping and turning to face the king, "why she would take it upon herself to unseat you, to be so blatantly disobedient to your commands. She seems to care for you very much."

"Aye, that she likely does," Malcolm mused quietly, looking down at his boots. "She's all I have left, Maisie. She and I are the last." He looked up but avoided Adrian's gaze, turning his eyes instead out to sea. "She's trying to make up for her mistake. But I fear she'll pay with her life, and that I canna forgive her."

Adrian, too, turned to gaze out through the mist. "The mistake of overthrowing your rule."

"Nay. The mistake she made at Midsummer." Malcolm puffed on his pipe for a moment. "When she first left Wyldonna."

Adrian blinked and turned his head to regard the king. "She left the island last summer? Before she came to find me?"

"Aye. She followed a duvenet man to the Outland," Malcolm said somberly.

Adrian's blood froze. Maisie had left Wyldonna in pursuit of a man.

He tried to speak calmly. "Was she in love with him?"

"I doona know if she was when she left," Malcolm said. "She'd said she was done waiting to expire on Wyldonna. There was naught here for her—no future, no hope of a family. I do know she cursed his name upon her return, only weeks after she'd left."

Adrian didn't know what to say. There was no doubt that Maisie had been a virgin when Adrian first claimed her body. Had she been in love with the duvenet and he'd refused her?

Perhaps a broken heart was to blame for the mistakes made by the queen of Wyldonna.

The idea of it made Adrian's stomach clench painfully. The way she'd physically loved him, with such wanton abandon; had it been nothing more than a balm to her wounded pride? A way to gain revenge on the man she'd wanted but who had rebuffed her affections?

"Something troubling you, lad?" Malcolm asked lightly.

Adrian gritted his teeth. "I'm just curious: You said her leaving at Midsummer was the mistake for which she is seeking to atone. Why would she have to atone for wanting a future? Where did she go when she left Wyldonna with . . . with that man?"

"An Outland city called Hamburg," Malcolm said, and he turned and looked at Adrian at last. "Where she first met Glayer Felsteppe."

Chapter 17

Maisie sat on the stone threshold of the castle's front entrance, gazing into the tree line, watching, listening. The mist was so bright today—a sign that spring hovered just beyond the horizon now. The days had grown incrementally brighter in the weeks before Ostara, when true day would dawn, and each sunrise and sunset thereafter would be observed and celebrated until the season turned slowly toward fall—and darkness—again.

Last Midsummer, Maisie had sworn that she would never again be witness to the darkening of Wyldonna. But she had been wrong. It was this year that was to be her last on the island.

She drew a deep breath and held it for a long moment before releasing it in a rush. Frightened. She was frightened. And she had been naught but frightened for months now, the first time in her life she could ever remember being so. Some days it was intense enough that she felt as though she were being slowly strangled. First she was frightened in the Outland, when she found that adaptation was not as easy as she'd thought it would be. Then she was frightened of the people she'd met, was forced to depend on for her survival. Once they'd seen her abilities, they'd sought to use her, intimidate her into cooperating with their plans. They'd frightened her all the way back to Wyldonna.

And then they had followed her.

Maisie was properly chastised now. In trying to escape the ancient laws of the island, she had only succeeded in bringing her fate about more quickly. So although she had finally accepted the inevitable, she was still frightened.

The only place she found any reprieve from her fear was in Adrian

Hailsworth's arms. He was a good man, and a brilliant one. He would go on to do great things to the benefit of many, Maisie was certain.

She hoped he would return to the castle soon, so she could forget her fate for a little while. She'd done all she could do, both to ruin and then rectify things. All that was left was to wait, and to gather whatever comfort she could.

She heard the rustling in the underbrush before she saw him emerge from the wood. He was without his shirt again—a wise choice when going among the folk—and Maisie appreciated the sight of his lean, muscled body as he approached her. Even the way he moved affected her; the swagger of his shoulders, the swing of his tattooed arms, the long stride of his legs, all caused a clenching sensation in her middle. Her excitement at his approach was lessened somewhat, though, when he drew near enough for her to see the anger chiseled into his handsome face.

She opened her mouth to greet him, but his pointing finger precluded any thought she'd had of civilized conversation.

"You have done naught but lie to me since the moment we met," he accused.

She drew a steadying breath. "That's nae true."

He came to a stop two paces before her, forcing her to tilt her chin to look up sharply at him. In other circumstances, perhaps she would have risen to her feet in order to escape such a submissive pose, but she found that she didn't mind, really, looking up at Adrian Hailsworth. She was finished with escapes.

"You lied to me about the treasure."

"I didna."

"You lied to me about your reason for bringing me to the island."

"Nay. I only delayed telling you a portion of it."

He placed his hands on his hips, and Maisie couldn't help but let her eyes fall to the front of his chausses. She knew what he was going to say—he'd spent the morning with Malcolm, after all. He was angry that she'd failed to mention meeting Felsteppe last year, probably justifiably so. She should have told him, especially once their . . . relationship had changed, deepened. But each time she thought to, she couldn't bear the thought of the disapproval she would see in his eyes at her foolishness. She'd never meant to deceive him, only to avoid his scorn and disgust at how stupid she'd been.

"You didn't tell me you left Wyldonna this past summer," he accused.

There it was, then. Good. But that simple accusation was not enough to satisfy him, apparently.

"To be with *that man*," he finished.

Maisie frowned and looked up at him again, startled by his words.

"Don't look at me as if you've no idea what I'm referring to," he ground out. "More lies will only make it worse."

"I know exactly what you're referring to," she said. "Are you implying that I sought a relationship with Glayer Felsteppe?"

Now it was Adrian's turn to frown. "No. God, no. Although I do have some questions about how he came to be drawn into this in the first place. What I want to know is why you did not tell me that you fled Wyldonna to be with a man you were in love with—the duvenet. And then, when he refused you, you used me as a balm for your wounded pride."

Maisie's heart seemed to warm and swell in her breast, but she kept her expression neutral. "I wasna in love with Jagger when I followed him to the Outland."

"I don't believe you," he said darkly.

Maisie huffed a breath of laughter. "Why on earth nae?"

"Because you are Wyldonna royalty. You left the only family and home you had to follow this man, this . . . *Jagger.*" Adrian spat out the name as if it was a foul taste on his tongue.

Now Maisie slowly gained her feet. Standing on the stone threshold brought their gazes level with each other. "Adrian, are you jealous?"

He reached out and grabbed her upper arms, causing Maisie to gasp, but not with fear. Quite the opposite of fear, actually.

"Why didn't you tell me?"

"Because I didna want to show you how much of a fool I truly am," she answered honestly, bending her bound arms at the elbows to place her hands on the hot skin of his waist. She had to touch him.

"Why would you be the fool when he refused you? No man who would do so is in possession of respectable intellect."

Maisie wondered if any would see should she make love to Adrian in the castle yard.

"He didna refuse me, although he certainly would have, had I proposed such intimacy with him," she said, her eyes roving the hills and valley of his upper lip. "Adrian, Jagger prefers the friendly company of a man."

His head drew away slightly, his frown lessening. "Why would you follow him then, if he was of such . . . devious appetites?"

"Because he had a place in the Outland. I knew him. I thought he could keep me safe, see me settled," she said, leaning her bodice against his chest, her toes now her only contact with the earth. "Were you jealous because you thought I was in love with him? Because you thought I wanted to make love with another man before you?"

Adrian growled deep in his throat. "Yes," he hissed. "I was mad with jealousy. I still am," he said in a warning tone.

Maisie leaned forward and kissed his lips gently. "The only man I want to make love with—have ever wanted to make love with—is you. And that is the truth, if ever I've spoken it. If you'll only take me inside, I shall prove it to you."

He released her to sweep his arm beneath her legs and then turned to maneuver her through the narrow doorway. In moments they were dashing through the hall, Maisie running her fingers through Adrian's curling hair as she kissed his neck.

"Good day, Reid," Adrian said brusquely over the top of Maisie's head.

"And to you, Man," Maisie heard the giant's polite if confused reply. "Is there aught I can be of assistance to you?"

"Thank you, but I believe I can manage," Adrian said. And then threw over his shoulder, "Cairn sends his regards."

Maisie giggled against Adrian's skin and held him tighter. He was so perfect here, now. So perfect, and he was hers, if only for the little time she had left.

It took the use of all Adrian's will to slow in his lovemaking once he had Maisie Lindsey on the bed in her chamber. He wanted to take her quickly and roughly, but the idea that she had ever desired another man—regardless of how untrue that idea turned out to be—motivated him to imprint himself on the queen of Wyldonna. He wanted to bring her such pleasure that she would never desire anyone but him, would never think of another man in her bed.

For the rest of her life, perhaps.

And so he forced himself to linger over her body, to savor the smells and tastes of her creamy skin, until they were both panting with impatience. Then, and only then, did he join with her, pacing himself, increasing his insistence until she cried out with her release at last and Adrian quickly followed her.

She lay in his arms afterward, lazily tracing the designs on his skin. And although he didn't wish to disturb the intimate peace their lovemaking had created, they had only this day before Ostara dawned on the morrow, and Adrian needed all the information he could gain, even if Maisie herself thought it unimportant.

"Tell me about Hamburg," Adrian requested in the quiet.

Maisie's hand stilled, and then she lay her palm flat on his stomach and gave a little clearing of her throat.

"Jagger was employed there. By a deserter elf who was at one time a mercenary but had since taken up the occupation of innkeeper, using his business as a shield to protect the illegal goods and people he smuggled on the river there.

"When we arrived—only days after the solstice—the elf was to play host to a convening of soldiers at his inn. Jagger had asked permission for me to stay there, and even though the elfin man had left Wyldonna when I was yet a girl, he welcomed me. Despite everything, he seemed very kind."

Adrian's mind whirred and clicked. Last summer, a meeting of mercenaries on the river in Hamburg . . .

"It was the Queen's Inn, was it not?" Adrian asked against her hair, curling and fragrant under his chin. "The elfin innkeeper's name was Hamish."

Maisie tilted her face up, surprised. "Aye. How did you know?"

"My friend, the Spaniard—Valentine—he, too, was a friend to Hamish. He and the woman who is now his wife were at the Queen's Inn that night as well. Nearly captured."

Maisie stilled. "He was at the inn? I knew he was close—but I thought Prague. I had nae idea. . . ."

"Maisie, was it you who told Glayer Felsteppe that Valentine was traveling with an Englishwoman?"

"Aye," she said. "Jagger told Felsteppe that I could be of help to him in locating the men he sought. There was a large bounty offered and Jagger said he'd split the reward evenly with me, help me to settle myself in the city. So I . . . looked. I could feel the presence of the man—your friend. His connection with Felsteppe."

Adrian was quiet for a long moment. "By some miracle, Felsteppe didn't discover them that night," he said at last. "Did he then press you to . . . help him search further?"

"He did," Maisie said quietly, lying her head back on his chest. "Although he didna use such gentle terms. He would have used me for a slave. Likely worse. I grew afraid. And my fear of the Outland and its cruel people was larger than my childish desire to be free of Wyldonna."

Adrian didn't have to ask for further clarification of what Glayer Felsteppe likely had in mind for the naked beauty at his side.

"So you returned."

"Aye. I doona know that he bribed Jagger, or tortured him, but he somehow forced him to reveal where I had fled, and how to reach me here. He wanted me to finish the job I had started in Hamburg. I could scarce believe he had found me when he arrived in the winter. I thought, when the Autumn equinox had passed without threat . . ." She let the sentence trail away. "I had to then tell Malcolm everything. What I had done in the Outland. How I brought Wyldonna's destruction to our very door."

Adrian at last felt as though he understood Maisie Lindsey's plight. "And so you felt that if you looked for Valentine again and delivered him or another of us to Felsteppe, he would leave the island in peace and your brother would not make war."

She nodded. "I see how naïve I was. It wasna real to me before—offering up an innocent man to a devil like Felsteppe. But when I met you—when I saw what had been done to you because of him . . ." Her words trailed away again, and her hand slid across his stomach to clutch at his ribs, pull him closer.

After a moment, she continued. "I know he will never stop until you and your friends are dead. And I willna allow anyone else to pay further for my foolishness. Nae you, nae the folk, nae Malcolm. It is my crime. I alone shall bear the punishment."

Adrian frowned. "What do you mean?"

"You ken my meaning," she said. "You've read the book. There is nae treasure to give Felsteppe. If you surrender to him, you will be killed. If you doona, Wyldonna will go to war, and who knows how many of the folk will lose their lives. I'll trade myself . . . for them all," she finished quietly.

"No one wants that," Adrian argued, feeling a tightening in his chest. Something like panic perhaps, but he refused to let it take complete hold of him. "Not your brother, not the folk—certainly not me. Maisie, what shall Felsteppe force you to do once he has you under his control? You know about the abbey now."

"I am nae so innocent as I was when I first left Wyldonna," she said with a rueful tinge in her voice. "I set word among the piece bloods before I came to Melk. Some are against me, certainly, but many are still loyal to their roots, loyal to Wyldonna. Either way, they all know the threat Glayer Felsteppe has made upon us. The world has hopefully become a more dangerous place for that evil bastard."

"That's not a plan," Adrian said with a frown.

"We have what we have, Adrian," she said, resting her chin on his chest and looking at him once more. "I wouldna change anything I've done now. It's brought you to me, and glad I am of that. More glad than anything that's ever happened to me in my life."

Adrian leaned up from the bolsters behind his head and kissed her mouth. "I'll not give you up so easily," he said, hearing the roughness of his voice, the bluster that only he knew was an attempt to conceal the seed of fear that had been planted in his heart. "Neither will Malcolm. I saw the machines he and the folk have constructed. We worked on a plan of defense for the island when Felsteppe comes. It's a good plan, Maisie. Let us rise now and return to the mountain together. Make peace with your brother before the morrow."

"I've a better plan for the moment," she said, sliding her body up along his until she was lying atop him. She leaned down and kissed his mouth slowly, pulling at his lips until he stirred beneath her. "I think you'll prefer it."

"I think you're right," he said, happy to temporarily forsake all thoughts of the island for the attentions of the woman who had so completely consumed him in such a short time. He reached his left hand down to skim her leg to her knee, readying to flip her over onto her back, and then caught sight of Dragon, lying in the near corner. Her yellow eyes were trained on the cold hearth, which she had again left upon Adrian's arrival with Maisie.

The thoughts came unbidden to his mind, cooling his passion.

Dragon is small . . .

If Wyldonna's treasure is as vast as the tales tell, she couldna hide it verra well, could she?

He recalled seeing Cairn at the entrance to the mountain cavern: *Such a large opening would require a large guard. . . .*

"Maisie," he said flatly.

"Mmm?" she murmured, nuzzling him and reaching her hand down, impatient for him.

He'd been all over the castle. No, the plans hadn't made sense, and yet he'd found the secret doors, the hidden chambers behind the walls and beneath the floors.

They'd even gone so far as to pull up the floorboards in the chamber.

Adrian's eyes flicked to the thick carved beams along the ceiling, supporting the tightly seamed wooden boards. Then he looked back to the small creature curled in the corner.

Dragon was watching him.

"Maisie, get up," he said, pushing her off him.

She gave an offended huff as Adrian threw his legs over the edge of the bed and reached for his chausses.

"What is it?" she asked. "Where are you going so suddenly that you would leave me in such a state?"

He pulled on his boots while his mind raced. "Nowhere."

"You're getting dressed," she pointed out. And then, in a more in-dignant tone, "The shirt, too?"

He gave her a grin as he stood and pushed his head through the opening. She was sitting upright in the bed, her breasts bared and rosy. Good God, there was nothing so delicious on the earth as Maisie Lindsey. He leaned forward and braced his hands on the mattress to kiss her mouth firmly.

"One moment," he promised. Then he pulled away from the bed and crossed the floor to the hearth, where he crouched down.

The opening was perhaps not quite three feet tall, although it was a bit wider than that. Still, it would be a tight fit. He ducked and leaned his head inside to look up and saw nothing but narrow black-ness.

His mind went to the images of the plans of the castle, and he con-sidered the floors that were missing from the drawing in the book, the orientation of the tall ceiling of the corridor beyond the chamber door. He swiveled on his heels to face the room and then brought his left foot back to brace himself as he tucked into the opening.

"Adrian, what are you doing?" Maisie demanded from the end of the bed, where she'd crawled to watch him.

He winked at her. "Back in a thrice," he said, and then stood up in the tight space.

The sooty air immediately closed around him, as if he had been buried alive, the residual heat from countless fires emanating from the stones that were only inches from his skin—and seemed to draw closer as he reached up. Adrian could feel the familiar tightening of his chest, but he forced himself to breathe slowly through his nose—in, one, two; out, three, four—as his hands crawled along the crumbly, sticky prison.

Then he felt it. Shallowed by years of smoke, the depression was just deep enough for Adrian's fingers to hold to his first knuckle. He reached a bit higher with his other hand and felt the next. He braced his back against the stones and stepped up against the chimney, wedging himself inside. And then he began to climb. Two handholds, four, eight, until his next scrabbling reach met not a warm stony depression but a smooth, greasy surface, inset in the chimney itself.

Adrian rapped on it with the backs of his knuckles, and although the sound was spongy, it was still hollow. He pushed with first one hand, then both, but the barrier didn't yield. And so he shimmied up the chimney until his feet were on the bottom lip of the partition. Drawing back his right leg until his knee was beneath his chin, he kicked.

The barrier gave the faintest whisper of movement.

He kicked twice more, and on the last effort, his leg disappeared into the wall past his shin, where a faint gray light could be seen in the pitch of the chimney.

Adrian raised his buttocks higher against the stones behind him and hinged forward, gripping the insides of the opening. He brought his right foot to the wall behind him and pushed, while simultaneously launching himself into the unknown passage.

He slid through on the broken partition, his entrance heralded by a soft, clinking shush of sound. He put his hands down to lever himself up and pull himself in fully, and sank to his wrists in deep cold. Adrian dragged his knees in and slid to his feet, throwing his arms out for balance when he stepped off the tar-soaked piece of metal-clad wood.

Small round portals—no bigger than his fists—were set at the top of the low ceiling, letting in the soft, misty light of the sky beyond the castle. He turned in a circle, sliding on the slanting mound beneath his feet. The chamber was as wide, but three times as long, as the one he'd just left.

And it was filled with gold.

Chapter 18

Maisie heard two muffled thumps from somewhere inside the chimney where Adrian had disappeared. Clouds of dust and chunks of soot rained down onto the hearth. She thought he might have given a grunt, and then she heard nothing at all for several moments.

Prickles erupted over her skin, causing her to shiver, and she pulled the coverlet up over her chest as she sat on her heels at the end of the bed.

"Adrian?" She thought of how close a space he had disappeared into, and remembered his struggles with being trapped. What if he became wedged inside the stone passage, unable to breathe?

. . . who trades the death of the Queen . . .

A cold chill seemed to descend on her, freezing her in place so that she felt she could not have moved had the room been filled with afternhangers. In a flash, her mind imagined his lifeless body, and Maisie could feel the ripping of her heart with each slow thump.

"Adrian?" This time his name came out as little more than a breathy squeak.

But then the soot fell in the chimney again, and a tinkling of something else falling, bouncing on the hearth. She heard the scrabbling sound of an object sliding haltingly over stones. Maisie clutched the coverlet to her chest more tightly as she saw one of his boots emerge to crush the dead coals, and then—

His blackened, bare foot?

She frowned as he squatted out of the chimney, covered in the darkest filth. His clothes were ruined, his hair and face coated with thick, greasy smears of grime. He clutched against his chest his missing boot, and when she met his eyes, the crinkles at the edges amplified by the layer of soot on his skin, his teeth gleamed in a wide smile.

"What were you doing?" she demanded, her recent fear dissolving into unreasonable anger. She rose up on her shins as he approached the bed, leaving crisp black prints across her floor.

He reached her then and grasped her chin and jaw with his crusted hand, holding her face captive while he kissed her mouth. It felt like a necessary thing to life for her then, and perhaps it was for him too. As food to one dying from hunger. Then he pulled away and brought his fingers to splay against her collarbone, pushing her back playfully onto the mattress.

"What are you about?" She laughed now, leaning on her elbows.

"I have a gift for you, my queen." He grinned at her and then, with one swift movement, he seized a fold of the coverlet and whisked it from her body, leaving her nude before him. And then he brought up one knee, then the other, gaining the mattress at her feet.

"You'll ruin my bed!" she protested at the black stains he was grinding into the fabric covering, but it was only halfheartedly. He'd called her his queen. "Are you to paint me with soot so that I can be Man's consort?"

"Oh, I'm going to cover your beautiful body," he promised, as he held his old boot over her, the terrible, bloody stains now covered over and completely hidden by the filth from her chimney. The very idea that they could be erased forever gave her a sudden thrill of excitement.

And then Adrian turned the boot sole up, pouring a shower of gold onto her stomach.

Maisie gasped as the cold, tinkling coins slid over her skin and pooled at the seam of her body and the mattress beneath her. She sat up fully as the last coins bounced and rolled, grasping handfuls of them while Adrian threw the boot to the floor.

"Great gods," she breathed and then looked up at him, her fingers clutched around the pieces. "Is it . . . ?"

He nodded and fell to his hands on either side of her legs, crawling up until his face was even with hers. "Silly woman—don't you know? Dragons are guardians of gold."

She let the coins fall from her hand as her arms went around his shoulders, pulling him atop her back onto the mattress with a musical tinkle of the gold all around them.

* * *

Neither Maisie nor Adrian saw Dragon rise from the floor, her long tail swishing soundlessly just above the boards as she lumbered toward the door. They didn't see the creature dissolve beneath the crack at the bottom, her tail waving as it slid from the room.

Indeed, no one at all was witness to the sight of Dragon as she made her way slowly through the corridors and stairwells of Wyldonna Castle, working laboriously in her old age to reach a small, secret door too small for an occupant of appreciable height to have noticed before. Dragon made her way across the prickly winter grass, which would soon soften under spring's gentle winds. The feel of it on her belly was foreign, cold stone having been her cradle for hundreds of long, lonely years.

And yet the memory of it revived in her enough of an age long ago, when the world was covered in mountains and rivers, of trees that were taller than Wyldonna Castle, cathedral-like spires to the towering peaks from whence she was born. The time when she had claimed a true name and was not referred to by the simple description of her nature. A time when everything was magic, and there was nothing to guard but life itself. Life was the only treasure, love the only wealth. And death was naught but a future thing yet to be realized, many, many years away.

Dragon clambered over the rocky edge of the cliff, her old claws, stiff from disuse, only slipping twice. She reached the pinnacle of the island, Wyldonna Castle behind her, as the soft gray mist deepened to the color of smoke in a dream, the same color that drifted up from Dragon's nostrils as she lifted her long muzzle and smelled the sea air.

She crouched down and her spine arched, her scales trembling as she labored. Minute cracks appeared down the bony protuberances of her shoulders, like a statue that has been struck and is slowly shattering. The accumulated years crumbled and fell away with the quiet sound of pebbles rolling and bouncing down the cliff face, and her wings at last loosened.

She spread them wide and stretched out her body, raising her face to the sky. She smelled the air again, listened to it. In the wind she heard that, again, the only treasure was life, the only wealth of any value left to guard was love. That once unknowable future that had taken so many lonely seasons to arrive had come for her at last.

What had her name been? She could not recall. But perhaps the sleeping children she carried in her belly could tell her. Perhaps they would give her a new name, if she was only strong enough to find that safe place to awaken and bear them at last, somewhere in the new land beyond the mist. The magic was fading fast from this place, which had been her home for so very long. Soon it would be gone entirely.

She opened her jaws, and a long keening roar came from her, a sound of mourning but also of freedom.

Dragon crouched low once more and then sprang from the rock. Her wings flapped awkwardly for a moment, twisting her body in the air as she dipped, her tail whipping wildly for balance. She lurched and struggled with her wasted muscles, pulling at the wind, seeking the draft, her breath wheezing in her armored chest. Then the translucent skin between the ribs of her wings strained with the fullness of air, and she rose.

She climbed higher, pulling herself up on the current, rowing at the mist with her now elongated neck, paddling with her claws, running alongside the roiling clouds with the sweet sadness of her mission urging her up, up, up.

And then Dragon was gone.

Glayer Felsteppe paced the width of the ship's deck, pausing at each rail to glance at the Saracen who faced the bow. The dark man was holding a small square card of wood at the end of his outstretched arm, aimed at the nearly invisible horizon. A knotted string emanating from the center of the wooden square was caught between the man's teeth, and he turned minutely left, right; shifted his arm stiffly up, down.

It was taking too long. Why was he taking so long? The sky was clear this night, and the Saracen had already made use of a number of strange navigational tools and charts, over and over and over. The cold wind grabbed the hem of his cloak and thrust itself inside, prompting Glayer to snatch the opening more tightly around him with a growl. He began to pace once more.

At last the Saracen lowered his arm and began wrapping the string in a neat coil around the card.

"We are here," he said easily.

Glayer spun on his heel and strode to stand before him. "Are you certain? You must be certain."

"I am certain as anyone could be," the man said with an air of calm, one that Glayer himself could not claim. "It is difficult to navigate this far north. I am confident this is the approximate location to which you traveled at the year's end."

"*Approximate*," Glayer muttered as he turned to squint over the rails of the boat, bow, port, starboard. "I see nothing. Only water. Check your calculations again; if we are too far off course, we might not make shore on the morrow."

"I have checked enough," the man said with bold finality as he finished winding the string and tucked it into a fold of his long robes. Glayer might have been tempted to berate another for speaking to him so boldly, but he knew better than to test the Saracen. "If you do not believe me, you have only to look at your beast." The man's eyes flicked to the port rail.

Glayer's head turned to follow the man's gaze and, in truth, the long, sinewy Jagger seemed resigned, defeated, as he leaned his bowed and now bony spine against the railing. His clothing was little more than rags now, his feet bare, his unusually textured black hair matted and clumped around his head. The wide metal collar about the creature-man's neck—a very useful gift from the Saracen general at Glayer's side—had dug into his brown flesh when it was first put to use; now it sat on the bony protrusions of the thing's collarbones.

It was still a necessity, though. The creature-man was prone to strange fits. Disturbing, demonic displays that caused Glayer nightmares of long fangs and spotted, hairy hide. He'd had several crosses burned into the thing's flesh to no avail.

"Jagger!" Glayer demanded. The creature-man's head turned almost imperceptibly sideways, looking at him with large brown eyes whose deep hue was intensified by the startling brightness of the whites surrounding them. "Is the general correct? Have we arrived?"

"Why should I tell you anything?" the thing drawled in his strange accent. Glayer thought it similar to the Persians, but not exactly. His English was perfect, but his enunciation was gentle, as if the words became soft and rounded upon being spoken by those full brown lips. "You kept me locked in the ship rather than free me to my people as you promised to do when last I led you to Wyldonna."

"Surely you understand that I could not let you go when I had yet to return to collect my funds," Glayer explained easily. "Of course I will release you to your people—your *lover*," he emphasized, "once

your friend the queen has delivered to me what she has promised."
He walked across the deck to stand before the man and then crouched
down. He spoke quietly, gently. "You want that, don't you, Jagger? To
be returned to your little island of freaks? I'm certain it should be a
glorious reunion with your unnatural paramour, even with you as
wretched as you've become."

The man was looking down at his crossed ankles again, but he
nodded, and Glayer thought he heard a hitching breath, a choked sob
only just held in check.

"Now, now—don't start sniveling again. I'm only stating the obvious. If you could see yourself, I'm certain you'd agree." The creature's shoulders jerked once and Glayer rolled his eyes.

"Oh, I'm sure he shall be happy to see you any matter. Perhaps it's
not all so bad. I shan't tell him that you've been . . . unfaithful. I shan't,"
Glayer promised, using his most kindly tone. "Only confirm or deny to
me now that we are near to Wyldonna. Once we are landed, I will produce the key that's right here—" Glayer patted the secret compartment in his leather hauberk, over his heart—"and you shall be free to
scamper away to the woodland, as liberated and gay as dearest Pan,
taking with you my own heartfelt gratitude. *I promise.* Now, won't
that be delightful?"

"You should not have returned to Wyldonna," Jagger said quietly.

"What's that now?" Glayer chuckled. "Nonsense. You've obviously not been getting your rest. Now, have we arrived or nay?"

In the next instant, the creature-man's head flicked up, but his face
could no longer claim the flat, smooth cheekbones and wide proboscis
of his usual appearance. Instead, a hairy muzzle shot forward, long
fangs bared, and snapped only a whisper from Glayer's own pointed
noise, spittle and wiry whiskers flicking his cheeks.

Glayer fell back with a shout and then scrambled quickly to his feet,
his cloak tangling about his legs and hampering him for precious seconds. He stood panting, staring at the thing that appeared to be only a
man once more, although his brown throat bulged and pulsed over and
below the metal collar—witness to the wisdom of his incarceration.

Jagger could not change completely while so restrained.

Glayer felt the eyes of the ship's crew on him, as they had all ceased
in their duties at the sound of the imprisoned beast's snarl. His cheeks
burned with humiliation. He heard footsteps behind him, and then the
smooth, placating tones of the Saracen general.

"You have no need for this demon's confirmation. I tell you—at the rising of the sun, you will receive what you have come for."

Glayer wanted to believe the man. After all, had it not been he who had expedited the attack on Chastellet, he who had kept Glayer's identity secret all these years? He who had given the name of Constantine Gerard to Saladin himself as the betrayer of the Christian king of Jerusalem? If there was any man alive on the planet that Glayer Felsteppe could trust, it was General Abdal.

As if the general had read his mind, he said, "You must know that I, too, have ambitions to locate the men you seek. One man in particular, who has escaped me once and will not again. I vow it to God."

Glayer felt his own sneaky smile creep over his face. "It sounds as if someone is intent on revenge."

"Indeed," the general said with a nod. "I will find Ad—"

But his words were cut off by a sizzling in the air, and then cries of astonishment from the crew. The sky flashed, as if lightning had struck the water, and all aboard turned their faces to the stars.

A sound like stiff sails in the breeze shot the air just over their ship, and when Glayer looked up, he saw the black outline of an enormous bird against the starlit sky.

A bird with an impossibly wide body and a long arrow-tipped tail waving behind it like a sky-borne serpent.

"What in the bloody hell?" Glayer muttered to himself with a little shiver.

But then the creature-man, Jagger, lurched to his feet with a panicked jangle of chain, his already wide eyes appearing in danger of coming completely free of their sockets as his gaze tracked the bizarre bird. His head whipped back and forth.

"No," he moaned and began bouncing on the balls of his feet. "No, no." His throat bulged around the metal collar. "*Ray-gone,*" he seemed to say, but it was difficult to be certain, as his voice no longer held any of the gentle roundness of before.

"Oh dear," Glayer said, noticing a creak in his own voice. "That seems to have upset him greatly. I wonder, should we not also be concerned."

"Felsteppe," the Saracen general called, drawing Glayer's attention from the agitated Jagger. Abdal's eyes were trained once more over the bow. "Look."

Glayer blinked several times to be certain what he was seeing was real and not simply a product of his imagination. The dark outline of an island was so close to their ship that Glayer fancied he could have swum there had he the need to. An island boasting the silhouette of a tall slender castle, six spires seeming to point to the stars above.

"How—?" Glayer began, but decided he didn't quite know the question he was about to ask, let alone the answer. So he looked back to the Saracen, whose eyes were now scanning the empty sky above their ship, where the winged creature had flown and then disappeared into the night.

"I know not," the general muttered. Then he faced Glayer. "But I would advise that we proceed to shore. It is possible the island will not remain visible for long."

"Now?" Glayer clarified.

"Now." The Saracen's teeth gleamed in the night. "Everyone does love a surprise."

Chapter 19

Maisie paced the width of the hall while awaiting Adrian's return from the mountain. She trembled so that she had need to pause every dozen paces and steady herself with a chair back. On the table in the center of the floor, where the queen normally took her meals, sat a small wooden chest, into which she and Adrian had scooped the gold he'd retrieved from the secret chamber above her own.

They had won.

Maisie paused again, her fingers gripping the wood, her eyes closed. She had to fight against the weakness in her knees about what the Painted Man's victory might mean for her.

. . . who trades the death of the Queen . . .

Such an ominous stanza before, but now Maisie hoped—Adrian had found Wyldonna's treasure, and by ensuring that she could give Glayer Felsteppe what he demanded, was it possible that Maisie would not have to sacrifice herself for the island, or for Adrian's life?

Perhaps she could leave Wyldonna again, for good this time. Not to follow a naïve Wyldonian into a dangerous, foreign Outland but a man of brilliant intelligence, of noble birth, of honorable nature, who was returning to a land he knew well. A man of passion and wit, who could do nothing less than succeed in his crusade against Felsteppe. A man who had never been loved by a woman the way Maisie could love him.

The way Maisie did love him.

Once she was gone from the island, Malcolm could once more take the throne. She could never again live on Wyldonna, but that was her wish. And it was no less than she deserved for the chaos she had brought upon her brother and her own people.

The only question was: Would Adrian want her outside of the castle? She drew a deep breath and continued her pacing.

Maisie would ask him this night, before the equinox dawned on the morrow, and she must once more face that demon Felsteppe. She must know, for if he returned her gentle feelings, they would have need to leave before the sun set on that day, lest the fabric of the island be rent again, and further chaos ensue.

If he didn't want her . . .

Her hand shot out to steady herself once more.

She had composed herself by the time she heard the door slam shut, and Maisie dropped her hand to her side, a trembly smile coming over her lips as her eyes watched the doorway.

Malcolm came first, barreling through the opening in his typical blustery way, his boots stomping the stones. But Maisie could tell immediately by his pale face that Adrian had at least shared a hint of why she'd summoned him. Malcolm's eyes landed right away on the small wooden chest and he stopped in his approach. Adrian followed a bit more leisurely, his hair still blackened with soot, as were his chausses and boots, although he'd removed his ruined shirt before heading into the wood to fetch Maisie's brother.

If Maisie had her way in the future, he'd be without a shirt as often as could be arranged.

Malcolm raised his eyes from the trunk on the tabletop to look at Maisie, his expression one of astonishment. "He found it."

Her smile widened and she nodded. Her brother began walking once more toward the table, but this time his steps were cautious, almost hesitant, as if he feared the wooden box would disappear should he move too quickly. He reached out with both wide hands and gripped the edges of the chest, turning it toward him.

Maisie looked over her brother's bent head at Adrian, and found that he was watching her intently, his painted arms crossed over his chest, his dark hair brushing his shoulders. It was as if he was studying her, the way he had studied Wyldonna's book. There was no longer any hint of the scarred, damaged man she'd brought to the island weeks ago. No, this man was strong and whole and powerful and perfect.

Her smile gentled for Adrian, but he did not return it, and that caused Maisie's stomach to tumble about in a panic. She looked quickly to Malcolm, who had now opened the lid of the chest and was staring with wide eyes at contents that came halfway up the wooden sides. Adrian had told her the amount in the trunk alone was enough to purchase a small city.

Malcolm raised his face to look at her. "There's more?" he asked her in a hushed tone.

"A hundred fold," Maisie said. "A thousand."

"A hundred thousand," Adrian said, dropping his arms and walking closer to the table. "It would take days to exhaust the chamber I found." His wry grin flashed and Maisie's heart clenched at the sweetness of it. "Especially considering the means of ingress and egress."

Malcolm left the lid of the chest standing open as he took two long steps toward Maisie and pulled her into his embrace.

"You're safe now, Maisie," he said into her hair. "Thanks be to the gods—you're safe. I never wished ill upon you. Never. I swear it."

"I know," she said against his shoulder, squeezing her eyes against the tears that threatened. She mustn't start crying now; she mightn't stop for some time. "I am so sorry for leaving the way I did. So sorry for what I caused. The shame I must have brought you. I tried my best to remedy it."

"Aye," Malcolm said, pulling back from her and smiling through his beard. "You brought the remedy, you did." Then his arms left her as he turned to face Adrian, and in moments, the Painted Man was gifted with a hearty embrace from the man who was at one time king of that magic place, and who—Maisie hoped—would be once more very soon.

"I thank you, Hailsworth," Malcolm said gruffly. He broke the embrace and held out his right hand, which Adrian took readily. "You have saved my sister's life. You have saved my people from war. You will always be welcomed on Wyldonna, for as long as you shall live."

"I am honored by your graciousness," Adrian replied, and Maisie's heart swelled with pride for the man he was. "But I doubt that I shall ever have need to visit such a place that so threatens to destroy my many years of dedicated learning."

A cold weight seemed to fall into Maisie's stomach, but she had no time to deconstruct Adrian's meaning.

Malcolm threw back his head and laughed. "Canna have the truth interfering with your *knowledge* now, can we, lad?"

Adrian grinned. "'Twould be a shameful waste of my father's money, I fear."

"Be that as it may, you are welcome here." Malcolm clapped Adrian's shoulder before turning back to the chest and picking up a slight handful of coins to study in his palm. "Perhaps once you've put an end to your own business with Felsteppe. I canna fathom the origins of these coins. Lad?"

Adrian stepped to Malcolm's side then, and Maisie felt as if both men had completely forgotten she was in the room as they discussed the imprint and strike marks of the coins and volleyed theories between themselves.

"I regret that my studies have touched little upon nomisma. Sumerian, perhaps? Or later—from Rome?"

"Much older than the time of your Christ, I'd wager me beard, lad."

"He's not *my* Christ. Definitely from the Mediterranean region, though."

Adrian wished to never return to Wyldonna?

Did he also never want any reminders of his time here? Of her? Perhaps what they had shared together had truly been nothing more than physical recreation for Adrian. Exercise of a sort, to heal his wounded courage.

No. No, he wasn't that shallow. He couldn't be. She had seen his struggle in the Damascene dungeon. His honor ran deep in his heart, like the bloodstains on the old boots he'd forced himself to keep. Even after escaping that certain death, he had come all this way, risked his life again, to avenge the betrayal of not only his friends but of men he hadn't even known. Adrian Hailsworth fought for truth, for right. Maisie couldn't love him so otherwise.

"But what about me?" Maisie interjected into the men's scholarly conversation.

Both their heads came up at once, looking at her curiously.

She swallowed. "What are we to do?" She looked from Malcolm to Adrian, and her mouth quirked in a nervous smile as she twisted her fingers in the folds of her skirts. "About . . . about me, now?"

Adrian's gaze grew intense, wary, but Malcolm's eyes crinkled above his beard.

"You shall give the bastard what he asked for," her brother said, motioning with his handful of coins. "This and nae more. It shall keep your word."

"Aye. But then what?" Maisie pressed, glancing only briefly at Adrian. He had said nothing, and her anxiety grew.

Malcolm looked nonplussed. "I wager you'll do as you like. You always have." There was a hint of resentment in his words. "You are still the queen, after all."

"I doona want to be queen, Malcolm," she said. "I never wanted any of this."

His bushy brows lowered. "Mayhap you should have thought of that before you took the throne."

"Maisie did what she felt she must," Adrian said at last. "She's sought to undo the harm she caused and save the island folk from war." He looked between the brother and sister. "From where we now stand, I would say she was successful."

"Aye," Malcolm allowed, some of the fight going out of him. "But there is naught that can be done to indulge her change of heart. She successfully took the throne from me. She is queen, and that canna be undone while she still resides on the island."

"That's it, though," she said. She drew a deep breath. "I doona wish to remain on Wyldonna."

Malcolm was quiet for a moment, considering her with a grave expression. "Have you learned naught, lass, from when you left us the first time?"

"It wouldna be the same," Maisie argued. "If I leave on the morrow, on the equinox, the throne can be rightfully returned to you."

"But you couldna come back," he said quietly.

Maisie tried to give him a smile. "I could. To visit."

"You could never make a home here again."

Her smile grew wistful. "I canna make a home here now, Malcolm. The folk hate me."

Malcolm looked back down at the gold in his hand, bounced the coins a few times. "They doona hate you." His eyes raised to hers again. "You well know how dangerous the Outland is now. Where would you go?"

Maisie looked to Adrian at last. "With him."

Adrian's expression did not change. He only stared into her eyes.

Malcolm, however, seemed scandalized by her request. "With the Painted Man?" he exclaimed. "Maisie, you canna simply attach yourself to a stranger because you believe he might help you. Has he nae done enough already?" He turned to Adrian. "I apologize, Hailsworth. I doted on her, and she oft behaves like an indulged child."

"I'm not a stranger to her, Malcolm," Adrian said, but his eyes never left Maisie. "And Maighread is no more a child than are you."

It was quiet in the hall, the heavy thudding of her own heart the only sounds in Maisie's ears.

"Ah. I see," Malcolm said quietly at last.

Adrian's jaw flinched.

Maisie lifted her chin a fraction. She felt as if she stood naked before him again, but now she felt vulnerable, unsure.

"I must give chase to Felsteppe once he leaves the island," Adrian said. "You know that."

"I'll go with you," Maisie said, her worst nightmare rushing up behind her, and yet she struggled to outrun it. "We shall follow him together. Away from Wyldonna, I can do things, Adrian. You saw it yourself on the crawler. There is nae place Felsteppe could hide. We could—"

But Adrian was already shaking his head, and Maisie felt her heart shatter like ice dropped onto stone.

Malcolm cleared his throat, tossed the coins back in the chest. "I'll leave you to your privacy," he said and began to turn away.

Thunderous, running footfalls interrupted the king's departure as Reid lumbered into the rear of the hall. A gaggle of squealing elf maids burst from the doorway behind him like startled birds, swooping around the giant and reuniting to fly down the main aisle.

Reid's usually robust complexion had deepened to the color of seaweed washed up on the rocks, his eyes wild, his cheeks wet.

"Dragon," he choked, and his gaze went to Maisie as he swayed on his feet. "My queen—*Dragon is gone.*"

"Gone?" Maisie repeated. "What do you mean? I left her in my chamber." Maisie looked to Adrian.

He was shaking his head again, and Maisie had the urge to slap his face. "I didn't see her when we left."

The maids reached them, then, and fell into a low bow before Malcolm.

"My king," the boldest sighed. "Thank the gods! Have you been restored?"

"Nae," Malcolm said irritably. "Maighread is your queen, and your queen she shall stay."

The group fretted amongst themselves while the bold one turned to Maisie. "Then we are taking ourselves back to the village. The equinox is nigh, and the queen canna protect us." Without waiting for reply, the elf maid turned and herded her wards toward the vestibule.

A crash echoed in the hall, and Maisie enjoined her gaze with the men's as they turned to see Reid collapsing onto a tabletop, his enormous head on his forearms.

"*Dragon,*" he wailed.

Adrian turned back to regard Maisie. "I cannot imagine his upset is due solely to sentiment. What does it mean? If Dragon is gone?"

Her lips were numb, her throat constricted so that she wondered if she would be able to answer him. "If she has left the island," she choked, "it means that Wyldonna is nae longer safe. The enchantment would have been broken when she passed through. It is well that the treasure has been found, for we now might nae have the luxury of waiting for the dawn."

"Why?" Adrian pressed. "She didn't protect the island."

"Nae, lad," Malcolm said, pulling out a chair and sitting heavily. "That wasna her purpose. She protected the treasure, which doesna need protecting any longer."

Maisie heard the elfin maidens' faint screams of fright coming from the direction of the castle's entrance and she spun to face the front of the hall. The maids came flying back through the room along a far wall and disappeared into a doorway that led deeper into the castle. Maisie hoped she was wrong about what had turned them from their intention of escaping to the village.

But she didn't think she was.

"Adrian," she said, with a measure of calm that she certainly did not feel, "go at once to my chamber. Stay there until Malcolm or I come for you, whatever happens."

"I can't do that," he insisted in his maddeningly logical tone. "Malcolm and I still have need to ready the engines. I daresay we cannot be too careful. If we go now—"

"It's too late, lad," Malcolm said quietly, even as the sounds of scores of boots on the stones rebounded overhead. "The best we can do now is pray."

Adrian gave a snort of laughter. "Pray? Malcolm, I thought better of yo—"

Then Adrian fell silent as the redheaded man strolled through the doorway of the hall, pulling his gauntlets off in a leisurely manner. He was followed by what appeared to be two very different crews of men, some in the chausses and tunics of English soldiers and some wearing the long robes and head scarves of the Holy Land.

At his elbow strode a tall dark man with luxurious robes and ornate weaponry hanging from his belts.

"Blessed Ostara!" Glayer Felsteppe called out jovially, his arms spread wide. He halted at the end of the table and bowed. "Queen Maighread, how pleased I am to see you again. I would apologize for my early arrival, but I see that I underestimated your resourcefulness." He grinned his terrible, ugly smile at the open chest on the table and then turned it on Maisie. "You knew the moment I arrived, did you not, my beauty?"

Adrian felt the blood quickly leaving his head, and for a moment he wondered whether he might faint. It was not the sight of Glayer Felsteppe that shook him so but the presence of the man at Felsteppe's side.

Adrian's sword held before him in a two-handed grip as the brown face rushed at him, its mouth twisted in a battle cry. The curved scimitar rising, rising . . .

One swing.

The whine and slap of a beaded whip . . .

The thin leather strips, wound round and round his arms . . .

You are not dead. I am impressed, infidel . . .

Wet slime, crawling with maggots . . .

I have great plans for your conversion, indeed . . .

"I keep my promises."

Maisie's voice shook him from his nightmarish memories, and the strength of her words reminded Adrian that he was no longer a prisoner. No longer at the mercy of an army of foreign soldiers.

Adrian's hands clenched into fists.

"I never doubted you for a moment." Felsteppe smiled at her. Then he lifted a finger and motioned toward the chest, speaking over his shoulder. "Fetch the trunk."

"Wait," Malcolm called out as he rose from his chair, knocking the wooden lid closed and then turning to face Felsteppe. "I want your word: By accepting this coin, you shall never return here. Never to send any in your stead. You forget Wyldonna exists."

Felsteppe cocked his head and gave a contrived expression of confusion. "And who are you again? Not the king, I'd wager. He was *deposed*, as I understood it. And I don't take orders from the *peasantry*."

A roar sounded from the back of the hall as Reid gained his feet. He flipped the table he had recently been languishing on up into the air, and it crashed into splinters under his massive boots even as he tromped through the debris toward the group of soldiers. He drew his arms along his sides and leaned down, stretching out his neck like an attacking goose, although his warning was considerably more terrifying. He roared into the faces of the men so that their hair blew back and they swayed as if caught in a gale. Those not already armed scrambled to free their weapons from their sheaths.

If Adrian had learned anything, it was that giants valued courtesy.

His warning cry at his breath's end, Reid took yet another menacing stomp toward the group, and the stones beneath Adrian's feet trembled.

"Hold your ground!" Felsteppe commanded the men behind him, although his face blanched white. "He cannot harm us!"

"*You will not speak to my king in such a manner!*"

Felsteppe leaned forward, his head like a grape compared to Reid's wide visage. "He is not your king any longer. Move, mutant."

"He doesna recognize you," Maisie said to Adrian under her breath. "Draw nae attention." And then she stepped forward, placing herself between Adrian and the man of his worst nightmares.

Maisie was right. When last Felsteppe and Adrian had met, Adrian had been clean-shaven, the sides and back of his head shorn in response to the sweltering Syrian clime. He'd been well-fed, his clothes fine, although he'd never paid his costumes much mind. Adrian had remained largely aloof to all the fighting men save for Constantine, and all other tasks save Chastellet's completion.

Now Adrian stood in the hall of a castle that, by all logic, should not exist. His hair was long, wild, his face disguised by his beard. He was only half-clothed, and the skin that was exposed was covered with Song's swirling magic and the lean muscles carved by three years of cloister and anxiety. The gentleman of Chastellet was dead now. Here stood a different man.

But that man was without any weapon at all.

"Malcolm is nae longer king," Maisie said, "but I am queen, and you will show respect to my brother and my manservant."

Felsteppe looked Maisie up and down appreciatively, and Adrian wanted to strangle him with his bare hands.

"My most sincere apologies, Maighread." He smirked. "You have indeed been most accommodating. But alas—you have not done what I most hoped for. Where are the men I seek?"

"Here is your treasure," Maisie insisted. "All that I can lay hand to. Take it and go. My command is as my brother's: Doona return to Wyldonna."

Felsteppe motioned toward the chest again, this time turning toward the Saracen. "Would you mind, General Abdal?" He looked to Maisie as the dark man stepped forward to seize the heavy chest. "Yes, about that. I've had a thought. It seems to me that my silence is worth more than such a small bit of coin. It's likely not even pure gold."

"We had a bargain," Maisie ground out.

"Hmm," Felsteppe whined skeptically.

The Saracen grasped the handles on the ends of the trunk and straightened, and as he did, his eyes met Adrian's. The man froze, staring.

Adrian stared back. He found he could look nowhere else other than into those eyes he had seem so many times in his nightmares.

"You see, I really do need to locate them," Felsteppe argued. "It's as if they've disappeared from the face of the earth, and I know of only one woman—one beautiful, beautiful woman—who might help me find them."

"I canna," Maisie said. "And I willna."

"Which is it?" Felsteppe asked.

The Saracen gave a bemused smile. "I am interested to know," he called out, interrupting Maisie's answer, "who is this creature with the strangely painted skin."

Maisie spun on her heel, and Adrian clearly saw the way she looked at his face, the horror that dawned there as she understood who the man in the long robes was.

Could she see into his mind as well?

"He is my lover," she said dismissively. "From the village." Her eyes bored into Adrian's. "You may go."

Adrian's feet remained planted on the stones, even as the Saracen—Abdal, was it?—protested gently.

"No, no," Abdal said, setting the chest back on the table and stepping closer to Adrian, the black eyes he remembered so well searching his face. "I feel as if I know you. I do. I know you." He stopped only one pace from Adrian. "Speak, beast."

"You doona command my people!" Maisie shouted.

But Adrian could no longer remain quiet.

"I am no beast," he said softly, clearly. "I am a scholar."

Chapter 20

Maisie didn't hear Adrian's response to the Saracen general, but whatever he said was not well received.

The robed man's hand whipped up from his belt and then slashed through the air, a curved blade rushing in a downward arc aimed at Adrian's chest. Maisie screamed and lunged toward the Saracen, but Malcolm grasped both her arms from behind and held her firm.

"You canna, lass," her brother warned.

Adrian threw up a forearm in a blur of motion, blocking the blade, and then brought his other hand up to join the first in grasping the underside of the Saracen's arm and twisting. In a blink, the man's robes billowed around him as he was yanked from his feet and tossed onto the stones on his back. Adrian advanced, readying himself to stomp the man's outstretched arm still holding the blade, but the Saracen gathered himself quickly, rolling away before Adrian could reach him and gaining his feet once more.

"Abdal!" Glayer Felsteppe shouted from behind Maisie, his reedy voice betraying his alarm. "Stop! If you attack them, they can then retaliate!"

Maisie watched as Abdal circled Adrian warily. The Saracen held his hands aloft, the blade gleaming dully in the torchlight of the hall. But Adrian only turned calmly, his arms relaxed at his sides.

"Have no fear, General," Abdal called out almost happily. "None shall raise a weapon against us for this one's sake; he is not of their kind. Indeed, the queen has served us both well."

"What *are* you talking about?" Glayer cried.

Abdal lunged again, but Adrian leapt back to avoid the blow, coming to his balance in an instant and sweeping his leg in an arc at the Saracen's knee. The attack met, but only briefly, as Abdal lifted the leg Adrian had targeted and kicked out. The kick glanced off the left side of Adrian's ribs, causing him to clutch at his side and stumble back. But as the Saracen advanced, Adrian straightened, ready once more.

"You are more lively than when last we met," Abdal observed with a wicked grin.

Adrian did not return his smile. "A man tends to fight back against his attackers when he has the use of his arms and legs."

"This is true," Abdal acknowledged, thrusting with the blade quickly, but it was little more than a feint. "Which is why we prefer our infidels bound. They are infinitely more persuadable." He thrust again, this time closer.

Adrian took a leveraging step forward and reached out boldly to grasp Abdal's blade arm. With one swift rise of his knee, the Saracen's forearm snapped audibly, and the dagger clattered to the floor as the general cried out in pain. Adrian kicked it to the shadows beneath a table and stepped away once more, his arms again relaxed at his sides, his gaze steady.

The Saracen panted, holding his arm close to his abdomen. "You have just added to your debt, infidel."

"I am giving you opportunity to leave this island with your life," Adrian said slowly, and his voice was such that Maisie had never heard it before. Gravelly, low, threatening—he could have been kin to Reid. "What you did to me in Damascus you did in the madness of grief, the sick duty of war."

"Damascus?" Felsteppe squawked.

Adrian ignored him. "But you have aligned yourself with a devil, and I cannot allow you to further aid him."

"*You killed my son,*" Abdal ground out, his earlier facetiousness vanished. "My only son! I saw the moment when your sword met his neck!"

"I was preserving my own life," Adrian said. "I cannot return your son to you. But I can let you live."

"Hailsworth?" Glayer ventured hesitantly.

The Saracen roared at Adrian, and Maisie saw the mad tears in the man's eyes. "*It is you who shall not live!* I will command you unto the very moment of your death, and then you shall endure the torture of my vengeance for all eternity!"

Felsteppe seemed to startle, as if awoken from a daydream. So shaken was he that his words tripped over themselves as he stabbed his bony finger toward Adrian. "S-s-seize! S-seize . . . k-k-kill h-h-him!"

Two of the English soldiers came around Felsteppe's back, their swords at the ready.

"Adrian!" Maisie called out, straining against Malcolm's firm hold. "Behind you!"

Adrian glanced over his shoulder and saw the men approaching him. He sidled to the left, keeping the Saracen in his sight as he readied for Felsteppe's soldiers to attack.

"Malcolm," Maisie pleaded. "They'll kill him!"

"By all means, Queen Maighread," Glayer said, his words breathy and full of anxiety, "make your best move. I have six ships waiting in your bay, all full of trained warriors who are eager to storm your pathetic shore upon my signal."

Maisie felt Malcolm tense behind her. Six ships. How many men did they hold? Two hundred? Three? Even if Wyldonna's folk could hold the shore and force the ships to turn back, at what cost of life? How many good folk would die?

The soldiers raised their swords and began moving away from one another to surround Adrian, who looked at them calmly.

"*Kill him!*" Glayer Felsteppe insisted.

"No!" Abdal shouted. "I never finished with him, and he suffers so well." He looked toward the group of soldiers standing now to either side of Felsteppe and gave orders in a strange language, his good hand going to the numerous thin leather belts about his waist. "He will leave the island with us."

Maisie thought Adrian must have understood what the Saracen said, though, for the color drained from his face. Two robed warriors approached Adrian, and one reached a hand into the air to catch the tangle of leather tossed to him by Abdal.

"Perhaps my men can find the grooves left by my belts, eh?" Abdal taunted. "I am certain there is still some trace left, no matter how much you have tried to erase my marks from your body. I own you, infidel."

Adrian did not move as the dark-skinned soldiers walked around the Englishmen holding him at swords' point. He would not meet Maisie's eyes, keeping his gaze pinned to Glayer Felsteppe, who was all but chortling with glee.

"Adrian," Maisie choked as one of the Saracens reached out to pull Adrian's arms behind his body. She recalled the glimpse of his nightmare, the way he had been so cruelly restrained for weeks.

Adrian's eyes closed, as if he, too, were seeing the sandstone dungeon again.

"Malcolm," she pleaded again, twisting her head to look at her brother.

"Shh, lass," Malcolm hushed, his eyes still locked on the scene before them. "The Painted Man would nae give up so easily, now would he?"

When Maisie brought her gaze back to Adrian, his head had bowed as if in defeat. But then she realized the faint glow about him—a rippling, expanding halo of first red, then gold, then a bright, pure white—hugging precisely the outline of his body.

"It looks like . . ." Maisie swallowed, not knowing how Adrian was conjuring energy such as she had shown him on that first day in the turret room.

"Everyone is magic, Maisie," Malcolm whispered in her ear. "And none save us can see it."

And then, as the other Saracen touched the first leather strap to Adrian's skin, Adrian raised his head, and his eyes were like glittering black stones.

He whipped around, dragging the soldier still holding his arms with him. The English soldier lunged with his sword, and Adrian jumped backward, pushing the Saracen onto the blade and using the leverage of his skewered body to lift both feet and kick away the other robed man holding the leather ties. He twisted away, landing on his feet with a spin and sending out his forearm into the other English soldier's throat, grabbing the hilt of the sword and wresting it free. He plunged it through the ribs of the man, withdrew it, and swung in a wide arc behind him, severing the hand of the Saracen who had gained his feet and had been flying at him with a dagger.

Another backhanded swing found its target in the abdomen of the first English soldier, who had only now freed his weapon from the Saracen's body.

"Kill him!" Glayer Felsteppe cried out to the men behind him, prompting three more English soldiers to rush forward.

Adrian set his stance as the men ran at him. Maisie watched him bring his weapon low before him, gripping the hilt with both hands.

His tattooed skin gleamed in the torchlight, his eyes glittering like ebon treasure as he waited, waited.

Beware the Painted Man, my child . . .

With a terrifying battle cry, Adrian swung the broadsword, once, twice, and then paused as the two helmed heads thudded to the stones and wobbled there, and the third soldier skidded to a halt with a strangled cry. His boots slipped in the blood spraying across the floor from ragged necks as he sought retreat, causing him to crash to his hip. He skittered away like a crab before gaining his feet again and running from the hall.

Malcolm was no longer restraining Maisie now but only holding her hand tightly in his own. The thick, sweet stench of blood stuffed Maisie's nostrils and she raised a hand to cover her nose.

Adrian stood facing Felsteppe and the Saracen general, who had skirted the hall to rejoin the safety of the unit with which they'd arrived. There had once been a score of men; now their number was nearly halved.

"Come, then," Adrian invited. "You wanted me—here I stand. *I crave more cowards' blood upon my steel!*" he finished in a stone-shaking roar.

"I must go," Malcolm whispered in her ear. "The soldier who escaped—he will surely give the word that their men are being attacked. I canna let them take the shore."

Maisie glanced at him nervously. "Be careful, Malcolm."

Her brother squeezed her hand briefly and then slid away, stepping back into the shadows and then, in a blink, Malcolm had disappeared.

"Hailsworth, you cannot hope to prevail against a dozen men," Felsteppe reasoned in a strangled voice. "Surrender to me now and save yourself an agonizing death. I mean to do nothing more than release you to the governing authority of the Crown."

"I needn't prevail against a dozen men," Adrian growled. "Only the pair of them that I shall first reach." He took a single step toward them. "For I find I've no intention of releasing either of you to any authority save my own. And that means *you will die.*"

"What in the bloody hell is happening?" Glayer exclaimed, throwing out his hands and looking around wildly. "When last we met, you were little more than a bookish, mealy scribe! And now you presume Zeus!"

"He is no mere scribe," Abdal said, relieving one of the Saracen soldiers at his side of a long thin dagger. Then Abdal, too, took a step toward Adrian, brandishing the weapon in his weaker left hand.

"He is a scholar." Abdal braced his feet and nodded to Adrian. "You are not the man I captured at Chastellet."

"You are right. But I am no longer just a scholar, Abdal—on Wyldonna, I am the Painted Man. And I am to be feared."

The Saracen's throat convulsed. "Then perhaps you should thank me for allowing you to achieve such potential. It is clear to me that you will not so easily be captured again, but I cannot leave this place while one of us still lives. We should not haunt each other's dreams any longer. Let us end this now."

"Very well," Adrian agreed, dropping once more into his ready stance, the sword held vertically before him. "At your move."

The Saracen glanced up and muttered a high stream of unintelligible words before giving forth a loud cry and charging toward Adrian.

For one terrible, eternal instant, Maisie thought Adrian was not going to move. He stood in the hall as if he was nothing more than a statue as the dark-skinned soldier raised his dagger, running, running. Another pair of steps would bring him close enough to take Adrian's life.

But then Adrian released his two-handed grip and swiftly lowered the sword with his right hand, turning sideways to brace himself and holding its full length before him.

Maisie saw the Saracen become aware of the move.

And still, General Abdal ran full upon the blade with a cry that sounded almost triumphant.

Glayer Felsteppe cried out at the horror of his most valuable ally's gristly end as Adrian let his fingers open wide, dropping the sword and the skewered body of the general to the floor.

Maisie's eyes filled with tears as she watched Adrian stare down at the man, as if he could not believe that his nightmare was over. There was a cold, hollow ache in her stomach at the gravity of death in her hall; never had she been witness to such carnage, and this at the hand of the man she had loved with her body, her heart. What had it done to him, to his soul?

Perhaps he was not capable of loving her.

Then Reid stepped to her side and his deep voice rang out with an ominous warning. "I invite you to avail yourself of my queen's generosity by taking what you came for and removing yourself from the hall. I will allow you the courtesy of collecting your dead first, if you wish."

"This man," Felsteppe said to Maisie, pointing to Adrian, who had yet to look up, "is wanted by the Crown. If I return with word that Wyldonna is harboring one of the traitors of Chastellet, your little island of freaks will know no peace."

Maisie let her lips curve in a cold smile. "Perhaps at first. But what think you will be the outcome when the queen of this little island, her brother, her servants—all the folk who live here—reveal that this man—" she also pointed at Adrian—"was never a traitor? That the king's so-called loyal man Felsteppe has been in league with Saladin's army since Chastellet, and indeed, on his death, General Abdal confessed that it was you who orchestrated the siege of Chastellet? Hmm?" Maisie cocked her head. "What would your Baldwin do for you then, I wonder?"

"Abdal said no such thing!" Felsteppe protested.

"Then it shall be your word against mine," Maisie presented calmly. "For Abdal is clearly dead. I am willing to take my chance. Are you?"

"I will not have him so close at hand only to leave him behind!" Felsteppe shrieked hysterically. "He will tell me where the rest of them are hiding!"

"Take your coin and be gone," Maisie commanded. "My patience is quickly fading, and I do wonder how encouraged the men in yonder boats would be to make war on such a strange place as Wyldonna when their leader and financier is dead."

"I have yet twelve armed men to defend me!"

"And I have a giant ready to stomp you all like grapes, and a man who has already killed seven of your defenders. I am not afraid of you, Felsteppe."

"You would not risk it," Glayer taunted.

Adrian at last stepped to her side and she looked up at him, laying her palm along the side of his shoulder. His face was stony, but he brought up a hand to cover hers.

"I would," he said to Felsteppe.

On Maisie's other side, Reid gave his answer by raising one foot and slamming it down on the stones so that the very floor shook.

Felsteppe's throat convulsed as he swallowed and glanced nervously at Reid. "As I see it, we are at an impasse. I need that coin to pay the men who have accompanied me. But if I or any of my men come near, Hailsworth will strike us dead, true?"

Adrian nodded once. He squeezed Maisie's hand and then let his arm fall.

"If you will leave at once, I will bring it to you," Maisie said and stepped toward the chest.

"No, no!" Felsteppe said quickly, holding out a palm. "You might use the proximity to touch me and turn me into some beast, you hoary sorceress. I saw your charms once."

"What you saw were the simple tricks of a young, foolish girl. I am queen now, and therefore I canna use magic," she assured him. "But if I could, any beast would be a vast improvement to your present character, I assure you."

"You can't use magic?" he said, looking at her sideways. "At all?"

Maisie shook her head. "I would suffer the same effects as any whom I used it against."

"Maisie," Adrian warned in a low voice. "Don't."

Felsteppe sheathed his sword. "Very well. If you deliver it, all my men and I shall leave the castle at once."

"I'll follow you," Adrian warned. "I'll never let you rest."

Felsteppe gave him a queer smile as Maisie once more stepped to the chest and lifted it with great effort.

"I expect no less," the red-haired man assured him.

She reached him then, and Felsteppe's hands came up. But instead of taking hold of the leather handles, he reached for Maisie's curly mane, jerking her head back painfully and yanking her to him while his right hand produced a dagger from his tunic.

The chest crashed to the floor and spilled a tinkling wash of gold over the stones as the cold blade touched the thin skin over her windpipe. Maisie heard the soldiers behind Felsteppe fall on the coins, scraping them from the floor.

"I'm not hurting her! I'm not hurting her!" Felsteppe screamed at Reid as he dragged Maisie back several steps. "And I shan't harm her so long as Hailsworth agrees to accompany me away from this island. I told you: I will not have him so close at hand without capture. And I will not be forced to look over my shoulder the whole of the return to England *to damn this entire bloody place to the king!*"

Tears spring into Maisie's eyes as scores of hairs were pulled from her scalp, and Glayer mercilessly jerked her head back farther. She felt the bones in her neck grinding together and she couldn't swallow. All she could see was the ceiling of the hall. He was walking her backward toward the vestibule.

"Release the queen!" Reid roared.

Adrian must have advanced, for Glayer warned, "Stay away, Hailsworth! Stay away until I am safely aboard else I will slit her throat—I swear it!" Then he commanded, "Hurry up, you clumsy idiots! Hurry!"

"Adrian!" Maisie screamed, the sharp angle of her neck causing her words to scrape like rusty blades against her straining throat. "Doona follow us! He will kill you!"

Felsteppe jerked her head sharply even farther and growled into her ear. *"Shut up, bitch."*

Maisie heard the scrape of wood against stone, the loud crash of coins being jostled about the inside of the chest, and then the tromping of the soldiers' boots as they rallied around their despicable leader.

"Raise your shields; form a barricade," Felsteppe gasped as they passed out of the darkness of the vestibule.

Then Maisie's eyes saw not the black, shadowed planks of the castle's ceiling but the wide-open sky of night. Instead of the inky darkness of the hour before dawn, a faint, sparkling glow emanated from the wood as Felsteppe dragged her toward the trees.

"Now we shall see, lovely Maighread," he growled into her ear, "if your people care as little for your life as I."

Chapter 21

The treetops seemed aflame as Adrian and Reid ran from the hall and into the castle yard. They both stopped and Adrian looked up at the sparkling lights.

"What is it?" he asked.

"Faeries," Reid answered gravely. "They're watching. The king must be ready."

They marched toward the path that curved away from the village directly to the shore—the same trail on which Adrian had followed Maisie Lindsey and gained his first glimpse of Wyldonna Castle. Adrian led the way into the shimmering forest. He was still shaking inside from the massacre that had just taken place in the castle hall. His muscles trembled and his arms were splattered with blood. And Glayer Felsteppe had taken Maisie from beneath Adrian's very hand.

Adrian looked up again at the glowing balls of light in the branches and saw tiny winged creatures, sparkling like gentle stars. Their faces were so small and their glow so hazy that he could not make out their features. He was bolstered by their watchful presence all the same.

"The folk will surely come to her rescue once they see that she is held hostage," Adrian declared, as if he was trying to convince the giant crashing down the path behind him instead of himself. "The trolls, the elves, the duvenets . . ."

"Nay, Man."

"She is their queen," Adrian insisted angrily.

"She left them," Reid replied.

Adrian stopped and turned on the path, challenging the giant. "She is trying to save the island from war!"

Reid looked down and his expression was sad, resigned. "I know this, Man. But Wyldonna's ways are not your ways. You do not understand."

"I understand that this woman has risked her life out of duty and loyalty to an ungrateful lot of entitled bastards who feel as if they've the right to control her."

"I love her, too, Man," Reid said, his voice rough with emotion. "I've known her since she and the king were babes. And I understand why she left. It is why I remained to serve her. But leaving Wyldonna is seen as a rejection of all that we are—all that Maighread is. The folk will not protect her because she discarded her birthright. Her magic."

"That is *bollocks*," Adrian said with a stab of his finger at the giant. He turned around and began walking again. "And well you know it, Reid."

"Forgive me, but I don't recall stating that it wasn't bollocks." He crashed brush behind Adrian once more. "What are you going to do, Man, if I may be so bold as to ask of your plan?"

Adrian continued down the path as he considered Reid's question. Maisie had said she wanted to leave the island with him. Why? Was it because she liked making love with him? Because she was desperate to be away from the island any matter and he was convenient? It wasn't as if she was accustomed to a normal life on Wyldonna, so the secrecy, the covertness of movement necessitated by the accusations leveled against Adrian and his friends likely wouldn't faze her at all. Even being cloistered at Melk would probably seem a great freedom to her.

For all Adrian knew, Maisie only wanted someone to help her once more attempt to get her bearings in the Outland, be her crutch until she had settled herself somewhere in an inconspicuous life, and then she would likely set him free. She'd offered to help him apprehend Felsteppe—perhaps as payment for him assisting her in being away from Wyldonna?

But Adrian couldn't fulfill that request. He didn't want payment for taking Maisie away with him. He didn't want to feel as if they were doing each other favors any longer, making good on promises just until each of them achieved the ends to which they set out. He didn't only want her body, her strange magic. He wanted *her*. All of her.

Adrian had been resigned to the idea that he would die in Saladin's prison. And yet, somehow, he had lived. Perhaps he had been given strength by a God as yet unknown, unfounded, unexplored by him. Regardless of the how of it, he had lived to become entangled with the three other men who made up the Brotherhood of the Fallen Angels Abbey. Yes, it was appropriate that they should be called brothers. Roman had freed them, carried Adrian's body; Valentine had shown him great compassion and produced the means of asylum for them all; Constantine had led them, had encouraged Adrian to live, even as he was being thrust into his own black hell.

Had Adrian not sacrificed himself to come here for Constantine, for Roman, even for Valentine and his new bride, even if it had at first been under the guise of saving face? He'd had no idea he would place himself in such danger by accepting this unbelievable mission, but even if he'd known, he would have come if it meant sparing his friends.

Indeed, it had been nothing short of a miraculous chain of events that had allowed Maisie Lindsey to find *him*, Adrian, the only man who had been able to solve her riddle. The Painted Man, whose coming had been foretold centuries before either of them had been born. He had come to Wyldonna full of his own foolish pride, only to be frustrated and stupefied and shocked by how much he simply did not know. Things Adrian had yet to discover and study. Things such as giant men, talking cats, children with pointed ears.

And love.

> *Beware the Painted Man, my child,*
> *Who trades the death of the Queen.*

Maisie Lindsey had taught him that love wasn't always reciprocated. Loving someone—a brother, a people, a ruler, a place—did not guarantee that your feelings would be nurtured or returned. Indeed, sometimes love meant doing what you must, what you were born to do, even knowing that you would be hated for it.

Adrian thought it was perhaps the most important lesson he'd ever learned.

Glayer Felsteppe's great scheme was failing. He was not yet finished, but Adrian could not let his brothers' location be discovered until the men were ready to mount an offense against him with the knowledge Adrian now held.

Which meant he needed to solicit Malcolm Lindsey's help.

"I suppose I am boarding a ship," he said to Reid at last. "I'll need to speak with the king first."

"He shall be there, Man. On that you can depend," Reid said, and then both men were quiet as they came out of the wood and onto the wide rocky slope leading down to the shore.

The scene ahead was alive with flickering light, from the tall torches stuck into rock and the little flares bobbing on the ships waiting menacingly in the harbor, as well as the flitting glow of the faerie light about the fringe of the wood. Besides Maisie's crawler, left abandoned and listing on the sand where they'd landed near the wooden pier, only one ship had been brought to the dock itself, and Adrian squinted to try to make out the figures on the deck far below.

Somewhere there was his enemy.

Somewhere there was his love.

The mist, the gray fog was gone, and above the inky, flashing sea, the sky was velvet, pricked with bright starlight, even as the horizon was highlighted by a startling line of light. Adrian could not recall seeing the deep heavens so displayed, and he wondered how close the equinox was, and if its arrival would be heralded by some further strange phenomena.

On the beach itself, the skeletal arms of the trebuchets stood in stark contrast to the plush blanket of sky. An army of marvelously bizarre beings milled about the engines, and along the rocky cliff of the island a solid line of elves crouched, their bows at the ready. A small figure, like that of a young boy, waved at Adrian.

Edel, Adrian thought. The boy who also longed to one day escape from his magic home.

Then his attention was directed toward the bearded leader of Wyldonna, who was marching up the slope toward him, his brows drawn together.

"He's taken Maisie aboard the ship," Malcolm announced before he'd even reached Adrian.

"I know. I'm going after her now," Adrian assured him.

Malcolm stopped before him, his hands on his hips, his beard bending in the breeze. The fact hung in the air between them, and neither wished to speak of it.

Adrian going aboard Glayer Felsteppe's ship would likely mean his death.

And so Adrian gave the king a half smile. "It's what I'm meant to do—said so clearly in your book. You really should do something about the pathetic state of that cupboard you refer to as a library."

Malcolm shook his head and huffed a low laugh. And then he reached for Adrian and drew him into an embrace.

"You will be saving the whole of the world, lad," he choked.

Adrian didn't care about the whole of the world; he was only saving Maisie. His throat felt thick and so he pulled away from the king. "I need you to do something for me."

Maisie feared never reaching the beach alive.

Glayer Felsteppe held the blade to her throat as he attempted to maneuver them both down the dark steep path through the wood. The unfamiliar terrain caused him to stumble several times, nicking Maisie's skin, crushing her feet and ankles beneath his heavy boots. She'd fallen a dozen times because he had trod on her, and each time he cursed her, jerked her to her bruised feet, shook her, threatened her.

The faeries were about, always such curious creatures. Some of the more daring ones swooped down from the trees to hover above Maisie's face or around the soldiers, who cried out and swatted at the little glowing wings.

One faerie hung in the darkness just over Maisie's nose, illuminating her face. Tiny green eyes sparkled and looked at her curiously, the heart-shaped face tilting from side to side.

"Help me," Maisie mouthed. "Please."

The faerie flipped and then swooped away like a swallow.

"What be they?" one soldier demanded in a panicked voice.

"Naught but insects," Felsteppe assured him brusquely as he pushed Maisie down the path. "Pay them no heed. They can't harm you."

She heard a tiny, nearly inaudible *crunch* and then the shriek of a grown man.

"It bit me! It bit me face! I'm bleedin'!"

"Shut up!" Felsteppe commanded, but he must have been troubled by his soldier's injury for he pushed even faster, kicking Maisie's bruised ankles.

"I'll cause you nae trouble should we board your ship and cast off immediately. You have my word," Maisie said, her words jarred by the descent and strangled through her raw throat. "You doona need Adrian Hailsworth."

"Your concern for him is touching," Felsteppe sneered breathlessly near her ear. "I was wise enough to notice the way you cared for each other in the hall. It should please you, then, that I fully intend on leaving the island with you both. It shall be most beneficial to my agenda to torture one against the other until I have the information I seek. So, you see, I most certainly do need him."

"Adrian will never tell you anything, you cowardly pig," she gasped. "And neither will I."

"We shall see," was all Felsteppe said, and Maisie was dismayed to hear the wicked smile in his voice.

What *wouldn't* she do or tell or reveal to save Adrian from further suffering? Her blood ran cold when she could not answer her own question.

Felsteppe could not be allowed to leave the island with both of them.

Indeed, if Glayer Felsteppe was lucky enough to depart Wyldonna at all, Maisie determined then and there that neither she nor Adrian would be accompanying the bastard.

They came upon the rocky slope above the beach then, and from the corner of her eye, Maisie could see the tall wooden constructs Malcolm had kept secreted away from her in the mountain. The island folk crowded together on either side of the path she traversed in Felsteppe's clutches. As she was pushed through the living corridor, the folk bowed.

"My queen."

"My . . ."

". . . queen."

"My queen."

Hundreds of voices acknowledged her as she was forced toward the dock, but not one hand was raised to stop Felsteppe.

After all, Wyldonna's folk obeyed the laws of the island.

Maisie squeezed her eyes shut against the tears that swelled there. When she opened them, she saw the pointed bow of her crawler jutting up from the sand before the dock at a sharp angle. She knew it was resting upon a long, half-buried rock that infringed upon the path just enough.

Turning her foot inward beneath her already bruised ankle caused an authentic cry of pain from her and she stumbled to the left, feeling Felsteppe's blade slice just under her chin, where it sent forth a warm rivulet of blood down her throat. But he lost his grip on her hair as he flung out both arms to break his fall, stumbling over Maisie's body and then the rock as her own hands reached out to catch herself on the bow of the crawler.

She hung there for precious seconds while Felsteppe struggled and cursed her just at her back, and as his fist twisted into her locks again, she lifted the fingers of her right hand and tapped the smooth pale wood twice. She felt the vessel tremble as he lifted her away from the crawler and to her feet once more. Maisie screamed and instinctively brought her hands to her scalp.

"Keep your feet beneath you, you clumsy bitch," he hissed in her ear with a vicious shake, his dagger point once more dimpling her skin beneath her chin. And then their footsteps echoed on the wood of the pier.

He shoved her up the gangway, and as they came to the deck of Felsteppe's ship, Maisie could just see the pale line of dawn drawing a horizon between sea and sky. The sun would rise very soon—in moments, perhaps—and although Maisie had desperate hope that the dawn would bring with it the help Wyldonna needed, she knew she had no choice in what she planned to do.

Wyldonna must stand or fall on its own now.

"Take up the plank," Felsteppe commanded his crew. "Send over a rope instead. Hailsworth shall not bring any companions with him, nor shall he have a ready means of retreat once he is aboard. Untether all but the minimum of lashings. We will need to be away with the dawn."

Then he placed a hand between Maisie's shoulder blades and shoved, sending her to her hands on the deck.

"Stay down," he commanded unnecessarily, placing his booted foot on the back of her neck. "Rope! Bring rope!"

"We had an intruder while you were ashore, General," one of the soldiers muttered low behind Maisie's head as her hands and feet were bound together. "Tried to free the freak."

"What?" Felsteppe hissed. "Where is he?"

"There." A pause. "We resolved it. None on the shore were aware."

"Good." Felsteppe's hands returned to her hair, pulling her awkwardly to sway on her feet. "Don't move," he said solemnly, and then a grin broke over his ugly countenance at his own humor.

It was then that Maisie saw the large heaps of fur against the railing of the ship. Two beasts, it seemed, were curled together motionless on the deck. One had the size and deep brown pelt of a bear, its fur dark and matted in its side, where a wash of blood had flowed. The other claimed the bristly, spotted coat of a hyena, its neck bulging above and below a metal collar. The hyena's tongue lolled from its open mouth, fat and purple, its eyes dull and staring. The bear's muzzle was hidden beneath one of the hyena's forelegs, buried under its elbow as if in fear.

"Jagger," Maisie whispered. Then she looked to the beach, where the long arms of the wooden machines were being pulled back to the sand and carts of rock were being wheeled nearby. And in the midst of the commotion, Maisie saw Adrian walking toward the dock, Reid and Malcolm to either side of him.

Perhaps she could stop him now. Maisie drew a deep breath.

"Jagger and Ossal are dead!" she screamed as loudly as she could. "Felsteppe's men have kill—"

The blow to the side of her face silenced her words, but as Maisie blinked to clear her vision, she thought she saw several faces turn toward her. She looked back to Adrian; he had reached the dock now, leaving Reid and Malcolm behind on the beach, where a dwarf was speaking to the king and pointing to the ship.

The deck was growing lighter, and a glance behind her confirmed to Maisie that dawn was only moments away. She looked over her other shoulder and saw Felsteppe's ships in the harbor.

She must do this correctly. There was no room for rash mistakes.

"Six of you, at the ready for when he emerges over the rail," Felsteppe ordered the men nearest him. "Go, go! Have a care that you don't get too close; he has honed his skills since the time I knew him. Six of you, yes, good—weapons drawn. Once he is aboard, stand between him and the railing. Four more of you now; bring the chains and a manacle."

Then Felsteppe leaned over the railing. "Stop right there, Hailsworth. Let's have a turn-around so that I can be assured you carry no weapons. All right, up the rope."

"I want to see that Maighread still lives," Adrian shouted up.

"Oh, fine," Felsteppe huffed. He marched to her and seized her arms, dragging her along the splintery deck until her head was over the railing. "There you are. Happy?"

"I'm here—let her go," Adrian said.

"The deal was you must first be aboard the ship," Felsteppe reiterated angrily, shoving her behind him. "Now do get on with it lest you wish for me to cast off with her!"

Felsteppe was apparently satisfied with what he saw on the side of the ship, for he rejoined Maisie with a sly smile. He straightened his tunic, brushed at a blood splatter, its failure to disappear bringing a slight frown. Then he squared his shoulders and took a deep breath and glanced at Maisie.

"Wonderfully exciting, isn't it?" he offered.

She only stared at him, feeling the swelling in her face, the shooting pains in her ankles and feet, the throbbing of her hands where they were bound, her sore scalp where the patches of missing hair seemed to crawl and sting.

"No?" he said with a pout. "Ah, well . . . perhaps you will be a bit more lively when I set you afire once we are out to sea. That's what is done with witches, you know. I'm not certain who will talk first, but I'd wager one of you will."

Then he directed a broad smile toward the bow of the ship as Adrian's head appeared over the railing. "Ah, the guest of honor. Welcome aboard, Hailsworth."

Adrian set his boots on the deck and straightened, his path of escape cut off by the crowd of soldiers that moved immediately behind him, urging him forward with their swordpoints.

"Release her," he said, but his eyes would not meet Maisie's as the first rays of true dawn moved over his face, turning his skin to beautiful gold.

The equinox had come.

Maisie's head whipped around to look over her shoulder again, almost in the same moment that one of Felsteppe's soldiers called out in a worried voice.

"Ah, General? Were you expecting reinforcements?"

Out of the dawn light, the prows of no fewer than six ships appeared through the sparkling mist, coursing through the waves and separating Felsteppe's mercenary vessels from one another. And the decks of the arriving ships were full of eager beings pressed to the railings facing Wyldonna—impossibly tall men, marvelously small ones, beasts with hair and cloven hooves, women with long gossamer wings. Common-looking folk, too, mingled with the magical, both men and women, their gifts unseen, and yet Maisie knew that each being upon the ships carried a piece of Wyldonna in their hearts.

And all of them were armed. A shaking smile broke over Maisie's face and tears spilled down her cheeks at the poignant sight of the ships.

The piece bloods, the deserters—even the exiles—had come home to Wyldonna at last.

Felsteppe's next hurried commands caused Maisie to whip her head back around.

"Cast off! Cast off!" he shouted. "Secure Hailsworth!"

Adrian rushed forward and was seized by no fewer than four men, who hung on his arms and shoulders, struggling to attach chains.

"Let her go, Felsteppe! You swore you would let her go!"

"Sorry." Felsteppe arched one red brow. "I lied."

The time was now, Maisie realized.

"Adrian! Adrian!" she called to him, gaining his attention at last. His dark brows furrowed as his eyes took in her assuredly dreadful appearance.

"It's all right! It's going to be all right now!" She tried to smile at him. Out of the corner of her eye she could see the first of the piece-blood ships drawing alongside Felsteppe's, and a familiar-looking blond man climbed upon the railing to somehow balance there on his feet, his arm raised high in the air toward the shore.

"*Hamish!*" a young voice echoed down from the cliff.

Hamish waved his arm in a wide arc. "Edel, me brother! I've come for ye!" And then he turned toward the ship on which Maisie stood. He saw her and bowed. "My queen."

All the figures on the deck behind the blond man echoed both his gesture and his sentiment. Beyond the craggy slopes of Wyldonna, the castle glowed blue and gold in the dawn.

Maisie drew a deep breath and blinked at the tears in her eyes, letting them flow freely. This was to be her finest moment as queen, as a woman. The occasion deserved her full depth of emotion.

She spoke as loudly and clearly as she could.

Chapter 22

Maisie Lindsey's vibrant red curls swirled in the morning breeze, her beauty luminous despite the bruise on her face, the splotchy tracks of her tears cutting through the drying blood on her graceful neck. Adrian felt the chains locking around his arms, but this time he did not feel imprisoned. Nay, the only things that held him helplessly captive were the clear, strong words coming from the mouth of the woman he loved as her eyes scanned the shore beyond Adrian's back.

"I shall protect the people of Wyldonna, the kingdom, and its wisdom.

"I shall forever preserve the ancient tribes, and abide by their traditions.

"I shall honor—" she choked a bit here but cleared her throat and then swallowed before continuing, even more loudly than before—*"I shall honor the blood of all my kin, be they of like tribe or nay.*

"By accepting this charge, I shall forsake all power gifted to me. For the good of all living things, both in spirit and in flesh."

"Maisie?" Adrian asked, hearing his own voice as if in a dream. The air held such stillness, the simple sound of her voice seemed to vibrate in the golden light.

Her eyes at last found his and she smiled. "Thank you, Adrian, for coming for me. I love you."

"Glayer Felsteppe!"

Adrian's attention was drawn by the sound of the blond man's voice. Hamish, who was no simple criminal but of Wyldonna blood. Adrian thought he should have guessed; Valentine Alesander could know no humble thief.

The keeper of the Queen's Inn pointed a finger across the water separating the two ships, his other arm holding an object down by his thigh. "You flaggin' devil's spawn! Prepare your goats for slaughter, bastard, for hell is opening to you this day!"

A roar went up behind Hamish, and also behind Adrian, from the shore; and from the sea before him, as the passengers on the approaching vessels gained the railings, bows drawn, swords waving, beastly screams filling the air.

Hamish himself brought up his bow and pulled an arrow from the quiver strapped to his back. He knocked it, and all the soldiers on Felsteppe's boat crouched as the blond man pointed his weapon to-ward the sky.

"*Save the queen!*" Hamish shouted and then let his arrow fly.

Two successive crashes echoed over the water, and then a heart-beat later the nearest enemy ship suffered a devastating blow to its mast and the sea lurched forth with foam.

Adrian's eyes flew back to Maisie. Her hands were somehow freed now, as Felsteppe turned in frantic circles, ordering his crew to return fire, and the *whip-whip* of arrows cut the air over the ship.

"I love you, Adrian," Maisie said again and then raised her hands.

Adrian saw a faint golden glow growing between her palms. It was a ball of light, much the same as she had shown him in the turret room, only this time there was no green, no fear. The ball rose from her hands and hung suspended for a moment. And then Maisie held her right palm behind it, as if readying to push it.

Adrian's heart stuttered.

Its effects should be turned back upon me equally.

"No!" he cried out. "Maisie, don't!"

"Go," she said softly and thrust the light toward him.

The ball hit him, seemed to absorb him. Adrian felt the hard metal of the manacles fall from his wrists as he was lifted off his feet and shoved backward through the air.

He caught the briefest sight of a green gown, red curls flying above the deck in much the same manner, only in the direction oppo-site from Adrian. He plunged over the railing of the ship, arrows whizzing past his body yet not touching him. Down, down he went, although he wasn't so much falling as being pulled.

He landed hard on his back, smooth yellow wood beneath him that immediately began to lurch. He got to his feet as quickly as his shocked limbs would allow, struggling to stand against the wind and the movement of the crawler, its oars rising and cutting through the air with a *whoosh* before sinking beneath the waves.

"Maisie!" he cried out, looking about him frantically for where she had landed as another pair of crashes from the trebuchets on shore heralded their volleys.

Then he saw her. Lying much as he himself had landed on the crawler, only her resting place was no wooden deck of a magical ship. She was draped over the jagged peak of a rock emerging from the surf, her red hair black from the waves buffeting her limp body, the foamy water licking at the stream of red pouring from beneath her head.

Adrian rushed to the side of the deck where the cabin's roof sloped, for the first time in his adult life praying to something—anything—that he could reach her before the waves took her. As the ship drew near, he realized it was picking up speed.

"No! Slow down!" he commanded, pounding on the cabin roof.

He saw that one of her legs was bent up beneath her gown, her now slipperless foot pointing in the wrong direction. Her right arm lolled in the waves, and when the water swept her hair back from her face and pulled her head against the rocks, Adrian saw Maisie's eyes.

Open, wide, still.

"*No!*" he screamed, leaning out over the water.

> *Beware the Painted Man, my child,*
> *Who trades the death of the Queen . . .*

And then a white-green hand, seaweed clinging to the webbed skin between its fingers, emerged from the water and slapped onto the rock. Then another, and another, until a trio of grotesque sirens were scaling the rock, singing their gruesome song. They gathered the body of the queen against their fish bellies, turning her, wrapping her in shrouds of seaweed with incredible speed as the arrows sang overhead, the roar of fire erupting, the clang and shouts of steel on steel ringing out, the trebuchets firing.

"*Maisie!*" Adrian sobbed as the sea monsters wrapped the last of the long slimy strands over her face, hiding his last glimpse of her unseeing eyes.

Then they slipped back into the water, pulling their package beneath the waves.

Adrian stood aright and held his arms out from his sides, screaming into the tempest created by the passing ships, the increasing speed of the crawler.

"Maisie!"

And then the sky seemed to go black in an instant, filled with white-hot stars that streaked past his body, and with an echoing, sucking sound that Adrian vaguely recognized as seeming to come from inside his own head, he was pulled backward into darkness and a door slammed shut.

Adrian didn't know how long he slept, only that in his long, long dreams, Maisie was once more in his arms.

They embraced beneath the waves, the deep water muffling their kisses, their caresses, into silence. Her skin was warm against his as the cold water buoyed them along in their secret haven, where there was no need for words. Her hair was long, dark, tangled silk over his shoulder, the sunlight far above rippling over her face.

And then she was gone, and there was nothing but the blackness behind his eyes, the quiet not of the ocean's depths but of an empty room. Adrian didn't want to open his eyes; he wanted to return to the sea, where his Maisie lay somewhere far below.

But the dream was gone and his eyes opened at last to behold the pale wooden planks above his head. Adrian found that he was lying on his back on the floor of the cabin, near the cauldron which hissed quietly with flame. He sat up slowly, his body creaking—how long he'd been lying there he didn't know.

The cabin was as they had left it, Maisie's curtain pulled wide, her berth in disarray from when she had gathered her belonging upon their arrival at Wyldonna. The provisions trunk stood open beyond the overturned table and chairs. Adrian gained his feet and staggered toward it.

It was empty.

He turned toward the hatch and mounted the ladder, wondering if the door would slide easily or balk at his attempt. He waited for the panic the thought of being trapped inside the crawler alone would bring, but nothing happened. His breathing remained steady, even if his heart was leaden. He pulled at the bolt and the door slid free.

Bright, warm sunlight blasted Adrian's face so that he threw an arm up to shield his eyes. He emerged onto the deck, feeling the spring air on the skin of his still bare chest. He squinted and saw a river, its opposite bank somehow familiar. Then he turned around.

Melk rose above him over the Danube, its towers and walls so formidable and fortresslike after the elegance of Wyldonna Castle. His eyes stung.

Adrian stumbled from the crawler onto the shore, falling onto his hands and knees in the soft muck. He was so weak.

Splashing sounds drew his attention, and he turned his head back toward the river in time to see the oars on the side of the crawler facing him raise in unison. The vessel drifted away from the shore and then the long wooden arms cut into the murky water, pulling itself rhythmically into the middle of the river. It seemed to shimmer, as if consumed with a sudden, violent heat, and then the crawler simply vanished, its oars in midstroke.

Adrian gained his feet and stood staring at the spot in the river where the crawler had disappeared for what seemed like hours. The sun warmed his skin even as the stiff spring breeze raised gooseflesh intermittently. He didn't know why he still stood there, staring. It wasn't that he expected it to return. But he knew it was the last place he would see a connection to his time on Wyldonna, his time with Maisie. And that idea rendered him unable to move.

Sometime later, a voice called out behind him. It was a familiar voice, but in his present state Adrian could not place it.

"Hello, there! Hello? My friend?" The accent was not English but something else. A hint of warmer climes, of reckless humor. "You seem as though you, ah, could use some assistance, yes?"

Adrian turned slowly and saw a man with dark hair and long brown monk's robes walking toward him. A woman in a plain gown, obviously with child, stood on the path behind him, her delicate forehead creased with apprehension.

"I do no know if you are aware," the man continued as he drew near, "but you are missing most of your clothes, and I believe the villagers would find your . . . ah, highly decorative appearance distressing."

"Valentine," Adrian tried to say, but his words came out as a rusty creak.

Valentine Alesander stopped, his easy smile freezing on his swarthy face. "Adrian?" he asked cautiously. "Ah, *dios mío!*" Then he rushed toward the river, his tooled boots sinking into the mud, his hands out and just taking hold of Adrian's arms as Adrian fell to his knees on the riverbank.

"Valentine," Adrian sobbed. He grasped at his friend's robes, burying his face in the coarse brown wool as he squeezed his eyes shut, his loss overtaking him at last.

"Maria," Valentine said over his shoulder, "fetch Stan. Tell him to bring a robe with him. As quickly as you can, *mi amor*." He turned his attention back to the man weeping before him. "It is all right, Adrian. You have returned. Whatever has happened, we will all face it together."

"Forgive me, Valentine," Adrian choked. "Forgive me, I beg of you. You are a good man."

"There is nothing to forgive, I am certain," Valentine said easily, gently. "Once we are safely inside the abbey we shall figure everything out. Do no torture yourself so."

"She's dead," Adrian wheezed. "I loved her and now she is dead."

Chapter 23

Adrian stared out the window of the little library, his senses filled with the quiet, the smell of the manuscripts, the creamy sheen of the candles that would be lit at the end of the day. A book was open on his lap, but he hadn't truly looked at it since opening it more than a pair of hours ago. His cup of wine sat on the stone sill, likewise unattended to. He seemed to have lost his taste for the grape.

He'd been returned to the abbey for two months. In that time, he had slowly shaken the catatonia and unreasonable hysterics that had taken hold of him after encountering Valentine on the shore of the Danube. In many ways, his life was largely returned to the state in which it had been before his ill-fated journey to the magical Scots island. He spent much of his time in this chair once again, reading, studying, thinking. When he was obligated to venture out, he participated in the responsibilities required of him in return for his asylum. His limp was gone, and so he took his turn in the rotation serving meals, and worked in the fields and industries of the abbey as needed. He slept in his same chamber.

The only differences between then and now were that he found himself attending the scheduled prayers of the brethren in addition to the other activities. He didn't know to what or to whom he was praying—or what for, for that matter—but the repetitiveness of it was a balm for his fevered mind.

The other difference was what he studied when he was alone in the library. Whereas before he had concentrated on pure mathematics, languages, philosophy, now he almost exclusively explored the intricacies of and the correlation between ancient mythology, astrology, time, the relationship between matter and force. Energy. The human will.

Life after death.

Adrian could now quote verses from the holy books in regular use at the abbey. Not only that, he could cite correlating stories from other philosophies. Theories of creation and deity that paralleled the culture in which Melk was founded and steeped.

He still didn't have any answers. But he was learning.

It was all very normal, save that Brother Song was no longer in residence. Indeed, it had been assumed that the Chinese monk had illicitly accompanied Adrian on his mission. But the man who had painted Adrian with the mysterious signs that had protected him while on Wyldonna—and cast him as the Painted Man, for good or ill—had then vanished without a trace.

Perhaps, Adrian thought, if he'd looked more closely at the ships arriving with the dawn on the equinox, he would have seen a familiar face.

His snideness had largely left him. His anger with the past. His fear. If anything, his love and appreciation for the men he called his brothers had grown, and even Mary Beckham held a place of esteem and respect in his eyes. She had sacrificed her comfortable life to become Valentine's wife.

At the idea of such a noble act, the bruised, aching heart that resided in Adrian's chest clenched.

He'd never told Maisie that he loved her. Foolish pride! He had refrained, thinking that she only wanted to use him to be free of the island. But what would that have mattered? Even if it had been true, why should that have prevented Adrian from admitting his feelings for her? She had declared her love for him before all—twice.

And then she had died saving his life.

Adrian swallowed and took a breath before reaching for his chalice. But the cup seemed to scoot away from his fingers as they drew near.

Adrian frowned and reached again. Again the cup skittered over the stones, but he was quicker this time and seized it.

"Blasted thing," he muttered. "Be still." He raised the cup to his lips and sipped. But he quickly spat the liquid back into the cup and held it from his lips, looking down into its flashing surface and then sniffing.

"Water?" he muttered crossly.

"It was supposed to be mead," a voice called from the room behind him.

Adrian's head whipped around, and the cup fell from his hand, spilling its water onto the floor. The manuscript in his lap fell to the same fate as the ghostly vision spoke again.

"I fear I'm nae longer as good at some things as I used to be."

Maisie brought her hand to her mouth as she caught her first sight of Adrian sitting alone in the small, quiet library to which Constantine had led her. The secret shelves clicked shut behind her, giving them privacy, but Adrian hadn't noticed the little sound, so absorbed was he in the view through the narrow window.

To her dismay, his fine physique was disguised by the same brown wool worn by all the men here, but his hair still curled over his shoulder, even longer than when last she'd seen him. His jaw was smooth now, and Maisie found she rather enjoyed the sight of him clean-shaven. She couldn't wait to run her fingers over the invisible stubble she knew she would feel just beneath his skin.

He sighed and brought up his hand to reach for the cup on the windowsill, and so Maisie, too, raised her hand.

The cup went out of his reach the first time but not the second, and she smiled at his curse. Then she swirled her finger toward him and waited.

"Water?" he growled and she winced.

"It was supposed to be mead," she said, and he turned to look at her at last. She wasn't surprised at the shock she saw on his face, the way his cup fell to the floor, his book tumbling away, forgotten. "I fear I'm nae longer as good at some things as I used to be."

Adrian's handsome face took on a pained expression. "Are you real?" he asked in a whisper.

She nodded, feeling her throat constrict. "Aye."

He stood slowly, as if any sudden move might cause her to vanish like the spirit he likely thought her. "Are you truly real? Not an imagining of my tortured mind? If you are, though, only an imagining, please stay until I reach you. Please . . ." He began walking toward her, his hand out, his eyes sparkling. "Please, stay. Until I—"

He reached her then, grabbed her and pulled her quickly into his arms and held her so very tightly.

"Maisie?" he breathed against the crown of her hair.

She drew away from him only far enough to look into his eyes. "I lo—"

But she couldn't finish her declaration, for he brought his hand to her lips.

"Shh." He swept his thumb over her chin, then smoothed her hair back along the side of her face while his eyes searched hers. Then he grasped her face in his palms. "I love you, Maighread Lindsey. Whether you are real or not, I must tell you now because I failed so many times before to do so. I love you. I'll love you forever. Please stay with me. Don't go again," he said in a choked voice. "Please."

Maisie raised up on her toes to press her lips to Adrian's, and in a heartbeat he had crushed her to him, kissing her with such sweet passion that Maisie felt as if she would fly away if he let her go.

He pulled away at last. "You are real."

"I am real," she agreed.

"But I saw you . . ." Adrian hesitated, swallowed. "On the rocks. You were dead. The sirens . . . they wrapped you, took you."

Maisie shook her head. "I wasna dead. The sirens saved me, Adrian. They kept me safe and nursed me while the war raged on Wyldonna."

Adrian stilled. "Malcolm?"

She let her smile return. "He is well. Nary a scratch on him, thanks to the duties of your friends the afternhangers. Indeed, the king is returned to his throne."

"Thanks be to God," Adrian breathed.

Maisie's eyes widened.

He gave her a boyish grin. "I have come to acknowledge that there are things I have yet to understand or explain. Until I can do so, I feel it wisest to err on the side of caution."

Maisie smiled. "I am glad of that. But I must tell you, others on Wyldonna were nae so fortunate as my brother."

Adrian took her hand and led her to his chair, and Maisie could tell he was noticing her limp as she crossed the floor and sat down. He knelt before her, taking both her hands in his now.

"Reid," Maisie said. "He was surrounded by a group of Felsteppe's mercenaries, out in the water, trying to help his tribe overturn the boats. They targeted him for his size, likely. Overpowered him. I suppose he wasna big enough after all," she finished in a small voice.

Adrian gave a tight nod. "Who else?"

"Half of the trolls. All but four of the afternhangers. A large number of elves."

"Edel?" Adrian asked.

Maisie hadn't known Adrian was familiar with the little elf lad. "Edel is well. Hamish took him and his mother back to the Outland with him."

Adrian's eyebrows rose. "How did Malcolm feel about that?"

Maisie took a breath. "The war has changed Wyldonna. It will never be the same. Many of the folk left after we prevailed against Felsteppe's army—and they went with my brother's blessing."

"I don't understand," Adrian said. "Leaving Wyldonna is a betrayal."

Maisie shook her head. "Nae longer. There was a council of the tribes. It was determined that Dragon did, in fact, leave the island. When she did, she rent the veil, and that is what allowed Felsteppe to surprise us as he did. With the last dragon in the world gone from Wyldonna, it was a sign that the island could nae longer carry on as isolated as it has been these many years. In order for the magic to survive, the tribes must flourish. The island has been shrinking for years. Rather than the tribes vanishing, they must spread to the Outland."

"But what about the piece bloods?" Adrian asked. "It's taboo for the folk to intermarry."

"Nae longer." She gave him a smile. "Besides, everyone is magic, Man."

He pulled her face to his and kissed her lips firmly. Then he pulled away and stroked her cheek with his thumb.

"That saddens me," he said. "The thought of Wyldonna and its wonderful strangeness simply diffusing into the Outland like smoke."

Maisie gave him a genuine smile then. "I want to show you something. It's in my bag there." She motioned toward the satchel she'd left on the floor by the entry.

Adrian brought it back to her, and Maisie produced the thick book of Wyldonna's history. She handed it to him solemnly.

"This is a gift to you from the king. He thought you would find it useful to study." When Adrian took it, she added, "And he wanted me to tell you he is working on the library."

Adrian laughed and ran his hands over the black swirls of the cover.

"Open it to the lineages," Maisie directed. "The last one."

Adrian sat the book on Maisie's lap and flipped through the pages. He stared at the drawing before him.

"Do you see?" she asked.

Where once Wyldonna Castle had taken up the whole of its page, complete with its six turrets, it was now only a small structure in the center, its roofline topped with only two towers.

But all around the castle, in small outlines representing landmasses near Wyldonna as well as across the oceans, towers were sprouting. Near cities, on islands. Not only towers but shapes of trees, of creatures, outlines of beings with wings.

"And look," Maisie said, pointing to a long range of jagged peaks resembling mountains. Her rounded nail stopped next to a sketch of a creature with a long tail and neck, flames coming from its open mouth.

Adrian looked up. "Dragon?"

Maisie nodded. "We think it must be."

He studied the page for several moments before he asked. "What of Glayer Felsteppe?"

"We doona know," she admitted quietly. "His body was never found, and one ship did escape us. He could have been on it, dead or alive."

Adrian raised his eyes to hers. "I must find him."

"You will." Maisie took his hands. "*We* will."

"I want to be married to you. Here, at the abbey, by Victor. I want the ceremony. The vows. The prayers."

Maisie nodded and smiled. "We need all the magic we can get."

"Tomorrow," Adrian said. "No, today. Right now." He set the book aside and then pulled her to her feet. "Let us go find him."

Maisie laughed and stayed him with her arms about his shoulders. "Can we nae wait an hour?"

His hands slid around her waist. "Only an hour? Once I get you alone in my chamber, I may never let you leave. I've lost you once. I daren't let you out of my sight again."

"Then take me there now," she said, running her hands through his hair. "I long to once more see the Painted Man in my bed."

"This time he's not trading anything for you."

"This time I'm nae the queen." She smiled against his mouth.

"No," he agreed. "But you're mine. And I'm keeping you forever."

* * *

Maisie and Adrian snuck out of the secret library and through the corridors of Melk, giggling like children. They disappeared behind Brother Adrian's locked door.

When Adrian was absent from the nightly meeting that evening, the rest of the Brotherhood, along with Victor, were not surprised.

Roman picked up the thick, strangely decorated book left on the windowsill and returned to the table with it, studying the page that seemed to be a map of sorts. While the other men talked gravely about the next step in locating Glayer Felsteppe, Roman ran his finger along the shape of the landmass he thought represented where the abbey lay. Its fortifications and river beyond were clearly identifiable. As were the figures, which seemed to hover over the rendering of the holy house.

A woman with a crown and what appeared to be a man whose skin was covered in swirling designs.

Then Roman closed the book, stood, and walked to a shelf. He slid the thick manuscript into a snug spot and returned to his place at the table.

Epilogue

The torches burned dimly in the close chamber, the smoke swirling with the heady scent of incense that seemed to only heighten the air of danger for the naked woman as she stood at the earthen bowl, washing herself in preparation for the man lounging on the mat that was her bed.

It would be the last time she did so, even if it meant her death.

She turned to him at last, pulling her long black hair over her shoulders, stroking it over her breasts as she swaggered to the mat. She walked around and around him while his head swiveled, following her with his eyes, glazed with lust and drink.

"I am honored to serve such a brave warrior," she said softly. "It will surely be my greatest pleasure."

He nodded, as if he expected no less. "It gladdens me that you are no longer under Abdal's hand. Now that he is dead, you will be mine. And I will come to you every morning, every night. I will see you grow fat with my love. You are twice the beauty your mother was."

Isra smiled down at the man and then came to kneel at his side, taking a colored bottle of oil from a basket near the mat. She was relieved he had not mentioned Huda, else she doubted she could have contained her rage long enough to do what she must. She poured some in her trembling palm and then set the bottle aside, warming the fragrant liquid in her hands. Then she leaned forward and began stroking the man's chest, trying to push away the memory of the sight of her young sister's slim body, covered in bruises and dried blood.

"Tell me again of your victory over the infidels," she prompted, pressing his flabby flesh with firm, smooth strokes as she'd been taught.

"They were as rats in a hole, frightened, weeping, crying to their false god," he said. "I alone saved the ship of men, even the infidel Felsteppe. But he will bring me great glory with our leader."

"Yes?" Isra let her hands slide down to the man's thighs.

"It is his plan to kill the king of Jerusalem," the soldier said, closing his eyes and raising his hips, seeking contact between his erect flesh and her skin. "I have agreed to help him and receive a portion of the gold he hoards. As well as honor from our leader."

"Ooh," Isra sighed, the passionate sound belied by the lack of emotion on her face. She indulged the man by gripping his small member and then, with one hand, reached for the bottle again. She poured the oil directly on him. "Will you receive your glory soon?"

"Yes. Soon," the man groaned.

Isra moved faster. "How soon?"

"When the Christian king comes to council with his bishops," he panted.

"Ooh, yes," Isra said flatly, no longer bothering to pretend passion.

She reached into the basket again, this time withdrawing a short dagger. She held it near her thigh.

"Who accompanies you?" she demanded. "When you are to do this thing?"

"The white infidel himself," the man grunted. "Give it to me now, whore. Give it to me."

She leaned down close to him. "Here it is," she said, plunging the dagger home.

She shot to her feet and stumbled back, her heart pounding so that her vision trembled as she watched the man die before her. She found she couldn't swallow and wanted to bring her hands to her mouth, but they were covered in oil. She fetched a long silk scarf from the end of the mat and wiped her hands frantically and then leaned down and retrieved her mother's blade from the man's still chest while her stomach tumbled. Isra pulled the silken scarf over him as if he were asleep. She backed away again, gathering her clothes as she went.

Once she had reached the doorway, she paused to toss the blade into the bowl of water while she pulled her clothes on and adjusted her hair cover. Then she wiped her blade dry and returned it to its jeweled hilt. She stared at the dead man, the first she had ever killed.

Her feeling of vengeance quickly faded. Her mother had been dead for three years; Huda, six days. Isra was truly alone in the world, and soon she would be wanted for murder.

She had only months to find the one man who could help her now.

Isra turned and fled into the dark streets of Damascus, remembering the face she had seen there only once three years before, but every night since in her dreams. How she would reach him, she didn't know.

Isra had to once again find Roman Berg.

Please turn the page for an exciting sneak peek of
ROMAN
the next novel in Heather Grothaus's
BROTHERHOOD OF FALLEN ANGELS series
coming in July 2016!

Prologue

August 1179
Syria

The wall came down no more than fifty feet behind Roman, the already hot air contracting around him like a shroud, then exploding with a roar of flames. The blast lifted him from his feet and sent him flying over the bodies of the slain workers who were, only a moment ago, being prepared for burial. He slammed into the hard packed dirt and then skidded and tumbled for several yards, his rough brown tunic seeming to melt into his skin.

He realized the instant he came to a stop that it wasn't a friction wound he felt—the back of his tunic was afire.

He slapped at the flames and flung himself onto his back as a pair of screaming pillars of fire ran past him, but Roman could barely hear them above the loud squeal the explosion had stuffed into his pounding, spinning head. They weren't flaming pillars; they were men. Men on fire.

Roman pushed himself up on his elbows and looked at the southeast corner of Chastellet's bailey. Where carefully crafted rectangular stones—many which Roman Berg himself had set—once comprised the fortress's key defense, the wall sagged, framing an inverted wedge of white-hot Syrian sky beyond. Roman's eyes burned and his nose ran as the air was filled with the stink of naphtha and burning sand, burning flesh.

His head jerked as a hand gripped his right bicep. He hadn't heard his apprentice approach, hadn't been able to hear the slim man's shouts over the twisting whine still swelling in his ears. But

Osbert's mouth was moving widely, his teeth flashing behind cracked lips as he pulled futilely at Roman with one hand while gesturing with the pick in his other to the barracks left standing against the eastern wall. Roman glanced in that direction, but the shelter held little interest for him as his gaze fell upon a hunting falcon tethered to a post just outside one of the doorways. The bird of prey's hood swiveled and twitched, as if listening to the commotion that Roman could not hear. Roman found himself fascinated by the creature's movements . . .

A hand struck Roman's cheek, and he reluctantly turned his attention back to Osbert.

Come on! his apprentice mouthed, spittle flying, his eyes bulging.

Roman frowned, hesitated. He was confused. What was happening? Why had the wall fallen? Why were there little shadows, like insects, crawling across Osbert's face, across the dirt of the bailey . . . ?

The arrow shaft appeared in Osbert's neck so suddenly, it was as if by magic. Blood spurted out of the hole on the side opposite of the fletching. Although Osbert's mouth opened once again in what Roman surmised was a terrible scream of agony, he doubted any sound emerged. The apprentice pitched forward onto Roman, the man's pick arcing smoothly down into the dirt, and he felt Osbert's hot blood soak through his tunic and run down his chest as arrows fell like rain on the bailey.

Roman pushed the apprentice's body from him as he skittered backward. A zinging pain shot up his left arm from his smallest finger and he jerked his hand from the yard, looking at the arrow that had shot a wedge of flesh from his hand before it had buried itself in the dirt. Another landed precisely between his bent knees. Roman's head swam, throbbed; his tongue seemed to swell in his mouth. Stay still? Move? What sort of nightmare was this?

Roman looked up and saw Chastellet's remaining workers, Templars, servants—all that were left on this sixth day of siege—crisscrossing the bailey frantically, many of them pausing midstride to demonstrate the bow-backed pose of defeat before crumpling to the ground, their bodies stubbled with arrows. Roman staggered to his feet at last, shook his head violently despite the pain it caused.

His hearing came back with a slow whoosh, letting in the roar of screams, pounding feet, clanging metal. Reality crashed upon him as surely as the wall which had crushed the men standing just behind him: *Chastellet had been breached. The wall had been the first wave of attack.*

The arrows falling around him with whistles and pings: *second wave. Which meant . . .*

Roman again raised his eyes to the collapsed section of wall just as the undulating crowd of Saracens crested the rise and charged toward the opening. Some were on horseback, some afoot. All with weapons raised, and yelling their terrible, unintelligible screams.

Third wave.

Roman reached down and retrieved Osbert's pick from the dirt, all the while keeping his eyes on the force advancing toward him. The warrior monks were already engaging the invaders, their long, double edged swords swinging without hesitation. But even Roman Berg—never a warrior until six days ago—knew the sheer numbers of Saracens pouring into Chastellet's walls meant that defeat was likely.

He thought briefly of Lord Adrian Hailsworth, Chastellet's architect and Roman's principal at the site, and he wondered if the brilliant man would live to see the total destruction of his latest design.

He thought of Lord Constantine Gerard, a layman general of noble rank who was to have left Chastellet a week ago. Was he already dead?

They were both good men, noble men, casually treating Roman as their equal. Even Hailsworth—arrogant as he was—made it a point to defer to Roman's skill and experience. Now whatever differences in their backgrounds and pedigrees were truly washed away, as Roman would battle as they battled, fight as they would fight, to defend the place that Roman considered to be the pinnacle of his life's work. He could die, this he knew.

He began to stride toward the line of Templars who were miraculously holding back the onslaught against them. Perhaps God would protect them, after all. Without pause, he reached down and pulled a broadsword from the limp grasp of a fallen soldier. But he kept the pick in his right hand—it was familiar there, and he knew just how to utilize it.

As if his earlier thoughts had conjured the man, Roman saw Constantine Gerard leaping and sidling through the fight toward him. His helm was missing, but he held forth his long shield as he dispatched a rogue attacker. Somehow, Roman must have caught Gerard's eye, for the general paused and banged his sword against his shield before raising it in Roman's direction.

"God be with you, brother," he shouted at Roman.

Roman lifted his weapons and crossed them with a clang over his head. "For Chastellet!" Roman returned against the cracking of his voice.

And then General Constantine Gerard was gone, the last of him Roman saw was his tawny mane flowing behind him as he threw himself into the thick of the battle. Roman turned once more toward the breach, walking deliberately, his weapons flanking him like the squires he could never claim.

Yes, he knew he could fall this day. But for as long as he was able to swing his tools, he would swing.

He stopped then and braced his feet as a Saracen soldier broke away from his comrades and galloped toward him on horseback. The man's robes rose and fell in rhythm to his mount's charge, and he held a long scimitar in his right hand, a small hatchet in his left, guiding his fine horse with nothing more than his knees.

Roman crouched lower, holding forth the broad sword and drawing the pick behind his head. He opened his mouth to let out a cry of attack . . .

He came awake with a gasp, inadvertently sucking in some of the silty dirt from the floor of the cave. Roman fell into a coughing fit as he sat up fully, noticing that he clutched at his shoulder out of habit. He released his arm and reached for the now nearly empty skin of wine the Spaniard had left behind for him.

"To pass the time, yes?" Valentine Alesander had said with a wry grin as he'd tossed it down from atop his horse. Then he'd disappeared down the trail in the spreading dusk.

A bird's short, creaking chirp echoed in the cave, interrupting the memory.

Roman gained his feet and walked to the opening of the cave where the hunting falcon was tethered. He stroked Lou's back with one gentle finger as he looked down on the walled city of Damascus that would soon lie in shadow once more. Three days. Valentine Alesander had left Roman in the cave three days ago.

"They will be praying soon," Valentine had said. "It is my best opportunity."

Roman scrubbed a hand over his bristly face as if he would wipe the thick air and his troubled thoughts away. Then he sighed and placed his hands on his hips. It was of no use; the cave seemed to be full of ghosts now: days past living on in his dreams, voices in his head.

Something had gone wrong. Either the Spaniard had been caught, or he had not even attempted to gain entry into Saladin's prison to free Adrian Hailsworth and Constantine Gerard. Perhaps he had instead maneuvered his horse around the wall and gone on past the city, taking the sack of Chastellet coin with him. He'd already proven he could disappear into the native population—Roman had nearly killed Alesander himself upon their first meeting, thinking him Saracen.

Roman stalked to the back of the cave, squatted down and checked his bag again—it was still cinched tightly, the other sack of gold secure inside. Then Roman rose and paced the width of the crude shelter.

Whether Alesander had absconded with the coin or been captured himself, there was clearly no one to rescue Roman's friends. And if the Spaniard *was* caught, his blood was on Roman's hands. Roman's shoulder ached where the man had reseated the joint for him, dislocated for weeks, and he kneaded the bicep which seemed so much smaller than it had been only weeks ago.

Valentine Alesander had rescued him from the midden heap of Chastellet—its cisterns stuffed with corpses and its walls adorned with carrion birds; rescued him from the cesspool of his own mind which echoed with screams of the dying; the sounds of arrows finding deep flesh; the shame of being the one left behind, the one left alive. The Spaniard had made Roman's body whole again, despite the healing gashes and still-dark contusions beneath his tunic and chausses. And he had led Roman to Damascus, where the only two men on earth Roman could claim as friends were being held by the conquerors of Chastellet.

If they weren't already dead.

Roman, like Chastellet, had fallen. Had he not been struck so many times to the temple, perhaps he would have realized the true folly of dragging himself into the exposed bailey once more to save the life of the hunting bird left abandoned and tethered to its perch— the same one that now stood guard at the cave's entrance. But in Roman's swollen, fevered reasoning, there had been naught else for it. His weakness and injuries had rendered him incapable of saving Chastellet, but there had been a creature before him—one totally innocent of man's folly and politics—that he *could* save. He had decided to let the attempt be on his soul then, and damn him if it would.

Lou chirped again—a questioning sound—and Roman went once more to the falcon, who had come to mean so much to him since that bloody day.

"Naught else for it again, is there, Lou?" he said quietly, stroking the bird's feathers. The falcon tolerated Roman's touch, but Roman knew he was impatient. Lou needed to fly. And so did Roman.

He looked back to the opening of the cave. If he did nothing to save the three men hidden somewhere in the city below, he might as well return to the ruin that was Chastellet and drop from a rope hung from its highest crumbled wall. It would be better than rotting here in this cave, waiting for the Spaniard who was clearly not coming back.

Roman returned to his satchel again, picking it up and looping the strap over his back before donning the leather hood that fit tightly over his skull and draped onto his shoulders like a short cape. He had no robe, no cloak, nothing else to disguise his large body and Anglo coloring. The hood would have to do. The guards would likely kill him as soon as he passed through the gates any matter, if even he made it that far.

He had no gauntlet for Lou, but the falcon had been content to ride upon Roman's shoulder from Chastellet. He picked loose the leather tie keeping the bird captive, and then leaned down, easing the falcon onto the edge of the leather hood.

"Going on an adventure, Lou."

The bird didn't respond, but sidled a bit higher on Roman's shoulder, closer to his ear. Roman found the weight of the creature, the grip of its talons, comforting, as if he truly had a comrade in the falcon.

"I'll not keep hold of your tether though," he said, turning and walking out of the cave without hesitation and setting his boots upon the narrow, twisting animal path that led down the hillside. "I'm likely walking into my own death, and I'd not have yours on my conscience, as well. I'll remove your hood before I enter the city. You'll be free."

Roman considered as he tromped down the mountain in the lengthening shadows that, if he were being truly magnanimous, he would remove the bird's blind now. But he could not yet bear it—the thought of being totally alone at what could again be the last hour of his life. It had been that way since he was a boy, had it not—the alone? He thought with some shame that he should be used to it by now.

He walked quickly among the dunes dotted with scrubby brush at the base of the mountain, seeking the shortest path to gain the packed road leading into the city. Roman guessed that a lone man afoot with nothing more than a single bag was unlikely to draw immediate scrutiny from the guards atop the wall. The sun was swiftly sliding down the sky behind him, throwing a long, deep shadow on the road before him, and Roman hunched into it, made it his companion along with the falcon on his shoulder.

When he was within a stone's throw of the wall, Roman stopped abruptly and, before he could think himself out of it, he reached up and gently slipped the leather string from Lou's leg, and then the hood from the falcon's head. The bird blinked and tilted its head wildly, seeming to drink in the sight of the wide open sky.

Roman gave a shrug of his shoulder. "Go on, then." The falcon flapped its wings for balance and then settled back against Roman's ear. "Go on." He shrugged again.

This time Lou crouched low and leapt from his shoulder, the quiet whoosh of its wings sending a crisp flip of air across Roman's face. He watched the falcon fly low over the ground for several yards before flapping in earnest and pulling himself up, up, up into the darkening east over the walls of Damascus. The falcon cried out once, and it caused Roman's heart to flinch.

But then he tucked the falcon's hood and tether beneath the flap of his bag and headed into the night himself, his head down, his eyes only on the road. Roman had lost any traces of hesitation he'd felt in the cave. He had set his aim now, freed his obligation, and there was no fear in him of what might happen once he reached the gates, the streets of the city, the prison. His feet fell like hammers beneath his gaze, working to chip away at any obstacles he had once imagined.

So intent was he upon his purpose that it was quite a surprise to realize he had passed through the walls and was in the city. The spicy, fecund smells pressing around him and the sounds of his footfalls muffling gave him a physical start, as did the blaring of a horn that shot the thick, still air, and then another, and the warbling sound of a song in the familiar yet still foreign tongue. Roman glanced sideways and behind him to see the guards closing the gates to the city, not twenty feet beyond his heels, shutting out the last rays of the sun disappearing over the rolling land.

The horns continued to sound, and Roman realized he was caught up in a current of citizens all heading in the same direction. His heart pounded despite himself, and he hunched his shoulders farther, crouched lower on bent knees as the slimness of the general population became glaringly apparent. The narrow black space of an alley between sandstone buildings came upon his left side suddenly, and Roman stepped into it as swiftly as a gust of air, slinking back into the deep shadow and straightening his aching back against the wall of the building.

He watched from the shadows as the stragglers, mostly boys and young men running in the center of the street, hands clapped down on their caps, hurried to answer the call to prayer. Another moment and the ruddy street would be deserted.

Then what? He had no idea in which direction to go. Wandering aimlessly through the maze of pathways connecting the straight and orderly streets might only be enough to render him completely lost, and then when the faithful flooded the city again on their way to their homes . . .

He dared lean toward the opening to glance in either direction. There were no clues whatsoever as to where the city housed its prisoners. He pressed his back against the building once more with a sigh. And then his heart stopped as he caught sight of the woman standing against the wall directly opposite him, so close that he could have touched her without fully extending his arm. The last slash of sunlight slunk away from her face, hidden in veils, as the alley was dipped in indigo. He didn't know how she had come upon him so suddenly, so silently.

"Pardon me, mistress," Roman said brusquely and looked away, turning toward the street once more. There was nothing for it now but to go. He could not inhabit such a close space with a woman of this culture—it would certainly mean his death, and likely hers, if he were caught.

Not that he thought to be spared if found alone, either.

But before he could step from between the buildings, he felt a hand upon his arm, staying him. Roman paused, but dare not turn to look at her.

"What is it you require of me? I do not speak your language."

"Not to worry—I speak yours," she replied. "I will not raise an alarm to betray you, you must believe me." She tugged on his arm so that he turned to face her once more. "We have not much time before it is discovered I am gone."

"I fear I am unable to give you whatever it is you seek," he said, feeling her touch conspicuously upon his arm. He could smell the soft, heady, feminine scent of her in the close alley and it made his skin flush beneath his coarse tunic.

"It is I who shall give to you," she said, and then slid her palm down his forearm to grasp his fingers, stepping backward as she did so, pulling Roman's arm away as if she would lead him.

He understood then. She was a whore.

Roman pulled free from her grip. "I cannot tarry with you, woman. I am looking for someone in the city."

She dropped her arm to her side and stared at him for a moment. "I know why it is you've come. I will take you to your friends, but you must come with me now."

Roman hesitated. If she was a whore, the only place she would likely take him was to her keeper, where Roman would be certainly robbed and probably killed. She couldn't possibly know who he was looking for. But she'd mentioned friends, plural, when Roman had only mentioned he was looking for some*one* . . .

"Where is this friend of mine?" he challenged.

"They are still imprisoned, if that is what you are asking."

A chill shook his spine. This smelled of a trick to Roman. Likely the guards atop the wall had caught sight of him entering the city but lost him in the crush, and had sent this woman to seek him out during the prayer. He couldn't risk it.

"You're wrong," he said, and began backing away from her, toward the edge of the buildings where ambient light in the sky from over the mountains urged him to quit wasting time and *search now*.

"They die at dawn," she called after him. "The two soldiers. A Spaniard as well, if you know of him. One may not live to see morning, he has been tortured so."

Roman paused. "Who?"

"I have heard him called Hails-worth."

Lord Adrian Hailsworth, Chastellet's architect.

The woman continued, as if she sensed his hesitation. "I can convince you not standing here. You must trust me, and you must follow me now. If you do not, I shall have no choice but to leave you. You will soon be discovered on your own, and they will have no mercy on you."

"How can I know you will not betray me?"

She shook her head, a rounded shadow in the already dark alley. "We must go now now." She held out her hand.

Roman understood that he had two choices: deny the woman, and strike out on his own, or follow her. If he followed her, she could lead him directly to his own death. If he denied her and she was in league with the guards, she would raise the alarm immediately.

But perhaps the worst outcome of all was if he denied her and she was telling the truth . . .

He stepped toward her suddenly and took her hand. "If you lie, or if we are caught, you will regret it, mistress."

"That I well know." She didn't waste time with mincing steps, and soon they were running between the close-set buildings which leaned together like crowded molars in a dark, humid mouth of a beast. She led him around sudden corners, pulled him across wide, deserted thoroughfares until they came to an enormous long building on the north side of the city, its pitched roofs black and sharp looking in the gloom.

Over the growing sounds of night, Roman could hear the droning prayers emanating from inside the building. The entire male population of Damascus was contained within its walls.

"Are you mad?" he demanded, pulling free from her in the street.

"Do not slow—no! Hurry!" She grasped his hand again and yanked, but she could not move him.

"Why would you take me here? Why should I believe that you are helping me rather than leading me to my death?"

"You will be the cause of your own death and your friends' if you do not come out of the street!" she hissed angrily and then marched toward him to look up into his eyes. In the next moment, she ripped the veil from her face, and Roman could see the cuts and deep bruises on her delicate cheeks, the swollenness of one eye. "They beat me, tortured me, too! They have killed those whom I love! I will have my revenge!" She was nearly gasping in her anger.

"Who?" Roman queried, shocked at the woman's delicate beauty crushed beneath the heavy weight of the violence visited upon her.

"The prison is below," she said, ignoring his question and pulling on his arm again as she refastened her veil with her other hand. Roman fell into a trot once more—he had no better option at the moment.

"Follow the corridor at the bottom of the stairs," she continued as the very building they ran past seemed to watch their flight. "Then turn right at your first opportunity. The cell you seek is at the very end—the only one. There should only be a lone guard in this moment. You must dispatch him quickly though, and do not exit the corridor you enter—it is the way the others shall return."

"Then how are we to escape?"

She pulled him behind a short wall that seemed to enclose a small garden beyond, and also served as the lintel for a black rectangle of doorway that led down into further darkness. The woman was gasping, and Roman could feel her trembling in his grasp. For all her demands and vows of revenge, she was terrified.

"You must pass this entrance, and continue on through the entirety of the prison. There is another exit."

"Only one corridor?"

She shook her head. "No."

"Which one do I take?"

"I know not. I have never been below."

Roman dropped her hand with a breath of agitation and turned in a short circle until he was once more facing the black doorway. The chanting from the domed building had stopped.

"I thank you for your help, mistress," he said gruffly. "If indeed, you are helping me. I will be in your debt." He stepped toward the descending stairs.

"Wait," she called, once more laying her hand on his arm. "I have a message for the general."

Roman felt his eyebrows raise. This woman had a message for Constantine Gerard?

"He must not return to his home. England is against him now, as they are the other one—Hails-worth. The general has been marked a traitor and is wanted by his own crown. His family is being watched."

Roman nodded. "Very well. Again, I shall be in your debt."

She let her hand slide from his skin slowly. "Do not forget me then."

A screeching cry split the night and then a dark shadow shot from the sky and lighted upon the wall above the doorway. It sidled awkwardly along the rough surface, bobbing and ducking, until it was near enough that Roman could determine its character.

"Lou?" he asked softly.

The falcon flapped-hopped the short distance separating it and Roman, settling on the leather of his hood once more, fidgeting, adjusting, its weight obviously increased.

The woman stepped close to Roman and hesitantly reached up toward Lou with one hand, her wide sleeve sliding up to reveal a slender arm adorned with metal bangles that tinkled in the thick air. The falcon ducked away at first, and then shot its beak forward, nibbling curiously at her fingers.

"Lou," she whispered. Then she stroked his wing with one finger while speaking a stream of foreign words to the falcon, who seemed to listen intently, swiveling his head to look at her and then the sky with alternating eyes.

The woman abruptly stepped away and began walking backward, looking at Roman as she went, as if she was loath to lose sight of him. "Go now. You have only moments."

Indeed, Roman heard the distant sounds of a crowd, and although he could see nothing over the wall when he turned his head, he knew that the time of prayers was over.

He looked back for one final glance at the beautiful, mysterious woman who had brought him thus far, but the street before him was empty. She had already disappeared into the city.

Roman ducked through the doorway, pushing all thoughts of her away as he descended the stairs as quickly as he could. A moment later, he had found the right hand turn, and now he ran through the corridor, his wide shoulders nearly brushing the walls, his hood only inches away from the undulating ceiling. A haze of torchlight shone around the corner ahead, but Roman did not slow.

And so he took the guards by surprise—two instead of one. They rose from their crouched positions before a wrought door, one still rolling the woven mat he had knelt upon. Roman came to an abrupt halt, and was unable to stop himself from glancing through the bars to his left.

There, chained by his neck to the back wall, was General Gerard, his tawny mane now long and stringy around his face as he lifted his head to investigate the crashing footfalls. A shadow against the far left wall of the cell grew taller, and then Valentine Alesander stepped into view, his Saracen robes swinging.

Near the Spaniard's feet lay a long, crumpled pile of rags.

Adrian Hailsworth.

One of the guards shouted at Roman, his foreign words challenging, yet hesitant, as if he was unsure what to make of the giant man who had appeared in his prison with a falcon upon his shoulder.

Roman glanced down at the man's waist and saw the ring of keys dangling there. Then he looked both guards in the eyes in turn.

"I've come for my friends."